PANDION

PANDION

A NOVEL

William Michael Ried

CKBooks Publishing

Publisher's Cataloging-in-Publication Data
Names: Ried, William Michael, author.
Title: Pandion / William Michael Ried.
Description: New Glarus, WI : CKBooks Publishing, 2022.
Identifiers: ISBN 978-1-949085-54-9 (paperback) | ISBN 978-1-949085-55-6 (ebook)
Subjects: LCSH: Ponzi schemes--Fiction. | New York (N.Y.)--Fiction. | Mystery fiction. | Suspense fiction. | Bildungsromans. | BISAC: FICTION / Coming of Age. | FICTION / Mystery & Detective / General. | FICTION / Thrillers / Suspense. | GSAFD: Bildungsromans. | Mystery fiction. | Suspense fiction.
Classification: LCC PS3618.I39228 P36 2022 (print) | LCC PS3618.I39228 (ebook) | DDC 813/.6--dc23.

LCCN: 2022909460

Osprey image by Lorenzo Contessa
Cover design by César Pardo

CKBooks Publishing
P.O. Box 214
New Glarus, WI 53574
CKBookspublishing.com

Prologue

Atticus Forester had never before been late for a flight on the company jet when his father Hugo was at the controls, but the Thanksgiving after he turned twenty he *was* late, and that changed everything.

It was in what Atticus later would recall as the "Apex," the days when Hugo was the "hedge fund king" and the Foresters ruled the world.

"I'll give you an extra hundred if we make it," he said to Joseph, one of their regular drivers.

With his snout on Atticus's leg, Ghost looked up as if to say there was no use fidgeting. The dog was right, of course; there was nothing more he could do. And there was no sense calling ahead. Hugo wouldn't wait. He'd do a final instrument check, curse his irresponsible son and order the door closed. He'd take off on schedule and see Atticus if and when he found his own way to Pandion. He wouldn't even mention the incident later, to show his son he alone was responsible for his own actions.

But Atticus would hear about it from his big brother Bode, for sure. He was such a jerk sometimes Atticus wondered how he could really be his brother.

The minutes ticked away. The general aviation airport at Teterboro was small, and they wouldn't be held up for security, but the timing was still close. Even light traffic could clog the Lincoln Tunnel entrance.

If his mom had a say Hugo would wait. Atticus knew she found his rules draconian, but she wouldn't tell *him* that. She did everything possible to avoid conflict in the rare times she had with her husband. Atticus sometimes worried this made her give up too much of herself.

"Here we are and three minutes to spare," Joseph said, screeching to a stop curbside.

Atticus saw no way to make it, but he jumped out of the car, not even shutting the door.

"Hey, what about that hundred?" Joseph called out.

"Yeah, *if* I make it," Atticus shouted without turning back.

He ran with his backpack falling from his shoulder and Ghost close beside him. People jumped out of their way and laughed as they rushed past. They were sure to miss the flight. This was a disaster.

He kept going over the morning. He'd been all ready to go until Ghost got sick. Bode would have let the housekeeper or a driver take him to the vet, but Atticus couldn't leave his dog behind, not when he was sick. He was just being responsible! Isn't that what his father wanted? He took his dog to the vet instead of leaving it to the staff. And for that he might waste a whole afternoon stuck in nowhere New Jersey? He wondered if he should take flying lessons, like Bode, and someday pilot his own family up to Maine. He'd never leave *his* kid behind.

Bursting through the door to the tarmac he spotted the Gulfstream already on the runway! Hugo must have left precisely on time and would take off right in front of him, like a big slap in the face.

He stood frozen to the ground, panting. Sweat trickled down his sides. He knew he shouldn't wait; he should be checking when Uncle Ted was flying so he could hitch a ride on his charter. Otherwise, he'd have to cab it to Newark Airport and try to find a commercial flight.

He knew his father's rules: at company functions you played the dutiful son and made small talk with investors; you never embarrassed your mother or interrupted Hugo when he was doing business; and you were never ever late for a flight when Hugo was captain.

But this time he *was* late, and Thanksgiving be damned, he was on his own. At that moment Bode would be sitting back in comfort, laughing that Atticus was left behind. Hugo would be focused on his checklist for takeoff. Atti's mother would be staring out the window, waiting for him to call. But calling would serve no purpose until he figured out how he'd get to Maine. He set his backpack against a fence and dialed Ted.

At the far end of the runway, his dad's jet sat behind what had to be an Arab royal, given the markings on the plane. There was some justice in this; Hugo couldn't hold up five minutes for his son but he'd have to wait his turn to take off.

"Atti?" Ted answered. "I thought you'd all be in the air by now."

"I'm glad I caught you, Uncle Ted. My dad is just taking off, but I got here late."

"So, he left you."

"Afraid so."

The Gulfstream powered up and started down the runway. Atticus paused to watch and then said, "So, I was wondering...."

"Of course you should join us. I chartered a flight at four, so you'll have to sit tight for a few hours. We'll see you then."

He hung up and kept watching the jet. He had often flown on his father's aircraft but had never seen one takeoff from the ground. For some reason he thought of *Foreign Correspondent*, the Hitchcock film where the hero goes down in a clipper plane shelled by the Germans. But he dismissed that morbid association and looked down at Ghost.

"We've got a ride, buddy," he said. "Just have to kill some time." The dog paid no attention, distracted by the airport smells.

The Gulfstream rolled by and lifted effortlessly. It rose and banked to the north, and Atticus turned to leave.

But someone shouted, and a marshaller in a yellow vest pointed up, mouth open wide.

Atticus turned back. The Gulfstream careened, flames trailing, and plummeted. A heavy boom shook the air. The jet hit out past the runway with a flash and another blast.

He dropped the leash and grabbed absently at the fence, unable to turn his gaze from the squiggly, pure white cloud lingering in the sky. Wild barking came as if from far off. Ghost stood between him and the wreck, snarling and yapping like a mad dog. Even in the sudden chaos, everyone shied away from them.

Sirens sounded. People shouted and rushed in all directions. Atticus fell to his knees and gathered Ghost to him, his heart and the dog's beating together like two angry drums. He couldn't know it then, but this was only the prelude.

Chapter One

At his seventeenth birthday dinner, Atticus laughed as a man in a chef's hat sprang into the dining room to ask if they needed anything. Hugo shook his head with a patronizing smile and the man disappeared.

"Who was that guy?" Atti asked.

"Han Chung, you dope," Bode scowled. "He has that cooking show. Dad finally let him buy in."

Hugo and his brother Ted ran Pandion Capital, an exclusive hedge fund with an extraordinary record of growth and a reputation among those in the know for consistent returns. The Foresters' Carnegie Hill townhouse was steps from Central Park and blocks from Earlington, the private school Atti attended. The neighbors were bankers and celebrities. Those who came to the house generally had two things in common: more money than they could ever spend and lust to make more. And some, like Chef Chung, showed up to pay homage to the man who kept their money safe and growing. Atticus enjoyed watching his father play these people, insisting the fund was closed to new investments and then watching them grovel for an exception.

"Your birthday dinner is Chef Chung's way of saying thanks," Hugo said. "A fitting gesture and, I must say, a beautiful meal. I hope it tastes as good as it looks."

"And he's quick," said Bode.

Hugo laughed. "Yes, and it's a good thing he can cook. All he knows about money is I get him more consistent returns than his brother-in-law, the broker."

"To money," Bode said, holding up his water glass.

What a pompous ass his brother was, Atti thought. He looked for support to his mother, who lowered her eyes in an almost imperceptible plea to let the moment pass. Hugo meanwhile grinned and tilted his wine glass at Bode, who beamed in response.

Atti wished his father would look at *him* that way. It was *his* birthday, after all. He returned to his meal, hoping Bode would choke on his lobster tail.

Atti paused to glance at the new Patek Philippe on his wrist. It was certainly expensive, but he had asked for an Apple Watch. What good was a hunk of jewelry that couldn't text or tell the weather? But his other birthday gift made him smile. His father rented a chalet in Cabo San Lucas for Atti and a few chosen friends from his soccer team. They'd have a housekeeper and a driver for the week and Hugo would let them use the Gulfstream, which would impress even his Earlington friends. His mother was not wild about the plan, but she wouldn't go against Hugo. His father had many inviolable rules, including that no one second-guessed his decisions about his sons. His judgment, after all, had opened a world of wealth and luxury to the whole family.

The week in Cabo was spectacular. The weather was hot, the beach fantastic and there was no age restriction in the bars. Atti and his friends Emerson, Haskins and Lincoln applied their chemistry on the soccer pitch to team trolling for girls in night spots and on the beach. With parents thousands of miles away and a fabulous house with an infinity pool, it was easy to lure girls from the resorts to join them. His best friend Emerson said it was the most dope vacation ever.

Atti slept all the way home and still needed two days to get back to normal. He told his mother he was recovering from Montezuma's revenge because he had mistakenly used ice in a drink. She was skeptical but let it pass. She disapproved of how Hugo let his sons do pretty much as they pleased but she would do anything to avoid confronting her husband. Whatever mess Atti got into, his mom would just be glad to get him back in one piece.

Atti was back on his game in time for the "Summer Splurge," the party Hugo threw at their house each year before the family left to spend July and August in Maine. This event promoted Hugo as ruthlessly successful in business and yet approachable and kind on a personal level. This reflected what he taught Atticus and Bode about succeeding in finance; it required discipline and guile. "Think of the osprey," he said. "We see nature's grace in its slender body and sculpted wings. But when it spies a fish, it doesn't hesitate. It plunges and snags that fish from the sea. In business you go right for the fish, but let the world see only your grace and humility."

A jazz quartet played in the garden. Out front uniformed valets parked expensive cars. As a special thank you to Hugo, the owner of a Michelin three-star restaurant arranged the catering. The staff looked like the actors they probably were, better dressed and more attractive than the invitees, who were mostly investors in the fund. The guests grazed on caviar and quaffed champagne while some waited for their minute in the library with Hugo, as if he were a mafia don. Atti wondered if any of them kissed his big diamond ring.

A few days after the party, per tradition, they would fly up to Pandion. That was Grandfather's name for the family compound he built on the southern coast of Maine. He had earned a fortune shipping goods on sea routes others feared to ply and built Pandion as his legacy to be passed down. There was some sort of Greek mythological connection with the name, but Hugo always said it referred to the provincial osprey, *pandion haliaetus*, to honor the sea as the source of Grandfather's fortune. The property covered twenty acres on a peninsula overlooking the ocean to the south and the sheltered Christmas Cove harbor to the northeast.

Hugo and his brother Ted had founded Pandion Capital, a securities firm named for the Maine property and Hugo's love of flying. When they hit it big, Hugo was in demand for financial news shows and courted by institutional investors. His cascading wealth opened all doors to Bode and Atti. They attended an elite boys' school on the Upper Eastside where the Forester name smoothed any trouble they caused. They wore the latest clothes and played on the newest gaming systems. And even though Bode got a Porsche for his twenty-first birthday, chauffeurs were always on call.

Bode had been co-captain of the football team his senior year at Earlington. Hugo donated a scoreboard that year and attended games with the head of school and chairman of the board of trustees. Atti was not big enough for football so he played soccer, and he did well on a team competitive in the Ivy Preparatory School League. His mom encouraged him and even practiced with him when he was young. His father never attended a game or even asked about the team.

Atti had trouble with his ears when he was very young, which led to a speech delay. Trouble communicating made it hard to avoid disappearing into his big brother's shadow. But his mother hired specialists and therapists, and by fourth grade he was done with what she called "elocution lessons." Atti then spoke quite well, but was still more inclined to listen than talk, and he sometimes stuttered when he was nervous, especially around girls. In middle school Atti was too scared to ask a girl on a date. He was afraid he would stutter, she'd laugh and he'd look like a fool. "Don't you get it, d–d–dummy?" Bode chided him when Atti started high school. "Even with your s–s–stammer, any girl will date you because of our money. All you have to do is tell her who you are and what you want."

The only girl Atti felt completely comfortable with was his cousin Elle, because they grew up together with a need to join forces against their older brothers. He could always count on her to be on his side.

Atti had a crush on a raven-haired beauty named Violet DeMorsey for as long as he could remember. In seventh grade they went to the same church and traveled in the same group of friends, but she hardly said three words to him that whole year.

Over eighth grade and the following summer he grew almost six inches, which gave him a new perspective and made kids and even grownups more deferential. Still, he was not happy about attending his first Earlington mixer.

"It'll be fun, Atticus," his mother said. "We'll buy you a new suit, since you've gotten so big. It will be good for you to meet some girls your age."

That was what scared him. "But I'll never dance, Mom, so what's the point?"

She gave him a look mixing patience with amusement. "You don't need to dance, but please go to the party, for me. I want to see how my handsome young man cleans up."

His mother rarely insisted on anything, so he had to go. He loved her and trusted her to do what was best for him, so maybe there was a point to it. Anyway, he needed to keep her on his side as a buffer against his father.

He was enormously relieved to find Elle at the mixer. It gave him someone to talk to. But then she turned on him, saying, "If you don't dance with me, I'll tell everyone you keep a teddy bear in your room."

That was unfair. There *was* a very small bear on his shelf, but only because it reminded him of a day Elle and Atti had spent with their families at Tivoli Gardens in Copenhagen: Atti won a mechanical rabbit and gave it to her, and she won the bear and gave it to him. He was pretty sure she wouldn't rat him out, but her mischievous look made him nervous, so he stepped onto the dance floor.

Dancing turned out to be okay. He didn't know what he was doing and so just jumped up and down, but she did too so it was fun. When they stepped off the floor, out of breath, Violet was watching. "You got tall, Atti," she said. "And I didn't know you were such a good dancer."

Someone shoved him from behind, so he was face to face with her.

"He wore me out, Violet," Elle said over his shoulder. "You better take over."

Before Atti knew it, he was dancing with Violet.

He couldn't believe she suddenly liked him. They danced a lot that night and over the next few weeks talked and texted all the time. His middle school crush was a spring breeze compared to his new gale-force devotion. He wrote her name over and over in notebooks and fell asleep picturing how she flipped her long black hair from her face.

His parents threw a party a couple of weeks later for families from their church. The DeMorseys came and Atti was proud to introduce Violet to his parents and Bode. That was a big mistake.

"Aren't *you* all grown up," Bode said, and she blushed.

From that moment Atti felt like a potted plant someone forgot to water. When he managed to speak to Violet, she kept glancing around as if she had lost something. She asked for a glass of punch but, when Atti returned with it, she had disappeared. He looked everywhere in the house and then tried the garden. In three weeks he hadn't gotten up the nerve to kiss Violet, but now he found her backed into the wisteria with his big brother. He went up to his room so no one would see him cry. He hated Bode.

His mother came upstairs to find him. She somehow knew what had happened; maybe she saw Bode and Violet together. It didn't matter. She had a way of rescuing his ego without embarrassing him. She made him laugh and feel loved and in the end ready to rejoin the party, all without mentioning his brother or his ex-girlfriend.

By his junior year, Atti had learned the trick with girls, who really did fall in line once they knew Hugo was the hedge fund king. Cast aside by Bode, Violet had turned her attention back to Atti, but he got his revenge. He went out of this way to date her best friend.

He still didn't talk much, mostly because he didn't know many people who could carry on an intelligent conversation. Girls just thought he was a good listener, which added to his appeal. He only had to nod once in a while for a girl to go on talking about herself. And that same ability to listen as if he cared proved invaluable at the Summer Splurge, where he had to make small talk with grownups.

Atti didn't understand the intricacies, but he knew Hugo ran a "fund of funds," which invested in other funds. Hank Salaban ran one of those related funds in California and had the gold jewelry and tan to prove it. "You've gotten so tall, Atti," Hank said. Atti smiled and nodded.

Ed Blankley grabbed his hand. He was CFO and a decent enough guy. He liked to talk Knicks and Yankees with Atti, but it was obvious he did this mostly to stay on Hugo's good side. Ed spotted someone across the room and left with another smile and nod.

Charles Tilson stepped past a large woman and came face to face with Atti. He was wide though not very tall. He always dressed in a way to make clear he was from Texas, even when he took off his cowboy hat. Tilson ran a feeder-fund for Pandion in Houston that brought in lots of money, so he was always full of himself. Atti could remember him scowling over rimless glasses when Atti and Bode were at the age "better seen than heard." Now that they were grown, Tilson seemed to wonder how they fit into the pecking order.

"So," Tilson said with a drawl, "are you going to follow your brother and be the next Bulldog in the family?"

There was a subtle jab there, reminding Atti he was the little brother who was expected to follow his brother to Yale. Through the years Tilson's quips often barely disguised his scorn, only now Atti understood the sentiment and resented it. "Ah, I don't know, Mr. Tilson," he said and then added sarcastically, "but it is *so* good to see you again."

Jazz wafted in from the garden. White-jacketed waiters circulated with drink trays and hors d'oeuvres. Hugo held court in his library, with Uncle Ted leading in one supplicant after another.

"Nice suit," Elle said emerging from the crowd.

"Hey, thanks," Atti replied. "I wanted to come in board shorts but…"

"But we *are* Foresters."

"And what could be better than that?"

The tiny freckles on her tanned nose and cheeks, and her big, warm smile made Elle a fresh spring day in this overdressed, Botox crowd. Since she always looked out for him, he felt it his duty to corrupt her. "What do you say to ducking out?"

"Well, the dads are doing business, Jillian is preening, and your mom is running the show. I guess the only ones who might notice are the brothers. But Martin is probably off smoking weed, and Bode seems preoccupied."

"Yeah, he's really into the crown prince act," Atti sneered. "I wonder what he's up to?"

"Too much Kool-Aid?"

Atti laughed. Bode was all-in on Pandion Capital. Still, he seemed unusually attentive this year to the investors slopping up Hugo's liquor.

Elle glanced past his shoulder. He turned and saw his friend from school, a tall, skinny boy, out of place with hair sticking out at all angles and a wide floral tie loose around his neck. Atti bumped fists with him and turned to his cousin. "Elle, meet Q."

She smiled. His eyes went wide.

"Q, this is my cousin, Elle."

"Q?" she said, holding out her hand. "That's an interesting name."

"Er, ah," he said.

Atti punched his arm. "We call him Q because 'Paolo Giaquinto' doesn't fit the rebel musician image."

"You're a musician?" she said earnestly.

"I am, but don't tell my father."

"He doesn't get a lot of parental support," Atti said.

"Welcome to the club," she laughed.

Elle spotted someone across the room and said she'd be right back. Q turned to Atti in awe. "Jesus, man, you said your cousin was nice, but you never told me she's a freaking goddess!"

"Yeah, she's okay."

"Okay? Are you kidding? Those luminous eyes! I'm in love. Do you think she might run off with me to Costa del Fuego?"

"No chance in hell. A dork like you?"

"You're right. I should write her a song first. She must have a boyfriend, right?"

"She's dating some guy from Collegiate…or was." Atti thought the world of his cousin, except for her taste in boyfriends. "Either way, you have zero chance of dating her, but we might lure her upstairs for some underage drinking."

Elle eagerly joined their foray to an upper balcony overlooking the garden. Atti left them to free his dog from bedroom banishment. Ghost was a three-year-old Australian shepherd, smart and fast, with one blue eye and one amber. Atti's biggest problem with him was his coat needed constant brushing to keep from matting, but there was always staff to help with that, and the groomer made house calls.

Ghost was deliriously happy to see Elle and Q.

"They locked him up?" Elle said, hugging the dog.

"Hard to believe, right?" Atti said.

"And he's such a party animal," Q said, taking his turn to tussle while Ghost growled playfully.

Atti popped open a bottle of champagne, sending the cork in a parabolic arc that almost hit the musicians in the garden. The drummer looked up with a big smile and without missing a beat.

"Those dudes are the bomb," said Q. "I dig that tenor sax."

"They won a Grammy last year," Atti said as he poured.

Elle reached out again to pet Ghost. "So, my stepmother's off-the-shoulder dress is causing quite a stir downstairs."

"She's your *mother*?" Q asked, incredulous.

"*Step*mother. Jillian is only twelve years older than me."

Elle's mother had died of cancer when she was ten. Jillian took her place three years later. She was shapely and knew how to wear jewelry and expensive clothes, but otherwise she paled in comparison with Elle's mother. Bode said she was after Ted's money, and he was a deluded old fool. But her marrying Ted proved what Bode often said: women would overlook anything for enough money.

Q watched Elle, transfixed, until she turned her smile on him again. "So, what's your plan to become a rock star?"

"Haven't quite worked that out. A friend downtown says he could get me gigs, but I'd have to find a place to live. My dad will kick me out if I don't go to college. He says I should be an engineer—I guess because I tinker with electronics—but he won't even talk about supporting me if I do music. We have some pretty heated discussions on the subject."

Q's parents had enough money to send him to Earlington but nothing like the Foresters. He'd have to support himself someday, and his father saw music as a distraction. And the "heated discussions" were more like World War I trench warfare, sometimes driving Q to crash at Atti's house. They spent a lot of time there listening to music, playing chess and trying out Q's inventions for amplifying and recording his guitar.

At school Atti spent his time with his teammates and mostly avoided Q. All the guys knew whose parents had money, and that mattered more than Q being smarter than the rest of them, although smart in a quirky way. His eccentricities would have added to his image if he were higher up the social ladder, but in Q they came across as weird. Atti accepted this as the natural order, and it was reassuring to compartmentalize and have one friend away from school always sure to follow him around like a puppy. Also, Atti's parents were used to Q staying over, and that summer Hugo said he could fly up to Pandion with the family.

Once they had settled in with their champagne and grew tired of roasting party guests, Elle asked, "So, Atti, have you decided what schools you're applying to?"

"Oh, dude, what a buzz-kill," Q said, downing his glass and reaching for the bottle.

She squinted to acknowledge the faux pas.

"Give it a rest," Atti said to Q a bit sharply. He turned to Elle. "Haven't given it much thought. I *could* always go to Yale."

"And hang out in the Forester Business Library?" Q interjected.

Atti gave him a stern look, and said through a grimace, "But that would mean trailing along behind Bode. I'd rather go somewhere with less family and better weather. What about you?"

"I've been rating colleges by how far away they are from all things Pandion."

"You mean Pandion *Capital*."

"Of course. You know I love Maine."

As the youngest children in the family, Elle and Atti had spent their summers and holidays together at Pandion. She had been a tomboy and a perfect friend for Atti. They sailed, explored the woods and rode bikes, and she was also a natural swimmer, even in the frigid ocean. Her laughter stood out in so many of his memories of Maine.

But he had no idea how important she'd be to him when it all went to hell.

Chapter
Two

Atti sent Q and Elle downstairs while he gathered the glasses and bottle to hide among the party detritus. But then he stepped off the balcony straight into his cousin Martin.

"So, a little private party?" Martin said derisively. "You and my angelic sister...."

Atti shook his head and turned toward the staircase.

"Oh, yeah," Martin sneered after him, "I saw you. Hope no one catches alcohol on your breath."

"Martin, screw off. What's it to you?"

"Nothing, except my sister can do no wrong, while my father hires people to watch me."

"I guess he has a reason, right?"

Martin snarled and pushed past him. Atti looked over at Ghost, who sat passively and watched. Atti liked dogs better than most people.

After he closed Ghost back in his bedroom, Atti headed downstairs. On the staircase he met Harry Gooden, the chief compliance officer, who was as usual a little short of breath. "Your father is ready to speak," Harry said urgently, checking his watch and a clipboard in his hand. Atti swept past him.

In the main room downstairs, he joined the crowd just as Hugo and Ted appeared. The band stopped playing and Harry handed Hugo a microphone.

"On behalf of my lovely wife, Marie, my two boys and myself, I want to thank you for joining this year's Summer Splurge and to welcome you once again to our humble abode." A few titters. Obsequious smiles all around.

"This year marks two milestones for the Forester family and Pandion Capital. My brother Ted and I are more than pleased to announce Pandion Capital has surpassed forty billion dollars in managed assets." A collective intake of breath and then enthusiastic applause. Men shook hands. Couples kissed. Many attendees had their fortunes invested in the Pandion Fund, so *its* success was *their* success.

"Equally important in my eyes," Hugo went on, "I am pleased to say in September my son, Boden Forester, will take on the role of Special Assistant to the President." More applause, polite rather than enthusiastic. Those standing near Bode shook his hand or clapped him on the back. He beamed with typical arrogance. Atti shrugged in response to Elle's inquiring look.

Hugo held up his hands for quiet. "Although," he went on, looking at Bode, "we expect the newest member of our executive team to complete his studies at Yale University before joining the firm fulltime next June."

After the speech, Q left in search of crab cakes. Elle nodded at him. "He's nice, your friend. How come we haven't met before?"

"He's kind of a nerd," Atti replied. "Doesn't hang out with my friends. He's something of an acquired taste."

"That sounds very superior. He seems to think the world of you."

"Yeah, sure. But then we *are* the imperial family."

Elle looked disappointed, which stung a bit. He had only asked Q to the party because Nick Emerson was in Aruba for the month. But it was no surprise Elle would adopt Q, the same way she supported so many lost causes. Anyway, Atti had more important things on his mind than the chance he might offend Q. The news about Bode was a shock.

Already a millstone around Atti's neck, joining the company would make his brother insufferable.

"What does a Special Assistant to the President do?" Elle asked, jerking Atti back to the conversation.

"Ah, who knows if it even involves work?" All that was certain was Bode would lord the appointment over him. It wasn't so much he'd get paid; they could both pretty much buy what they wanted. It was how he'd flaunt it. He would now be part of the company while Atti was just a kid.

Atti could see Bode's appointment ruining the summer. Large as Pandion was, he doubted it was big enough to hold *three* masters of the universe. With no real friends in Maine—the locals were feeble-minded, and the old money yacht-club kids resented Hugo's fortune—Atti would have to rely more than ever on Elle. In consequence, he felt like a genius for thinking to invite Q after Emerson turned out to be traveling with his family. Elle liked Q and maybe he'd bring some energy to the summer.

Harry Gooden came over to Atti and offered his hand. "Sorry to be abrupt on the stairs. You know how your dad is about being on time."

"I know it all too well, Uncle Hal. My bad." It felt odd still calling the man "Uncle Hal," but he knew Harry liked it and Atti felt a little sorry for him. Harry had been shaken by his wife's death five years before and never quite seemed to recover.

Harry ate it up. His whole long, jowly face smiled, pinching up his funny salt and pepper mustache. He had been with the company from the start. Atti remembered playing hide and seek when he was young with a fun "Uncle Hal," but over the years the man became just "Old Harry," who worked for his dad and always overdressed, as he did now in a serious business suit and hard shoes.

"He knows where the bodies are buried," Bode chided. "No other reason he's still at the company."

That was unkind—the man had been "Uncle Hal" to Atti's brother as well—but Bode's instincts for what went on at the company gener-ally proved out, so this colored Atti's perception of Harry. Besides, why would a chief compliance officer at a major financial firm run around an investor party carrying a clipboard? Bode was probably right about

Harry just taking up space. Atti hated admitting it but he had a lot to learn from his brother—when he wasn't being an ass.

Atti continued to circulate, his small talk on autopilot, while he thought about where he'd rather be. If he had the guts, he'd chuck it all and sail around the world like his grandfather. He had enough to live and travel, but not enough to buy a respectable sailboat. He'd want at least a forty-footer, to make an impression when he came into port. And he'd need someone to crew, and there would be all sorts of expenses. If he didn't have to wait until he was twenty-five to get his hands on his trust fund, he could leave now and sail for years. Later he could always return to some job at Pandion Capital that didn't require much effort, or else his father could set him up with one of the clients always falling over themselves to do him favors. What was the sense of being a Forester if he had to work for a living?

All this was interesting to think about, but who was he kidding? He had everything he wanted. Soon he'd have a driver's license and his own car, maybe like Bode's Porsche or something even faster. His father would bring him into the company, and maybe he could get posted to London or open a new office somewhere with room to breathe. None of this was far off.

Two of their usual chauffeurs drove the family to the airport for the flight to Maine. Joseph drove Atti, Bode, Q and Ghost.

"I don't know why I have to ride with you runts," Bode sneered and made a show of looking out the window. His brother disregarding them was fine with Atti; he was easiest to take when he ignored everyone. Q was the opposite. His excitement spread across his face, like a kid. Atti wished his friend wasn't so awkward, because it reminded him how his own stuttering made him conspicuous, but Q's enthusiasm was refreshing.

Atti didn't know what was wrong with Ghost, something he ate or just driving in the car, but in the tunnel he heaved on the mat.

Bode scoffed, "Can't you train your dog to do that shit outside?"

"Except it isn't *shit* and it's not his fault."

"It's gross. I'd make you take a cab but that would leave me with the mess." He plugged in his headphones and turned back toward the window.

Ghost seemed okay after that, and Atti was grateful they didn't have to hear more abuse from his brother. The upchuck was on Q's shoes, of course, which caused him to curse under his breath. Atti laughed at his hapless friend, always on the receiving end when the shit was flying. But his father would blame Atti if his guest got on the plane with barf on his shoes, so he opened the bar and handed Q napkins.

They made it to Teterboro Airport in plenty of time and walked directly through the small terminal building to the tarmac.

"Isn't there any security?" Q asked.

"This is general aviation, hardly any commercial flights, so no TSA."

"I don't have to take off my shoes?"

Atti laughed. "Right, but you can if you want, and you can also smuggle a couple of kilos."

"No dogs either?"

Atti stopped. He looked at Q as if that were an insensitive remark and gestured toward Ghost. But the dog was paying no attention and they both laughed. "But seriously," Atti said, "there are Port Authority cops, and I hear the FBI watches for human trafficking—so try not to look like a hostage."

Atti then pointed out the new Gulfstream. "Holy shit," Q said. "That's really yours?"

"The 'PC' is for Pandion Capital, of course."

"Not 'politically correct'?" Q laughed.

Atti laughed too, enjoying Q's cynicism. "No. My father and uncle *are* Pandion Capital and own practically everything, usually with a mess of companies in between. I tried to get Bode to explain it all, but he said it was 'confidential.'"

"Well, the important thing is we get to fly in it," Q said.

"And we're on time."

"Another Hugo rule?"

Atti chuckled. "And this one's set in stone."

Chapter
Three

Hugo used Brunswick Executive Airport in Maine because it was close to South Bristol and he owned a hangar on land leased from the operator. When the family deplaned there, Gabriel Oak was waiting by a black SUV. An imposing, barrel-chested man in a flannel shirt, he welcomed them all with his broad, honest smile.

"Good to see you," Hugo said, shaking the caretaker's hand.

"You had grand flying weather, Hugo," Gabriel responded, in his way of sounding more like an Irishman than someone who had lived his whole life in Maine. He then greeted each of them in turn. Atti introduced Q, while Ghost stretched his legs running circles around them all.

Gabriel was on salary, but he and his father before him had run Pandion for so long he felt like family. He was the only one of their domestic employees who called Hugo and Ted by their first names. He was also attentive to Atti's mother, who always had a smile for him. For his whole life Atti had turned to Gabriel as a safe harbor when storms rocked the family. Only Bode ever had an unkind word to say about him, probably because Gabriel stepped in over the years to temper his bullying.

The gardener Enrique stood with Gabriel. He had come in Gabriel's Jeep and started loading bags into the two cars. Q watched to make sure Enrique handled the guitar case gently.

Gabriel turned to Hugo. "We've had a bit of trouble," he said. "There were surveillance cameras planted at the Barn."

"The Barn" was Grandmother's name for the grand Victorian house at Pandion that stood up to the sea wind from a bluff overlooking Christmas Cove and the village of South Bristol. The Barn faced the ocean to the south, the cove to the east and north, and a big lawn to the northwest. Scattered over the compound's twenty acres were thickets of trees and trails and outbuildings. There was a boathouse on the harbor side and a changing hut his grandmother named "The Lookout" by a narrow beach of coarse sand on the ocean side. Trails through the trees led to small stone guest cottages Grandmother had given names like "The Old Buck's Eyebrow" and "Be Thankful." When Atti was young "Cliff Dweller," on the ocean side, had been the summer refuge of Grandfather's old college professor. At the entrance to the property stood the stone two-bedroom gatehouse Gabriel occupied year-round.

They quickly packed into the cars for an hour's drive up the coast and down the peninsula. Bode maneuvered himself into the front seat of Gabriel's SUV so he could ride with Hugo and Marie, which left Q and Atti to enjoy the drive in peace, though Atti struggled to understand what Gabriel had meant by finding cameras at Pandion. Who would do that?

He put this aside and opened the window to the smell of lush forest and briny sea and the ubiquitous call of seagulls. Q had never before been to Maine and gazed out the window for glimpses of the ocean. Ghost stepped up on Atti's lap to stick his head out the window. Atti could not understand why the dog liked that so much but hated when you blew at his face.

At Pandion Gabriel showed Hugo where the cameras had been found, one on the porch aimed at the front door, another under the eaves aimed at the big lawn, and a third pointing into Hugo's office at the north end of the ground floor.

"Were they wired? "Hugo said.

"They ran on batteries and the police said they appeared to broadcast a signal to a receiver in the area. They impounded two of the cameras but left this one." He passed to Hugo a device that fit easily on the palm of his hand. "The detective said they don't have the resources to track this down."

"Get hold of Ed Warner. Tell him we need a team up here tomorrow morning to sweep the house and the grounds and test the range of this camera."

The surveillance incident tempered the usual excitement of moving into the house for the summer. Atti's father told him to look around for anything suspicious, so Atti took this excuse to take Q through the house. His friend couldn't believe the number of rooms in the sprawling structure and the enormous bedroom assigned to him. "I may move in for good," he laughed, trying out the bed.

"And we may need you to stay," Atti said, "to upgrade our alarm system."

After lunch Atti and Q wandered the property. They were out by the tennis courts when the cars pulled up again. "The rest of the Foresters," Atti said. "Uncle Ted doesn't fly with us; something about asserting his independence. It's really dumb because he and Jillian wouldn't be caught dead flying commercial, so he has to charter a jet for the fifty-minute flight."

"Dude," Q said, "you live in a lofty world."

"What can I say?"

Atti's uncle was a toady when his father was around but acted "lord of the manor" at all other times. Atti could sympathize with living in the shadow of a big brother, but Ted was still sometimes hard to take. He acted erratically and would fire staff for small offenses. The summer before he dismissed a young Mexican man working with the boats because Jillian found him a little too interesting.

While each brother owned half of Pandion, Atti's dad and mom always occupied the best wing. Atti figured this was because his father paid most of the bills although, like the jet, house expenses probably ran through a company account.

Q and Atti walked across the lawn to greet the new arrivals. Ted acted the benevolent uncle to Atti and paid no attention to Q. Jillian jiggled about, shaking her ass in red leather pants to make sure Q noticed, which he certainly did. Martin barely nodded to Atti as he told Enrique to carry his bag into the house. But none of that mattered once Elle greeted Atti and Q with hugs and her electric smile. She then dropped to her knees to return Ghost's welcome.

Ed Warner arrived next morning with three technicians. They found nothing in the house and determined the cameras could have transmitted up to two thousand feet, which meant the receiver had to be either in the compound or just over the property line. This prompted Hugo to bark instructions.

"Atti, take Q out past the tennis courts and down near the boathouse. Look for any kind of electronic device or evidence something has been hidden."

"Are we only looking outside?" Atti asked.

"No, of course not. Look in the cove-side cottages and the boathouse. These things could be anywhere."

He assigned other areas of the property to Elle and Bode and Enrique, and he was peeved Martin was nowhere to be found. He said to Gabriel, "You take Ed along the fence and beyond the property to the limit of the transmission range. You'll be able to smooth this over if you run into a neighbor, but I'd prefer you not share any details."

"Understood, Hugo," Gabriel said. "There won't be an issue."

After the security scan found no receiver and the team departed, the normal rhythm of summer returned. The days passed as always at Pandion, the kids having no responsibilities beyond amusing themselves. Josie, the cook, always had something heavenly baking in the kitchen, two housekeepers handled the indoor chores and Enrique managed the gardens. Elle tried to entice Atti to join her in jogging or aerobics with the old exercise discs, but he was firmly devoted to sleeping in, sailing their three boats in the cove, leisurely bike rides and walks, and meals served on the ocean-side terrace or in the big dining room. Gabriel popped in and out, always wearing a tool belt or carrying a clipboard. A week after their arrival Bode's Porsche was delivered from New York, which thankfully allowed Bode and Martin to spend time away from the compound, scouring the coast for trouble.

One morning Atti woke as the sun was rising. Hugo had flown back to the city the evening before and taken Bode. Everyone else was still in bed. He and Ghost wandered down the cliff trail in the crisp morning air. Atti thought he'd take out a rowboat in the sheltered cove by The Lookout. Ghost liked looking into the water for fish and a little exercise would give Atti an appetite for breakfast.

The sea was calm. Gulls circled and cawed. The big rocks along the shore blushed a rich gold before the rising sun.

Ghost barked and ran ahead as if he'd seen something. Around the back of The Lookout Atti found him with Marie. She sat on a rock petting him, her face flushed.

"You guys came to my rescue," she said, sounding flustered.

"What happened, Mom? Are you okay?"

"I am. I came out for an early walk and twisted my ankle a bit." She turned her leg, but Atti could see nothing wrong.

"I was just catching my breath," she continued.

Ghost turned to the trees and barked again. He ran up the trail toward the gatehouse.

"Marie! Atticus!" Gabriel's deep voice boomed from the trail. "You two are out early!"

Gabriel came out of the trees with Ghost right behind. He seemed oddly out of breath but stopped and said, "Am I interrupting a mother-son-man's-best-friend moment?"

"Oh, no, Gabriel," Marie replied. "I was resting after a walk when my men found me."

"And she *twisted* her ankle," Atti added, unwilling to make light of the injury.

Gabriel looked concerned. He not only cared for the house and the grounds, but through all the years of bumps and bruises had been the master of first aid. He kneeled and took Marie's ankle in his hands. "Is it bad?" he said, gently manipulating it. "Does this hurt?"

"It's fine," Marie replied. "I just needed to rest it a bit."

"I don't see any swelling," Gabriel said, "but it would be best to elevate your leg and ice it, just in case. Let's help you up to the driveway, and I'll get the Jeep."

Marie looked as grateful as Atti felt that Gabriel had happened along. Gabriel took Marie's arm to help her up the path and Atti followed. His mother never dwelled on her own aches and pains, and he marveled at how she acted as if the ankle didn't bother her at all.

Atti waited with his mother, and then he and Ghost walked along behind the Jeep. By then he was ready for a pile of Josie's pancakes.

The odd thing about that morning was not so much Gabriel showing up; he always materialized when he was most needed. But later Atti's mother pulled him aside and said, "About this morning, Atticus…."

"When you hurt your ankle?"

"Yes, and Gabriel drove me to the Barn…."

"What about it?"

"Well, I'd rather you not mention it to anyone. People will make a fuss, especially your father. No telling; he might rush me off for x-rays."

"Yeah…sure," Atti said, although the notion of his father fussing over his mother's ankle seemed far-fetched.

Two days later Hugo had returned and was gone again. This time he flew to Boston with Ted. The morning was sultry with a forecast for much higher than usual temperatures. Elle and Atti agreed on a trip to the beach and Q was eager to join them. The hot day would make the frigid ocean more tolerable and an afternoon away from Pandion would be a way to avoid Bode and Martin who, with both fathers gone, were certain to be a bother.

"So where is this beach?" Q asked as they walked to the garage to look for working bikes. "And isn't the water a little cold for swimming?"

"Oh, *it's cold*," Atti said, "but today will be really hot. You'll like it; trust me. Back Bay is out past the other side of the village, a half-hour ride."

They found two useable bicycles in the garage, and Gabriel and Q quickly got a third working. Soon they had left Pandion and were pedaling through the village when someone shouted Atti's name. It was Father Jake out front of St. Bernard's. His real name was Giacomo, but Atti started calling him Jake when he was little and couldn't pronounce the Italian name. The nickname stuck; it felt like a bond between them.

Marie always went to church on Sundays, and when the boys were young, she took them with her. When Atti was eleven, she talked him into joining the church choir. His voice was changing and his sense of pitch suspect, but none of that mattered because Father Jake made it fun. The priest became a friend, and in later years Atti saw him when Marie invited him to dinner or to the Picnic each year, or when Atti stopped in to talk. The priest always singled him out for special attention and lent an ear whenever Atti needed it. There was also something serene and comforting about the old church when it was empty, although it had become a little shabby because Father Jake put all the parish resources into reaching out to locals. He watched over a wide assortment of neighbors, never seeming to distinguish his parishioners from the others who struggled through the winters, when the big houses were empty, work was scarce, and a cold wind raked the shore.

"I heard you folks had arrived," the priest said affectionately. "Hello, Elle, I trust your family's well."

"Thanks, Father," she said. "Same as always, I'm afraid."

"Please give my regards, and mention to Martin he owes me a visit." It was an open secret Martin had at one time attended meetings for ex-addicts in the church.

"And I see you've brought me a convert," the priest said, turning to Q.

Q looked around for support. Atti suppressed a smile. He was sure Q hadn't seen the inside of a church since his confirmation.

"Yes, Father," Atti said. "This is Paolo Giaquinto. He's looking for spiritual direction."

"Paolo!" the priest exclaimed, grasping Q's hand in both of his. "*Credo che il tuo amico ti stia prendendo in giro.*"

Q looked desperate, as if he were being shanghaied into a monastery.

Atti laughed. "It's okay, man. Whatever the padre said, I'm sure he was kidding."

"I apologize," Father Giacomo said. "I assumed with a name like that you'd understand I said, 'Your friend is pulling your leg.'"

Q was so visibly and comically relieved that they all laughed.

"So," said Atti, "out enjoying the day, Father, with so much of the world yet to be saved?"

"Yes, I needed a break from wrestling with *Organo.*"

"Some things never change," Atti laughed.

"I'm convinced there is some mechanical reason I can't get our old friend quite tuned," the priest sighed.

"Father," Q said hesitantly, "could I lend a hand?"

The priest looked at him in surprise. "Do you know pipe organs?"

"Not specifically...."

"But," Atti interjected, "Paolo is a musician and a mechanical wizard."

"A mechanical magician musician," the priest laughed. "It seems the Lord led me into this glorious morning for more than a breath of air. Paolo, I humbly embrace your help."

Q agreed to return the next day, and Father Giacomo excused himself to meet the volunteers setting up a community garden, "made possible through a generous donation by Atti's mother." That prompted Elle to say she'd help; she was a sucker for any kind of local-sourcing enterprise. Atti, on the other hand, took this as his cue to say they'd all catch up with the priest later. Father Giacomo's knowing look reached deep inside Atti and reminded him he had promised to assist with a canned food drive. Atti was not naturally altruistic, like Elle, but the priest would poke at his conscience to make him feel an obligation to give back to the village. The priest acted like the Foresters were feudal lords responsible for the many souls on their land. But that was nonsense; rescuing the downtrodden was his job, not Atti's.

Back Bay was just up the coast road from the village. They left the bikes by the road, not bothering to lock them, and bounded down the sand cliff to the beach. The sand was coarse but still a break from the huge rocks strewn along most of Maine's shoreline. Other than a fisherman casting into the surf and a family with two small children, they had the narrow beach to themselves. Sandpipers raced along the water line and noisy gulls circled overhead. They laid out towels and enjoyed the brilliant sunshine until Elle announced she was ready for a swim. She stood, peeled off her T-shirt and strode toward the water.

Q looked stunned.

"You okay?" Atti said.

"I can't believe you!" Q stared at her receding form. "Oh, my God! She's the most gorgeous girl I've ever seen!"

"Right," Atti said. "Should I remind you again she's my cousin, not to mention I grew up with her?"

"Dude, you're comatose!"

Atti followed his stare. Q was right; if he didn't know who she was, he *might*… But that kind of thinking went nowhere. Atti got up and stripped to his bathing suit, and Q jumped up to follow.

"By the way," Atti said as they walked toward the water, "don't let her sucker you into a race. She was on the boys' swim team at the yacht club. You couldn't keep up with her in a rowboat."

They all stood in the edge of the waves until the cold had numbed their legs and then dashed into the water. Out past the breakers they jumped and splashed, and then Atti and Q returned to dry sand.

"Bunch of babies!" Elle called after them and started swimming along the shoreline.

Next morning Atti and Q were on the tennis courts, knocking balls over the fences more than playing a legitimate game. When they tired of chasing balls, they sat in the sunshine with their backs against the fence. "There are a lot of visitors to that cottage," Q said. He was gesturing toward Be Thankful, nestled on a rise overlooking the harbor, a van parked beside it.

"That'll be Jillian," Atti said. "Her masseuse or her yoga instructor."

"You're kidding."

"No. You can always tell when Jillian's here. Bode says she sets herself up in a cottage so we won't notice who's coming and going."

"Maybe she stashes away a gigolo?" Q said, his loosed imagination evident in his eyes. "She *is* a lot younger than your uncle."

"And he's no prize at *any* age," Atti grinned. "But…I wonder. Jillian's visitors seem to know their way around the compound pretty well, how to get in and out without being seen…."

Q's lascivious grin turned curious.

"What if…?" Atti said and paused. "What if one of them set up those cameras?"

Chapter
Four

Marie insisted each summer on an annual catharsis. The whole family would all spend one entire day, morning through evening, outdoors at Pandion. Gabriel, of course, was in charge of setting up what Marie called the "Picnic." In Atti's memory the weather had always been fine. His father wasn't allowed to take calls. Bode had to lay off picking on him. "And you," his mother once told him, "must make your mother laugh."

Gabriel programed activities, which had to get more elaborate as the kids aged. When they were little, a three-legged race worked, or a balloon-toss. When they got older, he brought in ponies and jugglers. Even through their jaded teenage years, he came up with amusements to keep everyone engaged.

Then there was always croquet, a simple pursuit taken deadly seriously in the Forester family. Several matches would take place over the course of the day. Some of these would be friendly. Marie enjoyed playing and having Hugo play with her, which would *only* happen at the Picnic. Jillian would occasionally pick up a mallet, as long as she could play a color matching her outfit. Father Giacomo would join in sometimes, though he lacked the killer instinct of the young players. Marie would even drag Harry Gooden out to play, although it had been years since he actually seemed to enjoy it.

But as evening approached, the croquet became serious. The crowning event of the day was the annual championship match. Played right before dinner, this was reserved for the kids but everyone else would cheer or heckle. Bode had by general understanding aged out when he turned twenty-one, but he agreed to continue playing with the "children" because it was another opportunity to dominate his sibling and cousins. Though increasingly churlish as the years went by, Martin still joined as well because the prize might be worth having.

The prize was Ted's creation. Like Gabriel's amusements, the reward got more elaborate as the kids grew. What started as a special cake or a trip to the ice cream store in Gabriel's Jeep became a gaming system or a mountain bike and, two years back, a block of IBM stock. Ted never let on what the prize would be until he handed it over. Atti suspected he decided to award an extravagant emerald brooch last year only after Elle took the match in dramatic fashion.

The day arrived. A salty breeze blew in from the sea, making the temperature perfect. Songbirds filled the trees. Caterers were setting up tables under the big elm tree. A string quartet played on the gazebo. A white-jacketed young man poured coffee and took breakfast orders.

"So, let me get this straight," Q said, "we play croquet and the winner gets, like, a car?"

"Well, Uncle Ted might not give *you* anything."

Q's smile drooped and Atti laughed. "Don't be such a dope. If you win the match, you get the prize."

Q was visibly relieved. "So, what else happens at the Picnic?"

"*That* is a question only Gabriel can answer."

Atti was sitting with Q and Elle, finishing an omelet, when a panel van pulled up, "Falmouth Falconry" painted on its side. From the driver's door emerged a big man dressed all in khaki, one side of his floppy hat pinned up. Two young assistants in khaki overalls began setting up equipment on the lawn.

"Let the festivities begin," Elle said with a knowing smile.

The big man approached. Erect on his heavy leather glove stood a bird ten inches tall with beautiful brown, gray and black plumage and a face so expressive it seemed about to speak.

"Folks, meet Finn the Fowler," Gabriel said to the family.

"Doesn't look Finnish," Bode said under his breath.

Finn glanced quickly at Bode and turned a wide smile on them all. "Good morning, Forester clan!" he said in a booming voice. "We are so happy to be here this fine morning. For today's holiday, we'll be flying a variety of raptors. The birds will be on holiday as well, since today they won't have to hunt their breakfast." He paused, as if for a laugh. "Tough crowd," he said to the bird and turned back to them. "Some, like Bob here—an American kestrel and member of the falcon family—fly for the pure joy of it but will always return to hand when offered a treat. Some of the others—like Arthur the ferruginous hawk—won't fly for nothing. In the wild he sits in a tree conserving energy until hunger drives him into the air to catch a meal. He then immediately returns to the tree to digest and ponder. Arthur is a great thinker."

"Did you bring a sea hawk?" Hugo called out.

"Ah," Finn responded, "I anticipated that question, given the name of this beautiful estate. It is *possible* to fly a sea hawk, also called a western osprey or *pandion haliaetus*, but its natural food is live fish, so that might cause complications here, so close to the sea. But we have brought a variety of hawks and owls who prefer the beef on this morning's menu."

Over a leisurely two hours Finn handed the heavy glove around and showed them how to fly the birds. Each took off from the gloved hand and flew in wide circles within the outer reaches of the lawn and up over the near trees. Once a bird landed, Finn would load a piece of meat onto the glove of whomever was wearing it and step away, and the bird would swoop in and land on the glove to eat.

"It's amazing," Elle wondered aloud, always enamored with nature, "how a bird so big can fly so fast yet land so softly."

Finn spiced his instructions and bird stories with one-liners. He mentioned having to pick up supplies in New Hampshire, which led to a riff of insults against the neighboring state. "They call themselves Granite Staters," Finn laughed, "but Bob and I think Granite-heads is more like it."

Hugo flew a snowy owl and then coaxed Marie to join in. She agreed but only if she could fly Bob the kestrel, whom she found "much the most personable of the lot." Q was fascinated with the process of weighing each bird before and after it flew, bringing mathematical precision to the ancient sport of kings. Even Bode couldn't act aloof with a raptor on his hand.

"Got a golden eagle back at the barn," Finn said. "Name's Rosie: a real troubled case. Hates everyone and came to me as a last resort. We get along because she thinks I'm her mate, but even *I* don't turn my back on her and she never flies free. The one time she did she knocked down a golfer, who fortunately thought it was a great story to tell. Another big bird could do damage by accidentally knocking you down or clawing your arm, but Rosie *wants* to hurt you. She's about the meanest creature you'll ever meet—other than my second wife."

Finn's assistant prepared to shoot video when he untethered Arthur. The bird was dark brown and stood over two feet tall, a leather hood covering his head. Finn moved him from his perch to Bode's glove, while the other assistant placed meat on a railing forty yards away.

"Now this fella will only be *taking off* from your hand. If he landed, he'd knock you down."

Bode scoffed, as if a bird could take *him* off his feet.

"The very instant the hood comes off," Finn said, "old Arthur will go for the meat on the rail. Be ready; he'll launch before you know it."

Finn gestured everyone to step away and prepared to remove the hood. Bode puffed out his chest, like a Mongolian falconer galloping over the steppes.

Finn yanked off the hood. Arthur instantly spread his huge wings, startling everyone and sending Bode diving for cover. The bird covered the distance to the rail in two beats of its wings.

Bode stood up, brushing off his pants and his dignity. "You try holding that thing!" he snarled.

They all laughed, but Atti and Q had much the same experience flying old Arthur and no one else chose to try.

The only one who didn't enjoy the hawking was Ghost. He understood these animals were guests and could not be chased or eaten but he kept a close eye on them, especially when one was near Atti. And then there were the local birds. "Have you noticed," Elle said, "how all our songbirds have disappeared?"

"A hawk show has got to be a finch's worst nightmare," Q replied.

Father Giacomo arrived for lunch, and Hugo invited Finn and his assistants to join them at the one long table on the lawn, with filmy sunshades placed strategically overhead. Gabriel, Josie, Enrique and the two housekeepers also sat with the family. This was common for Gabriel but only a semi-annual tradition for the rest and a special treat for Josie to be served someone else's cooking.

Over lunch Finn kept up a stream of hawking stories and jokes about New Hampshirites and his three wives.

Late in the afternoon Uncle Ted announced the championship match. The play was cut-throat, as always. Old rivalries outweighed strategy when one of them would spend a bonus shot to knock another ball far across the lawn, aiming for the trees. But this was nothing new, and it evened out in the end. Annoyingly, Bode won and so everyone had to see his shit-eating grin.

Ted put down his drink and shook Bode's hand. "This year," he said dramatically, "the annual croquet prize goes to Boden Forester for—what is this, about the tenth time?" He smiled at Bode, who smirked. "Anyway, the prize this year is five front-row tickets." He paused and looked around, raising his eyebrows.

Bode looked at Ted listlessly. "What, to like Parson's Ice Cream Shop?"

"No, no, we researched this." Ted sought out Gabriel's affirmative nod and waved a white envelope. "And we have arranged for five fortunate individuals to drive to the airport, fly to New York and take front-row seats at Radio City Music Hall for the Scrags one-night-only show!"

"Holy crap!" Q burst out and then covered his mouth, looking sheepish. Q loved the Scrags, an alternative rock band that had crossed over to the pop charts. They had famously given up performing live two years before, so a one-time show would be momentous. But then, it was Bode who won the tickets.

Ted was still waving the envelope and cleared his throat. "I'm pleased to see you appreciate that Uncle Ted scored these tickets, and, of course, you will thank Uncle Hugo for lending his jet for the night. But I think you'll appreciate even more an idea put forth by one of the ladies of the house," bowing his head toward Marie, "that this prize should be *shared* by the five young people who have spent this month together at Pandion."

Q jumped in the air and shot up his arm. Bode looked around in dismay but seemed to catch Marie's eye. She smiled like a proud mother, and he went along. The rest of them shared big smiles.

The Picnic was Saturday. The concert was the next Thursday. On Wednesday morning, Atti found his father alone in his office.

"Dad," he said, "I was thinking about those cameras…."

Hugo looked up with interest.

"Well, it's really only a thought, and I didn't want to say anything in front of everyone else, but…."

"Out with it," Hugo said, his attention beginning to wane.

"It's just…you know how Jillian has personal trainers and hair stylists and all sorts of people at Be Thankful…."

Hugo inhaled with a pained look.

"They always seem to come and go without anyone noticing. Could one of them have set up those cameras?"

Hugo squinted and turned his head, rubbing his chin. "You may have a point, Atti, but you were right not to mention this to your uncle, and certainly not to Jillian. I'll have our people do some background checks. Good thinking."

Atti came away from this talk brimming over, not so much that he had come up with a lead about the cameras as that his father was actually pleased with him.

That afternoon Hugo and Ted left again for meetings in Boston. The next morning Bode pulled Atti and Elle aside, with Martin circling at a distance like a hyena waiting to feed.

"Yeah," Bode said. "I should tell you things have changed."

"*What* things?"

"Well, the concert...."

"Tonight? What are you saying?"

"You see, Marty and I went up to Damariscotta last night and met these two girls...."

"And?"

"And, well, they're gorgeous...and eager."

"So?"

"So, they're coming to the concert."

"What the hell!" Atti yelled.

"You can't do that," Elle objected.

"Yeah," Bode said somberly. "Yeah, I can because, like, I *did* win the tickets, and the old men are gone until Saturday. And, well, somebody could complain to my mom and destroy her moment of familial harmony, but no one would have the heart to do that. Anyway, the dads will understand and would probably do the same themselves. And look, we still have one extra ticket...."

"Oh, screw off," Atti scoffed.

"I wasn't asking *you*, little brother, but Marty and I could always escort another hot date." He raised an eyebrow at Elle.

She exhaled forcefully and stomped away.

"You're such an asshole," Atti spit out and turned. Beyond exasperation with his brother—an all too familiar feeling—he was sorry for

Q. His friend had been picking out Scrags songs on his guitar all week, and Atti cringed at having to tell him they weren't going to the concert.

But Q was surprisingly sanguine. "Realistically," he said, "I'm lucky even to be here. And the Scrags, well, that almost seemed real too, but no loss. No worries."

"Man, you have turned truly Zen here in Maine."

Atti later found his mother reading in the sunroom. "Bode and Martin are *not* taking us to the concert," he told her.

She looked up from her book, less surprised about the news than grateful Atti had not turned the matter into a ruckus. "I love both my sons, Atticus," she said thoughtfully, "but you are *so* different. Bode takes after his dad, which makes him impetuous and strong in his way. But you, my joy and my solace, you have always been wise beyond your age. Maybe the glare attracted by your brother allowed you the space to learn to rely on yourself. It taught you about resilience, and this strength will serve you well."

She reached out a hand and pulled him down to kiss his cheek. It felt like a balm soothing the sting of Bode's sellout. He wondered how his mother could always do that.

After dinner Jillian disappeared. The kids played Parcheesi with Marie, but their heart wasn't in it. Q then wandered off—possibly to sulk in private.

Elle looked at Atti. "Want to watch a disc?"

One of Hugo's rules was that Pandion was a television-free zone, to build independent thinking. The Barn thus never had cable service. But a monitor in the back parlor would play DVDs and over time box sets of *Harry Potter* and *Star Wars* appeared, along with exercise tapes and classic movies, particularly two box sets of the movies of Alfred Hitchcock, whom Hugo called the greatest motion picture director of all time. The repeated viewing of this director's movies introduced a family lexicon of references and pop quizzes about the films. The intended victim and murderer have the same name? The leading lady is rescued off Mount Rushmore?

"I've seen each of those movies at least five times," Atti complained.

"Que sera…," Elle said musically.

"*The Man Who Knew Too Much*," he shot back. "But after our falconry last week, maybe we should watch *The Birds*?"

"Oh, not tonight," she said, sucking in her lips. "That one still scares me. Maybe we should call it a night?"

"I guess, but it feels wrong, like I need a minute to get over missing the concert. Sounds dumb, right?"

"Not at all." She turned away from the house and pulled him by the hand. "Come on," she said, "let's get over it together."

They walked around the frog pond and sat on the bench Atti used to get away from his family. They watched the sea. The air was cool, and waves lapped in a soothing rhythm. The gulls had mostly left off cawing for the night. Geese flew overhead in jagged formations silhouetted against the sky. It was hard to be too upset about *anything* in this setting. Nonetheless, Atti blurted out, "It just sucks."

"I know," Elle responded fatalistically, "but nothing new, right?"

"Exactly. Our brothers: they've always been such jerks."

"And they feed off each other. But what can we do? Martin never really got over Mom dying and, at this stage, he's just sad and getting worse. Bode will end up running the company and lord it over everyone. But we'll soon be free, away at college, away from everything."

"From everything, but not from each other," he said seriously.

She turned to him with a crooked smile. "And you're supposed to be the smart one in the family?"

He pulled her to her feet and laughed. "How did you and I become the last best hope for the Foresters?"

"The dynasty goes all downhill from here," she laughed.

They wandered along the cliff trail and circled back to the driveway. The night was still. Fireflies hovered over the lawn. As they approached the Barn, ethereal music blended with night sounds from the woods and the pond. They looked at each other curiously as the music became more distinct. When they reached the gazebo, they saw Q lying on his back in the wooden structure, strumming his guitar.

"That's enchanting," Elle said.

"What?" said Q, opening his eyes. "Oh, the night was pulling chords from my axe. I was a bystander."

"Then the fortune is *all* of ours," she said warmly.

Q sat up and beamed, then looked embarrassed.

"Well, I'm to bed," she said. "Good night."

She turned to go inside, and Q stared after her.

Atti elbowed him. "Shouldn't leave your mouth open like that. Lots of swarmy things around after dark."

Q shook his head. "But, seriously, dude, I think your cousin has ruined me for other women."

"Yeah," Atti laughed, "you and me both." He threw his arm around Q's shoulder, and they walked into the house.

Next afternoon Elle watched Atti and Q finish a chess game in the gazebo. As Q declared checkmate, Atti looked up at her lamentingly. "Do you think he's ready?"

Q's eyes went wide. "Ready for what?"

Elle looked at Q affectionately. "Oh, yeah, *he's* ready."

In a horror-movie voice, Atti said, "*The secret chamber.*"

Q looked from Atti to Elle. She nodded solemnly. "But you must swear not to tell how we get there or we'll have to kill you."

They entered the house by the kitchen door. The chamber was actually a wine cellar cut from the stone beneath the house. Years back Elle had seen her father stash the key to the door in an old clock in the hallway. When she and Atti first explored the dark, cool cave years before it had been spooky, but over time it became their refuge from the big brothers.

Barrels served as tables and seats. Dusty bottles lined shelves on the walls and wooden cases were stacked on the floor. It was an extensive wine collection, considering Hugo and Marie drank so little, but Uncle Ted did his best to carry the load.

Hugo would not abide with children drinking alcohol except in the presence of their parents, and Elle and Atti never touched the wine in the cellar. But they loved sitting in the coolness among the musty old bottles, hidden from the world. There were bare electric bulbs hanging from the rough-hewn ceiling, but they preferred to use the candles scattered around. A couple of times they replayed the wine cellar scene from *Notorious*, but typically they used the cave to share secrets or makes their secrets more mysterious.

Atti smiled at how Elle enjoyed Q's wonderment. "I think it's time we took a taste," he said with conviction.

Elle looked up in surprise and admonishment. "Those bottles are worth a fortune!"

"Hey, we're Foresters. Who better to drink up a fortune?"

"But my dad will know, and then we'll lose our hideout."

"Okay, look, we'll take one of the newer bottles. Here's an open case with two gone. No one will notice if it's three. We just have to finish it and bury the body."

He found a corkscrew and opened the bottle, picked up a glass, blew out dust and poured. Then he held the glass up to a candle, as he had often seen his uncle do, swished the wine around, wafted the smell over his face, sipped and chewed at the wine.

"Ah, an excellent vintage," he said, though he couldn't tell one red wine from another.

Q laughed but reached out his hand. Atti looked for two more glasses and poured one for each of them.

"To hiding out in the underworld," Atti toasted.

"In our Secret Garden," Elle rejoined, her mischievous eyes catching the candlelight.

Chapter Five

Q went back to New York at the end of July. He had gigs lined up around the city and hoped to back up a friend at a benefit concert at the Beacon Theater. Atti missed him more than he had expected. After dinner the next night, Hugo rose from the table and said, "Bode, stick around. We may want you to listen in on a call."

"Yes, sir," Bode said, turning to Atti with a smug look.

As soon as Hugo and Ted left the room, Atti ducked onto the terrace and hurried along the driveway. He circled the frog pond and headed for his bench, out of sight of the Barn. He was muttering to himself about Bode when Gabriel appeared, focused on a wooden contraption in his hands.

Gabriel looked up with a gentle smile. "Hiding?"

"You know how it is. Don't rat me out, okay?"

Gabriel laughed softly and took a seat. "Never would do, Atticus; you can always trust me."

The caretaker's serenity contrasted with the usual tension and competition in the Forester family. He had run the property Atti's whole life, and was the one who always fixed things, even Atti's childhood troubles and then his teenage angst. Gabriel always had time for him and encouraged him to see a world beyond big houses and fancy cars.

"Why is my father so strict, and why does he treat me like a kid?" Atti whined.

"To be fair, Atticus," Gabriel said, holding his implement up to his eye, "you *are* a kid."

"Legally, yeah, but he treats Bode like part of the company and he's only twenty-one. He just ignores me, or he lumps me in with what doesn't concern him."

"And what would you have him do?"

"Give me a chance! I'm part of the family. I have a stake in the business and could do as well as Bode, probably better than Uncle Ted."

"But is that what you want: to be a partner at Pandion Capital, sit in an office with a secretary and wear fancy suits?"

"And beat my brother."

"Ah, Atticus, that's disappointing. Your brother's not your problem. He's an energetic young man who no doubt will follow in his dad's footsteps, and you should take pride in that. You share his blood and his success. But there is something more substantial in you. Even though Bode is older and bigger, you seem better able to handle life, real life beyond Pandion Capital. You still have a lot to learn but I think someday you'll set yourself apart from your brother and even your family."

"You sound like Father Jake. Both of you act like I have to be *more* than a Forester man."

"Well," Gabriel said with a wise smile, "they call me a 'caretaker,' so I try to take care."

"Okay," Atti said, feeling content for the first time all day and gesturing at the device in Gabriel's hand. "So what are we working on now?"

"Atticus, I thought you'd never ask."

Two days later Hugo pulled Atti aside and said, "Crossing tomorrow."

"Five o'clock?"

Hugo nodded. "And dress warm; it looks like we'll have some weather."

For as long as Atti could remember, he and Bode had tried to discover where his father and uncle disappeared to for two days each summer. When Bode and then Martin joined the disappearing act, Atti about went crazy, left at home with the women. Then, when he turned thirteen, his father finally invited him to join an expedition they called the "Crossing." By his seventeenth year, the Crossing had become a routine part of Atti's summers, and he had already set aside what he needed for the trip.

He woke before dawn and met the men in the kitchen, where Hugo was preparing the annual breakfast—the one time all year his father cooked anything. While Hugo fried bacon and eggs, Ted tuned in the marine weather report. The forecast was for early morning rain and squalls. Winds were expected at close to the level triggering a small craft advisory.

"No worries," Hugo said over his shoulder. "Calypso is hardly a *small* craft."

Ted seemed to gird himself to echo Hugo's confidence. "That's right," he added, "not with *our* crew."

Atti looked at the others to measure their concern. Ted and Bode avoided his glance. Martin looked queasy.

Hugo stopped midway through dishing out eggs and looked at them all. "Look," he said, "weather is part of sailing, like troubles are part of life. We've all been here before. We set the date and we'll stick to it! It's how the Crossing works. Did a little wind stop your grandfather from riding Hurricane Charlie into Cozumel?"

This reference to Grandfather's famous hurricane run didn't seem to comfort Martin, who looked chalky and left the room. Bode scoffed as if to say, if Hugo was game then they should all be. Atti wondered why they couldn't go back to bed and start the trip when the weather cleared. But he couldn't question his father. The risk of sailing in bad weather was part of the point; they were all beyond the age of wonder at sneaking off before dawn and camping out, so a bit of peril would keep them engaged. It hardly seemed worth tempting fate to honor some "noble" cause, but

Atti had spent his whole life proving he was a Forester man and couldn't back down now.

Martin and Atti trailed behind the rest as they walked through the rain to the boathouse. "You okay?" Atti asked.

"This is sick," Martin said. "We're not even on board and I've barfed twice."

"Well, at least you won't make a mess on the boat."

Martin stopped and looked at him. "Very funny, asshole."

Atti was grateful his father had dredged out a deep-water dock, so they wouldn't have to row to a mooring. But even tied up tight in the sheltered cove, Calypso moved uneasily, pitching in the choppy seas and snubbing herself against the dock lines.

The wind was blustering. Fat drops rattled loudly on the rain slickers and deck. Hugo checked the boat with the same precision he always applied to the Gulfstream. Atti wondered at the parallels and whether his father would risk flying in this weather.

Ted tuned into a weather advisory on the ship-to-shore radio. The report called for winds up to twenty-six knots with gusts to thirty. "Still below gale-force," he shouted to Hugo.

"Bode!" Hugo called out. "Run the checklist again!" Then he turned to the rest of them. "We'll have no drowned heroes today. Everyone into life jackets."

This was unusual. They were all experienced sailors and good swimmers and typically shunned life jackets on the Crossing, where the objective was to prove their manhood. But this sea was ominous, and Hugo was the captain so no one questioned his order.

They cast off like a shot. Beyond the protection of the cove, Calypso beat into a stiff onshore wind. The boat dipped into swells and took waves across her bow. Atti held tight to a rail while he mastered the rise and fall. Over the jagged waves he saw dim outlines of the cliffs they were leaving behind. Ted and Bode braced themselves on the windward rail.

They quickly tacked to starboard. Calypso's side dipped to the water line. Water splashed over the deck. The high winds made it impossible to set full sails so Hugo had ordered two reefs in the mainsail. A few times they tried to set the headsail as well but had to give it up. Just too much wind. Swells continued to bang the boat.

Atti was busy following Hugo's orders so he had little time to think about what might go wrong or why they were even out in these seas. Such was life with a man who demanded obeisance, even from nature.

Atti often had moments of bliss on the Crossing, taking in the blue-green sea and the big sky, leaving his troubles on shore. Even in rough weather he could look at the horizon and be lifted by the magic. But this voyage was different. The danger was imminent, and as the hours passed, he had to monitor his thoughts to ensure they didn't become too bleak.

Both the wind and waves were on Calypso's nose, and one swell after another threw them around the boat. One sudden jolt knocked Hugo from his feet. His head hit the bulwarks and he came up bloody. With his hands off the wheel, the boat turned its broadside dangerously toward the waves.

"Grab the wheel!" Ted shouted as he bent to his brother.

Bode rushed to the helm. Atti hurried below for the first aid kit. He stumbled twice in a few short steps as sharp gusts jerkily lifted the deck and tossed the boat on her ear. Reaching the hatch, he braced himself to descend into the dim light below. Even on this spacious boat, the cabin had a cramped feel and the sickly-sweet smell of diesel fuel.

Martin was in the cabin holding tight to a rail. Atti pushed past him and yanked open a cupboard for the first-aid box. When he turned back, Ted was helping Hugo down the ladder. Blood streaming down his face, Hugo collapsed onto a bench.

Atti had no experience as a doctor but ripped open the seal on a large bandage and held it against the cut. "Keep pressure on this," he said to Hugo and turned again to the box.

He doubled up two more large bandages and doused them with an antibiotic cream. With a roll of surgical tape in hand, he turned again to his father. "Okay," he said, "pull that away and I'll wrap it."

His father, dazed, did as he was told. Soon Atti had bandaged the cut and wrapped gauze several times around his dad's head.

"Enough," Hugo said. "You better get topside."

Atti felt an enormous weight lift from him. He was proud of how coolly he had acted under fire. But the boat jolted again, knocking his elbow painfully against a cabinet.

Gnarly weather would not force them to return home, but their only hope of making progress was to proceed under power. "Otherwise, we have to bear off to ninety degrees!" Ted shouted to Bode. Bode agreed, though he seemed reluctant to show any weakness while he had the helm. He cranked up the engine and ordered Atti to add a third reef to the mainsail.

Under power, Calypso made halting progress and within an hour Bode brought her into Peregrine Isle's sheltered bay. They dropped anchor as the rain and wind eased off and the clouds began to thin.

Hugo came up from the cabin, his head wrapped in gauze but looking alert.

"Our captain's gone buccaneer," Ted laughed.

"Only a scratch," Hugo replied, "but I'm thinking I like the look."

That was typical of Atti's father. Gashing his head wouldn't slow him down. It was clear why Bode acted the same. Did that really show strength or just a tenuous link to reality?

With skies now clearing, they moved supplies ashore. As if to show its sense of humor, the sun then burst through the clouds.

Once they had laid out their rain gear to dry, they set up camp. The young men retrieved the large ammo box they buried each year under a big tamarack. Inside were tools wrapped in canvas, tarps and rope, cans of food, bottles and a short-wave radio. Ted once laughed that Peregrine Isle would be their last refuge when zombies overran the mainland.

Hugo took it easy in the shade while Ted and Bode assembled a lean-to, Martin built up the remnants of their old stone firepit and Atti looked for dry wood. It would have been easier to keep the lean-to and firepit in place each year, but Atti's grandfather had set the tradition of leaving the island each year much as they found it.

After they ate grilled bratwurst, Atti hiked to the far side of the island. Self-reflection was supposed to be at the heart of the venture, so he should be thinking about where he'd go to school and what classes he'd take. Should he study business to prepare for joining the company? Working at Pandion Capital would provide substantial income but it would mean taking a back seat to his brother his whole life, just like Ted had done. But what else was there? His father and uncle had started their jewelry business when they were still in college, but Atti didn't think he had the drive or imagination for something like that. He'd much rather travel and enjoy life until the trust fund paid out.

For dinner Ted grilled steaks and buried potatoes in the embers and they had a tub of cold Brussels sprouts Josie had pre-cooked. It was all good if you overlooked a bit of sand. Hugo seemed fully recovered by then. The cut on his head didn't appear to require stitches, which was a relief to Atti since he had been drafted as the medic and he couldn't even sew on a button.

The fire burned down, and they sat back watching the embers, weary with winning the day. A breeze shimmered the high branches. Owl hoots mixed with quiet sounds from the woods. Hugo leaned against his sleeping bag. Unlike Ted, he was not much of a drinking man but this trip was always singular in many ways. He pulled a bottle from his bag and unwrapped it from a sweater. "This Macallan was distilled around the time my father was born," he said, turning the label toward them. "This bottle cost as much as one of the small boats in the cove."

From the ammo box Hugo pulled five nested glasses and nodded for Bode to hold them while he poured. He then held his glass up so the scotch sparkled in the firelight and toasted, "As we have done since our father first brought Ted and me to this island, we take time away from our lives each year to commemorate how our fortune came from the sea, remember the hardships behind and look forward to the rewards ahead."

He tipped his glass toward each of them. "We, none of us, know how long we will have, so we take time to pause and reflect. The Crossing is a tribute to our ancestors, our toils and our luck. To these we toast, and to the sea."

"Even with occasional bumps on the head," Ted laughed.

Hugo smiled, tilting his glass to his brother, and added, "And I'd like to add all our thanks to Bode for seeing Calypso safely into harbor."

Atti toasted sincerely. He had to admit Bode did a masterful job, and he was the one Atti would want handling a boat in that situation, maybe even more so than his father. Still, he wished Hugo had also thanked *him* for jumping into action to bandage his head. Apparently, his father wasn't hit hard enough to bring on that degree of sentimentality.

Ted later told a story about a sailing trip he and Hugo took with Gabriel when they were teenagers.

"Has Gabriel ever come on the Crossing?" Atti asked.

"Gabriel?" Bode sneered.

"No," Ted said. "Grandfather reserved the Crossing for Forester men—but we sailed a lot with Gabriel when he wasn't busy helping his father."

"In fact," Hugo added, "we're blood brothers." He smiled at Ted.

"That's right," Ted responded. "In the cave out past Back Bay, we swore allegiance to each other and to our goals in life. Hugo and I always knew we'd find our place in the world, though we had no idea just *how* successful we'd be. But Gabriel…he was a caretaker's son; all he wanted was the life he already had."

Ted sniggered. Hugo cast him a knowing smile and continued. "Mansions or gatehouses," Hugo said, "a lot of that comes from where you start. Gabriel's ideal was the kind of life his father, old Joseph Oak, had at Pandion. Sad he never found a woman to share it. But at core we all agreed the thing was to reach beyond yourself. We swore we'd take on the world in a real, physical sense and leave it a better place than what we found, for ourselves and those around us."

Uncle Ted chuckled. "Of course, we didn't know then what it would be like to live *on top* of the world."

"Too true, brother," Hugo said, holding his glass again up to the firelight. "Before we knew it, Pandion Capital took off and blew our plans from the water."

Atti was confused. Were Hugo and Ted dedicated to improving the world or had financial success become their only goal? He decided he was too drunk to sort this out.

As the embers burned down, the scotch put Atti to sleep, but he woke later to quiet voices. He half-opened his eyes and could see Bode and Martin were in the lean-to but his father and uncle still sat by the fire. He kept still despite the root sticking into his side.

"So what about those cameras?" Ted said quietly.

"You mean who put them there."

"And what are they after?"

"If we could figure that out, we'd know who it was. Given how they gained access to the property and the sophistication of the equipment, it's clear they're after something."

"It all makes me nervous."

"As it should. Someone digging into our operations could bring it all down. I think I'll put our own investigator on this and take a good look at everyone with access to the compound." He paused and looked over at Atti. "Let's move the young one into his sleeping bag."

Hugo nudged Atti and guided him to the lean-to. Soon a cacophony of snoring blended with the waves, but Atti lay wide awake. What did it all mean?

Chapter Six

Marie stayed behind at Pandion for three weeks after Labor Day, when the rest of the family returned to New York. Atti worried she'd be lonely, but he guessed that was the price she paid for her wealth and position. Hugo would be off on business as soon as they got home, with no time for her, so why shouldn't she stay at Pandion? She had friends in the city and loved music and theater, but she seemed most herself in Maine.

"You are my darling boy, Atticus," she said, "but I'm happy here. I love seeing the seasons change. And I won't really be alone, not with Josie and Father Giacomo and the army of gardeners and painters Gabriel has preparing for winter."

Atti's senior year started on a great note when his soccer team won its first three games. On the field celebrating a win over Dalton, he ran into Elle. "Since when are you a soccer fan?" he said, hoping she saw the goal he scored.

"I could say I came to support my favorite cousin," she said with a roguish smile, "but actually I'm dating one of your opponents, and here he is!"

Dalton's center midfielder was tall with broad shoulders. He came up to them and nodded suspiciously at Atti as he took Elle's arm, conceding the game while claiming the bigger prize.

"Atti, this is Peter Becker," she said, hugging his arm. "Peter, I guess you've more or less met my cousin, Atti Forester."

Peter looked mildly relieved. "Good game, Forester," he nodded. "I thought we had you there at the end."

Dalton's coach called his players to their bus. But before Peter left he kissed Elle demonstrably.

Once he was gone, Atti turned to her with a smirk. "So this is the latest?"

"Isn't he cute?"

"Big, at least, and a strong right foot."

Elle took hold of Atti's arm, congratulated him with a kiss on the cheek and said she had to run. He watched her hurry off, shaking his head and hoping she had found a decent boyfriend for a change. But Peter's cocky look made that doubtful.

The school year flew by. Elle was gleeful at getting into St. Andrews in Scotland. Atti surprised everyone by choosing the University of Pennsylvania over Yale. He told his father this would allow him to take classes at the Wharton Business School, but his main reason was to get away from New York and out of Bode's footsteps.

The summer at Pandion was quiet. Bode stayed in the city to work, which should have been a relief, but Elle was also off taking a summer course at St. Andrews. Nick Emerson came up for a week but he had to return for an internship in the city. Even Q was unavailable, except for a long weekend at the fourth of July. That left Atti with Martin, which was pretty much like being on his own. He felt like the last one left at the playground when the sun was going down. He wondered if he should have taken a job; his father could easily set that up. But he didn't really want to work, not when he could kick back at Pandion and rest up for his first year at Penn. He spent a lot of time with Gabriel building devices or coming up with schemes to improve the property, marveling at the caretaker's constant ability to look at things with new eyes and make them better. He stopped by the church a few times to see Father Giacomo and once enticed him to play chess, but that wasn't very challenging. He finally resorted to mapping out his college plans and started to see how going away to school could be an opportunity to both escape his family and learn how eventually to take a substantial role at the company.

To get the escape part started, that fall he moved into a dorm, like everyone else, determined to play down his family name as much as he could. To his pleasant surprise, when his suitemates learned Hugo was his father, they didn't really seem to care. Wealth was significant to them but not their primary way to value someone. They seemed to care more about what he believed and brought to the conversation than how much his father earned. Atti worked hard at his courses and explored new interests outside the classroom. He played intramural soccer. A classmate from Virginia introduced him to cigars and jazz. He shared his love of classic films with a friend on his hallway and discovered there were great directors *besides* Alfred Hitchcock. As to his love life: there were mixers and parties and cute girls in his classes, but without relying on the all-access pass of the Forester name he felt like he was back in eighth grade, shy about asking girls out. Simply smiling and nodding no longer worked, so he had to force himself to act self-assured. With time he got the hang of it and for a while dated a woman who worked for the school paper and then a theater arts major who took him to student plays and workshops.

He went home once in a while to do his laundry and see his mom. Elle and he spoke over FaceTime. She was thriving in Scotland and talked about taking courses the next summer somewhere in Europe. He missed Ghost, who was staying at the gatehouse with Gabriel so he could be outside with space to run. Atti called after a week to check up on him.

"Ah, the dog is grand," Gabriel said in his oddly Irish way. "He has the run of the property and is great company for an old man."

"Gabriel, you are far from an 'old man.'"

"Brilliant company, nonetheless. We've been up and down the coast together."

"Well, you know we both appreciate it. I'll live off campus next year and he should be able to stay with me. But for now, I'll be up and see you both at Thanksgiving."

The summer before his sophomore year Elle took classes in Madrid, and Q could only come up to Pandion for a week. Atti still loved Maine but it felt lonely. He exchanged visits with friends from Penn and spent some weeks in the city with Q and his old soccer teammates, all home for the summer. Even Marie, who loved her serenity, sensed too much quiet at Pandion that year. After Labor Day she announced her wish that the whole family spend the month of July at Pandion the next summer. Atti had to laugh at how gently she got the word out and yet knew for certain everyone would show up.

The one disquieting note that summer occurred one morning when Ghost found a dead osprey on the lawn.

"It's nothing I've seen before," Gabriel said, clearly troubled. "Looks like the poor thing's neck was broken, but I don't see how it would happen."

"Could someone have killed it and left it here?" Atti said.

"Aye, that would seem to be the only way." Gabriel gazed around the lawn, pondering.

"Do we tell the police?" Atti said.

Gabriel grimaced and shook his head. "It'd be a mess of bother and all for a bird…sad as that is."

Ever since Gabriel found surveillance cameras in the Barn two summers before, Pandion no longer felt like the impregnable refuge Atti had always known. He wondered if this was partly a result of growing up and realizing Pandion was no fantasy Arcadia. Those cameras had been real and unsettling. And now the osprey with a broken neck deepened the shadow over his languid summer days.

In his sophomore year Atti and four friends rented a house off campus. The senior who organized everything was happy to have

Ghost join them, and the dog became a recognized feature on campus and around University City. Living across the Schuylkill from Center City, the housemates welcomed the security of a big dog, and having five young men eager to take Ghost out made caring for him easy. Atti's new Mercedes—a birthday present from his parents—also expanded his range in and around Philadelphia. He realized driving the Mercedes blew his cover and it quickly got around that he was Hugo's son. But by then he felt assured he could be his own man without relying on the family. With that concern out of the way, it wasn't such a hardship to drive a fabulous car and have people know he was rich. Besides, his main focus was economics in all its forms, from calculus to statistics, macro theory to political economy.

He did, however, find time to date a woman in his film class, and they together produced a short documentary. Atti wrote the screenplay, which focused on the economics of anticipating new technologies like blockchain and electric cars. They won a department award and posted the film on YouTube.

That summer the family-reunion commenced in New York with the Summer Splurge. Atti was struck by how different it felt from earlier years. He was no longer intimidated talking with investors. He simply told them he was enjoying college and asked something inane to switch the conversation back to them. Turned out it wasn't only shallow high school girls who bubbled over talking about themselves.

Q came to the party—less likely than ever to pass up free food since he lived on his own—and Elle was there, winsome as always and *not* trailing a boyfriend.

"Going stag, huh?" Atti said with a smile.

"I've only just got home. But you know what?"

Atti opened his mouth and shook his head.

"I met a guy!"

"What a surprise…and he's not good enough for you!"

She laughed. "You'll see. His name's Oliver MacNash. He's great, and I know you'll love him."

Atti wasn't ready to go that far; he'd have to see for himself. Men were always flocking around Elle but her boyfriends never treated her as well as she deserved. She seemed happy this time, though, which was all that mattered.

Atti's mother came across the room wearing the enigmatic smile she had perfected for Hugo's business events. The smile turned real when she hugged Elle, then she turned to Atti. "You'd better go rescue your friend. Darla Rose has him cornered."

He laughed, picturing Q fending off Mrs. Rose's perfume and pawing. But he caught himself at his mother's scolding look. Despite all their money and her leading position in society, his mother never seemed quite comfortable at large parties. He didn't know why this was, but it made him want to do whatever he could to help out.

"I've got it, Mom," he said and charged across the floor like the cavalry.

Atti extracted Q from Mrs. Rose with an excuse about needing his help in the hallway. As soon as he was free of her clutches, Q turned with desperate eyes. "Jesus, man, I remember her from years ago, but she never circled in like that."

"Since old Mr. Rose kicked the bucket, Bode and I never get within arm's reach."

Q laughed uncomfortably, and they both noticed one of the men stationed at the front door handling a large package.

"What's that?" Atti asked.

"Don't know, Mr. Forester. A man dropped it off. Said it was a present for the family."

"A man? Who was he?"

"He didn't say."

That was the kind of idiot you got with rental security guards. "Okay," Atti said with annoyance, "I'll take it."

Q came with him into Hugo's library, which was full of leather-bound books and ponderous ebony furniture. Atti was going to leave the package on his father's desk until Q said, "Aren't you going to open it? He said it was for your family."

Atti was used to people sending Hugo gifts of all sorts and hadn't focused on what the doorman said. But Q was right; there was nothing wrong with taking a look. He unwrapped the brown paper to find an oil painting of a beach cut into a rocky coastline, "Ithaca" burned in big awkward letters into the wooden frame. He propped it on a bookshelf. "That's near Pandion," he said, mostly to himself.

"Is the beach called Ithaca, like the city?"

"No. I can't imagine what that means. It's the beach at Back Bay, just past the village. You remember."

"Oh yeah, that's where I fell in love with Elle for the fourth or fifth time."

When they left the library, Q went looking for Elle, and Atti approached Hugo, who was speaking earnestly with a distinguished man in a bow tie.

"Ah, Atti," Hugo said, finding his son at his elbow. "Meet Mortimer Shankel, Director of the Guggenheim. Mortimer, this is my son, Atti."

"Nice to meet you, Mr. Shankel," Atti said. "Dad, can I speak to you for a minute?"

Hugo turned with a look of impatience. "Someone brought a painting for us," Atti said. "I put it in the library."

"Why are you bothering me now?" Hugo said but paused. "A painting? What are you talking about?"

"I don't know. It looks like Back Bay."

Hugo's jaw dropped. "Are you sure?"

"Well, on the frame it says 'Ithaca,' but I recognize the beach."

Hugo strode toward the library. Atti followed, intrigued by his father's reaction. With the door closed behind them, Hugo stared at the painting. Then he barked, "Find your Uncle Ted. And close the door on your way out."

Atti did as he was told and followed Ted back into the library.

When his uncle saw the painting, he almost dropped his drink. "Where did this come from?" he said in a hushed voice.

They both looked accusingly at Atti. "One of the d–d–doormen," he stuttered, feeling suddenly defensive. "He said some old man dropped it off."

"Tell him I want to see him right now," Hugo said, turning a serious look at Ted.

When Atti brought the doorman into the room, Hugo eyed him closely. "Describe the man who left this package."

"Ah," the doorman stammered, "I didn't pay much attention, Mr. Forester. He said it was a gift for the family. I asked who sent it and he laughed and said, 'They'll know,' and walked off."

"That's it?" Hugo said impatiently. "You can't describe him at all?"

"Well," the doorman said, looking nervous, "he was pretty big, almost as tall as me, but he was older and stooped over. He wore a long coat, and a hat hid his face."

Hugo peered at him, clearly demanding more.

"Oh, yeah, when he turned away it looked like he was missing an ear, or it was disfigured or something."

Ted looked stunned. Hugo's expression turned hard. "That's all," Hugo said, and the man quickly left the room.

"You too, Atti," Hugo added, dismissing his son with no more ceremony than the security guard. All Atti heard before he shut the door was Ted grumbling they should "fire the firm that sent that moron." It was clear the painting was important. But like so many times before, when something serious came up, Hugo sent Atti from the room. He hated that. He was too old to still be treated like a child.

No one spoke about the seascape again and it disappeared from Hugo's library. Atti filed the painting incident away as one more subject from which he was excluded.

Bode had arranged to work from the Barn, as necessary, during July. Elle took the month off from summer classes. Q was busy performing and doing session work at a recording studio, but he also cleared his schedule and finagled an invitation.

When Gabriel met the family at the airport in Brunswick, he looked troubled. "Sorry to have to greet you again with bad news," he said to Hugo as they stepped out of the jet. "Someone broke into the Barn."

"The Barn?" Hugo said with concern. "When? What did they take?"

"It was last night," Gabriel said, "while we were asleep. They cut a window in your office."

"What about the alarm?"

"Guess they disabled it."

"Did you call the police?"

"First thing. Sergeant Lucent came out right away. He brought two officers, who checked the grounds. They were running police tape around the terrace when we left for the airport. Lucent said a detective would arrive shortly. I said you'd meet him when you arrived. I figured there was no use bothering you until you landed."

"You did right," Hugo said, looking somber. "I can't think of what they'd be after, except…"

"Jewelry?" Marie suggested, stepping into the conversation. "You kept some things in the desk."

Hugo screwed up his face in concentration. "Well, certainly… um…"

Before founding Pandion Capital, Hugo and Ted ran a business buying and selling precious stones and jewelry. At the house in the city, Hugo kept some of what was left from that company in a large safe, but it was no surprise there were other things at Pandion.

They soon rolled past the gatehouse and up the long driveway to the Barn. A man in a rumpled suit was standing on the lawn. "Good to see you, Mr. Forester," he said, offering his hand. "I'm Detective Horace, down from Wiscasset." He had droopy hound dog eyes but a kind face. "Looks like your intruder came up from the dock," he said, pointing with his thumb over his shoulder. "One man, size-eleven shoe." He led them around the north end of the house and gestured at the door. "He disabled the alarm here and used a glass cutter to enter this room. I understand you use this as an office?"

"That's right, Detective. Can you tell what he took?"

"Well, this is where we need *your* help, Mr. Forester. Most everything seems undisturbed, but the desk drawers were stacked on the floor."

"Oh," Hugo frowned. "The locked drawer on the left held a strongbox with jewelry and some cash."

"We found that drawer and the box broken open," Horace said, "but it's puzzling."

"How do you mean?"

"Can you itemize the contents? How much money? What jewelry?"

"Not for sure. I kept cash there as a convenience, maybe twenty thousand? And as to the rest, I'll have to think about it. We were in the jewelry business for years, so there are things left over, along with some of my wife's pieces."

"Well, here's the odd thing. The box was cleaned out except…," he hesitated, pondering, "except one ring that looks valuable."

Hugo said nothing but the blood drained from his face. "A ring?" he said softly.

"Yeah. I have it here." He held up a plastic evidence envelope containing a gold ring with a large oval sapphire designed to look like an eye, diamond slivers forming the eyelashes. Marie and Atti looked over Hugo's shoulder. They were all familiar with jewelry because of the jewelry business and Hugo's many gifts to Marie and others.

"How beguiling," Marie said. "I'm sure I've never seen it before."

Hugo's eyes flashed at her but then his look softened. "It's just an estate piece I picked up; I don't even recall when. I always thought it was gaudy. Almost forgot it was there."

Marie looked confused. "Oh, I like it, though it's not really my style. The sapphire is such a stunning deep color." She reached out for Horace to hand her the bag. "Isn't this an evil eye design or, what do they call it, a Greek eye?"

Hugo ignored the question and turned back to the detective. "Can we go in and check what else is missing?"

"Absolutely. Our team is done. Please look through the office and the rest of the house and let me know—along with listing as best you can what's gone from the strongbox. You'll need that to file an insurance claim, anyway."

"And the ring?" Hugo said, reaching for the bag.

Horace held on. "We'll return it, of course. But for now it's evidence, at least until we figure out why it was left behind. Anything you can remember about it might be helpful."

Hugo spread his hands and shrugged. "Like I said, some old estate piece."

A week later Detective Horace returned. Hugo immediately ushered him into his office along with Ted. Afterward, his father said the police had found no useful evidence but had put out notices on the stolen jewelry.

"And what about that ring?" Marie asked. "Did they figure out why it was left?"

"Not that they told us," Hugo responded ponderously, "but they returned it."

Although Hugo acted as if the ring meant nothing to him, he was visibly relieved to get it back and stash it away again.

The lack of any resolution about the burglary disquieted the compound, where doors were never locked and the outside world was supposed to be held at bay, but everyone gradually relaxed again into the familiar summer rhythm.

Marie's Picnic went ahead with a full cast for the first time in three years. In addition to the family and Q, Father Giacomo showed up after breakfast was served under the great elm. Harry Gooden also flew up for the day. He was his usual self, trying to make friendly conversation, but seeming nervous and making people uncomfortable.

Marie met him effusively as he got out of his car. "Harry, it's so nice to see you! Thanks for making the trip."

"I know how important it is to you," Harry said, put at ease by Marie's open affection, but then seemingly recalling a disagreeable task. "I don't see Hugo. He's here, of course?"

"He is if he knows what's good for him," Marie laughed. "I think he's down at the dock with Ted, where I trust you will make sure they are *not* talking business."

Harry tittered uncomfortably. "Of course, Marie. No business at the Picnic: we all know that."

Atti heard this encounter as he walked over to shake Harry's hand. The man wore a seersucker suit, with wingtips and a half-Windsor knot tied firmly at his neck. Atti wondered if that was why he was sweating.

"I think I'll pop over and say hello," Harry said, turning abruptly toward the boathouse and leaving Atti and his mother to exchange questioning looks.

As the morning wore on, they all amused themselves playing the two short golf holes Gabriel had set up on the lawn. At lunch Gabriel announced, "This afternoon there will be trap shooting by the tennis courts."

As usual, he had their attention and Atti and Q were first to head across the lawn.

"This gun is way cool, dude," Q said, cradling a shotgun with his usual goofy smile.

"Are any of these yours?" Atti said, holding up another gun to Gabriel.

"Ah, no, lad, the equipment comes with my man." Gabriel caught the elbow of the crew boss and introduced him. "Mr. John Blood will be your gunnery instructor and I caution you to pay close attention. These are *real* guns, so let's keep it to the pigeons, right?"

Blood had set up two tossing machines on the tennis court facing the cove and Be Thankful.

"I hope Jillian hasn't stashed a boyfriend in the cottage," Atti laughed.

"Today we'll be trap shooting," Mr. Blood said, "with clay targets traveling away from you at varying angles, and then we'll add an element of skeet shooting with rising and falling targets crossing each other."

Atti and Q hit enough pigeons to satisfy themselves and then handed the guns to Father Giacomo and Martin. "For a priest, the Father is so chill," Q said as they stepped back to watch, along with Bode and Ted waiting their turn. "When I helped him with the organ, which is amazing and of course he also plays and wrote his own toccata and fugue—but I guess you know that...."

"Father Jake and I and *Organo* go way back," Atti laughed.

"Well, you should have heard him play a bit from the *Organ Symphony*. I swear it shook loose the dust and some of the paint from the ceiling." Q paused and looked around. "So what's up with your dad...and Elle? Why aren't they shooting?"

"Elle doesn't like the idea of shooting animals, even *clay* pigeons. And Dad is off somewhere with Harry...but there they are."

Hugo seemed almost to drag Harry to the tennis courts. It was clear the compliance officer had something serious on his mind, but Hugo was sticking by Marie's rule of no talking shop at the Picnic.

"Just come over," Hugo pleaded, when they were close enough for Atti to hear.

"How can you...?" Harry said in exasperation. "I'm surprised you even trust me with a gun."

That got Atti's and Q's attention. They turned to watch the two men walk up to Mr. Blood and take hold of shotguns. Q grimaced at Atti, "Doesn't seem like a good time to hand Old Harry a gun."

Atti shook his head. "Hitchcock could do a lot with this scene."

The championship croquet match later in the day was as hard-fought as ever and for once Atti took the prize, which turned out to be a limited-edition iPhone. He thought about how his brother had screwed them all out of those Scrags tickets the last time they played. Atti thought about asking Bode if he was still in touch with those girls who went in their place but decided there was no point dwelling on the past.

After Ted's cheesy award ceremony, everyone drifted to the tables set for dinner except Q and Elle, who knocked balls around the course. Harry kept hovering behind Hugo's chair until Atti's father finally stood up, annoyed, and led his executive by the arm across the lawn. Atti couldn't hear what they said but they were clearly arguing as they disappeared down toward the boathouse. Next time Atti saw Harry, he was getting into a car with only Marie and Elle there to say goodbye.

It was unprecedented that Harry missed dinner but nobody seemed to miss him. They all lingered long at the table beneath chandeliers dangling from the elm, laughing, eating and toasting another successful Picnic. But Atti thought it must have been something serious to send Harry home early, and he knew Hugo would never explain it.

Later Atti asked his brother what it meant. "Bug up his ass, as usual," Bode replied. "The old man was *not* going to deal with more of his crap today."

As evening approached and fireflies twinkled over the lawn, Atti went into the Barn to use the bathroom. On his way back out, he noticed Hugo's office door ajar and heard voices. He stepped closer and heard Ted say, "What did the detective say about the ring?"

His father's voice replied, "Horace is convinced it means something the thief left it, but he didn't get any further. Since they didn't register sapphires in the twenties the cops would have to find an old photo and connect it to the records of the jewelry store or the insurance claim."

"But the setting! Damn it. Someone could easily recognize that. You said we couldn't keep settings."

"Easy, little brother. The cops won't connect the ring to anything. Too much time gone by."

"I hope for all our sakes you're right. But then we have the same question as the police…."

"Who left it behind."

"And why. It must connect to the painting."

"My concern," Hugo said, "is Lazlo Crane. He went up for thirty-five to forty, but that was in 1978. He got paroled four years ago."

"How do you know?"

"After what our doorman said about the deformed ear, I had an investigator check. And who other than Crane would have an interest in that beach?"

"We should tell the cops."

"Right! And what do we say without turning their attention on us? No, we'll get the investigator back on the case. *We'll* find Crane and scare him off…or buy him off."

Chapter Seven

Atti returned home from school two days before Thanksgiving so he could fly up to Maine with the family. There was no need to pack much for the long weekend, as he always left cold-weather clothes at the Barn. He brought along reading for his political economy class and his laptop so he could start working on a final paper.

Wednesday morning he was in the park with Nick Emerson and then called for a car to drive him home. He only needed to change clothes, pick up his backpack and Ghost and head for the airport. There was no sense questioning his father's logic for setting takeoff at one fifty-eight; it was only important to be on time. Arriving one minute late was the same as not arriving at all.

But Ghost didn't meet him at the door, which was worrisome. Then Atticus found his dog lying on the kitchen floor, having trouble breathing.

"He's been sickly all morning," the housekeeper said, worry distorting her face.

"What do you mean?" Atticus shouted. "Why didn't you call me? What the hell did you feed him?"

"Nothing, Mr. Forester. I mean…he had his usual food, nothing else."

"You must have given him something!"

Atticus knelt and held Ghost's head. The dog's eyes looked hazy.

"I don't have time for this!" Atticus growled. Should he leave the dog with the housekeeper and get to the airport or risk his father's rage and take care of Ghost himself?

"Call the vet!" he shouted. "Say it's urgent and we're in a rush. And tell Joseph to have the car ready!"

He ran upstairs to grab his backpack and then led Ghost gingerly to the waiting car. He hoped he wouldn't regret this decision but just couldn't leave his dog when he looked so miserable.

The receptionist immediately showed them in. The vet induced Ghost to cough up something he had swallowed and, after another look in the dog's eyes and a listen through the stethoscope, pronounced his patient "ready to rock and roll."

But all the rushing wasn't enough. Atticus was late, even if only by a few minutes. Those minutes were all it took. He and Ghost missed the flight that blew up in the sky.

As the sirens at the airport sounded and people sobbed, Atti knelt on the ground holding Ghost. After a while the dog licked his face, which reminded him he was still kneeling. He stood and picked up the leash and turned to walk with no notion of where he was going.

He wandered through the terminal building and along a road toward the crash. That was where he should be, with his family. But he felt dizzy and sat on the sidewalk with his arms around the dog. How could he reach them? Was it really their jet? Could they have survived? There must have been a mistake.

He had no sense of time. At some point a police cruiser pulled to the curb and a cop stepped out. "You okay, son?"

"I...," Atti muttered. "I have to get to the crash."

"The crash?"

"I'm meant to be on the plane...with my family...it blew up."

The cop returned to his car and spoke on the radio. Then he helped

Atti and Ghost into the backseat and took them to a low, nondescript building. People looked up from their desks as he passed through an office, holding Ghost on a short leash. The cop introduced him to a gray-haired lady with a kind face. Atti didn't catch what she said, but she walked him to an empty lunchroom and brought him a cup of coffee and dish of water for Ghost.

Atti felt warmth through the Styrofoam cup but didn't drink. A fluorescent ceiling light buzzed. He still had no sense of time. The window blinds were drawn closed, and he thought he should look out; he might see something to help him understand. But he didn't want to move. This couldn't be real. Any moment he'd wake up with Mom saying to fasten his seatbelt for landing. If he just closed his eyes tight enough.

Sometime later Uncle Ted rushed into the room, looking frantic. "Atti! Thank God!" he said. "I can't believe you missed that flight."

"Ghost was sick. He left us."

Atti had been late for a flight, and it changed everything. Death stole his family but left him. The thought struck him: were there even bodies after explosions like that? And what happens to someone like Atti, who should have been on that jet?

Ghost nudged his leg. He petted the dog's head. It was because of Ghost he missed the flight; so, in a way, the dog saved his life. But what kind of life would it be with no family? Everything he wanted—his father's respect, his mother's love—was smoldering on the ground. Even Bode was gone.

"Have you got a suitcase?" Ted asked.

Atti looked around. He couldn't remember what happened to his backpack so he just shook his head. A car drove them to Ted's apartment. His uncle spoke to him along the way, but his words made no sense. Atti just stroked the dog and stared out the window.

At Ted's apartment, Elle met them at the door with swollen eyes. When she hugged Atti, something inside him broke loose and he cried for the first time. Then he could hardly stand, he was sobbing so hard. She led him inside to a chair.

Martin offered his hand with sympathy, which surprised Atti; he seemed genuinely to share his cousin's shock and grief. "I'm sorry, man," he said, gripping Atti's shoulder.

Jillian kissed him on the cheek and stepped back whimpering, as if *she* were the one to be pitied.

Atti couldn't eat or drink and didn't want to talk, so they left him alone, Ghost on the floor beside him. He gazed out the window at wispy clouds floating like the smoke from the explosion, pure white on clear blue.

He heard Ted in another room on call after call, his muffled voice in turns agitated or angry. He was grateful his uncle was handling things; there must be so much to do.

By late afternoon the crash was all over the news, and calls came in from employees and investors. After answering the phone several times, Elle turned off the ringer. Ted's assistant soon arrived to field calls, responding to each that the police were investigating, Atti was safe but needed privacy and Pandion Capital would release a statement shortly. Ted took the call from the mayor.

The afternoon and evening passed in a haze. Atti didn't recall eating dinner and slept fitfully in the guest room, Ghost lying against the door as if to protect him. He woke several times in a cold sweat, panicked until he recalled where he was and then horrified when he remembered why he was there. Is this how things would be now, hardly sleeping or eating or living? Did they all expect him to go through the motions, like the day before, when he lived in a different world?

Thanksgiving morning the newspaper headline read, "Crash Kills Hedge Fund Titan." Atti couldn't bring himself to read the articles but broke into tears when heard on the radio all aboard were confirmed dead, along with two employees in a factory where the jet came down. The police had locked down the airport. The feds were opening an investigation. What caused the accident? Was it a mechanical issue?

Two police detectives came to the apartment. Ted spoke to the ownership of the Gulfstream—through a subsidiary of Pandion Capital—and who maintained the jet and the hangar space at Teterboro. Atti tried to explain why he missed the flight and didn't see the explosion, but only the jet falling…and the smoke. The cops wouldn't tell them much, except the cause of the blast was under investigation, and they were assisting the feds.

Atti's telephone filled with text messages and voicemails, but he lacked the focus to sort through them. There was no one he wanted to talk to, anyway. He tossed his phone onto a table as Elle entered the room.

"Can I help with that?" she said.

"Doesn't matter. So many people I don't even know."

"You've got lots of friends; they're just concerned. Tell you what, let's take Ghost out for some air."

He looked at the dog, whose ears had pricked up at the sound of his name. "Yeah," he said. "He needs to go out."

Descending in the elevator, Atti hoped doing something constructive like this would take his mind off his choking grief. They crossed the lobby, Ghost almost losing his footing on the slick marble floor. They could hear commotion outside, which registered with Atti as the usual sounds of the street. But then they emerged into a phalanx of reporters.

Cameras flashed. He found microphones shoved in his face. All around reporters and photographers looked ravenous, as if they would devour him if they could. They shouted over each other:

"What will happen to Pandion Capital?"

"Was it a disgruntled investor?"

"Why weren't you on the plane?"

Atti backed against the door. "I d-d-don't…," he stuttered, about to panic.

Ghost bared his teeth and growled. Elle pushed between Atti and the reporters and nudged him inside. He looked to her helplessly. She screwed up her face and then led the way to the rear of the lobby. They walked down a staircase to a parking garage and up again to a utility yard typically used by building staff. Atti and Elle sat on an old picnic table while Ghost explored the narrow yard and did his business.

One reporter's question echoed in Atti's mind: why wasn't he on the plane? It couldn't be because his dog was sick…or his father wouldn't wait. Those reasons made sense yesterday but today they sounded incredible. Was it chance…or fate? Why was he alive?

"They're vultures," Elle spat out.

"Just doing their job."

"They could show some empathy."

He shook his head. "They ask the right questions. What *will* happen to the fund? Your dad's in charge now, but it's hard to imagine Pandion Capital without my father."

Thanksgiving dinner was somber. Ted's housekeeper improvised a meal, but no one felt like eating, and it was hard to be thankful for anything. Martin pushed his plate aside and announced he was going to watch football and try to forget what a mess everything was.

Atti stood up to help clear the table, but Elle caught him by the elbow. "Leave that," she said gently. The sympathy in her expression again brought him to tears. He turned away out of embarrassment and went to join Martin, grateful for something to stare at besides the news.

Next day Pandion's general counsel arrived with the lawyer who managed the family trusts. With both his parents and Bode gone, the bulk of the estate would go to Atti, with bequests to long-term employees like Gabriel and Josie and several of his mom's charities. Atti would be the majority shareholder of Pandion Capital, which meant an enormous amount of money but also staggering responsibilities. Thankfully, Uncle Ted succeeded Hugo as president. Atti wouldn't have to take an active role in the business unless and until he wanted to.

Ted's staff handled the funeral details. There would be a mass at St. Patrick's Cathedral for New York friends, business associates and public figures. Then the family would hold a private burial in Maine. Elle would stay for both ceremonies before returning to school.

"When you're home from Penn, you'll live with us, of course," Ted said to Atti. "That house is too big for one person, and we'd love to have you. We're family, Atti, and we have to stick together no matter what. All of what your dad and I talked about at the Crossing? It may have sounded hokey sometimes, but deep down it was real and what holds us together."

"I don't want to give up the house."

"I don't mean we need to sell it, not right away. And you're no kid, Atti. You know you can retreat there if you need privacy sometimes. But day to day it wouldn't be healthy to wander that big house alone with all the memories."

"And Pandion?" Atti said, feeling tired and lost.

"The Maine property will go on, of course. You and I now share ownership…until Martin and Elle someday inherit my half. And Gabriel will take care of it for us all, as always."

"Gabriel!" Atti said, suddenly wishing his old mentor were there. "Will he use the money from Mom and Dad to move on?"

"Oh, not Gabriel. He never wanted anything more than what he has. You might not know this, but your grandfather left Gabriel's father the gatehouse and the acre it stands on."

Atti looked up in surprise. "He never said anything…."

"That's Gabriel Oak for you. But yes, he owns the gatehouse and the bit of land by the property line, right down to the water, so he'd probably live out his life there even if Pandion passed to someone else."

"Which will never happen."

"Of course not."

After a couple of days, most of the reporters stopped camping out in front of the apartment building. Pandion Capital released a statement memorializing its founder, dedicating funds to build a garden in Central Park in memory of Hugo, Marie and Bode, and assuring investors business would carry on as before.

The funeral service at the cathedral was somber but opulent. A fire department band marched on Fifth Avenue with bagpipes, as they would for a fallen hero of their own. Along with Ted and some business associates, the mayor and a former secretary of state eulogized Hugo.

"A great financial innovator and captain of industry," the mayor called him, "who met the world with humility and dignity despite his enormous success. He will be missed for all the good he has done for the city." Those words meant nothing to Atti, who retreated inside himself to avoid the glare. These people were all focused on Hugo, but the real tragedy was losing his mother. She had been the light in his world, his one source of unconditional love untouched by the competition for power that drove his father and his brother. Still, he couldn't grieve for her here.

He tried to keep his eyes straight ahead but couldn't avoid the strangers' faces on the cathedral steps. They looked more intrusive than sympathetic. So many of them held up phones to take pictures, as if he were a celebrity, as if the Foresters were some dynasty worth their trouble to notice. For once he was grateful for Elle's old boyfriend, Peter Becker, who had shown up and stayed close by her during the whole service. His size was effective at shielding Elle from the cameras. Atti wished *he* had one of the family's chauffeur-bodyguards to protect him from those eyes. It wasn't until his limousine started to drive off that he caught sight of Q squeezed into the crowd, his face contorted with concern.

The calls and messages kept streaming in. Ted's apartment was full of flowers. Nick Emerson and Tom Haskins had come to the funeral but he didn't talk to them. He later heard from his housemates at Penn and some old Earlington friends and kids he knew from church and the park. Even Violet DeMorsey sent a card.

Elle turned from setting the sympathy cards on a sideboard to ask Atti, "I was thinking: did you see Harry at the service?"

"I didn't look for him, but no, I didn't see him. He was probably with Ed Blankley and his wife."

"I suppose he got squeezed out by all the celebrities."

"Right; the rich and famous were not so broken up over the crash or nervous about their investments that they couldn't pose for the cameras."

A few days after the service, Nick Emerson called. "Hey Forester, you want to get together and, I don't know, kick a ball around...or just hang? And Friday there's a party downtown with some people from school."

"Thanks, man. I guess I'll be back to doing stuff in a while but now I can't. Too much going on with the family."

"Well, I'll be around when you need a break."

Atti was far from ready to return to normal life, but it was some comfort to feel support from his friends. And then there was Q, who had become a frequent presence at the apartment, ready to play a game of chess or watch a movie or just sit with Atti. He had been insulted when he wasn't invited to the funeral but, being Q, he quickly got over it. And he had the ulterior motive in coming to the apartment of seeing Elle, but that was okay. The poor sop really couldn't help himself, and Atti knew his *primary* motive was to be there for him.

Atti heard from Carnegie Hill neighbors and business associates of Hugo's who had known him his whole life. Ed Blankley's wife asked him to their weekend house. Several neighbors sent invitations to dinner. He tried to be polite but the last thing he wanted was to be the center of attention at some social gathering. Maybe he'd be up to it after a while, but even then it wouldn't be simple. Something made him recall Elle's question about Harry Gooden, and he wondered why Harry hadn't stopped by.

Ted famously didn't like dogs but he put up with Ghost, who rarely left Atti's side. Elle helped keep the dog clear of her father but Atti still sensed his uncle's displeasure. As the days passed, Martin also returned to his boorish self, and Jillian became distant even when she was present. If not for Elle, Ted's apartment would have been stifling.

Ted started going into the office but discouraged Atti from joining him. Elle tried to make sure Atti had what he needed and gratefully otherwise left him alone. Peter Becker also showed up again and it looked like he and Elle might be rekindling something. Atti wondered what Oliver would think about that.

A week after the accident, Ted chartered a jet to Maine, and they all flew up to bury Atti's family in the graveyard beside St. Bernard's. The weather was cold but there was no snow yet, and Uncle Ted brought in heavy machinery to dig graves in the frozen ground.

The Pandion staff attended, with many local friends and shopkeepers. Peter flew up with the family and was surprisingly kind to Atti.

Father Giacomo presided at the service. "I remember Bode as a precocious seven-year-old," the priest said to the packed church, "always in a hurry to grow up and take his place with his dad and his uncle, with the same drive that swept aside all challengers in the juniors' race at the Fourth of July Regatta. His passing snuffs out the promise of youth and carries this sad loss through to another generation.

"And Hugo. So much has been said and *will* be said of one of the great men of his age. He built an empire stretching around the world but always thought to help the rest of us join his good fortune. Those who rely upon St. Bernard's will benefit from Hugo's generosity for years to come. While I'm confident his brother Ted will carry on in Hugo's place, the great man's shoes will be hard to fill.

"Then there was Marie, a…" He paused and choked back a tear. "You all know Marie was a great help to St. Bernard's and the moral center of her family. You saw her gentle way of guiding her men and sprinkling kindness wherever she went. I…" Again he faltered. "I too saw the goodness she shared so freely, but I was privileged as well to know her as a friend, a very old and dear friend, who was strong in the face of life's trials, caring about the struggles of others and devoted to those she loved. Her loss leaves a void in my heart as well as our community."

Father Giacomo had asked Atti if he wanted to speak at the mass or graveside, but he wouldn't take the chance his emotions would make him stutter. He had mostly outgrown this impediment, but he still felt uncomfortable speaking before crowds of people. Anyway, his grief should be obvious to all, and he saw no need to put it into words.

As Atti stood at the grave and looked around the many familiar faces darkened by the gloom of the day, he again recalled Elle's question whether Harry had attended the St. Patrick's service. Atti may have missed him in that crowd, but it was clear he was not at the burial. Atti found this distracting and pulled the company's chief financial officer aside.

"Thanks for coming, Ed," Atti said.

"For your family, Atti? Of course."

"But I was wondering what happened to Harry. I don't see him and I don't think he came to the service in New York either."

Blankley looked suddenly uncomfortable. "I guess your dad didn't mention it. We had to let Harry go, or more accurately he resigned."

Atti was perplexed and silently asked for some explanation.

"Harry had put in his time and did quite well for himself. But differences arose about the business and in the end it made sense for him to move on. Don't worry; he got generous severance."

Atti thought about Harry as everyone left the graveyard for the warmth of their cars or homes. It almost felt like he had memories of two different people: Uncle Hal who used to play with them out on the lawn, and Old Harry Gooden, shrunken into a shell of himself. Lately, he had seemed increasingly bitter and nervous, and Atti had noticed him scowling when he thought no one was watching.

Gabriel broke into his thoughts to ask if he could speak with Ted and Atti. The caretaker looked heartsick, sadder than Atti had ever seen him. But Gabriel had known Hugo his whole life—and always had a special relationship with Marie—so his grief was understandable.

Ted assured him nothing would change at Pandion. The staff could stay on, and the property would be maintained. The family would not come up for Christmas but hopefully would visit in the spring and return next summer. In time things would return to some sense of normal.

Ted then went to find Jillian, and Gabriel cast a look at Atti saying he shared the young man's inconsolable sorrow. "Will you be all right?" the caretaker said gently.

"I don't know," Atti replied. "I feel numb and have no idea what's next. I wish you'd been there."

"I struggled with it but didn't want to impose on your family time."

"You know you're as much my family as anyone, Gabriel. You and Elle: you're the only ones left I really care about."

Chapter Eight

Atti returned to Penn but barely finished the semester. Luckily, he had done well enough through the term to pass his courses despite disastrous exam results.

Over Christmas break he decided he couldn't go back to school; he needed time to adjust to his new reality. What was left? For the rest of his life he'd have no parents, no brother. He'd always be on his own. He had often thought his father didn't care about him and maybe that was true. But Hugo did provide for him and teach him about the world and business. And his brother? He was nasty and bossy but maybe all little brothers think that. Atti wasn't always happy with his dad and his brother but without them he felt all alone in the world. And losing his mother was a shock he'd never get over. She was the only one who loved him always. What would life be without her? Could he fool some part of his brain into believing she was still alive, that she was just a phone call away? Wasn't that the best he could do?

Ted let him wallow in his grief through Christmas and New Year's, which passed with no celebration. But when it was time to return to school, he confronted Atti. "Look," he said, "we've all suffered unspeakable tragedy, especially you, but life has to go on. You have to pull yourself together, finish out the year, at least."

To keep peace with his uncle, Atti returned to Philadelphia in January. It was a relief to be away from New York, to a place where it didn't feel like all eyes were on him. Still, his friends knew about the crash and treated him as if he were something brittle they were afraid to touch. Conversations stopped when he entered a room. All the obsequious kindness made him want to run and hide.

One jackass on his hallway asked what it looked like, the explosion, as if it were in a video game. Atti couldn't answer but only had to close his eyes to see white smoke linger in blue sky.

Leaving an econ lecture a casual acquaintance came up to him with a greedy smile. "Dude, you must be filthy rich now!"

Atti had always had money and now he might have more but also so much less of a life…and more responsibility than he could fathom. What did it all matter? His family was gone.

He found himself overcome at times. He might cry in the shower or into his pillow late at night. Everything seemed to remind him of life before the accident.

It helped that his housemates still asked him to come out to the bar or play touch football. But Atti could see he was bringing everyone down when the dread would grip him. Besides, partying in the dorm or going to a bar felt frivolous next to the tragedy of the crash. The only one of his friends who seemed to get this was Q, back in New York playing his music. He called a few times and came down one weekend to visit.

Atti hoped schoolwork would leave him no time to dwell on his loss. Still, he was obsessed with news about the crash. One tabloid said investigators thought the jet was sabotaged, that it was no accident. He called Uncle Ted about this, who started to come unhinged, pleading, "So what are we supposed to do now, hire security?"

Atti tried to comprehend that his family may have been murdered. That made focusing on his courses impossible. What did statistics and public finance matter when someone might be trying to kill him?

Walking across campus one afternoon, Atti was accosted by a woman and a photographer. "Atticus Forester?" she asked.

"Who are you?"

"Alice Walker from the *New York Post*. I'd like to get your reaction to the news about Pandion Capital."

"What news? What are you talking about?"

"The news, Mr. Forester." She held her microphone up to his face. "The FBI raid? The irregularities? Have you any comment?"

He was confused. People had stopped to watch them, adding to his discomfort. "I d–d–don't know what you mean," he said and turned away.

The reporter followed and asked, "You have no comment about the Ponzi scheme?"

He broke into a jog and entered the first building he reached, lost the reporter and photographer in a maze of hallways and exited at the rear. He needed to find out what she was talking about.

He made his way to a carrel in the Van Pelt Library and checked his phone. The authorities were alleging fraud at the company! The story had snowballed through the morning to the point where it spooked the markets. The police had raided Pandion's New York offices. Company and family bank accounts were frozen.

He couldn't believe what he was seeing. What happened? What could Pandion have done so wrong? It was barely two months since his father died; things could not have gone bad that fast. He called Ted but it went to voicemail. He was about to call Uncle Hal but remembered he had been fired, so he tried Ed Blankley but no one answered. Then he called Elle in Scotland.

"Atti!" she sobbed. "What's going on? The news, even here, is talking about Pandion. I'm scared!"

"I hoped *you* knew something. I can't reach your father or anyone at the company. It looks like they closed the New York office. Maybe we should try London?"

"I tried calling when my dad didn't answer. I didn't know if anyone would talk to me, but they didn't even answer the phone. And now the news is saying this financial thing is connected with the crash, like it could have been suicide!"

"That's insane. Look, I'm going to get a train home…."

"Is that safe?"

"I don't know. I don't know anything. I'll go to the house. No one's living there so there shouldn't be any reporters."

"I'm coming home, too. I can't stay here when I don't know anything. My dad must be going crazy!"

"That's probably best. Try to keep your phone on as much as you can, and let me know where you are."

Atti walked back to his dormitory. He saw the *Post* reporter in front of the building and so entered through a side door. He went to his room and packed a bag and soon sat in the 30th Street Station. He had bought a Phillies cap and sunglasses and sat with his hood up and his back to the wall. He almost laughed despite himself when the reporter and the photographer burst into the waiting room, scanned the people moving about and ran out.

He took a cab from Penn Station to the end of his block, where he could see press vans double-parked in front of his house and people with equipment loitering on the sidewalk. One man was hanging over a railing pointing a camera through a window.

He called the house, but it rang through to the answering machine. Then he tried the housekeeper's cell phone.

"Hello," she said tentatively.

"Danika, it's Atti. Are you in the house?"

"Mr. Forester!" she almost cried. "There are people knocking and calling. It won't stop. What do I do?"

"Okay, Danika, now listen. It'll be okay. Don't answer the phone or the door. I'm outside, but I don't want the reporters to see me so I'm going to hop the fence into the garden and come in the back door. I need you to turn off the alarm and unlock the door for me. Can you do that?"

He made it into the house. Danika was agitated, so Atti told her to go stay with her sister. He then turned on the television. Reports said Pandion Capital had been under investigation for months but everything accelerated after the crash. Officials were alleging the company was built on an enormous Ponzi scheme. Atti couldn't make sense of this and kept switching channels. It seemed when Hugo died there was a rush of withdrawals, which used up cash, and the banks refused to lend more. Then Ed Blankley took a dive from his office window, leaving a note calling Pandion Capital "one big lie."

Reports speculated about billions in losses. News outlets raced to reveal names of celebrity and charity clients, along with a few university endowments. The talking heads dug into how Hugo had fooled everyone into investing by making the fund seem exclusive and delivering consistent—and illogical it now appeared—results. Even in the 2008 crash, when the markets were down almost forty percent, the Pandion Fund was up for the year, and through it all Hugo never failed to pay off a redemption and profits always met or exceeded forecasts. No one, the experts said, could deliver these consistent positive returns, regardless of the direction of the market. Atti caustically wondered why none of these "experts" had expressed those opinions when Pandion Capital was the darling of the financial world.

Money was going to be an issue from now on. Atti searched the house for cash but found very little. With Hugo gone and Uncle Ted probably going to jail, what was he going to do? What would he live on? There was no one to keep paying his tuition or anything else. He would have to support himself and feed his dog.

Hugo's fortune was largely self-made but Grandfather had given him a head start. Atti would have no support from his father and instead would be tainted by Hugo's crime. And getting back to the kind of wealth he had known his whole life could only be a distant goal now and probably a fantasy; the immediate need was to find a way to support himself.

He pocketed the key to the back door. When he reactivated the alarm system, he turned off the input from the garden fence so he'd be able to sneak back into the house. In his Phillies cap and sunglasses, he slipped over the fence.

Reporters were thick in front of Ted's building, and Atti could see no way around them, so he put his head down and pushed through.

"It's the son!" someone shouted, bringing the sidewalk to life like a kicked-over anthill.

A shrill woman's voice pierced the din. "Where did the money go, Mr. Forester? What about the investors? Don't you care about them?"

The doorman ushered him inside and led him to Ted's apartment. A security guard stood outside the door. Atti used the key Ted had given him to let himself in.

Ghost jumped up to greet him. Martin looked up from a sofa in front of the television. "Great," he spat out. "Just what we need."

He ignored the sarcasm and asked, "Is your dad here?"

Martin's reply was interrupted by Jillian shouting from the master suite. "This was not the deal!"

"Why blame me?" Ted shouted back. "It wasn't me!"

"But you'll land in jail with the rest of them! And then what happens to *me*?"

Atti looked back at Martin, who shrugged. "They've been at it all day. Jillian's afraid her friends who invested will take it out on her."

"My heart goes out to her. I trust she's hidden away her jewelry."

Martin sneered. He only seemed to ever find humor in other people's troubles.

There was more news in the afternoon. The SEC had once investigated the company for "front-running," trading for its own account based on knowledge of its clients' orders, but an examination found no evidence. In 2014 there was a charge Pandion hid its clients' orders from other traders while it was registered only as a broker-dealer, but the company resolved the charge by paying a fine and registering as a wealth manager. These matters seemed routine for a hedge fund as large as Pandion, which never stopped growing, or so it appeared. Reporters pointed to Hugo's deep reservoir of trust with investors and regulators, who never dug beneath Pandion's elaborate accounting statements. Those statements—it seemed remarkable in retrospect—were distributed *only* in print form, despite the fund's reputation for employing cutting-edge technology in stock picking and market timing. And Hugo's unobtrusive confidence lured investors not to withdraw money from the fund, for fear they might not be able to get back in. Now there was talk of multiple criminal and civil suits against not only Pandion Capital but also feeder funds that had funneled investors to the company.

Elle arrived home in the evening. She looked as if she hadn't slept in days, but she immediately took charge of the household. She straightened up the mess, started the laundry and got her father and Martin to sit down to a meal. Ted looked like a frightened animal, his shoulders twitching. Martin was clearly stoned, his look veering between amusement and boredom.

Elle motioned Atti into the den so they would have a moment alone. "How are you holding up?" she asked.

"I feel like I have to keep my head down, like I'm afraid of what happens next."

She sighed and held out both hands. "We'll get through this together."

Elle's strength pulled Atti through the next week. He couldn't believe how she managed her father and brother, looked after Atti and Ghost and still kept at her schoolwork, determined not to lose a semester.

"I've packed it in," he said.

"You're not going back to school?"

"I can't. And I couldn't afford it even if I wanted to. I'm lucky I've got a place to stay. Next, I've got to find a job."

Reports speculated that indictments would be handed down against company officers, starting with Ted. He was morose and drank hard. When the general counsel came by, Ted huddled with him in his office with the door closed.

Even in these horrific circumstances, Jillian managed to make things worse. She moaned and rattled dishes and sneered at everyone, especially Atti, as if he had engineered the scandal to injure her.

Going stir crazy, Atti started taking Ghost for long walks. The dog picked up on Atti's tension and bared his teeth whenever someone approached, which gave them some space from reporters.

One day he left Ghost with Elle and returned to his house. He spent time sitting in the great room, trying to recreate the feeling of living there, which he had never appreciated when it was his reality. This had been home his whole life but now was an empty shell. He'd have given anything to go back six months, even with his big brother needling him. And images of his mother filled the house. Just as she often seemed neglected by his father, she now appeared to him as the most innocent victim of all—well, the most innocent after Atti, who now faced a lifetime without any of them.

Leafing through an album of photos of his mom when she was young, he left tears on some of the pages. He put the album in his backpack, along with the stuffed bear Elle once won for him. Those photos might keep the pain fresh for years to come, but he treasured the connection to his mother. As to the bear: it would make Elle smile and might help them both remember a time when their families were intact.

Leaving the house through the garden put him on a quiet cross-street and then Madison Avenue. Up ahead he spotted his old teammates Lincoln and Emerson on the busy sidewalk. They both attended college in the city, but it was odd to find them on the Upper East Side.

"Nick!" he shouted out. They stopped and turned.

"Oh, hey," Emerson said awkwardly. "How's it going, Forester?"

"Yeah, dude," Lincoln added. "Been a while."

Atti shrugged. "Well, things have been pretty nuts. What's up with you guys? I texted you."

"Yeah," Emerson said uncomfortably. "School got pretty busy. Sorry I didn't get back."

"So, what's up?" Atti said.

Lincoln said, "Emerson's got this new girlfriend and we're…"

"Forester doesn't want to hear about that," Emerson snapped. Then he turned to Atti. "Like I said, we're just banging around. What about you? Why are you in the city? You leave school?"

"People were saying you went to jail," Lincoln added.

Emerson turned on his friend. "Don't be stupid, Link. That was his father or…would have been his father."

"Oh, yeah," Lincoln said. "Sorry, dude."

"Yeah, no," said Atti, "I'm taking a break." He paused. "So where are you guys headed? You want to hang in the park?"

"Ah, not right now," Emerson said.

Atti raised his eyebrows in question.

"Yeah," Emerson added. "Like, I suddenly remembered. I've got to go see this guy about some tickets."

"I understand," said Atti, thinking he understood all too well.

"So, take it slow, man," Emerson said and backed off. Lincoln nodded and turned to go with him.

"Right. You guys take it easy. Good to see you."

Atti stood on the corner as his former teammates crossed the avenue and melted into the crowd walking east. He couldn't believe these guys had dumped him. Didn't they remember the trip after junior year? They were a team, on and off the field. They flew on the Gulfstream and partied in the infinity pool. That birthday trip was a highlight of the Apex, the time when the world was ripe for picking. But now? Those guys were such jerks. Link had always been marginal, but Emerson? Atti had thought he was real. All through JV and varsity soccer they were tight. At Cabo he felt like a friend for life.

Atti used to laugh at the parasites sucking up to his father at the Summer Splurge, but his supposed "friends" from Earlington were no better than junior versions of the same, friends for what they could get out of him.

The only person he could think to call was Q. He was uptown visiting his mother and agreed to meet in Central Park. A half-hour later they sat on a bench watching nannies push strollers and kids play kickball. "I've got to get out of Ted's apartment," Atti complained.

"Can't you go home?"

"The sheriff locked up the house."

"So you can't even get your shit?"

"There are ways in besides the front door."

Three days later Atti, Q and Ghost sat on the fourth-floor balcony off the master bedroom. Atti handed Q a bottle of champagne. "Remember when I almost hit that drummer with the cork?"

"That dude's smile was the best part of the day…after meeting Elle, of course."

Atti laughed quietly. "See if you can hit the patio."

"Won't it spill?"

"There's more champagne than we could drink in a week. In fact, since we don't have any glasses, I'll get another bottle and we'll see who gets closer."

After they both hit the patio, they sat and drank, both spilling on themselves as they drank straight from the bottles.

Q laughed and wiped his mouth on his sleeve. "So when do you have to give up the keys?"

"I'm not giving up *my* keys, but the audit starts at the end of the week. Thing is, I don't have anywhere to move stuff, and everything of value is already marked for auction or carted off. I have a couple of suitcases at Ted's apartment and," he gestured toward his backpack, "there's this left. Looks like I'm traveling light."

"You sure there are no jewels hidden somewhere? Your family's got a history, you know."

Atti laughed. "You may have a point. Should we find a pickaxe and see what's behind the walls?"

Q considered this for a moment but said, "Nah, let's just nab some more wine. Anyway, traveling light will keep you nimble. Also, you don't have to live at Ted's if it gets really bad. I moved back from Williamsburg to Loisaida, on Ludlow north of Stanton. I've got a couch with your name on it, and we could find someplace to stash your stuff… and Ghost, of course."

"That would be more fun, for sure. I think I could be a Lower East Side guy. But Ted is family, and Elle could use the help."

"Well, I can't offer anything to compete with your cousin. In fact, maybe *I* should come stay with *you*." Q was still smitten with Elle, and she had put him off so gently he remained devoted to her. "Anyway, keep it in mind in case you need to escape the drama. The building's okay and the neighborhood's a lot livelier than the Upper East, if a bit dilapidated, and you get used to the stairs and the bathtub in the kitchen."

As Atti took another swig from his bottle, his phone buzzed. "Hi, Uncle Ted."

"Listen Atti, I get you're upset—like the rest of us—but you can't walk out and then we don't hear from you. Are you coming back tonight or what?"

Ted had become more and more caustic since the scandal broke. It was as if he blamed Atti for the collapse, even though he was a partner in the company and must have been in on the fraud. But Ted needed to place blame on someone and it would not be himself.

"I'm over at the house picking up a few things."

"How did you even get in? Isn't it locked up?" He paused. "Oh, never mind. Just tell me if we'll see you for dinner. Jillian's not feeling well, and we sent the housekeeper home so Elle is cooking chicken."

"Sure, Uncle Ted. I'll be back in an hour."

When he hung up, Q gave him a questioning look.

"Elle is cooking, and I have to go. I'd invite you along but I don't think you want to be there right now."

"Your uncle still in denial?"

"Yeah, big time. And Martin is no better; his solution is to sneak out to get high. On top of that, Jillian's having trouble adjusting to reduced circumstances."

"I can see that. How much younger is she again?"

"Ted is in his mid-fifties and Jillian's a little over thirty."

"Yeah, she looks like Elle's sister. In fact…the two of them together…"

"Keep it to yourself." Atti shoved him, only half-kidding. Jillian was way too good-looking to be married to a disgraced, paunchy ex-fund manager, but Atti would not stand for Q including Elle in his erotic delusions.

They finished the wine. Q took a few bottles back to Ludlow Street, and Atti headed for Ted's.

This time at Ted's building he ignored the cameras and shouted questions. A guard was still on duty in the hallway. Elle heard Atti open the door and came to meet him. Her anxious expression froze him in his tracks as Ghost squeezed past her. Without speaking she turned to lead him into the dining room, where Ted and Martin sat at the table looking peevish. A cardboard shipping box lay on the floor. On the table between them was a beige handbag with a horseshoe-shaped clasp and a chain shoulder strap. A photograph of a bright yellow flower was glued to the side of the bag.

"What's the matter?" Atti said. "What is that?"

Ted turned to him. "It's a Gucci bag; it came half an hour ago, addressed to Jillian."

"So what?"

Elle grasped his arm and grimaced. "Inside," she said in disgust.

"What's inside?"

"A special surprise," Martin said glumly.

Ted slid the bag toward Atti. He stepped up to the table and felt along the outside. There was nothing unusual except the flower picture and a skunky smell. He lifted the clasp holding the flap closed.

Elle groaned. Atti looked up. She had averted her face. He turned to the others, confused. Ted grimaced. Martin watched eagerly.

Atti lifted the flap and opened the bag. Inside was a dead animal, a bat maybe. It was covered with maggots! The smell poured out and gagged him. He dropped the flap and stumbled back.

Martin snickered. Ted looked pained and said, "What do you make of that?"

"It's disgusting! How did it get here?"

"UPS," Elle said.

"So, it means nothing to you?" Ted asked.

"Yeah, boy genius," Martin said. "We thought *you'd* be able to explain it."

Atti ignored Martin and stepped farther away from the table. "Have you called the police?"

"To say what?" Ted said coldly. "My brother was just blown up and our hedge fund collapsed in a global scandal, but could you come investigate a dead rodent?"

"But what if it's connected? This could be a warning…or a threat."

Ted glared at him. "Sure, and a long list of people wish they'd sent it."

Atti went upstairs to wash the smell off his hands and face and have a moment to himself. Ted and Martin were idiots. But Ted *must* have been in on the Ponzi scheme. He was Hugo's partner from the beginning, not to mention his brother; he could not have been blind to what was going on all that time. And now they would all pay. It was not enough they lost all the money and were disgraced as a family; now someone was harassing Jillian.

When he finally returned downstairs, Atti stared at the photograph glued to the bag. What did it mean? There must be something to it.

Elle took his arm. "Jillian was so excited," she said quietly, "that one of her *dear* friends sent a sympathy present. And Gucci is definitely her style. Then she opened it and lost her lunch. We all just stared, and she ran up to her room."

As if on cue, Jillian clamored down the stairs in a short skirt and high heels, carrying a shoulder bag and crashing a wheeled suitcase down the steps behind her.

"You're a sorry old shit!" she snarled at Ted once she hit the ground floor. "You'll hear from my lawyer."

Ted watched her go, and everyone on the thirtieth floor heard the door slam. After a moment Ted came back into the living room and started swilling bourbon. After three quick shots, he turned over his glass on the table and wheeled on Atti with unsteady eyes.

"You!" he spat out. "You're a grown man now. It's time for you to check your ass out of the Uncle Ted hotel…and take that hairy dog with you. I don't want to see you or be reminded of you *or* your father."

"That's not fair!" Elle objected.

Atti waved at her back.

"Fair?" Ted said, slurring the word. "What's fair about my brother ruining my life? What's fair about our friends shutting us out like goddamn lepers? Dogging our trail…sending dead animals…driving my wife away…."

"But…," Elle said.

"But nothing!" Ted shouted and turned on Atti. "Just go!"

Atti gave Elle a sad smile and went up to the guest room. She followed, knocked on the door and came in. "He can't throw you out!" she said urgently. "Where would you go?"

"Look," Atti said, reaching for her hand. "It's not so bad. I'll find someplace."

"But we're supposed to be a family!"

"It's okay, really," he said resignedly, trying to convince himself. "I hate to leave *you* but it will be a relief to get away from here."

She went back downstairs. He sat on the bed to consider his options. He couldn't call Emerson, not after the way his "friend" dissed him. And the rest of his so-called friends from school would be the same. The only exception seemed to be Q.

Q answered his phone. "S'up, dude?"

"Man, I've got to take you up on your invitation."

"Why? What's going on?"

"It's Jillian; she walked out. Ted blames me, or blames my father, which is all the same to him. This place is toxic. Can Ghost and I crash?"

"Well, it'll be tight. I wasn't really thinking about the dog and how small this place is. But that's crazy about Jillian. The perfect trophy wife! What happened?"

"I don't know. She signed on for a luxury cruise and wigged out when she got a shack on the beach."

"Man, you are a poet."

Atti laughed sadly. "Anyway, a package arrived for Jillian today: a bag with a bat…and maggots. It freaked me out. Oh God, the smell! It pushed her over the edge."

"A bat? Sounds like the mob. You reported it, right?"

"I'm about to call the police. Ted is too stupid. That's one reason I need to get out of the apartment; I feel like I've got a target on my head."

"But what about Elle?"

"Ted wouldn't let her go, and she wouldn't leave anyway. She has this undying need to take care of everyone." He paused. "So, can you put us up?"

"Yeah, I guess. Come on along. Can't have you sleeping on the street."

Atti hung up and called the detectives investigating the crash. Detective Lawrence said he would send someone to pick up the bag.

Atti returned downstairs with his backpack. Ted was practically passed out on a sofa. Martin stared at the liquor in his own glass, apparently not far behind.

"A Hallmark moment," Atti said acerbically.

Elle looked so heartbroken he immediately regretted his remark. "I'm sorry, Elle," he said and held out a hand to her.

She took his hand and buried her face in his shoulder. "I'm so, so sorry," he said, rocking her gently.

"I can't help thinking how different this would be if my mom was alive," she said. "Jillian would never have happened, Martin wouldn't be such a mess and even after the scandal, she would *not* let my father act like this."

There was truth in what Elle said, but no point in dwelling on what might have been. It was time to grow up. No one was going to step in and make things right. It was up to Atti.

"Listen, I'll be at Q's," he said and then added confidentially, "And listen, if someone is pissed off enough to freak Jillian out, then we could all be in danger. No one will find me deep in Loisaida, but you…."

"Don't worry about me, Atti."

"But you're the only person I *do* worry about."

"*You're* the one out on the street! How will you live?"

The shock of Jillian's departure and being thrown out paled against the pain of seeing Elle's distress. Her puffy eyes, normally so clear and bright, were deeply mournful. On top of all her troubles, she now had to care for two broken men who blamed the world for their failings, and yet *she* was worried about Atti. The one saving grace was her college account, unlike the trust funds, wouldn't be seized and could only be used for school, so she could return to finish her degree in Scotland and get clear of this mess.

Ghost was up and ready to move. Elle bent down to hug him, leaving tears on his coat. With one more sad smile, Atti led the dog out the door.

Chapter Nine

Atti took the subway to Q's building on Ludlow Street. A steel gate covered the storefront at street level of the five-story red-brick tenement. Clinging like an awkward appendage a rust-colored fire escape hugged the upper floors. Other than the cars dense along the curbs or snaking down the narrow street, it was easy to imagine this block a hundred years ago looking much the same.

"Yo, Atti!" came a shout from above.

Q was leaning out over the fire escape five floors up. "The buzzer's broken," he shouted. "Catch." He dropped a rolled-up bandana. Atti grabbed at it but missed, and it bounced under a parked car. He got down on his knees and retrieved it, finding a keyring wrapped inside.

From his knees he looked up at Ghost, sitting and watching with apparent amusement. "Suddenly, you don't fetch?" he said, but the dog didn't respond.

The building lobby barely fit the mailboxes for ten apartments, a staircase and the door to the backyard and basement. Atti's bags banged against the railing and walls of the narrow staircase as he made his way up. Half-way to the fifth floor, he paused to change his grip on a bag. "You go ahead," he said, dropping the leash. Ghost scurried up to the next landing and looked back.

From above they heard a door open and Q's voice. "You guys lost down there?"

Ghost looked once more at Atti and trotted up the stairs, clanging his leash behind. Atti followed and finally reached the top landing.

"You get used to it," Q said when his panting friend entered the apartment through the kitchen and dropped his bags. Ghost was drinking from a bowl on the floor.

Atti surveyed his new home. The railroad flat had a small living room to the left, narrow bedroom to the right and bathroom through the bedroom. He had hoped Q was kidding about the bathtub in the kitchen. It turned out the tub was the only water source in that room because the sink faucet didn't work.

Q poured a can of iced tea into two glasses and handed one to Atti. "To a new chapter!" he toasted as his fist squashed a cockroach on the counter.

"A declaration of independence," Atti toasted, grimacing as Q brushed the dead roach onto the floor and wiped his hand on his pants. Ghost sniffed at the carcass but left it alone.

Q showed Atti a couch covered in a faded floral design, crowded into the room with two shabby chairs and piles of books and electrical equipment. A window opened onto the street through crooked, filmy curtains and a steel gate, now open but meant to shut off access from the fire escape. On the wall were posters of Robert Moog playing a synthesizer and Django Reinhardt in a Paris café.

Seeing Atti peruse the posters, Q said, "I really should put up a shot of Lou Reed since he lived up the block."

Atti sunk into his new bed. His thoughts ran through the steady deterioration of his digs, from the big house in Carnegie Hill, to Ted's spacious Upper East Side duplex, to a worn-out couch in Loisaida.

Q watched Atti until he looked up. "You'll have to get your other stuff from your uncle's place," Q said.

"Yeah, some time when he's not around."

"He still putting it all on you?"

Atti nodded. "He was my legal guardian until I turned eighteen, but that doesn't mean anything to him now, not since he got caught scamming everyone he knew."

Q shrugged and joined Atti on the couch, scratching Ghost behind the ears. "Well, let me know when you need help moving stuff. We'll find someplace to stack it."

Apparently trying to lighten the mood, Q showed Atti a pedal he was rigging. "It makes guitar notes thick and raspy," he said. "It's like what they used to call a 'fuzz box' except there's a clear harmonic overlay. And I can daisy-chain this to a pedal that makes it sound like a drum and play percussion and distorted guitar at the same time." He flipped on an amplifier and played a flourish of notes and chords.

"You're a one-man rhythm section," Atti laughed, "but I don't understand what you said."

"Not important. It only matters that you savor the celestial sound."

After a while Atti gave Q more details about the bat in the handbag. Q grimaced. "It was some fancy pocketbook?"

"Apparently, and Jillian's style, which means it was expensive."

"But with the maggot residue, I guess it won't resell for much on eBay," Q smirked.

Atti laughed. "Anyway, I have to go talk to this detective tomorrow. Ted thinks the bag came from an investor blowing off steam, but it's more aggressive than that."

Atti hadn't eaten since breakfast, so Q boiled water and cooked pasta. "This bass player I know works at a food service. He gave me a twenty-pound bag of elbow macaroni when I helped him rewire an amp. Not sure where he got it, and I didn't ask. I've been trying to eat it before it gets moldy."

"I like pasta," Atti said.

"Yeah, well, I'll remind you you said that. It's better with some kind of topping, like cheese or vegetables, but plain it still fills your stomach."

In the morning Atti walked Ghost to Broadway and found an

ATM, but when he tried to withdraw money, a notice said his account was frozen. At another bank he tried each of his credit cards but couldn't get any cash.

"Damn it!" he yelled, drawing looks from passersby. How would he live? The two hundred dollars in his wallet wouldn't last long. Ted would be no help; he couldn't even care for himself. But Atti needed money for food and to pay his phone bill. He thought about what he might sell but his only possession of value was his watch. How could he get the best price for it?

On the way back to the apartment he bought a jar of tomato sauce and a bag of dog food. Eating plain macaroni was too much like sticking your tongue out the window, and no matter how lean things got, Ghost had to eat.

Next day Atti went uptown to the police station. Detective Sam Lawrence pointed to the table between them. "This is the bag you called about?"

"That's it."

"And you looked inside?"

Atti nodded.

"What do you think?"

"No idea. Everyone keeps asking *me*. It was at my uncle's apartment when I got there. They said UPS brought it addressed to my aunt. No one knew where it came from."

"Can you think of why anyone would send this to your aunt?"

"Not at all. A lot of investors were hurt. Ted thinks one of them sent it as a kind of fuck you…I mean, sorry."

Lawrence waived this off. "Ted, being your uncle?"

"Right. Edward Forester. He was there with my aunt and two cousins."

"So does a bat have any significance to you or your family?" The detective started to open the flap, which made Atti flinch.

"We removed the carcass," Lawrence smiled, turning the open bag toward Atti, "though I don't think we'll ever get rid of the smell."

"So," the detective went on, "no idea about the bat? What about this photo? Did you all talk about what it might mean to glue a flower picture to a handbag full of maggots?"

"We were all disgusted. I don't get any of this."

"Would it interest you to know this flower is…" he checked his pad, "a *lotus corniculatus*, commonly called 'birdsfoot trefoil'?"

Atti shrugged. Nothing was getting clearer.

"We did some research. There was a traditional means of communication through the use flowers called 'floriography,' where birdsfoot trefoil symbolized revenge, which would make it a nice garnish for a maggots-and-bat gift bag."

Atti understood the detective was trying to put him at ease, but he couldn't imagine what he was supposed to say.

"Still, revenge as a motive doesn't tell us if it was an investor. And another thing is interesting. My sergeant tells me this 'Dionysus' model costs thousands of dollars. Is this the kind of thing your aunt might own?"

"If it's expensive and exclusive, Jillian would want it. But what did you call it: Dionysus?"

"A Greek god, or maybe goddess, I don't know."

Atti thought about that. Didn't something else about mythology come up lately? He couldn't quite recall.

"So," Lawrence went on, "someone sent Ms. Forester a package that would appeal specifically to her, booby-trapped as some kind of revenge. But after the suspicious plane crash, we wonder if this targeted only your aunt or represents a broader threat to the family."

Images swirled around Atti's head: the mangled bat, the plunging jet, Elle's anguished face. "Sorry I can't help," he said sincerely. "Nothing makes sense anymore."

Lawrence looked sympathetic. "Okay, well, what can you tell me about Harry Gooden?"

This change of subject threw Atti off balance. "Uncle Hal? He's been the compliance officer at Pandion Capital since before I was born.

He used to be close to the family but drifted away as Bode and I got older. Now he's kind of a sad character, especially since his wife died."

"We have information there was friction between Gooden and your father. What do you know about that?"

"Nothing was smooth between Harry and the world. But now that you mention it, Harry was all torn up at the summer Picnic in Maine this year. He kept arguing with my father and then left in the middle of the day. It was strange. But Ed Blankley told me he lost his job. He couldn't be involved with the jet, could he?"

"We don't know that. We simply need to find Mr. Gooden and hear what he has to say; but he's disappeared."

"What do you mean, disappeared?" Atti was dumbfounded.

"It seems he sold his house over the summer and has been quietly closing accounts and moving money ever since. He sold his car last Tuesday and flew to Toronto and from there to Costa Rica. Then the trail went cold."

Atti couldn't believe Harry would do this. He was sad and agitated and he *did* get fired, but he wasn't mean, and why would he pick on Jillian?

"As chief compliance officer," Lawrence went on, "Gooden oversaw the firm's brokerage functions. Whether he was in on the Ponzi scheme is unclear, but lots of folks want to talk with him."

"So you think he sent the bat?"

"We're really more focused on the jet, and any connection with Harry is speculative. But given all the circumstances, we need to know more. He could have recently discovered the fraud or concluded he'd be swept in when it came to light. We just need to find him."

"I wish I could help, though I can't believe Harry would harass Jillian, or any of us."

"Well, nothing's certain. We're also looking at one of the early investors in the fund. Do you know a Charles Tilson?"

The name sent chills down Atti's spine. "Yeah, I know him. Texas drawl; full of himself. He always acted like he was on the inside of the business. Was he in on the fraud?"

"We can't say, but he was an early investor who eventually ran a feeder fund for Pandion out of Houston. Records show he closed up shop and cashed out twenty-two million dollars in August."

"Which means…?"

"It's not much to go on, but he did take out his money at exactly the right time—assuming the prosecutors don't claw it back."

"Well, he was scary when we were kids, and probably still is. I saw him last summer, and the meeting was a little icy."

"Yes, well, you keep your eyes open, and make sure we can contact you in case of developments."

Atti turned to go, feeling overwhelmed.

"And son…," Lawrence said.

Atti turned back.

"I know you didn't ask for any of this and don't deserve it. But keep your chin up; we'll figure this out. We'll find out who's doing this and put a stop to it."

Atti walked downtown rather than spending money on another subway ride. At 34th Street he turned toward the walkway along the East River so he could think without watching for cars. Why didn't they know what happened to the Gulfstream? Was the accident connected to Pandion Capital? What if it was? Would the police sort this out? Lawrence seemed capable—and surprisingly nice for a cop—but was there more to fear from the investors?

When he returned to Q's apartment from walking the dog next morning, Atti told himself things were improving because at least he didn't have to climb under a car for the key. But having a key to the door didn't count for much in the big picture with his mother and father dead and someone terrorizing his family. Was this penance? Would they all have to pay for Hugo and Ted's crimes? Hadn't they already paid enough?

In the tiny lobby, he removed Ghost's leash and the dog leaped up the stairs. He looked back eagerly from the landing above, forcing Atti to smile. He was thankful beyond words for the dog's indomitable spirit.

Ghost ascended out of sight, but as Atti passed the third floor there was barking from above. He bounded up and found Ghost on the fourth-floor landing, crouched in a face-off with a Dalmatian baring his teeth. Atti stepped up beside Ghost, signaling with his hand to stay down. The Dalmatian lunged. Ghost jumped in front of Atti and barked loud, ears flat and teeth bared. The other dog backed off but continued to snarl.

"Down!" Atti yelled. Ghost took a half-step back but remained coiled.

Behind the yapping Dalmatian a woman in a flannel shirt, curly black hair wild about her face, shouted, "Chauncey! Get back here!"

The Dalmatian kept growling as she hooked a leash to its collar. She pulled with both hands and shot a fiery look at Atti. "Who the hell are you? What's that dog doing here?"

"Sorry. We're visiting upstairs."

"Well, your dog should be on a leash!"

Atti looked down at Ghost, crouched on the step beside him, and then at the crazed dog struggling on his hind legs against his restraint.

"He was protecting me," he said.

She opened her mouth to speak but then cursed and yanked the Dalmatian away.

Atti waited until the woman's apartment door slammed and then continued up the stairs.

Inside the apartment Q was on the couch picking at his guitar. He looked up. "What's all the commotion?"

"Some girl with a feral dog."

"Oh, you mean Hippie Chick?"

"Is that her name?"

"No, it's Rooney. I call her Hippie Chick because she dresses pure sixties flower-power. She wears it well—don't get me wrong—but it's hard to see her fine bod under those baggy clothes. You wouldn't know it to see her now but she was really chill before she got that dog. The mutt has totally messed her mind."

"She didn't like me much."

Q laughed. "Give it time. She's okay."

"I have to admit there's something perversely alluring about a good-looking girl who wants to rip your heart out."

Q returned to scribbling notes on a sheet of manuscript paper. Atti filled Ghost's water bowl and settled into one of the stuffed chairs to scroll job listings on his phone. "I have to find something fast," he said in exasperation. "Start putting food on the table."

"Hey, whoa. You just got here. Maybe you need a break, huh? But as to a job: I know a guy named Henry, a little off but nice. He works at my favorite record store, around the corner, and I think someone quit last week. I'll call him. It's the Paradise Plum. I go there for the LPs, not to buy—because I don't own a turntable—but to handle the records and read the liner notes. Does that sound weird? Anyway, it's also a head shop. Might be they sell vinyl and CDs as a cover. Let me talk to him."

Atti took Ghost with him next morning to check out the record shop, but he couldn't see in the window. A solid metal security gate was locked in place. The gray aluminum was painted with graffiti and strewn with peeling stickers. A sign on the bricks above the gate said "Paradise Plum" with a primitive painting of a plum wearing headphones.

Later in the day Q called Henry, who said Atti should come by to meet the owner after twelve, when the shop opened. Atti returned without the dog. Out front on the sidewalk now were folding tables and milk crates holding record albums and a couple of boxes filled haphazardly with forty-fives offered at a dollar each. Behind filthy glass the display window contained an assortment of exotic water pipes, one having a bowl with the face of Jimi Hendrix. There were also LPs, looking as if they had been tossed rather than placed there, and concert posters for Led Zeppelin and Thelonious Monk.

Atti paused inside the door to look at a wall covered with flyers for dog walkers, movers and French lessons. Then he went to the counter and introduced himself to the owner.

Frank Bruno was a dark-haired man just turning gray, probably forty-five, whose body looked soft but whose face was hard. He had heavy black and gray stubble, not fashionable like a hipster or a movie star, but bristly and sloppy. He went out of his way to say he was a native of the Lower East Side so Atti said he lived right around the corner. When Bruno asked about his employment experience, Atti was ready with a story about working at a bookstore in Maine. That response, and the fact Atti had a social security number and didn't drool on himself, was all Bruno needed to hire him.

Bruno waved around the store. "The records and CDs are grouped by genre and then alphabetic; Henry will show you. The bongs and pipes are all priced on the stickers—and we *don't* negotiate prices. As to anyone wanting to sell used records: they have to see me. Any questions?"

Atti shook his head.

"Well," Bruno went on, "if you had any brains, you'd ask about the pay…and the hours. I'll tell you up front. The money's minimum wage, which is not great but it is what it is. There are sometimes side jobs for cash; we'll see how that goes. As to hours, you work five days, twelve to seven. We're closed Mondays, you're off Tuesdays and on Wednesdays you'll be here by yourself. The other guy is Henry. He's out getting coffee, but he'll be back in a minute to show you around. Are we good? Any questions, problems?"

Atti shook his head again.

"Not much of a talker, huh? That will be a relief after Henry."

Bruno looked him over again and nodded his head. "Listen, you show up on time, you don't do drugs on the job, you keep the place clean. You do that and we get along fine. We'll see; we'll see how it goes."

Henry returned with coffee for himself and Bruno and greeted Atti. He was shorter than Atti but seemed fit and had big features and a generous smile. He was eager to show Atti what needed to be done in the shop: sorting incoming records, answering the phone, filling email orders, ringing up sales, sweeping the floor.

"Frankie can be a little hard," Henry said as he showed Atti the stockroom. "He acts like a big shot, like he's connected or something, but all he's got is this dump."

"He said I might earn extra money on the side?"

"Yeah," Henry laughed, "that's Frankie. He could ramp up the mail-order business and stock records people are willing to pay for, exotic imports and bootleg concerts, but he buys crap and sells crap, and not much of it. He must be laundering money or I don't know how he affords the rent and our salaries. But then," he paused and looked around and continued more quietly, "the real business is drugs. He sells weed out of the stockroom, and he'll ask us to make deliveries. It's usually ten bucks cash to make a drop, depending on the order, and you do it on work time."

Over the next week, Atti settled into the job. He liked Henry and the ambiance of the shop. They played all kinds of music and attracted a mix of serious audiophiles and colorful passersby. The people who ran the Chinese takeout place on one side and the vintage clothing shop on the other were nice. The clothes shop employees would stop by to chat. Nobody in the other store spoke English but they smiled when they passed.

Bruno was in and out. He had a way of looking like he was making some shifty deal each time he cradled the phone against his shoulder and chewed an unlit cigar. But Henry was good company. He was a bit older than Atti and seemed rudderless but consistently hopeful a good-looking girl might come into the shop—which never happened.

"Grew up outside Wilmington," Henry volunteered, "but got out as soon as I could."

"So why New York?"

"I don't know. Something in the air." He paused to laugh. "And I don't mean that dumpster smell we get when there's no wind."

Atti liked looking at the old album covers and could see why Q frequented the place. "It was the art form of the sixties and seventies," Henry said, "like craft beer cans are now."

"So, you're an art lover?" Atti replied.

"Oh yeah, long as I can drink it or spin it on a turntable."

Bruno said he'd have to empty the mouse traps, and Henry pointed out they drew a bigger crowd than the records. As the newest employee, it was also his job to clean the "bathroom," a squalid toilet and tiny sink in a corner of the stockroom.

"This is the worst job," Henry said as he showed him the cleaning supplies, "but what Frankie said about you doing it because you're new is crap. We'll switch off each week—and it's not like anyone really *cleans* this shit hole."

When Bruno learned Atti had a large dog, he said to bring him to the shop. He apparently thought Ghost would chase mice…and provide security. Ghost was more than happy to come to work with Atti and quickly made friends with Henry. As to job performance, he excelled at greeting customers more than chasing mice.

Henry talked most of the time, though he didn't have much to say. At least he was good-natured, and Atti was short on friends since the Upper East Side crowd had dumped him. Henry showed him cheap places for dinner, but after Atti saw his first paycheck, he realized he'd be eating macaroni at home until it ran out. Henry also introduced Atti to a shifting group of mostly young men he met after work at Tompkins Square Park. This hodgepodge of street people and the marginally employed gathered on the benches and lawn behind the great elm, celebrated as the spot of the first public chanting session of the Hare Krishnas outside India. They played music and shared cigarettes and wine each night and weed when they could get it. Q joined them a couple of times but spent most of his nights working with musician friends.

Ghost always came with Atti and Henry to the park. He would run loose—unless Atti saw a cop or a park ranger—and was friendly to people, sometimes too friendly. One night Atti saw the dog wagging his tail with a couple of street people gone on hallucinogens or glue or something. Atti whistled for him and took him to the dog run, like a respectable pet. The "dog people" were sometimes just as odd, and often less friendly, than the park people, but Atti thought Ghost needed to do some hard running with his own species.

"I am so hungry," Atti blurted out one evening on a park bench while Henry and a scruffy young man shared a cigarette.

"You know they give away food here?" the man said. "It's not bad… for the price."

"I heard that," Henry said. "It's some political thing?"

"Bombs Against Hunger or something," the guy said. "They hand out meals every Sunday."

Atti was tempted to try this out. He needed a break from macaroni. But he looked at the people around the elm and wondered if he was far gone enough to join the breadline. He had a roof over his head and a job and enough pasta to fill his stomach, which put him in a higher income bracket than most of these people. He'd keep it in mind as a fallback, though.

One morning Atti was sitting with Ghost on the front stoop, gathering energy for the walk upstairs. Rooney approached on the sidewalk with another woman, a bit older than her with shoulder-length blonde hair, a kind of Hitchcock blonde hiding seductive eyes behind big-rimmed glasses. They started up the steps without looking at him.

"Good morning," he said.

Rooney looked up dismissively but kept walking. Her companion stopped and smiled at Atti and then looked at Ghost. "Roo, why doesn't Chauncey sit like that?"

Atti looked at Ghost and smiled back at the woman. "His name's Ghost," he said, "and he's sitting because there's nowhere else he has to be."

"Will you come on?" Rooney said, reaching for the woman's hand and pulling her into the building. The blonde shrugged and turned to follow.

"So, Hippie Chick has a friend," Atti told Q over the evening pasta with ketchup.

"Seriously tied-back blonde hair? Too refined for the neighborhood?"

"Yeah. You know her?"

"That's her sister, Jordan. The family sends her round once in a while to make sure Rooney hasn't gone over to the dark side. She's like twenty-five, graduated from Bryn Mawr, works for some rich investor dude."

"How do you know so much about her?"

"Rooney's a friend. We moved in the same day and hang out sometimes. She digs my music. Like I said, she's all right—not to mention she's got a fine ass."

"Yeah, I noticed."

"I don't know why she dislikes *you* so much," Q said with an overly serious expression, hardly hiding his amusement.

Atti didn't know either but wished he could find out. While he pondered this, his phone rang. It was Gabriel Oak.

"Calling to check in, Atticus. I know things have been hard for you."

"Thanks, Gabriel. Hard for all of us, I guess. Did you have any money in the fund?"

"I did, yes, but it was mostly what your father and uncle gave as Christmas bonuses in the form of shares. So, I lost paper profits but no real money of mine. Worse off is old Giacomo."

"Father Jake invested?"

"I'm afraid so. He had some small amount of family money, but he also invested a bequest that came into the church from the Schneiders five, six years back. You remember them?"

"Yeah, of course."

"Well, their estate gave a chunk of money to St. Bernard's in care of Giacomo, and your dad convinced him he could multiply it so he could fund all his programs *and* refurbish the church building."

"That sucks! I can't believe that devil was my father."

"Aye, it is lamentable. But as to whether Hugo was a devil, I suppose Giacomo would be the expert."

"I'm also sorry for you. But Ted told me you own the gatehouse free and clear, which is great."

"As to that, Atti, you know you always have a place here, even when Pandion is broken up for tract housing."

"That's really nice of you, Gabriel. I won't be moving in…but I may be by once in a while to visit?"

"Ever and always."

Q took a call in the bedroom and emerged excited. "I booked a gig Friday night at Buffalo Hall! You know, on Avenue C?"

"I know the place. That's fantastic. I'm there, definitely."

Q smiled sheepishly. "I was wondering if you might also invite your cousin."

"Good idea. She's going back to school next week and I want to see her. But…what about our neighbor?"

"Hippie Chick? You like her?"

"Yeah, maybe, if I could get her and her dog to stop snarling at me."

Q laughed. "Okay. I'll mention you have a crush on her and want her to come to the show."

Atti punched his arm.

When Atti called Elle, she said she'd love to go. "Q seems really talented, the little bit I've heard. Anyway, we—and particularly you—have *got* to support him."

"I'm coming to realize that."

"Took you long enough."

"You're right," he said and paused. "When the shit hit the fan, he never changed. He's just always there."

Atti hung up and thought about what Elle said. Atti really did have to do what he could for Q after all his friend was doing for him. With Atti's family gone and his housing pulled from beneath him, he didn't know how he would have gotten by without that help. And even beyond material assistance, Q filled a small part of the void left by his mother, or made Atti at least feel someone cared what happened to him. That was not to belittle Elle's place in his life—she had always been there for him and always would be—but with the foundation of his life gone up in smoke, he needed all the reinforcement he could get.

Q's show was celestial, as promised. He did an amazing cover of two Scrags songs, which was remarkable for a solo musician, but mostly he played his own compositions. His home-made fuzz box/phantom drummer also got some notice.

Elle dressed down perfectly for slumming on the Lower East Side. Rooney also showed up but with a guy Atti didn't know, who seemed kind of stiff. She was hot in a dress with a flowery pattern that *was* very sixties. She nodded at him from the bar but turned away.

"Who's that?" Elle said with her mischievous smile.

"Oh, she's a neighbor. She pretty much hates me."

"That look said something else."

"You think so?"

"Definitely. Keep talking as if you're into me, and I'll watch her."

He laughed. "I'm gonna miss you, Elena Forester, all the way across the ocean."

"Me too. By the way, I had to make up a story about where I was going tonight. I still can't mention your name around my dad."

"Why try?"

"To say where I was going, for example, but we also had a fight when I reminded him he is your guardian and your father's brother."

"Honestly, I could use the help but let him be. He's got enough to worry about with the criminal case. I read the DA is about to issue indictments against the senior employees."

"He's my father and I love him, but it's not fair, regardless of his legal problems. He's supposed to be the grownup. None of this was your fault. And now you didn't even finish college—which I totally don't agree with, by the way."

"Stop, Elle, please. I can't right now. I need to just live, quietly, with no photographers and no news stories. And I need to earn my way. I really, really will be all right. Get back to Scotland and stop worrying about me."

"That isn't fair either: I get to go to college and have a life while you're stuck here?"

He slow-punched her arm. "I'll be fine."

She smirked. "Well, I am headed back to St. Andrews Monday."

She said this as if it were an apology, but he smiled. He knew it was time for her to go, but it still hurt. He wished there were some way for her to keep clear of the Forester calamity without leaving him behind.

Chapter Ten

Atti didn't see Elle again before she left for Scotland, though she called to say goodbye. To take his mind off her leaving, he asked Bruno if he could fix up the Plum's display window. "It looks pretty tired," Atti said. "Some of that stuff hasn't been dusted since, like the Bush administration."

"Knock yourself out," Bruno said, "but I don't pay you to be a comedian. Put the albums and music stuff up front, bongs and water pipes behind."

Atti got started pulling out the old display. Ghost sniffed each item as Atti set it aside. The album covers were faded from the sun, and the records were warped. "Hey, Frank," he called out, "shouldn't we take the records out of the album covers before putting them in the window?"

Bruno looked up from his newspaper and sighed. "Put the records in new sleeves…and make sure you label them. Still, they won't be worth nothin' without the covers."

"Well, there *is* the music," Atti said under his breath. Bruno thought it more important how an album was packaged than the experience of listening to it, the kind of form over substance attitude that typified what had been wrong with Atti's prior life.

"Are you decorating or daydreaming?" Bruno grumbled.

Atti looked up, trying not to look surprised. "Decorating, boss. Just giving it some thought."

"Forget about thought and fill the window, albums up front and bongs behind. It's simple. In fact…leave it all for now and come back to my office."

It was part of Bruno's self-important image that he called the stockroom his "office." There *was* an old desk in the cramped space where he kept the books and packaged the weed, but the room was otherwise crammed with cardboard boxes, stacks of records and an old bicycle. The room could barely fit three people at one time.

Bruno handed Atti a sealed envelope. "Here's the deal. You take this to Building 283 in StuyTown, over near Avenue C and 14th Street. You buzz number 25 and wait in the lobby. The customer's a middle-aged guy, thinning gray hair with a stubble. He'll meet you in the lobby and pay you a hundred and eighty bucks, and you give him the package. Make it quick and keep your eyes open. Then you bring back the money and get your cut."

"What's my cut?"

"Depends on the size of the delivery and…other things. We'll see how it goes."

Atti took the bicycle from the backroom, and Henry agreed to watch Ghost while he was gone. Atti rode uptown, locked the bike to a railing in Stuyvesant Town and, after some looking around, found the building. The exchange was quick and easy. A timid guy in slacks and a golf shirt came through the inner door, nodded like he was being covert, handed over a roll of cash and took the envelope. The man disappeared without a word, so Atti called after him, "Have a nice day."

When Atti got back to the Plum, Bruno called him into the stockroom to hand over the money. "You counted it, right?" he said.

"No, I thought you said to make it quick. Is it wrong?"

Bruno counted the bills and scoffed. "It's right…this time, but how would you know? You always count it before you hand over the goods.

No way to go back and collect if we're shortchanged, and the difference comes out of your pay."

Bruno pocketed the cash and handed Atti a ten-dollar bill. "There you go," he said.

"That's it?"

"For a bike ride to visit a mousy accountant? Yeah, that's it. Hey, no one's twisting your arm. Henry can do the drops."

"Sorry, no, it's okay." Henry had told him Bruno would pay ten dollars for most jobs, but Hugo taught him to push hard at the start of any business relationship, to set expectations.

Atti grew tired of evenings in Tompkins Square and took to strolling the streets in the evenings with Ghost, listening to street musicians, watching pretty girls and checking out books sold from the sidewalk. He brought his watch to a pawn shop and a couple of jewelry stores, but it was worth much more than they offered so held on to it. In one store the owner acted like he thought the watch was stolen so Atti showed him the inscription on the back: "To our Forester Man, Love, Mom and Dad."

One day he caught sight of Rooney and Jordan again, dressed up and looking elegant. They were heading out when he and Ghost came down the street. Jordan petted the dog. Rooney watched, slightly less snappish than last time.

"He's such a doll," Jordan said. "You said his name's Ghost?"

"That's right. And I'm Atti."

"So then, Ghost and Atti," she said with an amused smile, "I'm Jordan." She nodded toward her sister. "And, of course, you know Rooney."

Rooney almost imperceptibly dipped her head, another baby step toward affability. Atti struggled to start a conversation, but she walked abruptly up the sidewalk, followed by her sister.

A couple of weeks later, Atti was at the front of the Plum sorting newly arrived LPs. Weed deliveries had become a routine part of the job, and he was thinking with satisfaction that the extra money meant he could buy food and pay his phone bill. He was still sad at heart and lonely much of the time, but he was coming to think things could be worse in his dystopian world.

"Atti, you got a delivery," Bruno called from the stockroom.

"Yeah, no problem," Atti said. The day was sunny and he was glad for an excuse to get outside.

Bruno handed him a fat envelope. "This guy wants an ounce of sativa, so I said I'd send this new Orange Kush. He'll give you eight hundred bucks. Make sure you count it; this guy is new."

"You don't know him?"

"No, but he had the number and the routine. His name is 'Mr. Actless'—which sounds made-up to me, but that's nothing new. He wants to meet in East River Park, so you know he's careful."

Until then Atti had delivered only to repeat customers at their apartments, where the exchange was familiar and private. This guy must be nervous about using his home address for his first delivery.

He wheeled the bike through the store. Henry called out, "Hey, Atti, can you pick up a pack of smokes? I'll pay you when you get back."

"Dude, those things will kill you."

Henry made a long face and he relented. Henry was a good guy and would certainly do the same for him. Besides, he kept an eye on Ghost when it was Atti's turn to make a delivery. And maybe it was a bit precious of Atti to give him a hard time about a vice like smoking when he on his way to deliver marijuana.

He pedaled east and crossed the bridge to East River Park at Grand Street. The park was empty except for runners and people walking dogs. When he got close to the meeting point at the south end, he rode along the river to avoid a construction crew working on the path by the highway.

The appointed spot was at the south end of the promenade, with a great view of the old office towers downtown. Atti got off the bike and looked around. Other than the work crew, the only person in sight was an old man on a bench wrapped in a coat. That was odd on such a warm day, and the man seemed to be watching him from beneath a wide-brimmed hat. But he was no threat; probably some sad old fossil with nothing else to do.

He removed the envelope from his shoulder bag and held it in his pocket, reminding himself he had to see the money before turning it over. Fingering the envelope while glancing down the river, he could see the Statue of Liberty by looking under the Manhattan and Brooklyn Bridges. From this vantage point it looked like the statue stood on the coast of New Jersey rather than its own small island. He played the Hitchcock game, prompting himself with "Statue of Liberty" and answering *Saboteur*.

There was no chance now of the city erecting a statue to his father, although in the Apex a few months ago that hadn't seemed far-fetched. Everyone had loved and honored Hugo. Now they acted like they knew he was a crook all along, everyone but the people trying to recover their money. Universal homage had turned to scorn, but maybe it was for Atti to dictate how that would affect his life. Would the shame follow him, linger like the squiggle of white smoke against the clear blue sky? Or could he find a way to leave it behind, set himself free of the old life and expectations?

He pulled out his phone to check the time. This Actless character was late. That was not good. Sweat started to drip down his sides. He reached into his pocket again and felt the envelope as the old man on the bench rose and shuffled away. So he wasn't a master police agent in disguise, after all. Atti laughed at his own paranoia. But as he scanned the park for his connection something felt out of balance. The construction workers had left their project and were moving toward him from two sides. It was a setup!

He yanked the envelope from his pocket, ripped it open and pulled out the plastic bag. A siren chirped. Two police cruisers raced toward him along the footpath, lights flashing. Atti shook the bag over the river. The weed blew out into the water. He threw the empty bag after it.

A hand grabbed his shoulder. Someone pushed him into the railing, jamming his ribs, and yanked at his shoulder bag. Hands ran down his sides and legs.

"What happened to the old coot?" someone said.

"Bugged out," came a response.

"Leaving what the fuck?" the first voice said, angry.

They searched Atti's pockets and found a joint in his wallet. A big cop spun him around. He held the wallet up to compare Atti's face to his ID. "So, Atticus Forester, is it? And what's this?" He held up the joint as if it were the smoking gun that would send Atti up the river.

Atti said nothing.

"And what went over the side?" He looked into the river. "You know it's against the law to throw trash in the water."

The cops looked frustrated. One pulled a long pole from the trunk of his cruiser and fished the plastic bag out of the river. Atti assumed they intended to catch him selling, but there was no customer and the weed had washed away. The most they had on him was possession of a joint and maybe littering. But still he was arrested! It had half-seemed like his life was getting back on track, or he was at least treading water, but now this!

The botched sting and Atti's refusal to say anything angered the cops. One slapped handcuffs on him and pulled him roughly toward the squad car. He held Atti's head down as he pushed him into the back seat. Atti thought about how many times he had seen that played out in police procedurals.

At the station house they booked him, took fingerprints and mug shots and left him alone in a cell. He couldn't believe they were holding him for one joint, or that they had mounted this operation to intercept an ounce. They must have been duped by whoever set this up and now were embarrassed and taking it out on him. Still, he was stuck in a cell. He wracked his brain to think of who could have set him up.

An hour later they let him make a call. Company lawyers always handled his father's business, except the estate lawyer, who wouldn't know criminal law. Anyway, the company was gone, and Atti had no money to pay lawyers. He thought about calling Bruno but was afraid the police would listen and connect him with the Paradise Plum and Bruno's operation—if they didn't already know about that. Instead, he dialed Q.

"I'm in jail. The cops found a joint."

"They pulled you in for a joint?" Q laughed. "What did you do, blow smoke in their face?"

"It's not funny...and it's complicated. They say I'll be arraigned tomorrow at eleven. Can you meet me in criminal court on Centre Street and bring cash for bail?"

"Ah...cash. I haven't got much."

"I know, man, and I'll owe you, but is there any way?"

Q paused and finally said, "Sure. I'll find some money. Yeah, of course. I'll be there. Did you tell them at work?"

"No, but I should let them know. Maybe you can call my boss." Atti hoped Q understood he was trying not to mention Bruno's name or the Plum.

"Right...," Q said and hesitated. "Yeah, I'll stop around. See you in the morning."

Atti sat on his bunk. Wouldn't his mother be proud, he thought, making the whole situation worse. Even more depressing, he had no mother or anyone else to care. He missed his mother. It wasn't fair she had been caught up in this, and it was really unfair Atti lost her when he needed her most. Every time life knocked him down, he came back to that fact: his mother and his whole family were gone. Wasn't it about time he got a break?

He tried to sleep by thinking of what other kind of job he could get. Waiting tables would pay better, but who would hire him? His police record was not going to help, on top of having no legitimate work experience. He was feeling crushed by one thing after another.

Late in the afternoon, a public defender came to his cell. She wore a lawyer suit and was distracted leafing through a file until she suddenly stopped and looked up at him. "You're Hugo Forester's son?"

He nodded sadly.

"Our first goal, then, is to keep this quiet. Tomorrow they'll simply charge you," she checked her sheet, "for possession with intent to sell, and I'll plead not guilty for you. Do you have any prior arrests? Are you employed?"

When the guard brought him into the courtroom next morning, Atti was relieved to see Q seated a few rows back, nodding eagerly, which Atti took to mean he had scrounged up bail money.

"The State of New York versus Atticus Forester," the clerk read off his clipboard.

Atti's lawyer rose and led him to stand before the bench. There was a small commotion in the back of the room, two men talking together urgently.

"Order," said the judge, pounding a gavel and directing her gaze at the men. One of them rose, bowed his head to the judge and exited.

"Reporters," the lawyer said quietly to Atti. "Just what we *don't* need."

The judge charged Atti with possession of a controlled substance with intent to sell. His lawyer pleaded not guilty for him.

"Given the lack of any permanent address for Mr. Forester and the short term of his employment at a..." the judge looked down at her notes, "record and paraphernalia store, as well as the possibility of substantial family resources to leave the jurisdiction, I am setting bail at five thousand dollars."

Atti choked. No way would Q have that kind of money; it might as well be five *million*. He looked at his lawyer in panic.

"Stay calm," she said. "I'll be in to see you tomorrow. We'll get this thrown out."

Atti was led from the courtroom by a beefy clerk, handcuffed and put in the back of a van. Back in his cell he wondered if he should have called Bruno. Q must have told him Atti was in jail. It was Bruno's business; it was in his interest more than anyone's to get him out. Otherwise, Atti was sunk. It was laughable to think his family had "substantial" resources or that Uncle Ted or Martin would lift a finger to help. Elle would give all she had, but she didn't have that kind of money either, and she was so far away. Could he get Q to sell his watch?

Chapter
Eleven

Late in the afternoon a guard opened Atti's cell door. He had made bail. After signing some papers and retrieving his possessions—minus the joint—he was released. Q waited at the front desk.

"Where did you get the money?" Atti said, incredulous.

"Not important. We need to duck the reporters outside."

The desk sergeant gestured toward a side door. Q went ahead to see if the way was clear, then they exited and jogged down a side street. After a block they blended in with the crowd on the sidewalk. Then Q suddenly stopped in his tracks. "I don't know how they got this out so fast, but you made the news," he said, gesturing at a news stand. The *New York Post* headline screamed: "Ponzi Kid Busted."

"My big ambition," Atti said sarcastically, "a nickname in the tabloids. But thanks for springing me…and you still haven't told me where you got the money."

"I'm not supposed to say. Long as you show up for your hearing, they give it back."

At home Atti waited on the sidewalk while Q walked up the stairs to let Ghost out. Atti whistled and the dog charged down.

Out front Ghost sniffed garbage cans while Atti looked up, waiting for Q to drop the leash. He caught it on the fly and turned to the dog, looking for kudos for the nimble grab. Ghost was unimpressed.

Then Atti saw Rooney at the top of the stoop, watching but not smiling. "Okay, I give up," she said. "How did you train your dog…?"

"Ghost."

"How did you train *Ghost* to behave so well?"

"I think it's how I treat him, and we've been through some things together. But he was probably smart to begin with; maybe it's natural to the breed."

"I wish I could do something with Chauncey."

"Well…I could try to help."

"Could you? I mean, would you try?"

"Sure." He struggled not to look too eager or stutter. He'd work with her looney dog if it meant getting close to the owner. He had developed a distinct taste for peasant blouses and tied-dyed tank tops.

"Have you tried music?" he said.

"What do you mean?"

"Animals can sometimes be calmed by music. Maybe we could give it a go, that and talking."

"I'm ready to try anything. He's driving me nuts."

Atti smiled. From a jail cell to an opening with Rooney, his day was looking up. "I need to take this guy around the block," he said, gesturing at Ghost. "Then I'll knock on your door."

Atti pleaded with Ghost to finish his business quickly, double-timed it up to Q's and brushed his teeth and hair. He caught his breath as he walked down to Rooney's apartment.

She opened the door part way, the dog yapping behind her. Her expression was welcoming and almost imploring. It suited her. She said, "I was afraid you were leaving me to the mercy of the beast."

He smiled and looked past her at the dog. "Okay," he said. "First, let go of the door and treat me like part of the pack. Chauncey will sense this and want to stay close. Don't fret, whatever he does, because he'll feed off you. Let him run out on the landing or down the stairs if he wants. Leave the door open and I'll take care of Chauncey…and then we'll see what kind of music he likes."

She looked at him with both cautious respect and trepidation, but she let go of the door. Chauncey pushed it open and rushed onto the landing, barking. Atti ignored him and entered the apartment. The dog soon came back, turned as if to bolt again but then stopped and looked at him, confused. Rooney was in the kitchen. Atti had taken a seat on a sofa. Chauncey approached him but growled quietly from out of reach.

"Can we put on some mellow jazz," Atti said. "Coltrane or something?"

"I don't know what I've got. I can try the radio."

"Here. I'll use my phone." Atti selected a soulful trumpet tune and sat back. The dog circled, keeping his distance. Atti held out his hand but didn't move toward Chauncey. The dog tentatively stepped close enough to sniff.

"So, we have a Miles Davis fan," he said softly.

The dog continued to smell his hand, which he moved slowly to the top of its head and petted. He spoke in a soft, even voice until Chauncey sat beside him.

Atti looked up at Rooney, poking her head out of the kitchen. "Amazing," she mouthed with a grateful smile.

Over the next week Atti returned to Rooney's apartment for several sessions with Chauncey. He borrowed a portable speaker from Q so the music wouldn't sound so tinny, although he wasn't sure the dog cared for audio quality as much as he did. He kept the selections soft, instrumentals to start but gradually adding vocals, and sometimes he sang softly in the same voice he used to talk to the dog. Chauncey was not overly bright but stopped growling at everything and eased off his frenetic energy.

When they started working on rudimentary commands, Rooney complained, "He never sits when I tell him unless I shout. It's like he doesn't hear when I speak quietly."

"Oh, he hears you. Look at the size of those ears. He's taking in a lot when you say 'sit': your body language, how loud you sound, how big and threatening your posture becomes. He knows you'll repeat the command, and get more excited each time, but also you won't get angry with him. You've taught him the first command is only a suggestion, and we have to break him of that. From now on don't repeat a command. If Chauncey doesn't obey, take something from him, even if it's just your attention. He'll understand, and he won't push it next time."

The second week he enlisted Ghost to help Chauncey socialize with dogs. The door to the basement opened onto a small yard closed in by brick buildings and a dilapidated plank fence to the rear. The patch of scrubby grass was drab, but the dogs had space to play.

At the end of two weeks, they could all walk together on the sidewalk without incident. "I can't thank you enough," Rooney said. "You really have a way with animals. Chauncey has become a sweetheart."

"He was scared and reacting to your tension. The words you say don't matter, but your tone of voice has to assure him there's no danger, that he can let his guard down."

"And the music?"

"You know what they say about savage beasts."

"'Soothe the savage beast': that could be the slogan for a dog whisperer, or a whispering service."

Atti laughed.

"No, really. Why not? Lots of people have troubled dogs. We could go into business. I line up customers; you program the music and whisper. We'll make you, like, the canine guru."

He smiled. The plan sounded dubious, but if they worked together, she might start to like him. He was feeling comfortable with her but so far she showed no interest beyond the dog thing. Her sister paid more attention to him than Rooney did. Jordan seemed to actually like him and was impressed by his success with Chauncey.

Atti had returned to work at the Plum. Bruno said he wasn't the one who posted bail but he would have if he had known Atti needed it. That was bullshit, of course. Bruno also said he regretted sending Atti to meet a customer they didn't know. "You lost product," he said, "which *should* come out of your pay. But we'll leave that for now. We just gotta be more careful."

We have to be more careful, Atti thought sarcastically, trying to contain his resentment. "How did Mr. Actless contact you?"

"He had the number and the name of a regular, but I followed up and got nowheresville. Our customer told someone who told someone else. It seems this guy put a lot of time into taking us down or taking you down by the looks of it. Either way, we're out eight hundred bucks."

"It didn't cost *you* eight hundred bucks."

With a smirk, Bruno said, "All the same: no more deliveries except to regulars."

"Well, I'm out of it. Henry will have to make the drops. I can't risk being arrested again."

He wondered how he ended up working for a greedy swine like Bruno.

"How much can we charge?" Rooney asked as they walked the two dogs around the block that night.

"When I lived uptown," Atti said, hoping to impress her, "we didn't even think about how much it cost to groom Ghost or take him to the vet. He was our dog and whatever it cost, some staff person just paid it."

"Nice in that world, maybe," she replied, clearly *un*impressed, "but most people have limited funds to spend on their pets, and we need to fit into their budgets."

That was a slap in the face. But with only his regular pay from the Plum, Atti barely had enough money to buy Ghost food, so what she said made sense. He needed a plan to get back to a real life, with houses and cars and a girlfriend like Rooney. It seemed a long shot, but he hoped dog whispering would be a start.

And before long Rooney lined up a client. Maureen was a woman of about thirty who worked with her. She had a nice one-bedroom apartment in a large building in the Village. When Atti showed up, she introduced Benny, a two-year-old Weimaraner.

"He's been aggressive since I got him a year ago," she said, "especially outside the apartment. Last week he nipped at the building porter." She held up a muzzle. "So now he doesn't go out without this."

"Oh no," Atti said sympathetically. "Looks like Benny and I have some work to do."

The dog looked at Atti suspiciously. Atti took a seat and observed how Maureen interacted with him. Benny was hyper and Maureen seemed overly concerned. It was a cycle: she was nervous, so he was hyper, which made her more nervous, and so on.

"If it's okay," he said, "I'm going to put on some quiet music and ask you to sit by me and treat me like an old friend. Maybe have some wine or a cup of tea, whatever helps you relax. Benny will take his cue from you."

In a few sessions Atti was able to work his magic with Benny—and Maureen—and along the way she fed Atti all sorts of cookies and tea cakes. Toward the end of the week she downloaded a classical playlist. "I've put it on each day when I spend special time with Benny. He seems receptive and calmer."

Atti soon had Benny walking outside without the muzzle. He then brought Ghost along to do his part. After a week Maureen felt secure enough to let Benny loose in a dog park. She was ecstatic.

"Rooney said I should pay through her," she said, "but I'd like to give you something extra, if it's okay."

Atti smiled, recalling the response Hugo had taught him to this kind of offer. "Oh, that's not necessary."

"But you've made such a difference in our lives."

"Well, okay, twist my arm. I should throw Ghost a bone." He gestured at the dog, who looked up at hearing his name.

Rooney proposed Atti take two-thirds of the fee, since he did the real work. That netted him a hundred and thirty dollars plus a twenty-dollar tip for about eight hours work, or twice what he earned at the Plum. It wouldn't make him rich, but it was legal—although he didn't plan to pay taxes so was it really legal? And Rooney seemed excited and maybe more receptive.

When she handed over his money, he said, "We should go out and celebrate."

"Absolutely. Let's do something next weekend, maybe with Q and Jordan."

The second assignment was with a couple in Murray Hill. Magdalena's poodle, Poochie, was the ten-pound terror of the neighborhood. Atti repeated his routine of working with the owners first and approaching the dog slowly. But the wife took offense to his suggestion her tone of voice—alternately coddling and shrill—was part of the problem. Even the dog's name was an issue, but Atti never got to bring that up. After two sessions, Poochie remained irascible, and the wife told Atti not to come back.

"I assume she paid for the two sessions," he said to Rooney the next day.

"Actually, no. Magdalena was quite unhappy. She said you were rude and insulting."

"What an asshole."

"She *was* the client."

"Not if she stiffed us. That witch couldn't accept that her dog's neurosis reflected her own."

"Well, we can't run a business insulting customers."

"Maybe our business is not such a great idea. Even with the Weimaraner, the money wasn't very good for all the effort, not when you figure in travel time."

They agreed to close up Soothe the Savage Beast, but Atti had learned a few lessons. First, he could never make a living at dog whispering, at least not with the kind of customers Rooney found. Second, working side-by-side gained him little ground with her; she was now friendly but still not interested. But most importantly, inventing might be his ticket out of sorting records and emptying mousetraps.

In the meantime he needed money from somewhere. He dug his watch out of the inside pocket of his backpack. He knew it was worth more than what the jewelers had offered. He thought about listing it online and found dozens of sites seeking to buy second-hand watches. He began sorting through user reviews and wondered if some industry source identified legitimate buyers. Something Hugo once said about jewelry stuck in his head: a private collector would pay twice as much as a dealer. With the trust fund gone, the watch was his last thing of value; he needed to make the most of it. How could he find a collector?

Q continued to pay the rent with money from his music gigs. He was performing every Thursday at a bar in the neighborhood and picking up random dates around the city. Also, some of his friends had a band making a name for itself and they hired him to set up their light show. After the whispering business fell through, Atti spent evenings in the park with Henry and his friends, walking around town with Ghost or helping out at Q's shows.

One evening Jordan took Rooney and Atti out for pizza. "Too bad about the dog therapy thing," she said to Atti. "What's your next idea?"

He was flattered she took an interest in him and wondered if he should redirect his attentions to her. But she was five years older than him and a little intimidating. She worked as an assistant slash private secretary for her uncle, who had sold his software company for a bundle and now amused himself with investments.

And Jordan's words encouraged him. He wouldn't have to waste more time in school if he could invent something that would sell. He tried to imagine what invention might improve each part of his day. Q's apartment needed space more than anything; with Atti's belongings piled in the corners and Ghost underfoot, there was hardly room to turn around. But Atti couldn't invent more space or smaller furniture. And trying to solve the roach problem was beyond him; he definitely was *not* qualified to mess with poisons and bugs.

The Paradise Plum was looking better with its updated window display, but he couldn't think of any kind of improvement to the shop that could be packaged and sold. He pondered the old bike Henry still used to make deliveries, but people put real expertise into bicycle improvements. And it made him laugh to think he should try to improve on the shop's mousetraps.

One evening, after he and Q finished a bowl of macaroni—this time with chopped carrots—they grew quiet, listening to rain pound the fire escape.

"You want to smoke a joint?" Atti said.

"Not in here." They generally didn't smoke inside because even *their* apartment was more livable when it didn't smell like stale smoke. "Does it seem to you weed smells a lot more than it used to?"

"It really does," Atti agreed. "And it makes me nervous about getting caught smoking, after being arrested."

"That charge won't hold up. They can't prosecute you for a joint."

"Maybe not, but I still have to go to court."

"Anyway, I don't want to smoke in the apartment, and I'm not going up on the roof in this rain."

Atti thought for a moment. "You know what the world needs? An effective weed camouflage."

Q started to laugh.

"No, I'm serious. If I could invent something to mask the smell… think of it!"

"Okay, so there'd be a market, for sure, but you're no chemist; how would you do it?"

"I don't know yet. I'll get back to you."

Over the next few days Atti read everything he could find about why marijuana smelled so much and about covering up odors in general. The cannabis flower, for better or worse, secreted chemicals to attract pollinators and ward off predators. These flowers were even more pungent when burned. It was the way of the world. But there had to be some way to burn it without such a strong smell.

"What about vaping?" Q said as they shared macaroni with hot sauce.

"Yeah, but people really like to *smoke* weed, and vaping just doesn't do it."

Q shrugged. "I guess you're right."

"Ideally the invention would combine three things: an air purifier to filter the smoke, a scrubber to sanitize the air, and a masking agent to substitute an innocuous—if not necessarily pleasant—smell."

"Why not use incense?"

"Incense is suspicious. People assume it's covering something illicit; why else would you burn it? But a strong smell you recognize like, I don't know, burnt coffee or fried onions, says someone screwed up in the kitchen rather than they are masking the smell of weed."

"Sounds a little complicated for your target customer."

"Dazed and confused, right? I know it has to be simple."

Two weeks of research and experimenting produced results. An air scrubber was too hard to build, but Q helped him construct a simple pipe that filtered the smoke, with an intake tube to exhale through the same filter. The device also had a tiny spritzer to release a masking odor. Burnt popcorn or stinky cheese were the strongest smells they could find but they were a little sickening. Then Atti found a synthetic oil with a strong smell of garlic.

They ran a final test when Rooney came up to collect Chauncey from Q's apartment minutes after Atti and Q had smoked through Atti's pipe.

"Come on in," Q said.

Rooney grimaced as she stepped through the doorway. She had become friendly with both Atti and Q but avoided their apartment, which was understandable given its state. Q closed the door behind her.

She watched the dogs, smiling at how they played together in such a small space, then she sniffed the air with a curious look. "Someone's cooking pasta sauce," she said, "heavy on the garlic."

Q and Atti bumped fists with big smiles. Rooney turned to Q, a questioning look on her face. He kissed her on the forehead.

"What the hell?" she said, stepping back.

"Oh, it's nothing, my beauty. You have confirmed young Atti here will revolutionize the world."

Atti replayed that scene over and over in his head. He was happy the pipe passed the test but annoyed Q had kissed Rooney…and that her reaction was not unwelcoming. Why was she interested in him and not Atti? And why was Q stepping in when he knew Atti liked her?

He tried to put his jealousy behind him next day at the Plum, where he described his invention to Henry.

"Sounds great but can you build enough of them to sell?" Henry said. "Can you make a lot of money?"

"I don't know. Maybe."

Bruno poked his head out of the stockroom. "*How* are you going to make a lot of money?"

Atti shook his head, not eager to discuss his invention with Bruno. "I don't even know if I can make these things cheap enough…or if anyone will buy them."

"Make what? Buy what?"

Atti sighed. "It's a way to cover up the smell of smoking weed."

Bruno's eyes lit up. "How do you do that?"

"It's this pipe—or really two tubes glued together—and a spritzer."

Bruno kept pumping him until Atti agreed to bring his pipe to the shop. Before he knew it, Atti had signed an agreement for Bruno and his "business associates" to assemble and distribute the pipes.

Within weeks the things started selling. They called it the "Camou-flager." Bruno had Atti put one in the window of the Plum with a hand-written sign. They sold three at the Plum, and Atti was proud to see the pipe for sale at two other headshops in the East Village.

"So, we're making some money?" he said to Bruno two weeks later.

"We *will* make money. I think we've got a good one here."

"But so far…?"

"We take in money on sales but it goes right back into making more pipes and marketing. We gotta jump ahead before we have competition. Don't you worry; they'll be plenty of money. Just sit tight and we'll see how it goes."

"Right, I understand all that. But isn't there *any* money now? I could really use some cash, you know, like so my dog can eat."

Bruno shook his head. "Look, kid, you signed a contract saying we'd split profits *after* expenses. So far, it's *all* expenses."

Atti walked home that evening dejected. He was sure Bruno had swindled him out of his pipe invention and doubted he'd ever see any money from it. Inventing was looking like a poor career choice.

As he passed the fourth floor in his building, he heard voices from Rooney's apartment and remembered she had invited him and Q for a beer. Thinking he could use the company, he knocked.

Jordan answered with a big smile and a quick hug. Q was there too, tapping out the rhythm of a song for Rooney. The two of them looked awfully cozy, and Atti considered going upstairs so he wouldn't have to watch. Chauncey was lying against Ghost, whose only welcome for him was two tail wags.

"Oh, don't get up," he said to his dog sarcastically.

"They spent an hour in the backyard wearing each other out," Jordan said, handing him a beer. She then asked about the camouflage invention. She seemed really interested in how he came up with it. "You know," she said, "I mentioned your dog therapy business to my boss. I'll admit I told it as sort of a funny story about 'some guy'.…"

"That's flattering. Thanks."

"But the point is he didn't think it was funny; he called it 'prepossessing.'"

"What now?"

"He really talks like that. It meant he's interested."

"And who is this guy?"

"Lloyd Prescott. He's my uncle. He made a fortune in a startup he sold to Microsoft and retired to this big house in Westchester. I'm his executive assistant. He invests in things, but mostly he studies stuff, takes an interest in things for their own sake. I think you two should meet."

Chapter Twelve

Atti liked days like this. It was Wednesday, Henry's day off. Bruno was out making, or at least pretending to make, deals. Atti had the Plum to himself.

There was an occasional call or email from a collector, but that took little time. Foot traffic was slow and, when someone did come into the shop, Atti had time to talk about Broadway cast albums or reggae imports.

By one o'clock he had emptied the mousetraps and swept the shop. He hadn't taken a call or seen a customer in an hour. Ghost was napping by the door, so Atti felt comfortable breaking up cardboard boxes in the stockroom. It was funny how the dog *did* provide some measure of security; he would never hurt anyone without being provoked but shoplifters wouldn't know that.

He was tying up cardboard and humming along with a Muddy Waters tune when his phone rang.

"Atti, is that you?" said a familiar voice.

"Detective Lawrence?"

"Yes, it's me. I'm afraid I've got some bad news."

"About the investigation?"

"No, I hate to say it but this is something else."

Atti said nothing. He didn't even breathe. After the crash and the scandal, what more could go wrong? He thought he should probably stop answering his phone.

"It's your uncle. He's at Lenox Hill in critical condition."

"How? What happened?"

"Poison. Apparently, he received a case of wine two days ago laced with arsenic. Someone added enough to each of the bottles to kill a horse. Luckily, your uncle sensed something was wrong and called for help. They rushed him to the hospital and pumped him out, but he's still in bad shape."

Atti's hand went to his face. How could anyone do that?

"And another thing," Lawrence continued, "the NTSB…"

"The what?"

"The National Transportation Safety Board is about to announce the jet went down because of a bomb. We're afraid someone's targeting your family."

"Holy shit! Am I in danger?"

"Probably not. You weren't part of your father's business, and you *are* living below the radar, so we don't want to raise the alarm. But you should be on the lookout for anything suspicious."

Atti thought about the setup leading to his arrest. He desperately wanted to clear his record before people found out about that, but should he tell Lawrence? It could be connected. Maybe the police knew who set up the bust?

Lawrence went on. "Apparently, Ted's son was at the apartment when the ambulance arrived but we haven't been able to locate him since. We could use your help with that. We also want to contact the daughter; I understand she's studying abroad?"

"Yeah, Elle is in Scotland. I can call her. And I have a phone number for Martin but no idea where he is. We're not close."

"Well, we need to find him. It appears *all* the bottles in the case were doctored, so we don't suspect anyone at the apartment was involved, but we have to look at everything. We'll need to confirm your recent whereabouts as well—I hope you understand. It would be best if you came to the station house, say later this afternoon? Then we can connect the dots and tell you what we know."

"I understand, and yeah, I can come in. I just…this is such a shock. I have to catch my breath. I'll get off work, and then I should go see Ted. So maybe fourish?"

"That'll be fine. I'm really sorry about this, Atti. You've suffered more than your share."

He hung up and stared into space. If this was payback for the fraud, maybe Ted got what he deserved. But that was harsh, even after how his uncle treated him. Stealing money was one thing, but poison?

And Elle! Oh, God. He had to call her with more bad news. He wanted to put that off and decided to wait until after he saw his uncle. But was she safe? Was *he* safe? Someone was hunting the family? Was it the same person who sent the bat to Jillian?

He needed to stop worrying and concentrate. He called Bruno. "My uncle was poisoned. He's in intensive care. I need to go see him."

"Sorry to hear that, but why tell me?"

"I have to go now, so I can't finish my shift. Can you or Henry come in?"

"Sorry for your troubles, kid, but on my end, no can do. I've got irons in the fire, things that can't wait. And didn't Henry say he was going out to Long Island today? If you find him and get him to come in, okay. Otherwise, you go see your uncle after you close up at seven."

Atti's jaw clenched along with his fists. "Did you hear me? My Uncle Ted might die! There's nothing going on here anyway. I'll bring in the crates and close up, but I have to go."

"Hey, kid, you go now, don't bother coming back. I'm serious."

Atti hung up without another word. He wrote "Closed for Bereavement" on a piece of cardboard and taped it to the metal gate after he locked it in place. He dropped Ghost at home and went uptown on the subway.

At the hospital a patrolman was posted outside Ted's room in intensive care. A nurse said his uncle was awake but weak, and he should limit his visit to twenty minutes.

Ted lay in a room with only his bed, a couple of chairs and monitoring machines. The bed was tilted so he was almost sitting. An intravenous tube hanging on a stand ran into his arm. His heartbeat pulsed on a display that beeped quietly. His eyes were closed.

"Uncle Ted?" Atti said softly.

Ted's eyes flickered open. His face was pale except for dark circles under his eyes. He coughed weakly. "Atti," he said in a rasping voice, "you came."

"Like you said, we stick together."

"I don't deserve that."

"You need to clear your head and focus on helping us figure out who did this."

Ted coughed violently. Atti recoiled, thinking he shouldn't have brought up the poisoning.

"Ah…my head," Ted said and focused watery, bloodshot eyes on Atti. "It's good you're here. Some things I should say."

"Hey, we're all good," Atti said, trying to sound upbeat. "Whatever you and Dad did in the business is not between us."

"Not that. It's how we built the company."

"I know. Dad always said—well you *both* said every year at the Crossing—our fortune came from the sea, from Grandfather's shipping business."

"No, listen Atti. The doctors… Well, remember when Hugo used to say none of us knows how long we'll have? Thing is, I know how little time and you've got to listen. Elle's not here and Martin is no help, but there's something I have to get out, so it has to be you. I'm one of only two people who know."

He coughed into a handful of tissues. His dark expression turned graver. "We swore never to tell but now…with Hugo gone and everything fallen apart…."

Atti tried to ignore the sickly-sweet smell of medication and decay while his mind jumped back to what he heard outside his father's office during the Picnic. Would he get the whole story now?

Ted looked up with unspeakable sadness, and then his eyes sank to the floor. "It was 1979. Hugo was fifteen, I was fourteen. We were going to take Guppy out one day but a storm blew in. Stuck in the house we heard about a jewel heist in Portland. There was a shootout and a guard died. The cops warned everyone to be on the look-out for two armed men."

"The storm was battering the shore, but we put slickers over our shorts and rode bikes to the marina. We were under one of the buildings, throwing rocks at a buoy, when two men ran along the wharf. They hurried onto the dock, looking into the boats, and then jumped into Jeb Paterson's cabin cruiser.

"Before we could do anything, they cast off. It was no day to leave the cove at all, especially in Paterson's hulk. But they motored out and past the jetty the waves nearly cracked them in half.

"Hugo said there was no way they'd get out to sea, and we should follow along the shore. We pumped our bikes through the wind up the coast road. We could see they were hugging the shoreline and the boat was riding low.

"From the cliff at Back Bay we could barely make out the boat when it rose on the swells. Then we saw bodies go over the side and lost sight of them. We ran down to the beach and up to the water but couldn't see over the breakers. Then a man washed up. He crawled up the beach and collapsed with his face in the sand. He was beat up and bleeding from where his ear used to be. He clutched a black bag. I wanted to go for help, but Hugo bent close to the guy and said it was too late."

Ted went into a spasm of coughing. When he recovered his breath, he went on. "Remember, Atti, we were young, younger than you are now. But we thought this guy was dead and he was a criminal, so we had every right to look in the bag. We pried it from him finger by finger. Inside there were small cloth bags and bundled cash.

"Hugo said that moment would decide our future. The thieves were drowned, and the boat would break up in the waves. No one knew the loot was saved; they'd think it went to the bottom.

"I was scared we'd get caught, but Hugo said we should hide it away and not say anything. He was my big brother—you know how that is—I had to go along. We rode out to the cave—we told you, it was our clubhouse. Out of the rain, we saw the smaller bags were full of jewelry and gemstones. Hugo said we should bury the bag and get back home… decide what to do when things settled down."

Ted coughed again and looked horribly drained. "Hugo said we could get away with it, and I believed him. And he was right—for a long time anyway."

He looked up with an expression pleading for some response. But what could Atti give him? Forgiveness? Sympathy? He decided he'd at least listen to the rest of the story. "So," Atti said, "you kept the bag? Did the cops come looking for it?"

Ted sighed heavily and strained to catch his breath. "We stuck to Hugo's plan, made up a story about spending the day damming a stream. That explained how we got so wet. No one ever doubted us."

"But then the news said the police found Lazlo Crane on the beach *half-dead*…."

It was the name Atti overheard at the Picnic!

"That freaked us out," Ted went on. "Hugo said there was no way he would recognize us from seeing us in a storm with his beat-up face in the sand, but I was terrified.

"Crane went to prison, but I had nightmares about him coming after me covered with sand and seaweed. Hugo always just gave me that look of his and said to keep my mouth shut.

"Later we went back to the cave. There was more than seventy-five thousand in cash. We had no way to value the jewels, but Hugo thought they had to be worth much more. The radio said the jeweler lost twelve million dollars in jewels but we didn't know if that was real or if it was all in the bag. But anyway we looked at it, it was a fortune.

"A few weeks later, we moved it all into a canvas tool bag and reburied it in the cave, deeper this time. We burned the black bag and buried the ashes. Then we waited."

"So," Atti said, "what happened to it all?"

"For years we checked to make sure nothing was disturbed. Gabriel spent a lot of time with us then, so we convinced him we should meet in the cave where we took our blood-oath—and that gave us an excuse to go there.

"Hugo and I started studying the diamond business. We read books and took a course in the city. Grandfather encouraged us. He sent us to Antwerp the summer before Hugo started college. We made connections and learned how gems and jewelry pieces were valued and registered and, most importantly, traded. By the time we were both in college, we could remove stones from their settings, which made most of them impossible to trace, except the registered diamonds. Then we formed a partnership to invest in precious stones.

"The summer before my sophomore year, we moved the loot from the cave to a house Hugo leased in New Haven. We started spending the cash and no one seemed to be tracing the bills.

"After he graduated Hugo worked in finance, but we both kept at the diamond business. We trickled our stones into the market, mixed with what we purchased, which made us look successful. On the strength of that and Grandfather's connections, and using the revenues as seed money, we started Pandion Capital." He looked wistful. "The loot started it all."

"Our fortune from the sea," Atti said, unable to keep the rebuke out of his voice.

"That part was true, eh?" Ted said and held up his right hand, with a pale spot on the finger where he always wore his Pandion ring, identical to the one that surely went down with Hugo. The authorities had seized Ted's jewelry, including his ring.

Ted went on ruefully. "We had the money to buy any jewelry we wanted, but the Pandion rings were made with *our* stones, as were engagement rings and other gifts through the years. But…" He paused in thought. "There was that one piece Hugo didn't break up, the Greek eye ring with the sapphire. Your dad kept it hidden, even from me. And we were spooked when the cops saw it was left behind after the robbery at Pandion. Why would a thief leave that behind? The cops were baffled but we knew it was a message."

The nurse stuck her head into the room, saying Atti would have to let the patient rest. He took Ted's bony hand to say goodbye.

"You're the last, Atti," Ted said, "you and Martin: the last of the Forester men. But…" He coughed violently and the nurse rushed into the room and directed Atti out.

Atti wandered downtown, devastated. He had always attributed the family wealth to his grandfather's guts and his father's acumen. And even after the scandal broke, he believed Pandion was a legitimate company that only corrupted over time. The conversation he overheard between Ted and his father seemed like a dream and came back to him only when Ted mentioned Crane's name. They thought he was responsible for sending the painting of Back Bay, because that's where they left him, and the ring because it was part of the loot. If that was true, what was Crane after?

But more distressing than any of that, it was clear the company was rotten from the start, built on stolen money. It was always a sham, which meant his whole life was a fraud, and now Hugo was gone, and the fortune was gone, and all that was left were ruin and corpses. His whole life he had strived to live up to the Forester name, which had now distorted into a badge of disgrace. Far from giving him a start in life, his father would reach out from the grave to hold him down. He had to erase his father and uncle from his life, free himself to make his own way without all the baggage. He had to make it on his own, regain the life he'd known, or else he'd lose himself in the gloom.

If his father and Ted really left Crane on that beach to die, then Crane had every reason to seek revenge. And if he was out for retribution, the painting and the ring could have been sadistic messages telling Hugo and Ted he was coming for them. A chill ran up his spine, and he looked behind him on the sidewalk. Was someone watching or was he being paranoid?

After walking south for ten minutes, he remembered he had to go see Detective Lawrence and so turned toward the subway. He also had to call Elle. He was sick at heart that every time he talked to her it was about some new tragedy. It was also expensive to call Scotland. With finances what they were—and no more weed deliveries or proceeds from the Camouflager—a fifty-dollar phone call would mean eating plain macaroni for some time. Should he use an online app? Or maybe he could call from the police station?

"You've had a rough time, son," Detective Lawrence said, setting two cups of coffee on the linoleum table between them. "I know you've caught flack for the Ponzi scheme, but I believe your dad and uncle kept that from you. They *had* to keep it quiet or the whole thing would have collapsed long ago."

"I appreciate that, Detective. Not many people believe in me; they treat me like fraud might be catching."

Lawrence smiled sympathetically and then turned serious. "So now," he said, "on top of it all, we've got the possibility someone is after your family. The NTSB report, as I said, concludes there was a bomb on the Gulfstream. They don't think it was terrorism. In fact, given the collapse of the fund they're focused on who might have benefitted. The feds are doing the financial forensics. This office is looking at physical evidence—fingerprints, video from the airport—and interviewing people who worked around the hangars…and now the second crime scene. At least with this poison attack there were no explosions to scatter the pieces. Oh…sorry."

Atti was startled by the sudden image of body parts scattered over the ground, but he girded himself to speak. "That doesn't matter, Detective, but I have something to tell you."

Lawrence took a seat and nodded.

"It's just…I d–d–don't want any more scandal." He gritted his teeth, angry he was stuttering. "But…I know who, who's been doing this."

The detective held up a hand, pushed a button on the table and said, "Jack, can you come in here." He turned back to Atti. "Detective Harlow is helping out on the case. He needs to hear this."

When the other detective was seated, Atti went on. "Just so I've got this straight: you're only investigating the crash and the poisoning, right? If I give you information, but it's about something that happened a long time ago, like forty years, does that have to become public?"

"Well, we can't promise anything. But we'll try to keep it quiet if we can."

Atti thought about his Uncle Ted…and Elle. Closing his eyes tight he saw a thin plume of white smoke in the sky. "Okay," he said suddenly, "here it is." He relayed what his uncle had told him about what happened on the beach. "His name's Lazlo Crane. He served time but he may have gotten out. I think he has because there's been this presence, like someone's been watching me."

"Wait," Lawrence broke in. "You've seen someone following you?"

"Not seen so much as felt. I don't know how to explain it."

"Okay. Go on."

Atti told them about the painting of Back Bay. "The guy who delivered it had some kind of mangled ear. Oh, yeah, and someone burned 'Ithaca' into the frame; I remember because it was so out of place, and I know a kid who goes to Ithaca College."

Lawrence looked up from his notes with a perplexed expression. "And this ties in with the bat in the bag?"

"Maybe. I don't know."

"Let's stick to what we *do* know. You're sure you haven't actually seen this man?"

"That's another thing." He described his finances after the scandal broke and his job at the Plum and admitted delivering weed. "And that last time, it seemed fishy all along and then suddenly it was clear I'd been set up. As far as I know the cops never clamped down on my boss, so it looks like it was all aimed at me. Am I in trouble?"

"Atti, we don't care about marijuana or some headshop. We're looking for a murderer, who may have more targets. Think. Did you actually see him?"

"I did, in the park, maybe. The only other person around—except for the undercover cops—was an old man in a long coat with a big hat. He looked homeless, but I didn't get a close look. Oh yeah, when he called in the order, the guy said his name was Actless."

"We'll run the name; could turn up something. And look, son, we really appreciate your coming in. This will help. If Crane got out of prison, there'll be a parole officer and a record of where he lives. Our focus right now is on finding Harry Gooden, but we'll look at Crane as well."

"And the stuff about my uncle and dad?"

"Like I said, we're looking at three current homicides and one attempted murder. I can't promise anything about the past, but we'll keep it internal if we can. And as to your arrest, I'm surprised they're even prosecuting with what you say they've got, and you may be right it's frustration about a bust gone bad. I'll see if I can get hold of the arresting officer and tell him you're a cooperating witness and we'd like to see the charge dropped."

"That would help so much!"

"So," Lawrence went on, "another question is about this poisoning. Can you think of any reason the assailant would deliver poison in wine bottles?"

Atti sighed. "Uncle Ted liked wine, probably too much. He had a cellar at the family compound in Maine. I never saw him drunk, really, but he always had a glass in his hand."

"So…what we'd call a functional alcoholic?"

"If that's a thing."

"Moving on, we *have* located Martin Forester. Between you and me, he doesn't seem the type to plan or carry out these attacks."

"Martin's no friend of mine, but I agree. He's inept."

Lawrence nodded. "And did you reach Elena Forester?"

"Yeah, right. I wanted to see Elle's father before I called. Is there any way I could use a phone here?"

"Sure. After we wrap up, I'll bring one in and give you some privacy."

"And," the detective went on, "to cover all the bases, you said last week you know Charles Tilson?"

"Yeah, unfortunately. But he was working with my dad. Killing my father could only hurt the company. Besides, the scandal broke *after* the bombing."

"Well, Tilson says he pulled out his money last summer because he suspected something was wrong—his accountant couldn't correlate fund returns with the market—but your father put him off. He said Hugo was angry and they had words, but that was the end of it. We have nothing tying him to the jet or your uncle's poisoning, but we'll keep digging."

"And what if it's Crane?" Atti said.

"We'll definitely look at him, like I said. But please let us know if you hear anything about Harry Gooden. I know you were once close to him. Time is running out for him to tell his side of the story."

Lawrence left to get a phone while Atti ran all the names through his mind. Charles Tilson was one person he had hoped never to have to think about again. But Harry seemed a more likely suspect. Atti saw him sweat and fidget around his dad, and then he got fired—no way he "resigned"—and that sounded like a motive. How much did Harry know about the fraud, and when did he discover it, and why was he fired?

But then how to explain the painting and the ring? Was Harry planning this long before he was let go?

In any case Atti needed protection. He wondered how to get a gun. Surely, Frank Bruno would know someone.

Ten minutes later he heard the double ring of the Scottish phone system, thinking how whimsical it would have sounded under different circumstances. Elle answered in a sleepy voice.

"Elle, it's me."

"Atti!" she perked up. "It's late."

"Yeah, I'm sorry, but…"

"What's wrong? You sound awful."

"Thing is, Elle, there's been another attack…."

"Another…wait, what do you mean *another* attack? Did the jet…?"

"Yes. They're about to announce there was a bomb on the jet. My family was murdered."

"You poor thing."

"Yeah, and now there's been a poisoning."

"Who, I mean…was someone hurt?"

"Yeah, Elle. I'm sorry. Your dad's in pretty bad shape. Someone sent spiked wine to your apartment."

"But…but how…? What's going on?" she wailed and started to sob.

"Listen, I saw him in the hospital today. He's in bad shape but he's conscious, and he's getting the best treatment."

"Is Martin there?"

"He is, yeah. I haven't seen him, but I know the cops talked with him."

"I'll get a flight in the morning."

"No, Elle…."

"What do you mean, no? I can't stay here when he's…"

"You *have to* stay there, Elle. The police think someone's hunting our family. We could all be in danger. But at least *you're* safe in Europe. Let the police work, and let Martin and me take care of your dad."

She paused. "I know what that means: *you'll* take care of him. No sense expecting anything from my brother. It's not fair to load this on you after the way he treated you and you losing your whole family. I need to be there."

"Elle, *please*. Please, for me, stay where you are. At least finish the semester. I'm going to help figure out who's doing this. But if you come home, I won't be able to do anything but worry about you."

"Atti, I don't know how we deserve you."

"So you'll stay?"

"For now, maybe, but first I have to talk to Dad…hear from him what he wants. I also need to talk to Martin and get him to step up. And you have to promise to keep me in the loop…and be careful."

"Absolutely. You sit tight. I'll get Martin to call you. Your dad's in room 409 at Lenox Hill Hospital. I can give you the number. Have you got a pen?"

When Atti got home, he felt drained. Ghost greeted him at the door with pent-up energy and needed to go out but Atti wanted to sit and think. So much had changed in how he felt about his father and the company and…just about everything. But the dog pawed at his leg, so he reluctantly took him down to Rooney's apartment, picked up Chauncey and put both dogs out in the backyard to play while he parked himself on the stoop. He wanted his former life back: the comfort, the prestige, the security, but mostly the peace of mind.

The dogs were tussling by the fence. He wished they'd play quietly and leave him to his thoughts. But Chauncey ran from Ghost with something hanging from his mouth. Atti was disgusted, thinking it was a rat. He shouted for Ghost to sit. Then he approached Chauncey, lying in the dirt and gnawing.

Chauncey jumped up and ran under a scraggly bush. Ghost rose to follow but Atti turned on him and shouted. Then he pulled his dog angrily into the building and shut the door. He turned back to Chauncey, who was still chewing his prize. Atti approached slowly, speaking in his whispering voice, until he could clearly see the dog had a slab of meat.

"What the hell?" Atti said out loud.

He cornered Chauncey and reached for the meat, but the dog snapped at him. He picked up a branch and moved in again. When Chauncey snapped again, Atti stabbed the meat with the branch and pushed Chauncey away with his leg. With the dog circling and barking, he lifted the branch and examined the meat. It looked like a steak you'd buy in butcher shop, not trash in a backyard.

Chauncey suddenly fell to the ground, making a scary gurgling sound. Atti leaned the branch against the building and knelt by the dog, who started going into convulsions.

He called Q. "Something's wrong with Chauncey! We're in the yard. Come down…or call 911 or something! Quick!"

Q soon burst out of the door right behind Ghost. "Rooney's calling!" he said breathlessly. "What happened?"

By then Chauncey was lying listlessly. "He had that," Atti said, nodding toward the meat.

Q stepped over to it and sneered. "Where did *that* come from?"

"No idea. They were fighting over it, and I called Ghost off."

"Ghost!" they said simultaneously and turned to him. The dog coughed something up and sat heavily on the ground.

"I'll get water!" Q said and rushed back inside, almost crashing into Rooney.

"The person at 911 sent Animal Control," she said, seeing Chauncey and bursting into tears.

A truck arrived twenty minutes later. By then Chauncey had stopped moving. Ghost was walking in circles, coughing and refusing to drink.

They rushed Ghost to the animal hospital. They wouldn't let Atti ride along so he ran to the corner for a taxi. With one look back he saw Q covering Chauncey with a blanket.

At the hospital they pumped Ghost's stomach and examined the gnarled meat. "He's fortunate," the vet said. The toxin in the meat would have killed him. Looks like the other dog got a bigger bite and never had a chance, but this fella only had a taste. We pumped his stomach and gave him some fluids. He'll be moving slowly for a few days but then should be back on his feet."

"Was the meat bad? I can't imagine how it got into the yard."

The vet looked solemn. "This is *not* a naturally occurring substance. I'm afraid we've had to report to the police the meat was poisoned."

Chapter Thirteen

They kept Ghost at the animal hospital overnight. Atti walked all the way home. He needed time to think. Everything was coming undone. It was hard to see his way clear.

His uncle looked awful. There was no telling if he'd pull through. Atti had lost his job at the Plum, which was no big deal except he needed money to live; he couldn't keep freeloading on Q. And now Ghost was hurt! That poison was surely meant for Ghost since the Forester family seemed to be the target, which meant Rooney lost her dog only because she befriended Atti. It was that simple and just not fair. If he ever got his hands on someone trying to hurt Ghost, he'd tear him to pieces!

When he got home, Atti stopped in Rooney's apartment to see if there was something he could do to help. She and Q were sitting quietly. She had obviously been crying. He was holding her hand gently but when he caught Atti's eye, his expression hardened. He pulled Atti aside to hand him a postcard. "I found this in the mailbox yesterday. I thought it was an ad. Now I'm thinking it's connected."

It was a Hayden Planetarium postcard, like they sold in the gift-shop. It pictured stars in the night sky with lines drawing constella-tions, identified on the back as Orion the Hunter and Canis Major.

On the back was also written in thick black marker: "This time Sirius precedes Orion."

Atti was sure the card had to do with poisoning the dogs, the timing was so close. He called Detective Lawrence.

"Our suspect is ramping things up," Lawrence said. "I'll send a couple of uniforms to pick up the card and check if neighbors saw someone near the yard. We'll also coordinate with Animal Rescue. You need to keep your eyes open and sit tight."

"I can't sit tight! This is everywhere!"

"I know, son. And look, I'm really glad your dog is okay…and I'm sorry about the neighbor's dog. I'll up the patrols in the neighborhood. My gut tells me you're right: the postcard connects these things. We *will* catch this guy."

Atti sat at the dining table for a long while, unable to focus. Eventually, Q came in. "I wanted to ask you something," Atti said. "You think Bruno could get me a gun, you know, for self-protection?"

"Are you insane? You just got arrested for dealing and now you want to buy an unregistered gun?"

"But I thought…"

Q shook his head. "No, dude. Not the way."

Atti was deflated. If not a gun, should he carry a baseball bat…or something? Or maybe he should focus on helping the police. They were still looking for Harry, but Atti was sure it wasn't him and decided to find out all he could about Crane.

There were some articles from the local Maine papers in an online archive. One described the jewel heist in 1979 but it was short on detail. Another traced each step of the robbery and flight, which showed Crane could have stashed loot anywhere along the route to South Bristol. There was also a feature about the motorboat they sank, which confirmed Crane washed up at Back Bay. But then in an expanded search Atti found something useful: a mention of a Professor Lazlo Crane from Saint Anselm College in New Hampshire joining an archeological dig in

Greece in 1976. He couldn't find Crane's name on the Anselm website so he tried calling and was forwarded to the Classics Department.

"Um, yes, Crane," a woman said. "I…um, I believe there was once a Doctor Crane here. It must have been some years ago."

"He would have taught in the 1970s."

"May I ask your interest in the professor?"

"It's a long story, but I'm trying to find out something about an incident long ago. It has nothing to do with your college."

"I see. Well, I've pulled up the records. Doctor Lazlo Crane did teach here for a decade starting in 1966 but I'm afraid there isn't much I can tell you. If I recall, he left under some kind of cloud. Perhaps Doctor McCracken could tell you something. He chaired the department then."

McCracken was retired but still lived in Manchester. With some cajoling Atti got his phone number—the professor did *not* use email—and Atti convinced the professor to speak with him about Doctor Crane, but only in person.

"I have to come along," Q said. "Rooney can take care of Ghost. Is there a train to Manchester?"

"Trains and buses but either way it's a day-long trip so we'd have to stay over on top of paying for tickets."

"We can get a room for two as cheap as for one, and it's worth the price of two tickets. You might miss something on your own."

They boarded a bus next morning from the Port Authority bus terminal for an eight-hour trip. On the way Q wrote down everything Atti could remember that might be connected: the Ithaca painting that looked like Back Bay; the Greek eye ring left behind at Pandion; the bombing and Harry Gooden disappearing; the collapse of the fund after Charles Tilson took out his money; the bat in the pocketbook; the strange weed bust at the East River set up by Mr. Actless; Ted and the dogs being poisoned; the postcard with the constellations; and Ted's story, which might possibly tie it all together.

"Are we wasting our time on this?" Atti said. "It's all a muddle."

"We have to do something. If the police can't pin it on Tilson and Harry Gooden isn't behind it all, what else have we got?"

Doctor McCracken lived in a small bungalow on the edge of Manchester. He had thinning grey hair but bright blue eyes suggesting a vibrant mind. In a cozy kitchen warmed by a wood stove, he brewed tea and set out a tray of scones for his guests.

"Might as well warm you up a bit, as I don't know there's much I can tell you about Lazlo Crane," the professor said, pouring their tea.

"Thank you, sir," Atti replied. "As I said on our call, we're not even really sure what we're looking for. We think Professor Crane encountered my father forty years ago but there are a lot of questions about what happened. We're looking for anything that might help us find the professor or understand where he was or what he was doing then."

McCracken sipped his tea and then said, "Lazlo and I taught together in Classics. He focused on ancient Greek literature but also had a hand in the archeological study of the area."

Q raised his eyebrows at Atti.

"Yes, old Lazlo," the professor went on. "He was a decent sort, or so it seemed. We socialized some, on a professional level. But then there was the incident. The FBI showed up on campus asking questions about him. I was his department head, so they came to me. They were interested in his personal finances—about which I only knew the modest salary we paid tenured professors in those days—and a particular dig he had joined a year earlier. I couldn't say much about that either, and the project leader later died in an accident. The next I knew Lazlo was charged with trafficking in antiquities. Apparently, he had unearthed artifacts worth more in trade than as historical relics and smuggled them home."

"Did they arrest him?"

"They did; pulled him right out of a lecture. He was arraigned and freed on bail, given his position on the faculty. But then he disappeared and it was only later we saw reports he had been involved in a jewel robbery in Maine."

"Right. That's part of what we're trying to find out about."

"Wait," the professor said, and he peered closely at Atti's face. "You're Hugo Forester's son."

"I am, and I'd really like to find out who's hunting my family."

McCracken paused, wringing his hands together. "I'm sincerely sorry for your troubles, young man, and there is one more thing. There were rumors Lazlo was on antipsychotic drugs. When I came to court to support him on the smuggling charge, his eyes darted around the room as if he couldn't focus. I think he had a serious condition. Add that to a brilliant mind and a long stretch in prison and you have a frightening recipe."

In their motel room that night, Atti said, "So how does all this tell us if Crane bombed the plane?"

"Maybe it doesn't," Q said, "but it shows this guy was disturbed long before crossing paths with your father and your uncle."

"And he's an ancient Greek scholar so maybe that explains the weird messages."

"Orion and Sirius, you mean?"

"Yeah, but also the bat bag: Lawrence said it was a Dionysus model. And Mr. Actless, who set me up: that sounds Greek too."

"Still a little thin. And how does it help us find him?"

"Maybe at least it will convince Detective Lawrence it's Crane and not Harry Gooden."

Dozing on the long bus ride home, Atti kept thinking about Hugo. Why hadn't he taken care of this when they got the painting of Back Bay? His father clearly connected it with that man on the beach. Why did he let that guy stalk them like freaking animals? Atti would never act like that. When he regained the wealth and power of his father, he'd protect the people close to him.

On the way home Atti looked over at Q, half dozing by the window. He was such a true friend and yet Rooney had been a source of tension between them. But Q knew her before he did, and she loved his music. Who knew why people were attracted to each other? Atti had to admit the strain all came from his side. He had to move on and find his own girlfriend.

"I'm sorry for giving you a hard time about Rooney," he said.

Q spoke almost as if he were asleep: "Dude, you've had it rough. I understand—we understand—just so you get over being a dick."

Atti punched his arm and closed his eyes for a nap.

When they got home, they stopped at Rooney's apartment. Q stayed with her. Atti brought Ghost upstairs and found a note from Jordan taped to their door: "Atti—My boss wants to meet you. Maybe a job? Call with a day we can take train up to Armonk together."

He was so accustomed to shocks at this point that this didn't seem odd at all. But how could he think about looking for work when he was chasing down the man who tried to kill his dog? Still, he kept thinking about the note. Was there really a job for him? With Jordan? That would be incredible.

He realized he hadn't eaten at all since breakfast and thought food would help him think straight. But the refrigerator held only one can of beer and an open bag of carrots. He skinned a carrot and took a bite, popped open the can and called Jordan. She had heard about the dogs and asked after Ghost. "He's home and looking like his old self," Atti said, "but I think I'd better stay with him tomorrow. Maybe we can meet later this week?"

He also called Detective Lawrence to tell him about the meeting with Doctor McCracken. "That's useful stuff," Lawrence said, "but you should leave the detective work to us. What I need you to do is keep your wits about you and your eyes wide open."

Atti arranged to meet Jordan at Grand Central two days later. The morning rush was beginning to ebb. He scanned the station but saw nothing suspicious. Then he tried to think of something positive, remembering how in the family's Hitchcock game he once tripped up Bode with a reference to the terminal's big waiting room; his brother jumped the gun with *North by Northwest*, when the response to the *whole* prompt was *Spellbound*.

Jordan was waiting on the platform for the 9:08 to Poughkeepsie. She looked ready for work in a pencil skirt and tight sweater under a suede sportscoat, hair pulled back and big tortoise-shell glasses. In fact, he realized she really looked like one of the dozen or so glamorous blondes who famously starred in Hitchcock's movies. He felt a thrill knowing she was there to meet *him*, and he was coming to feel like the hero of his own thriller.

But from the perspective of cinematography, he realized he looked pretty shabby. He had showered and his shirt was fairly clean, but next to Jordan he looked like a kid off the street. However, she didn't seem to notice or was too polite to comment. Instead, as the train rolled north along the Hudson she said, "Be yourself. Lloyd is hyper-perceptive so there's no sense trying to pretend."

"But what does he want? Why would he hire me?"

"I don't know. Something about your dog therapy business. Just meet him; this *can't* be a bad thing for you."

He recoiled at the reference to dog whispering but told himself that was his ticket to this meeting, and he had to put apprehension aside. Any kind of job was probably fantasy, but he had no other real options. Hearing his stomach growl, he hoped at least Lloyd would feed him lunch.

At North White Plains, Jordan called Uber, and they were soon pulling past a gate. Atti took it all in. Except for an ornate fountain in the center of the circular driveway, the house Jordan called "The Hall" seemed solid and functional with squeaky-clean windows catching the morning sunlight. To the side was a free-standing garage and a shed-like structure. The property was impressive but hardly on the scale of Pandion.

A butler met them as she opened the door. He stood with perfect yet effortless posture, chin angled upward. "Ms. Byrne," he said with a polite bow of his head.

"Morning, Jenkins. This is Atticus Forester. He's here to meet Lloyd."

"Of course, miss," Jenkins replied with another minor bow. "Mr. Prescott is expecting you, Mr. Forester. He is in the conservatory."

"Thank you, Jenkins," Jordan said. "I'll show the way."

They walked through a central rotunda with a vaulted ceiling. When Jenkins left the room, Jordan pulled Atti by the elbow. He was startled but wasn't going to complain. He had decided he liked Jordan and wondered if he had any chance with her.

But she placed him near the wall and backed off. "You stand there," she said, "and listen. I'll whisper in the corner of the library next door and you'll hear it."

"Like the ceiling outside the Grand Central Oyster Bar."

"Exactly. It's offbeat, like a lot of things around here."

She left the room and soon he heard her speaking. She was right: from wherever she was standing, her words came through clearly. That was quirky. He thought this place could be the haven he longed for from his troubles.

"So, what's with the butler out of central casting?" he asked when she rejoined him.

"Jenkins is a doll," she said with a sweeping smile, "though, as you've noticed, a little stiff. My uncle went to England to find a perfect butler to lend respectability to his unorthodox lifestyle. And now, when Lloyd no longer cares much about appearances, we're all so used to him that Lloyd keeps him on. He has this habit of adopting people to populate his domain. With a little luck, you'll see."

Through a hallway they reached a glassed-in room at the back of the house. When they passed through a fogged-up glass door, the temperature and humidity made it feel like a rain forest. Facing away from them was a tall man wearing a long rubber apron over an aloha shirt with a bird of paradise print as exotic as the plants lining the shelves. He turned with a wide smile that instantly put Atti at ease. Below the apron he wore shorts and sandals. Atti couldn't place the piped-in music, which sounded like a "classic rock" standard.

"Ah," Lloyd said, "Mr. Forester. Or may I call you Atti?"

"Of course, Mr. Prescott, whatever you like."

"And you must call me Lloyd. The only one around here who addresses me as 'mister' is Jenkins and," he added with a smirk, "you've probably already met Jenkins."

"Yes, sir. I understand." This guy was funny.

Jordan smiled at them both. "I'll leave you two to get acquainted," she said, and to Lloyd she added, "I'll get that correspondence out."

"Of course," Lloyd smiled and turned to Atti. "Jordan has the thankless job of keeping me on track."

After Jordan left the room, Lloyd said, "Let's step out on the terrace for some fresh air and perhaps you'd like a cup of coffee? Or a late breakfast?"

Atti's stomach growled. The faint taste of carrots and beer came back to him, and his mouth began to water. But his father always said it was unwise to eat at an interview, and Atti hoped that's what this would be. "No, sir. I've eaten, but coffee sounds great."

"Fine. But let's drop the honorific, as well. What I have in mind involves unfettered consanguinity."

"Sure, Lloyd, whatever you say." Atti wasn't sure what "consanguinity" was, but it sounded like cooperation, or something promising.

"So, I think I'm correct is saying you are Hugo Forester's son?"

"Yes," Atti conceded, "that's me."

"I apologize. I didn't mean that as an accusation. It's none of my business, really, except I knew your father and want to say I am truly sorry for your loss."

"You knew my dad?"

"Everyone knew Hugo. But yes, he and I met, and I also had the pleasure once of meeting your mother. Lovely woman. You have her eyes."

"Thanks. I miss her most of all." It stuck him that his mother was somehow playing a part in this drama, supporting him through the other side of the tragedy.

"In fact, I asked for our meeting today in one respect to repay a debt."

"I don't understand."

Lloyd smiled cryptically and led Atti to where Jenkins had set out coffee on the veranda overlooking a spacious garden. "I met Hugo years ago at a private equity conference," he went on as he poured a cup for Atti. "I was trying to drum up interest in my software company."

"You didn't invest in Pandion?"

"No, I was looking for *others* to invest in *me* and having little success. But your father pulled me aside—why, I never quite figured out. He put up seed money that bought us valuable time, but more importantly he gave me advice about my pitch, took the time to show me how appearances are sometimes more important than reality. I suppose that kind of thinking may have led to his undoing in the end, but it helped me enormously, and I always hoped to find a way to thank him."

"I don't know what to say. I don't hear much good about my dad these days."

"That is unfortunate. He was an innovative thinker and a charismatic man—and he was good to me."

"Thanks for saying that."

"Oh, no need to thank me. Also—a bit off topic—I am a casual etymologist, and I wonder about your name. Is 'Atticus' an homage to Harper Lee? Or no, given your ancestral estate is Pandion, it must come from the king of the Attic tribe Pandionis."

"That's right," Atti said, guessing Lloyd knew what he was talking about. "People connect my name with *To Kill a Mockingbird*, but no one ever guesses my mom got it from Greek mythology. She sort of followed up on this hobby of my grandfather's."

"And thus the Pandion name."

"That's right. Although we always thought it referred to the bird: the sea hawk."

"Of course, and the bird's Latin name *pandion haliaetus* no doubt derives from the mythical king of Athens, whose daughters turned into birds."

Atti was dumbfounded. This guy was some kind of genius.

"But let's move on," Lloyd said. "Jordan tells me you and Rooney started a business to provide music therapy for dissolute dogs."

Atti inhaled sharply, willing himself not to stutter. "Yeah, it seemed there would be a market, but troubled dogs tend to have troubled masters, and they didn't want to hear that from me."

Lloyd chuckled. "Not surprising."

"Right, and even when I could get the owner to cooperate, the process was too slow to be profitable. I guess it would work if we had clients in *this* neighborhood, where people would invest serious money to make Fido behave better than they do."

Lloyd chuckled. "Don't mistake owners of expensive houses for people eager to part with their money."

"I guess you're right."

"So now that we've established we are old family friends—and both dog lovers—tell me about this invention of yours: the 'Camouflager.'"

"Oh, she told you about that, too?" Atti was hoping to avoid the subject of weed but it was better than talking about dogs so soon after the attack—and Jordan had warned him not to hold back. "You see, even though marijuana is illegal, people still use it. And, well, it smells a lot, which makes it hard to smoke without drawing attention."

Lloyd's grin said he found this subject—and Atti's discomfort—amusing. "So again, you recognized a market and tried to satisfy it."

"Exactly. I built this pipe… Well, actually, my roommate helped me put together two tubes—he can fabricate anything—that filtered burning weed and also the smoke when you exhaled, and then we found an innocent odor to mask the smell."

"Innocent?"

"Right. Incense says you're hiding something; I wanted people to know they smelled something besides weed but recognize it as unsuspicious."

"Quite astute."

"Thanks. Anyway, garlic worked when we tested it. In fact—small world—your niece Rooney was our test subject, though she never knew it."

"We shall certainly circle back to *that* story, I assure you. But to the point: could it scale up? Could you produce your pipe in volume?"

"I never found out. My boss at the time, well, he kind of made himself my partner and then shared the design with these shady characters, and they started selling the pipes…."

"And they cut you out."

"Yes…and I notice that was a statement, not a question."

Lloyd tipped an imaginary glass in toast.

"Right," Atti went on. "I'm not sure the concept had commercial potential, but I contracted away whatever rights I had and don't even want to think about it anymore."

"A lugubrious but proverbial story. I was dispossessed of the rights to an invention once and know how that feels."

"Yeah, it sucked," Atti said and immediately thought he should watch his language.

But Lloyd only nodded with a sympathetic smile. "And finally, I was interested in your film…."

"My what?"

"Didn't you produce a short film on anticipating new technologies?"

"Yeah, at school. But how…?"

"We do some wide-ranging research here. I believe Jordan found your technology film on YouTube."

Atti had posted the film after it won the award, but he had no idea anyone actually watched it. Still, this put him at a disadvantage. Lloyd knew all about him but Atti still didn't know why he was there. He asked, "So, what kind of business do you do?"

"That gets to the point, and I must say I appreciate a man who gets to the point. You see, I made *my* money with an idea, essentially. I got help from people with technical ability, but it was the concept, the creative spark, that made the success. And success allowed me the luxury of living as I please and investing in other start-ups. I'm not involved in day-to-day business, but I'm still exhilarated by the hunt for the next big thing."

"What do you do when you find it?"

"It varies. Sometimes I offer advice or make contacts. I might invest angel money. Other times I just watch—like picking a hypothetical stock portfolio and keeping score. Lately, I've been focused less on investing for profit and more on probing into what works, what's possible. This is where a burgeoning mind like yours fits in."

"Ah," Atti said, fascinated but confused. "And how would that work?"

"We'll have to give it some thought. For now, tell me more about how you became an inventor."

Atti saw no reason to hide anything from Lloyd. He already knew about Pandion Capital and the Maine property, and certainly would know all about the scandal. So Atti talked about growing up helping Gabriel build tools and gadgets to maintain the compound and his fascination with Q's innovations for his guitar, and then how the dog whispering thing led Atti to believe inventing might be a path to regain his place in the world.

"So your aim is to find your way back to the big house on the hill?"

"Sure. I mean, I guess that's everyone's goal, right?"

When they finished their coffee, Lloyd took him for a tour of the garden, proud to show off his plantings. Atti talked about how he had redesigned the display window at the Plum to attract more street traffic.

"I'm curious to see this Paradise Plum, but for now Jenkins is signaling lunch is served. I hope you're hungry, and perhaps we can pull Jordan's nose from the grindstone to join us."

Atti's appetite urged him to rush up the stone steps to the veranda, but he politely held back. A table was set for three, and Jordan was already seated.

"I see you two are getting on," she said, amused.

"Your young man is as advertised," Lloyd responded, "an interesting amalgam of acuteness and precocity."

"See," Jordan said, turning to Atti and laughing, "I told you he talks like that."

Atti smiled. "I have no problem with big words when they come with lunch."

Lloyd looked at Jordan in mock affront but then smiled. "It seems we must feed our young man before we decide if we can put him to work."

The upshot of lunch—besides a gloriously full stomach—was Lloyd dangling a job, as yet undefined, that would involve Atti coming up to The Hall and working with Lloyd and Jordan in exploring opportunities. But first there would be a test.

"Show up Monday morning with an idea," Lloyd said, "anything from a better mousetrap to how to colonize Mars, and then perhaps we'll talk turkey."

Atti's hopes crashed to earth. This was the payoff. He had to contribute a "burgeoning mind" for Lloyd to keep feeding him, but where would he get an idea worth this man's time?

On the train home Atti watched the Hudson. The river views now seemed to represent a world of opportunities with eddying currents that could also pull him under. But his father had taught him a positive attitude was the first key to success. He wasn't sure how much he should rely on adages from a felon, but Hugo had thrived on the strength of his personality, so Atti couldn't discount his lessons completely.

Back in the city he convinced himself he would soon be solvent. So he sprang for a subway ride downtown and stopped to buy groceries to share with Q along with his news. That night they celebrated at the

Avenue B Saloon, where Q was rigging the lightshow for his friend's band. Rooney joined them. Atti sat with her while Q went backstage. She was still sad about Chauncey but was putting on a brave face. It was clear she was becoming quite attached to Q.

"So, you'll be working with my uncle?" she said with a smile.

"I only hope. I have to come up with some brilliant idea by Monday, and it's hard to know what he wants."

"He can be hard to figure, but he's always been great to us and close with my mother."

"And you see a lot of him?"

"On holidays or when he comes to town and takes us to dinner. Not nearly as much as Jordan, of course. By the way, she seems to have taken to you."

"You think so?" he said, a little too eagerly.

"Well, I wouldn't get all soppy about it. But yeah, she thought you were cute from the start."

Atti's imagination ran with this. He had thought Jordan way out of his league, but who knew? He pictured her at The Hall. She was hot in that skirt and sweater, and if she thought he was cute….

"Does she have a boyfriend?"

Rooney laughed. "She always has a boyfriend or two."

Q joined them, carrying three shots of tequila and slices of lime. "It's time to celebrate Atti's job!" he said, placing a glass before each of them.

"I haven't been hired yet," Atti objected.

"Dude, it's in the bag," Q insisted and poured salt on his hand.

Rooney also started to object but gave in. They raised their glasses, licked salt and downed the shots. Atti welcomed the warm feeling bursting within him; he wondered if it was from the liquor or the sense of belonging. He had he never before really had friends who cared for him beyond what it would get them, who would stick with him when things got rough. Nick Emerson had been a friend—Atti thought he was his *best* friend—until the shit started flying, and the rest of his former teammates were the same. The guys at Penn were less critical and less inclined to pin his father's crimes on Atti, but he was not really close with any of them. But unlike his other friends, Q and Rooney were genuine. They weren't going anywhere, even when it cost them in a serious way. And now he might have found a real job, with no experience other than sorting records and running drugs. Things were looking up.

When they returned home, Atti took Ghost for a walk. The dog seemed back to normal, though poignantly he stopped to sniff at Rooney's door each time they passed the fourth floor. They came back to an empty apartment, and Atti guessed Q must be downstairs.

He was unable to sit still and was suddenly inspired to straighten up the room—to the extent possible. He put on some music and cleaned the dishes, the sink and even the bathtub. Then he slept fitfully, one arm hanging off the couch on Ghost's back.

In the morning Atti was eating the cereal he had bought when Q came in the door. "Stop-off on the way home?" Atti said with a grin.

"Yeah. Seems Roo needed some help in her apartment. I don't know where the time got to."

Atti shook his head. "You never cease to amaze me, man."

Q was astounded at how clean the kitchen was and threw Atti a questioning look. Then he grabbed a bowl and joined his friend, looking content and sleepy. Half-way through his cereal, he said, "Anything new from the cops?"

"No, and I'm just sitting around waiting to get picked off…or run over or arrested again. The more I hear the more I think my freaking family deserves it."

Q shook his head. "Dude, that sucks."

"Oh, yeah, and did I tell you, my dad took money from Father Jake?"

"That's low."

"Right. I should change my name."

And then it suddenly scared him that Elle would come home soon to see her father, and after that there would be school breaks. Crane had the patience to wait for his opportunity. "You think *we* could find Crane?" he said. "Maybe there's some kind of crowd-sourced citizen watch?"

"I don't see how we'd get anywhere, except you *are* like the goat tied in a clearing, so maybe he'll show up to eat you for lunch."

"Nice image. I should ask Lloyd if there's a constellation representing the devil devouring a goat?"

Chapter
Fourteen

Monday morning Atti presented his idea to Lloyd. "I was reading an article about clothing stores," he said. "They use 'trend spotters' to predict what people will wear next season. That got me thinking. What if we built some kind of popularity predicter, an app or software or maybe a website? Something that..."

Lloyd had heard enough; he hired Atti for a trial period of six months. A weekly salary would enable him to rent his own apartment and eat regular meals. And he had Lloyd's promise of a fair return on any of his ideas they developed together. With coffee and a bagel inside him, Lloyd's infectious enthusiasm and Jordan growing increasingly attractive, it felt like things had turned around.

"In a way," Lloyd said, "a popularity appliance would encapsulate what I'm talking about: tapping into young, innovational thinking to discover what's next. But how do we build it and package it? It must have a commercial application."

Long discussions explored a business model: what they could build and how they'd sell it. Atti really enjoyed this work. It was a dream working with Lloyd and especially with Jordan, the modern-day Kim Novak in *Vertigo*. Starting with that first day on the platform at Grand Central, Jordan had rotated in Atti's imagination through Hitchcock blondes. But whichever role was his favorite at the time, he sensed she might be starting to warm to him.

One afternoon—when she was Grace Kelly from *Rear Window*—Jordan sat with Atti on the veranda. She was scrolling through websites, looking like a model out of a fashion magazine. He was sipping iced tea, appreciating the perfect afternoon and her shapely legs and the feeling he was safe in this hideaway. Frogs croaked in the pond and songbirds sang in the trees. It was a little like Pandion, with the lawn and the pond, though without the salt breeze or seagulls. That all seemed so long ago; how could that be?

"Easy to check popularity," Jordan said, typing. "Here." She turned her computer screen toward him. "Apple lists the most downloaded apps."

"But that's not the point. We're not talking applications or anything that can be counted. It's more than clicks or images on a screen. We want to identify what's popular in the real world…."

"Or more importantly," Lloyd added, joining them from the house, "what is *about to be* popular."

"Right," she said. "But how do we do that without a crystal ball?"

"Ah," Lloyd said with resolve, "the sixty-four-thousand-dollar question." He paused. "But you may have hit on a name for it: Crystal Ball!"

Atti and Jordan rolled their eyes and Lloyd shrugged. "A bit plebian? Well, how about 'Panomphæan,' as in the *Iliad*."

"He's kidding, right?" Atti said to Jordan.

"I fear not," she smiled.

Llyod *was* serious. "All the gods," he said, "squabbling over whom to favor in the Trojan wars, had to respect the ultimate master of the heavens, Panomphæan Jove. It means 'to whom belong all voices,' which is to say Jove held the key to omens and indications of the future."

Jordan considered this with pursed lips.

"Okay," Atti said, "I see the relevance, but who would remember it?"

Lloyd waived this off and went back into the house muttering in what Atti assumed was ancient Greek. Jordan returned to her laptop and Atti returned to musing. He stared at the dogwood blossoms on the breeze but felt a shiver seeing the pure white petals float like smoke against the blue sky. That brought him back to the postcard that came before the dogs were poisoned. He didn't want to tell Lloyd about all the threats—that would be a reason *not* to have him work at The Hall. But Lloyd might shed some light on the message.

"I was wondering," he said later in the day when he found Lloyd reading on the veranda, "do you know anything about Orion and Sirius?"

"Don't tell me you're reading the Greeks."

"No, well, not really. But this came up in regard to stars. I know they're both constellations but..."

"Both are figures in Greek mythology. Orion was a legendary hunter whose faithful dog was named Sirius. Orion's companion was so loyal that, when his master died and was given his own constellation in the heavens as Orion the Hunter, Sirius was awarded a star to sit by his side. Sirius is another name for the Dog Star, a binary that is the brightest star in the sky and anchors Canis Major, the Big Dog."

Atti turned to another subject, but his mind whirred. The note said, "This time Sirius precedes Orion." The Greek reference meant it had to be Crane. Did he intend to kill Ghost *and then* Atti? A chill ran up his spine.

He tried to shake off these thoughts and focus on work and his good fortune. Jordan was more attractive in each new Hitchcock roll. Lloyd was a Buddha, spewing wisdom. Lunch had become his favorite meal.

Lloyd was like Hugo in some ways but completely different in others. He didn't have the visibility of Hugo and he treated success differently. After *he* earned the right to do as he pleased, he stepped away from business rather than becoming a slave to it. Also, Lloyd *earned* his reward while Hugo was like an athlete who cheated his way onto the podium. Most importantly, Lloyd saw promise in Atti and was willing to overlook his youth and indiscretions. Hugo would never have stooped that far from his pinnacle, rickety as it was.

Feeling financially solvent and guilty about freeloading, Atti asked Q's help finding his own apartment. "Now that I can afford rent, I'll also repay the money you laid out," he said.

"What money?"

"Well, rent?"

"Like I wouldn't have to pay it, anyway?"

"How about food?"

"I should pay *you* for helping get rid of all that macaroni."

Atti sighed theatrically. "Look, man. You're impossible. If I just stepped in shit with this thing with Lloyd, by which I mean happened upon something great, you're coming along."

"Fine. Let me know when you reach Shangri-la. Until then, you save your money and I'll keep playing music. And as to apartments, I might be spending time downstairs for a while, so you should use this place, and we can split the rent."

"You and Rooney? You dog."

Q turned to Ghost. They both looked at Atti.

"Okay," Atti said, "poor choice of words." Q laughed but Ghost just kept looking at them.

Q grabbed his bag and headed out. When the door closed, Atti realized this was the first time he had ever had a place of his own. It felt good, freeing, and yet he was uneasy. When he closed his eyes, he saw the thin trail of smoke, white against blue, and then a bat covered with maggots, and a dog writhing on the ground. Nothing would be normal or safe until they stopped these attacks.

Saturday morning Atti's phone rang. He brought it to his ear, trying to wake up.

"It's Elle, sleepyhead. Aren't you out of bed yet?"

"Yeah. Sorry. Everything okay?" The clock said eight-thirty.

"I'm good. How are you?"

"Fine. Did you hear: your dad came home yesterday?"

"Yes. I spoke to him and got my brother to line up the nurse. Fortunately, Pandion had medical insurance Dad didn't lose. Have you been to see him?"

"I have and Martin was there and seems to be helping out. But I've gotten busy since *I got a job!*"

"A job! Where?"

"It's a little hard to explain. I work for this rich guy who dabbles in things. His assistant told him about the music therapy for dogs...."

Her laughter interrupted him.

"Yes," he continued, "he actually was intrigued by the dog whispering, and then he also heard about this thing I invented—I never told you."

"Never told me? Why not?"

"It has to do with weed, as do some incidents I should share when we get the chance. Anyway, this invention enables you to smoke without so much smell. My boss at the Plum, the 'man of the year,' basically stole the idea and started marketing the pipes."

"And you didn't tell me because...?"

"I didn't want you to think I'm like your brother, or a criminal or..."

"Don't be such a sap, Atti. I know who you are, better than you do yourself."

"You're scary, Elle."

She laughed. "But back to your story...."

"Yeah, so this guy was amused by the pipe as well. I had to go buy one to show him. I went to his house in Westchester, a beautiful place with a big garden. Jordan just introduced us and walked off."

"Jordan? Is she the woman from Q's concert?"

"No, but in fact she *is* her sister. She's older...."

"Older?"

"I mean she finished college—she's maybe twenty-five—and works for the investor guy, who's also her uncle."

"That sounds complicated, but I'm thrilled you got the job! Anything has got to be more legit than the Paradise Plum."

"Yeah, the Plum was kind of a low bar."

"So, what's the job?"

"Like I said, it's hard to explain. It's like he wants to tap into my brain, get a youth angle on things he studies."

"And this Jordan…?"

"I don't know. I like her but she *is* older and kind of mature."

"You're such a dope, Atti."

"But anyway, you said things are good for you?"

"Really good, actually. Classes are going well. Oliver is really sweet and has taken me all over the countryside. You must come see Scotland. In some places you feel like you're back a thousand years ago."

Atti's life couldn't compare with Elle's but it had fallen into an easy routine. Even the constant looking over his shoulder became a normal part of his day. He and Q experimented cooking dinners other than pasta, or he cooked for himself when Q was downstairs. Fortunately, the batteries in the apartment's fire alarm were spent so disasters on the stove caused no more fuss than letting the smoke out the windows.

Henry dropped by a few times to drink beer on the roof, but his interests were narrowly confined to girls, smoking weed and talking about what a jerk Bruno was. Atti had also become wary of the mangy crew in Tompkins Square, especially since a police sweep one night left the regulars grumbling about being persecuted.

Q had moved his electronics into the living room and some of his other stuff to Rooney's apartment so Atti could take over the bedroom. They didn't tell the landlord about any switch because he'd try to raise the rent.

A few days later Atti found Jordan in the kitchen at The Hall pouring coffee. "YouTube," she said, as if continuing a conversation from moments before, "measures the popularity of video clips by how much time viewers spend watching and how much of a clip they watch, whether they subscribe to the channel—along with 'likes' and 'dislikes'—and do they link to the website."

Atti shook his head. "That still says if you can't measure it, it doesn't exist. Numbers in, numbers out."

"Exactly. The academic papers on popularity all begin by defining it based on metrics. Same for the social networks. On YouTube it's ratings or numbers of reviews. On Amazon it's units sold or revenues. You have to put a number to it."

Lloyd had meetings all morning, and Jordan was busy so Atti wandered, thinking he might find inspiration out in front of The Hall. The property was well built and maintained. But gravitating to one dusty corner of the garage, he uncovered a cobwebbed croquet set on a wooden stand. It brought back vivid memories of the big lawn at Pandion. He had a sudden image of his mom beaming with her beautiful smile, playing croquet with her whole family.

Lloyd was pleased with the discovery. Jenkins polished the set, and next afternoon Atti set up a course.

Lloyd watched him push in hoops and remove mallets and balls from the rack. "So," he called out, "what features have you come up with for Panomphæan Jove? Oh, and I'll take green."

Jordan stepped out the door wearing a fashionable straw hat. As she sized up the red mallet, she said, "A new movie or book relies on a PR blitz. Lots of eyes on an image, testimonials from Barack Obama and John Stewart, quotes from reviewers—massaged, of course—and puffery about how people are lining up for it."

"You're saying it's all marketing?" said Lloyd.

"Exactly. Selling people something they didn't know they wanted."

"Creating an anxiety relievable by purchase," Lloyd said, almost to himself.

"What's that?" Jordan said.

"Oh, just a little David Foster Wallace."

Jordan looked at Atti to see if he understood. He had no idea who Wallace was and so just shrugged at another of Lloyd's obscure references. Then he pointed out, "But we won't be selling *anything*—other than a sense of what's to come."

Jordan looked frustrated. "So we want to be an influencer?"

"We aren't seeking to influence anything, just predict it."

"Then I'm still lost. What *is* our product? And Uncle Lloyd, wouldn't just 'Jove' be a better name than Pano…?"

"Panomphæan," Lloyd rejoined. "And more to the point, this grizzled old startup veteran wants to know how we monetize it."

Atti spent the rest of the day rethinking the popularity tester. Jordan was right; they couldn't sell a product or a service forecasting popularity without first defining it. And he began to wonder if popularity was even a useful concept. Like "celebrity," it seemed so often fabricated. He thought of what it meant to be popular. At Earlington it rested on how much money your parents made or how good you were at a sport. But why was that a reason to admire someone? And was being a "celebrity" a sign of popularity, or did it signify anything useful at all? At one time, celebrity may have meant something significant but now it seemed so often to connote simply being known, like you were famous for being famous. Atti was a celebrity because his father was a crook. Why was that a reason for anyone to care that he was busted for selling weed? Why did that sell papers?

On Friday after work Jordan and Atti shared a car to the station. Their reverse-commute assured them seats on the train and the ride along the river was peaceful. Even with a job out of his wildest dreams, it felt good to get to Friday and a weekend off. Atti needed to relax and do something other than think and—as only Lloyd would say—"descant." He was particularly looking forward to leaving his dictionary behind.

In the slow underworld approach to Grand Central, he got up the nerve to ask Jordan what he'd been thinking about all week. "You have anything on tonight? We could go to a movie."

"Sorry, Atti, not tonight."

"What about tomorrow? Q has a concert in Brooklyn; I'm sure Rooney is going."

"No, Atti. Look, it's sweet of you to ask but I'll see you next week. You have a good weekend."

She left to catch a cab, and he lingered in the station's waiting room. He loved spending time with her, but it was clear she had no interest in him. Rooney had mentioned she was seeing some lawyer with a hot-shot car and a ski house; Atti couldn't compete with that. Someday he'd have it all again; it was just hard to wait.

He gazed at the constellations painted on the ceiling, so far up, pausing on Orion the Hunter and then searching for the one panel they left as it was before the renovation in the 90s. That grimy spot could be Pandion Capital, which once lit up the firmament and then became a sordid footnote.

He took the subway downtown and walked to his apartment. Ghost lifted his spirits, overjoyed as always to welcome him home. They walked together to East River Park, where the dog chased squirrels, and Atti tried to wash clean the memory of his arrest. But he found himself instead trying hard to remember what that old man looked like. Crane seemed to seep into almost every train of thought.

Detective Lawrence called that evening. "Just wanted to update you," he said. "We still have nothing solid on Tilson; he's a pretty cool character."

"Like I said, he's always been scary."

"Right, but he's got plenty to be scared of himself these days. I understand he was named in the Ponzi indictment. And also named was Mr. Gooden, who still has not surfaced."

"But what about Crane?"

"Yes, well, we have confirmed he got out of prison in 2014 and failed to report to his parole officer, so we've issued an arrest warrant. Prison records put him at six-foot two with gray hair and a deformed left ear."

"Sounds about right. And that timing means he could be behind it all."

"Don't worry; we're looking for Crane, but we have to follow all the leads."

"Even with all I told you about Professor Crane and the Greek stuff, and him possibly being psychotic? How can you think it's anyone else?

The detective went quiet.

Checking a list on his phone, Atti added, "And then another thing about the constellations. I work for a guy who knows this stuff. He says Sirius was Orion's dog, and when Orion died and got his place among the stars, Sirius followed him."

"And the note...."

"Sounds like a threat to switch the order kill Ghost *before* me—and that's what he tried to do!"

"Well, the card was mailed from Manhattan but we got no prints, so we don't know who sent it. And look, this is all helpful, but you've got to back off playing detective. It isn't safe."

Atti's head felt about to explode. "Nothing is safe! You've got to catch this guy!"

"Look, son, you've convinced me we need to bring Crane in… and we will. But we still have questions for Harry Gooden, and we need to chase down withdrawals from the fund. These things almost always follow the money."

Atti was skeptical but said nothing.

"I'll make Crane the priority," Lawrence went on. "I promise you. You just keep safe, and smart." He paused. "And no more deliveries for Mr. Bruno, right?"

"You have my word. But I wondered: do you know anything about the charges against my uncle?"

"That was handled by our financial crimes task force—completely separate from homicide—and I think it's in the hands of the DA now. But given Ted's condition, I assume the case is on hold."

Chapter
Fifteen

Atti didn't feel like attending a concert after his call from Lawrence, but Q needed help moving equipment—and was excited about playing to an outdoor crowd—so Atti pitched in. Q, Atti and Rooney rolled amplifiers and instrument cases onto the subway and then several blocks to the venue, a stage set up between two Williamsburg warehouses. It was fun playing roadie for the evening, and Q's enthusiasm was contagious.

Once everything was set up on the stage, Atti walked through the neighborhood, mostly old industrial buildings with small coffee shops and hipster bars sprouting here and there. He was sad Jordan had turned him down but it would be best if he found a girl his own age. He had an apartment and a job now so he had something to offer. Maybe he could train Ghost to look cute to attract women.

On the way home, Rooney said to Q, "I thought your show was great."

"Me too," Atti agreed, "especially the piece with the loops playing over each other."

"But nobody listens to the music," Q complained. "They're on their phones, texting, taking selfies, whatever."

"That must be hard," Atti said.

Q held his hand over his heart. "It is the curse of the performer."

But then he brightened. "You know, a venue—for concerts or movies or plays—could really use some kind of blocking device."

"To shut down the phones?"

"Exactly. It would only need to be effective within the space."

"I think you've got something there…and I happen to be in the idea business."

Next morning Atti got notice his criminal charge had been dropped. It was an enormous weight off his mind. This left only apprehension about the attacks to cloud his day. But his fear never seemed to follow him to The Hall and so he greeted Jenkins and Jordan with a big smile. The positive feeling lasted until he found Lloyd sitting on the veranda, pensive.

"Atti," Lloyd said seriously, "have a seat. We need to talk."

He hated conversations starting this way. He was always afraid Lloyd would discover he was just a feckless kid with nothing to contribute and send him back to working in a headshop. But there was no use putting off bad news, so he sat and waited.

Lloyd was lost in some internal dialog but finally looked up and said deliberately, "We have reached a dead-end on Panomphæan Jove."

"What do you mean?"

"There are too many people trying to calibrate popularity. I don't see a viable product."

Atti was shattered. Was this the end of his job, his dream-freaking job? And just when he'd gotten used to eating real food again?

Jordan joined them. She looked sympathetic, so it was clear Lloyd had already given her the news.

Lloyd went on. "What tomorrow will bring we don't know, but for now I'm still looking for the next thing, what's the word for it?"

"The next 'dope' thing?" Jordan offered.

"Or 'sick,'" Atti said dejectedly.

"Well, in my day," Lloyd said, "we called it 'cool.' But whatever the adjective, if we knew what this thing was, we wouldn't need to give it five stars; we could just act on it and get out ahead of the trend."

"And you see a part in this for me?" Atti asked cautiously.

"That's what we need to determine. But I took you on for six months and will stand by that. As long as you're willing to work, I'll gamble on the perspective of a twenty-year-old former rich kid slumming with a musician. It gives us…call it a fenestella: a small window in the wall showing what's to come."

"I appreciate that but, just so you know, my roommate sort of moved in with his girlfriend."

Lloyd frowned. "Just what that girl needs: a musician boyfriend. But no matter. I still think this could work. I have a gut feeling. Jordan and I have enjoyed—and profited from—our talks with you, and we think you add value. If you are willing to apply yourself full-time, we'll call you…I don't know, our Chief Trending Officer…."

"Our 'Cool Tester,'" Jordan laughed.

He didn't care what they called him as long as he kept the job. It also was fair for Jordan to make up names for him—"Bad Tester" one day and "Dandy Tester" the next—since he gave her a whole new screen persona every few days. That day she was Eva Marie Saint in *North by Northwest*, early in the movie when Cary Grant still thinks she's one of the bad guys.

A mix of emotions filled Atti that week. He hated that Lloyd had killed the popularity app but was grateful he still had a job. For how long, he didn't know.

One night he dreamed he was kneeling on a vast green lawn before a pot of oily liquid set over a fire. He stirred the pot with a long thin branch, which left a graceful white trail on the surface of the oil. Then the trail contracted into the shape of the smoke that hung in the sky after the Gulfstream exploded. He dropped the stick, and burning oil splashed his arm. He woke screaming and clutching at his arm. Then he spent an hour staring at the ceiling in a cold sweat.

He tried to channel his grief and fear into vigilance. On the street or riding the train, he constantly surveyed the people around him, looking for anything suspicious but particularly for a tall old man or a disfigured ear. By Friday he had calmed down and that afternoon Jenkins found him in the library to say he had a visitor.

"Surprise!" Elle said when he reached the rotunda.

"Elle!" He stepped in to hug her. "You weren't due until tomorrow."

"Typical," she said in mock reproach.

Lloyd quickly joined them. "So," he said, "is this the famous cousin from the university of Marvelous Merchiston?"

"If that's St. Andrews," she replied, "then yes, Mr. Prescott, and it is so nice to meet you." She held out her hand to shake but he leaned in to kiss it.

"What a charmer," Jordan said sarcastically as she joined them.

"Ah, Jordan," Atti said, "this is my cousin, Elle. I told you about her. And Elle, this is Jordan."

Elle said she had arrived home that morning for a Christmas visit and driven north with a friend. He had business in Chappaqua and so dropped her off to say hello. She hoped she wasn't interfering.

"Interfering? Nonsense!" Lloyd bellowed and announced they would repair to the dining room for lemonade and then some lunch.

"Oh, I couldn't impose," she said.

"No use resisting," Jordan said. "Lloyd will have his way."

"So how do you find St. Andrews?" Lloyd asked Elle once they were seated.

"Oh, it's just north of Edinburgh," she said and smiled.

"North of…Oh, right; you're joking."

"I apologize, Mr. Prescott. That was cheeky."

He waved it off. "We have quite a lot of cheek around here." He peered at Jordan and Atti. "And please call me Lloyd."

"Thank you, Lloyd, but I have to ask: who is this Marvelous…?"

"Merchiston. John Napier of Merchiston—'Marvelous Merchiston' was a nickname—a sixteenth century Scot from St. Andrews who discovered logarithms."

"Logarithms?" she said.

Atti glanced at Jordan, who rolled her eyes.

"Of course," Lloyd said, "the inverse function to exponentiation. There would be no probability theory or statistics without an understanding of logarithms…not to mention psychology and the computer science underpinning quantitative analysis."

"And they must have some fun traditions at such an old university," Jordan interrupted, to the relief of everyone but Lloyd, who seemed about to launch into a lecture.

Elle turned to Jordan with a look of thanks. "We do. In October we have a 'Raisin Weekend,' when freshmen are supposed to give their mentors gifts—at one time a pound of raisins. Now it's a weekend of pranks and a huge shaving foam fight. That's always fun."

After lunch, Lloyd insisted Atti show Elle the garden, although nothing much was in bloom. Once out of hearing from the house, he turned to her. "It's great to see you. How's school?"

"Okay, but do you know if they'll go ahead with the case against my dad?"

"Given his condition, Detective Lawrence doubts it."

"He's probably right. It's just so hard; I feel like I should be able to protect him, whether he deserves it or not. He is my father."

"Yeah, and we both know it was *my* dad who pulled the strings, and Ted followed along. It's sad."

Elle was quiet. She reached to touch a dried flower hanging from a vine. "Well," she said finally, "I should tell you the 'friend' I drove up with is Oliver."

"Oliver?"

"I told you about Oliver. He's from an old Scottish family. They live in what they call the "Manse," but they also have a ruined castle on their grounds, which is pretty cool!"

"Wait, did you say 'cool'?"

"Yeah…why?"

"Nothing." He smiled to himself. "So, he…?"

"You'll see. He's handsome and rugged and has the cutest accent. He's very close with his family—although so far I've only met his sister."

"And rich…?"

"Well, there is the castle and all, and a lineage back to the Battle of Worcester."

"I'm really happy for you, Elle. I hope Braveheart…"

"Oliver."

"I hope *Oliver* knows what a prize he's got."

"He does," she said and blushed slightly, "and things have moved pretty fast. Maybe it's partly because of all we've been through, but I needed someone, and Oliver has really helped. But tell me about Jordan. She certainly is stylish."

"Yeah, this week she's Eva Marie Saint."

"*North by Northwest*?" Elle said, looking confused.

"Right! But so far only early in the movie."

"So, she plays Hitchcock trivia with you?"

"Seriously? No, she doesn't actually know we're playing, but she usually sticks the roles."

"I guess I can see that. And so, you two…?"

"Together? Not really. I mean, we goof around at work, but that's all."

She shrugged and took his arm, saying she was a bit cold and suggesting they return to the house, but he stopped her. "Elle, I'm really happy to see you, but you have to know what's going on with the police…."

"I saw Detective Lawrence at the hospital. He told me about Crane, and about Uncle Hal! Is that unbelievable? Oh, and about your neighbor's dog and Ghost! How awful!"

"Right. Also, the neighbor is Jordan's sister Rooney, who introduced me to Jordan and Lloyd. And on top of it all, Rooney is now Q's better half."

"You're kidding!"

"No, they are definitely together."

"Wow. I'd love to see him. But back to the dog, do they think the person who poisoned them was the same one who did those other things?"

"That's what I think, and I have a hard time believing it could be Harry, partly because there's this obsession with Greek mythology, and we found out Crane was a professor of Greek studies. But, whoever it is, you see why I wanted you to stay in Scotland? You *have to* keep your eyes open while you're here. There's no telling what could happen. None of us are safe."

"I promise I'll look out."

"I hope so. Anyway, Lawrence is on the ball. It should just be a matter of time."

Oliver arrived in a rental car to drive Elle home. Atti was disappointed he didn't have red hair and wasn't wearing a kilt. He seemed a pretty normal guy, though not quite as "rugged" as Elle had described. His Scottish accent sounded artificially upper-class, but Atti realized that might just be his bias against anyone dating Elle.

"The famous cousin," Oliver said, shaking Atti's hand.

"Well, 'infamous' might be a better word," Atti smiled.

"Well, there is *that*," Oliver said, without humor.

Elle took Oliver's arm in both of hers. "Oliver is in his last year at St. Andrew's," she said proudly. "He's studying finance and economics and thinking of working in private equity."

"Then you should get along with Lloyd," Atti said, "except he thinks everyone in private equity is cold-blooded."

"Atti!" Elle scolded.

"I didn't mean...."

"No worries, hen," Oliver said to Elle, "that's simply a bit a rubbish, now, isn't it? He didn't mean anything by it."

Atti paused. He had said what he meant: a career in business had hardened Lloyd to those people. But he had not meant to insult someone still in school.

"You see," Oliver went on unnecessarily, "I'll initially be stepping into a role managing our family's estate, and my father thought I should get a solid grounding in finance."

Elle introduced Oliver to Lloyd and Jordan but both quickly excused themselves on a business matter. So Atti alone walked outside with Oliver and Elle for an awkward goodbye.

"So that's the cousin," Jordan said, coming from nowhere to join Atti as the car pulled away.

"That's Elle."

"She's a stunner. Wonder why she hooked up with that British wanker."

"He's a Scot."

"Same difference. But anyway, come on in. Lloyd wants to descant."

Atti found it impossible to get any time alone with Elle over her visit. She was booked up showing Oliver the sights or with her father. Finally, he called her. "Are you planning a Christmas dinner at the apartment?" he said. "We could try to rustle up a plum pudding or mince pie for Oliver."

"That's sweet, but Oliver made a reservation at Per Se."

"You're taking your dad to a restaurant?"

"It's for two. Oliver wants it to be elegant and romantic. It's not what I would choose but he has this thing about my family—which is easy to understand."

"He doesn't want to sit at a table with a crippled father, a sullen brother and a cousin who can't keep his mouth shut?"

"No, that makes him sound insensitive. He's really just uneasy, I think, about the legal matters."

"Like it might impugn his managing the estate?"

"Atti, that's not helpful."

"Helpful to what? This is your family, Elle, and Christmas. You're here for not even a week and your dad…."

"I know. I know."

"How is Oliver with *his* family?"

"He's very loyal to his parents, though they're strict and a bit stuffy. He visits nearly every other weekend."

"But you said you only met his sister."

"Yeah, I haven't been invited to the Manse yet."

"What's *that* about?"

"Well, everyone knows about our family, and Oliver's trying to think of how to break it to his parents about us."

"I see."

"No, you don't see. It's not how it sounds. And the important thing is he's been great about it all; he says none of it matters."

Atti thought that was awfully big of Braveheart.

He only saw Elle once more before she left the country. She and Oliver had stopped by Ted's to say goodbye when Atti arrived with Ghost. She was with her dad in his room while Oliver sat in the living room looking at his phone. The dog circled the apartment and pushed into Ted's bedroom to greet Elle. She soon came out to the living room with Ghost at her heels.

"He may be at death's door," she said, gesturing over her shoulder, "but he still doesn't like you know who."

"Well," said Atti, "I think the feeling is mutual." They hugged while Ghost walked over to investigate Oliver. The Scot ignored the dog, who returned to Atti and Elle.

Elle spoke quietly. "I hate leaving you as the only responsible adult when my father is so weak. You've got to promise to keep me more up to date."

"I will; you know I will."

"Right," she said, her voice becoming louder and sharper, "like you waited a whole day before telling me he was poisoned."

"She's right, old chum," Oliver added, having crossed the room to interrupt.

Atti looked at Oliver with dull eyes and turned back to Elle. "They said he was 'stable,' but I didn't know what that meant. So, what could I tell you?"

"How about he was poisoned! That someone tried to kill him! You don't get to decide when to tell me something like that!"

"You're right. I'm sorry. I should have called right away."

"Now that that's settled," Oliver said, "can we get going, Elle?"

"In a minute."

"I'm keen on a long bath and a comfortable bed." Oliver looked impatient. His arrogance reminded Atti of his brother Bode. No one needed to tell Atti how intolerable this apartment was, but this guy could suck it up for one afternoon for the sake of his girlfriend and her ailing father.

Oliver and Elle nonetheless prepared to leave. Oliver shook hands perfunctorily with Atti and said he'd wait for Elle in the hallway.

"You could be nicer to him," she said after he was gone.

"He could be nicer to *you*."

"But that's not your concern, is it? He's been really thoughtful."

"Just doesn't want you meeting mommy and daddy."

"Look, Atti," she said with mounting anger, "this is *my* life."

"Whatever you say, Elle. You two have a safe trip." And a good life, he stopped himself from adding.

Chapter Sixteen

Lloyd read an article about electric scooter rentals and got the aroused look Atti had come to recognize. The descant for the next week was all charging stations and rental apps. Over lunch Jordan presented data on Bird and Lime, the California companies leading the market, which both planned EU launches in Paris that summer.

"But as to the business model," Lloyd said, "I have a concern. Dockless scooters operate through a phone app that broadcasts a GPS signal, so what does that mean for privacy? Should the rental company be able to track rides? Isn't that information private to the user? Sounds to me like surveillance, pervasive surveillance."

He looked gravely at each of them, then his face turned amused. "Pervasive surveillance," he said thoughtfully. "That's a great name. We should promote a security device with that name."

Jordan and Atti looked at each other and broke out laughing. Lloyd was surprised but laughed along.

"Atti," Lloyd said, "I'd like you to stay in the city the next couple of days. Identify key neighborhoods in, say, Greenpoint, the Village and the Upper West Side, and get us first-hand insight. Who rides scooters? How many? And where do they leave them? I understand rentals are not permitted in the city yet, so empty scooters should *not* be littering the sidewalk, but we're talking New York here so enforcement could be lax. Are any scooters already blocking sidewalks or knocked over in the street? Do scooter riders obey traffic signals, wear helmets? Who *are* the scooter riders?"

Lloyd had no specific angle. He just wanted to dig into the business to see what turned up. It made Atti recall Frank Bruno's classic line, "We'll see how it goes."

For three days Atti spoke with people on the street, took photographs and shot video. He stood on street corners counting scooters, talked to riders, looked up casualty rates. On the train Thursday morning he sat by a window reviewing his research, knowing Lloyd would want to "descant" when he got to The Hall. But his concentration was interrupted by a woman talking loudly on her phone. The banality of her conversation was killing him; she was distraught someone stole her yogurt from the office refrigerator. She complained about this over and over as if the person on the other end didn't believe her.

The interruption reminded him of Q wishing he could cut off phones during a performance. Could a phone blocker work? Why not?

When he reached The Hall, he didn't even stop for coffee before barging into Lloyd's office. His boss looked up, surprised and amused. "My Cool Tester has a nibble," he said, raising his eyebrows.

"A cell phone blocker!" Atti almost shouted.

Lloyd frowned. "A what?"

"Something to block mobile phones in a specific place, like a concert hall or movie theater, so people don't disturb others by talking and texting and shooting selfies…or to stop people from taking photos in a museum…or making calls on a train."

"And this can be done? I mean, it's possible to block signals *and* internal functions…in a confined space?"

"I think so. Why not? We'll need to figure out the technology."

Lloyd stared into middle distance. "Well, the technology of course is key, but then I think you've got it! Let's download all we can find on the science. I recall visiting an office where I could only use the landline and a computer on the local network, so some technology exists. We may only need to tweak it and make it portable."

"I'll dig in…unless you need me to stay on scooters."

"No, focus on this. We'll call it Cell Block. It has a ring to it. I'll see if Jordan can give us some time. And I have an old friend who can help us if we build a device."

As Atti turned to leave, Lloyd added. "And by the way, I've been thinking about your dog therapy business. Jordan tells me you had a very capable canine assistant?"

"Ghost, yeah. After the customer's dog got used to me, I brought Ghost in to get it used to other dogs."

"Given that our business relationship started with you *and* your dog, don't you think it's about time we met?"

"You want me to bring Ghost to The Hall?"

"Sounds like the simplest way. I have a feeling he'd add to the energy around here."

Atti had been feeling guilty about leaving Ghost home all day, especially after the poisoning, so it was a relief to be able to bring him to work. At the same time, Atti himself felt safer on the street with his dog beside him.

From that day on he and Ghost almost always commuted together. Ghost became a favorite with the conductors and loved watching the river. He and Jordan were old friends, so he was ecstatic every day to find her at The Hall or sometimes meet her on the train. Atti had to admonish the cook not to feed him too many treats, and even Jenkins loosened up to pet Ghost when he thought no one was watching.

More importantly, it was a relief to come up with an idea that excited Lloyd. No matter how much his boss seemed to like him or think he had a debt to pay, Atti needed to justify his cush job. So over the next few weeks he forced himself to focus on work.

In a way, thinking about the project so much made Atti tense, or nervous. He had no technical expertise to help with design or building. Jordan was more qualified than him to work with the lawyers. And, of course, he lacked Lloyd's market vision and business experience. So what was *his* role?

When Lloyd assigned him to research the industry, he dug into the work. "There are jammers on the market," he quickly reported. "Most transmit signals on the same radio frequencies as cell phones and disrupt communication between the phone and its land-based relay station."

"So, could we tweak this," Lloyd said, "to interrupt other functions like the camera?"

"I haven't seen that but I'll check."

"And there are legal impediments," Jordan interjected, "either outright bans or licensing requirements."

"Because it interferes with legitimate phone use?" Lloyd asked.

"Exactly, and getting a grip on this around the world will take time and money."

"So we focus first on the US—which makes sense, anyway—and address one set of regulations. Or do we have to look state by state?"

"Interference with radio communications violates federal law," Jordan said, "but there are state statutes as well."

Lloyd sat back in his chair. "I see. Well, give me what you have on the law, and I'll get hold of Ed Bailey; he's a friend at one of the big tech law firms. He'll find a way to make this legal. We'll need him also to look into patent protection."

"I don't see why the government stops you from jamming phones on your own property," Atti said.

"You keep working on the market," Lloyd said. "Let Jordan and me worry about the law, and how to get around it."

Everyone was working on the project, including several of Lloyd's contacts. Atti felt this product *had* to succeed; he needed something positive in his life. But trying to fall sleep that night, a nagging thought formed in his mind, and it came front and center when he woke up.

Was Cell Block really *his* idea? Didn't Q come up with it as a way to get attention from an audience? Was he taking credit for something that wasn't his, like a true son of Hugo?

Next day in the office he wondered what he could do for Q, something *other than* give him credit for Cell Block. Over coffee he told Lloyd about his friend. "He's the smartest person I know…other than you."

Lloyd bowed his head graciously. "Maybe there's a place for this genius in our venture. Do you think he'd come see me?"

"Absolutely. He's up for anything."

"Well then, invite your friend, and we'll see."

Lloyd and Q hit it off immediately, which was no surprise; they were like two awkward boy geniuses in a high school robotics club. Q listened with interest as Lloyd explained their work on Cell Block. Then Lloyd said, "And how would you feel about joining our efforts…to the extent this fits in with your musical career?"

Q looked astonished, with the infectious childlike wonder familiar to Atti. "I guess," he said slowly, "if I could really help *build* the thing."

"I think we might work that out. We'll start you out part-time and see how it goes."

Bruno's phrase again, Atti thought. But Lloyd hiring Q went a long way toward relieving Atti's scruples about the Cell Block idea.

Jordan and the lawyers continued to struggle with regulatory matters. Laws banned jamming devices in part because they prevented emergency calls, so Q and Lloyd's tech guys were working on a way to override the 911 block. The lawyers were arguing that property owners should be allowed to jam non-essential phone use within their own buildings—after seeking advance consent, if necessary.

It was looking like Cell Block could be economical to manufacture in a reasonably portable form and could block, not only Wi-Fi and phone signals, but also cellphone cameras. Lloyd was telling Atti about a deal to manufacture the device in Taiwan when Atti got a call.

"Mr. Forester," an officious woman said, "this is Nurse Halley at Lenox Hill. I am very sorry to say your uncle passed away this morning. The home nurse reported he had lost consciousness and by the time the ambulance reached the hospital he had died."

Chapter
Seventeen

Atti had only spoken with Elle once since she returned to St. Andrews and that conversation turned sour. They just couldn't get past the subject of Oliver. She was obviously serious about him, in a way Atti had never seen before, but it all seemed so rushed he believed it had to be wrapped up in all she had gone through lately. She needed something or someone to hold on to and apparently that was going to be Oliver.

"He's willing to overlook our family," she said again, and that incensed him. While their fathers deserved infamy, Elle didn't, and it was wrong to hold that over her head. And Oliver refusing to introduce her to his parents was insulting. They should thank God Elle had feelings for their son. But when Atti tried to bring this up, she shut him down. He concluded he should say nothing at all, as his criticism was just pushing her into Oliver's arms. He wished someone could tell him how to make her value herself without damaging his relationship with her. He couldn't face the prospect of Elle not being part of his life, especially now with just them and Martin left in the family.

Now he needed to tell her about her father. This really should be Martin's job, but he was wallowing in self-pity and that left it to Atti. He ran a finger over chapped lips, wishing he could close his eyes and have this done. Why was everything so hard? He needed to put this off, have time alone with his thoughts, but Elle was so angry he didn't tell her right away about the poisoning. He was the last one she wanted to hear from right now, but he had to call.

"Elle, its Atti...."

"Look," she said in exasperation, "I don't want to fight anymore; it's too hard...."

"It's not that. The hospital called. Your father died this morning."

After a long silence and muffled tears, Elle said she'd fly home and they agreed to meet in Maine, where they would bury Ted in the family plot. Martin would be frantic, of course, but Atti would get hold of him and make sure he was included.

"I'll call Father Jake," Atti said, "and find out how to transport the casket."

"This will cost money."

"Yeah, there's no way around that. I could get a loan from my boss."

"This is *my* obligation, mine and Martin's."

"You know Martin won't be any help. What about Jillian? They were still married and I'm sure she grabbed all she could on her way out."

"I'll call her, but I don't expect much."

"Well, then, I guess it's you and me."

"The last best hope for the Foresters."

He thought about the night he and Elle sat by the sea, when the biggest tragedy in their lives was missing a concert. But he roused himself and said, "What about Oliver?"

"He'll come with me, I'm sure, but I can't ask him to pay funeral expenses. That would be so wrong."

"You're right, Elle. And I'm sorry for intruding into your life. You know what's best for yourself. I only...."

"Atti, you don't need to say anything. I understand. I know you do it because you care about me. We've lost everyone else; we can't lose each other."

Detective Lawrence called while Atti was walking home from the subway. "I had a talk with your cousin Elle and know she's planning to come home from Scotland. She seems a good deal more capable than her brother and appreciates the gravity of the situation. We can't be following you folks around, so your safety largely rests with you."

"So have you found Crane or Harry Gooden?"

"That's my news. We learned Gooden reentered the country from Canada two months ago. He came in through Buffalo but his trail went cold. As for his assets, well, he is a professional and apparently good at hiding money. He's been named in the indictment and better show up soon with a good story.

"As to Crane, we know he skipped from a half-way house in Albany in 2015. After that we suspect he took a new name. We confirmed your information from St. Anselm, that Professor Crane was canned after he was arrested for smuggling. He apparently jumped bail and stayed out of sight until the heist. Whatever else Professor Crane is, he is patient and knows how to be invisible. We've put out mug shots of both Gooden and Crane and are just waiting for one of them to poke his head out of his hole."

"Okay," Atti responded. "So I assume Elle told you Ted's funeral will be in Maine. Martin and I will meet her there."

"She did, and if our perpetrator is watching, that may prove too tempting to pass up. I'll call the police in…where would that be?"

"The church is in South Bristol but you should call the Sheriff's Office in Wiscasset. There's a Detective…something. I'll get you the name. He investigated the break-in."

"Atti," Lawrence said, unable to mask his frustration, "*what* break-in?"

"Um, yeah. It doesn't change anything, but it's one more reason to know it's Crane."

"I'm waiting…."

"Last summer someone broke into Pandion and stole jewelry from a strongbox…but he left behind a ring with a big sapphire in a Greek eye design. My father said it was some old thing from an estate, but my mother didn't buy that, and she was sure she'd never seen it before.

Actually, the ring was part of the loot my dad and uncle took from the jewel thief. The police never figured out the thief left it behind as a message, telling my dad and uncle he was after them, and he didn't need the ring because money was no obstacle to his plans."

"Did they report this to the local police?"

"How could they, without admitting they stole the loot, not to mention left Crane to die?"

"I see."

"But" Atti said excitedly, "it was a Greek eye ring! It fits with a psychotic Greek scholar."

"So Crane, again." Lawrence nodded. "You know I'll need to discuss this with my counterparts in Maine, so they have the whole story. We'll also want to expand the notice to precincts up there."

"I understand. Sorry I screwed up again."

"Sure. But Atti...."

"Yeah?"

"Is there anything else you forgot to tell me?"

Atti responded with a shrug, then realized Lawrence couldn't see him over the phone and said, "Nothing."

"Okay and to confirm," Lawrence said, "you haven't heard from Harry Gooden?"

"No, and I can't believe he went underground."

When he got home Atti called to tell Gabriel about Ted. The caretaker offered to come down to the city and help with arrangements, but Atti asked him to stay and handle things in Maine. He then tried to figure out how to move the casket. He called the lawyer who handled his parents' trusts, who offered to make the arrangements with a funeral home in Portland. Atti told Elle he was going to sell his watch for the expense.

"You will not! This is on my brother and me. I've got that emerald broach—my croquet prize—and some earrings."

"If you say so."

"You're sweet, Atti."

They agreed Elle and Oliver would fly directly to Portland and stay in a hotel. He and Martin would fly with Ted's remains. Gabriel would drive Martin and Atti to the gatehouse, and they'd all meet at the church.

That evening on the Ludlow Street stoop Q said, "You don't mind if Roo and I come?"

"To the funeral?" Atti replied. "You don't have to do that."

"Dude, you need somebody watching your back."

"I have more guardian angels in Christmas Cove than anywhere else."

"Oh, right, you've got Father Giacomo—I'd really like to see him again, by the way."

"And Gabriel."

"And Gabriel, of course. Well, Roo and I were thinking of a road trip anyway, so we'll be driving up tomorrow. We rented a room in the village."

"Okay, then, thanks. Sorry the house isn't available...or the cottages."

"I understand. But all the same, Roo's curious to see the property. Where will you all stay?"

"Gabriel offered a room to Martin and me. Elle and her boyfriend booked a hotel in Bristol."

"Why so far away?"

"Apparently, they want to be close to the airport for an early morning return flight...or maybe Oliver prefers amenities unavailable in the village."

"I hear he's into long baths," Q laughed. "I'm eager to meet this Scottish dude. We have to watch out for our girl, right?"

"We do, but that kind of thinking has gotten me into trouble lately."

"Anyway, Roo and I will be there so let me know if there's something you need us to do."

"That's right!" Atti said suddenly. "Could you do me a solid and take Ghost in your car? I hadn't thought what a hassle it would be flying with a casket and Martin *and* a dog."

"Hey, no worries, but he'll have to be quick if he wants to call shotgun before Rooney."

"He'll be good in the back seat."

"Oh, right, he's a dog. I sometimes forget. So leave him in the apartment, and we'll pick him up in the morning. I have a gig tonight or we'd be gone already."

Atti asked Martin to meet him at a coffee shop before they left for Maine. His cousin showed up, which was a positive start, but he looked agitated.

"You okay?" Atti said. "I mean, none of us are okay but are you taking care of yourself? We'll see Elle Saturday, so that should help." He paused. "Help us both, really."

"How can I be okay?" Martin pouted. "Some psycho is trying to kill me."

"I know. Pretty insane, right? Hard to believe it's only you, me and Elle left."

"I miss her," Martin said and seemed genuinely in pain.

Martin's pathos struck Atti. He couldn't recall his cousin ever showing affection or empathy, but now he sounded sincere and infinitely sad. He had pretty much always been a jerk, but he had also been knocked around in the past few months, like the rest of them. Maybe being a target for a killer was starting to wake him up to how much he needed his sister.

"Listen, Martin, Elle is an angel and she loves us. And she's all alone now, except for us. But it's not *her* job to take care of everybody, though you know she'll try. You really should be nice to her when she gets here."

He expected a rude response, but Martin just stared and finally nodded and left. Atti watched him walk out the door and paid the check, wondering what would become of his cousin. What does someone like him do when he's on his own?

Chapter
Eighteen

Gabriel met Atti and Martin coming off the plane in Portland. How he got access to the gate area Atti didn't know, but he had friends everywhere. He escorted them out to the tarmac to watch the casket load from the jet to a hearse.

"Thanks for all this, Gabriel," Atti said. It was a relief having someone else in charge. All Atti had to do was play the dutiful child, accept a ride, carry his bag to the bedroom and change into his black suit. He paused for a sad smile, thinking about the suit his mother bought him for his first high school mixer, where he danced with Violet DeMorsey.

He was ready before they needed to leave and so wandered up the driveway for a full view of the Barn, standing lifeless like a grand, deserted lady. The weather was unseasonably warm for March, bringing an early "mud season" to Maine's southern coast. Atti stepped across the melting snow with his jacket unzipped. He gazed from window to window, recalling happy events in each room.

A grating sound around the edge of the house caught his attention. Enrique was clearing a drain so snow runoff wouldn't pool around the foundation. "Mr. Forester," he called out. "Good to see you again."

"Thanks, Enrique. I see you're still at it."

"Ah, you know, the new manager kept me on, and the snow melts and has to go somewhere."

Atti nodded and turned. He wanted to be alone. By the gazebo the sound of gulls brought him back to the hawks last summer flying circles around the lawn. He smiled at how embarrassed Bode was when old Arthur sent him sprawling. But it was good to see Enrique at work and comforting to know the seasons would follow one after another, unaffected by the storms rocking his life.

A car horn sounded from the gatehouse. He saw Q and Rooney step from a car, and then Q opened the back door and Ghost leaped out and ran to Gabriel, tail wagging furiously. He circled the group and ran back and forth between car and house.

Atti stepped out on the lawn and let out a sharp whistle. Ghost looked up and froze. He spotted Atti but looked back at Gabriel. The caretaker waved toward Atti, who repeated his whistle.

Ghost broke into a gallop, nose to the snow. Atti had to sidestep at the last moment to avoid a collision and the dog skidded comically to a stop. Then they came together, Ghost growling and Atti laughing. It was amazing how this animal always raised his spirits.

The dog stayed home while the rest of them drove to St. Bernard's. Father Giacomo greeted them in front of the church, taking special care with Martin, who seemed dazed. Elle and Oliver were already there. She introduced Oliver to everyone, and Q introduced Rooney.

Atti had always been able to read Elle's emotions on her face but now he could only wonder what she was feeling. Her father was a despicable person—like Atti's dad—but all the same she would now live her life without either parent, and he knew that hit hard. When she hugged Atti she whispered, "I'm so grateful you're here."

The church bell tolled, and everyone started to go inside. Atti noticed Detective Horace off at a distance and they exchanged nods. Then a taxi pulled up and Harry Gooden got out!

Atti shot an agitated look at Horace, who followed his gaze to

Gooden and then approached him quickly, speaking into his phone and dropping a hand to his holster.

Harry looked pale and almost unrecognizable. He had shaved his mustache and colored his salt-and-pepper hair dark brown. He wore his trademark business suit but part of his shirt stuck out from his pants. "Atti," he said stepping forward and reaching out his hand.

Horace caught hold of Gooden's wrist. "Harold Gooden?" he said forcefully.

"Yes, officer," Gooden replied looking dazed.

"You'll have to come with me."

"But…but the funeral."

"Yes, well I'm afraid that won't be possible. There are a lot of people looking for you, Mr. Gooden, and we have questions that won't wait."

Gooden's eyes dropped to the ground. He let two officers handcuff him and place him in a police cruiser.

Horace returned to Atti. "This could be a break," he said. "No use disturbing the service. You go in and I'll have my men secure Gooden."

Atti sighed deeply. This was such a release. Was it really Harry behind this all and could it now be over? But whatever Harry did, he wasn't capable of killing someone; seeing him now made that clear.

Atti suddenly remembered Elle was burying her father, and he rushed into the church. A few neighbors were sprinkled over the pews. He didn't stop to greet Josie, who sat with Enrique and Gabriel, but hurried to a seat in the front row beside Martin, Oliver and Elle. He kept picturing how lost Gooden looked and wondered how he could have done all this harm. With a sudden chill he turned to scrutinize the congregants again for a man with a mangled ear. Instead, he saw only shopkeepers and members of the yacht club, the same people who could have attended Sunday morning mass any time during his childhood. Seated across from Q and Rooney in the back row was Detective Horace.

Father Giacomo's eulogy was less effusive than four months ago. Instead of a financial icon, his beloved wife and boisterous son, they were there to bury a lone, sorry soul, so often sidelined in life and now disgraced in death.

But the setting was all too familiar, and thoughts of Atti's mother filled the space. He wondered if this would always happen to him in any church from now on, or maybe only at St. Bernard's.

The only real reason to be here, in the same pew as when he buried his parents and brother, was for Elle. Otherwise he could not have stood it, how the oppression came so quickly and endured what seemed like forever. He recalled his father once saying none of us know how long we'll have. Was that prescient or just more bullshit?

Once the ceremony began, Elle sobbed quietly. This brought tears to Atti's eyes, though he tried not to let anyone see.

"How to make sense of this latest tragedy?" the priest said somberly from the pulpit. "For a family torn by grief, evil has once again arrived at the door to snuff out a life."

When the priest finished, he offered his hand to Elle. She rose, took a moment to collect herself, and stepped to the pulpit. She looked otherworldly in her black dress with a veil pinned to her hair. She gazed up and down the pews, as if to connect with each person in the church. When her eyes met Atti's, her expression brimmed over with grief and thanks.

"First," she said, in a voice fragile but resolute, "I'd like to thank you all for coming—for myself, my brother Martin and my cousin Atticus. You all know how our world has turned upside down, how we've lost so many of the people in our lives, and you must know how very sorry we are for all the pain and heartache the Foresters have caused in the world and especially here in South Bristol. But all this falls aside when we have to say farewell…" She faltered and put a handkerchief to her eye. "When we have to say farewell to a man who had maybe more than his share of weakness but still did his best for us. We of the next generation in our family only pray we may find a way to make up for the wrongs of the past and that time may begin to heal…." It seemed she had more to say, but she shook her head and returned to her seat.

Atti didn't look around to see if he was the only one crying. It wasn't for his uncle; it was for his mother and himself and mostly for Elle. His heart burst to see her like this.

At the conclusion of the service Atti, Martin and Gabriel joined Father Giacomo's acolyte and two neighbors in carrying the casket around the side of the church. The early thaw had allowed Gabriel and Giacomo to have a fresh grave dug close by Hugo, Marie and Bode and under the watchful eye of Ted's long-departed parents.

Atti wondered if he'd merit even this kind of funeral when *his* time came…or would this cemetery and St. Bernard's even be here? Nothing seemed permanent anymore.

Detective Horace waited to catch Atti's attention until people were drifting away. He asked if all the cousins could spare a minute. Atti gathered Martin and Elle and they walked with Horace around the back of the church.

"As Atti knows," Horace said, "Harry Gooden showed up here, and we have him in custody."

"What?" Elle and Martin exclaimed.

"Yes. We didn't want to disturb the ceremony. We're not certain he was involved in the murders and everything else, but we'll dig into it. At least he needs to explain his disappearance and faces charges connected with the fund. At the same time, we've heard from Detective Lawrence of NYPD, and we think this other man, Lazlo Crane, almost certainly was involved and may be on the prowl. We want to be careful and ask you to keep us informed where you'll be while you're in the area. We'd also like to meet with you…tomorrow, after you've had your time to grieve."

"I'm sorry," Elle said, "but I have a flight out in the morning."

"That's right, Detective," Oliver interjected, having walked back to join them. "We'll be leaving early from the Algonquin Hotel in Bristol."

"That's all right," Horace replied, turning to scrutinize Oliver. "And you are…?"

"Oh, of course. Oliver MacNash. The young lady and I will be returning to Scotland, where we attend university."

Horace nodded and turned back to Elle. "Maybe it's best you leave the country. We're pretty sure that puts you out of harm's way. And we can hopefully get the information we need from your brother and your cousin."

Horace turned to Atti and Martin. "We understand you two will be staying on the estate with Gabriel Oak. That may be the safest place for you. Please keep your eyes open and alert us to anything out of the ordinary."

Gabriel invited everyone to the gatehouse for lunch. Atti thought Martin should go with his sister but Oliver drove off without him, so Martin and he got a ride with Gabriel. Father Giacomo said he'd gather the flowers left in the church and follow behind with one of the neighbors.

The mood lightened when they reached Pandion. There were still clouds in the sky, but the sun had poked through and the temperature was brisk but comfortable. Gabriel set out cold cuts and a tub of beer and soda and everyone relaxed. Atti went up to his room to remove his jacket and tie, and this encouraged the others to loosen their funeral clothes.

Atti was quite hungry. He sat with Q at a wooden table on the hard-packed snow eating a sandwich. "Sad you won't see this place anymore," Q said.

"I only have to close my eyes to see this place."

Q nodded toward the trees. "And it looks like Martin's been tripping down memory lane."

Atti turned to see his cousin emerge from the beach trail. "Tripping, possibly," he said, "but not on memories."

Martin approached with glassy eyes. "Hard to imagine it's not ours," Atti called out to him, trying to sound sanguine.

"Anymore, anymore," Martin said senselessly and walked past.

"I've got to find out where he gets his shit," Q said, shaking his head with a smile.

"It's not funny. I'm worried about him. He's got nothing left. But listen, now that the police have Harry, all we have to worry about is Crane. Should we go back through the list you made? Maybe Lloyd could help us with the Greek stuff?"

"That's it! We'll give *him* all the clues."

They followed Martin back to the house, where Q filled a plate and settled into a chair by the fireplace with Ghost close by, eyeing his food. Elle sat on a bench out front with Father Giacomo. Oliver stood in the kitchen with Rooney, speaking loudly enough to be heard in the living room: "…a bonnie spot, but not like the wide-open Highlands. Hardly going to bag a stag here."

"Hard to fit those damned stags in bags, anyway," Martin said, banging the screen door against the house as he entered the kitchen.

"What, are you…?" Oliver began and then looked at Martin condescendingly. "Oh, I see."

"You see *what*?" Martin said petulantly.

"It's clear who's in the bag, laddie."

Martin looked about to cause a scene, but Gabriel ushered him out of the kitchen, and Atti stepped into his place. "It's been tough on Martin," he said quietly to Oliver. "We're all looking for ways to cope."

Oliver shrugged and made no attempt to keep his voice down. "He might cope better if he dried out."

Rooney tittered, and Oliver gave her a self-satisfied smile. Atti thought about turning the onion dip over on his head but decided that might not improve things. Instead, he opened a can of soda and went to join Elle and the priest.

"Ah, Atti," Father Giacomo said. "Why don't you keep Elle company while I give Gabriel a hand inside?"

Atti suggested a walk around the grounds. Elle took his arm, and they strolled down the driveway toward the Barn.

"How many times have we walked this drive?" she said with a sad smile.

"Imagine being back there, nothing to think about but how to amuse ourselves."

She squeezed his arm tighter.

"So, what are your plans for the summer?" he said.

"First I should share my news!"

She was clearly excited, and Atti was afraid to ask why, so he just nodded.

She squeezed his arm tight and said, "Oliver proposed! Can you believe it?"

"No, I mean yeah. That's incredible." Atti's thoughts swirled. This was awful. How could she…and so soon…and with everything going on?

"You look less than pleased," she said.

"It's not that, Elle. I mean, I'm happy for you, of course. I'm… surprised is all. Aren't you rushing things, you know, with all that's happened?"

"Well, I didn't actually say 'yes' yet, and it couldn't be for some time anyway. He comes into his inheritance when he turns twenty-five, and before that he could only marry with his parents' consent."

"And that's an issue?"

"We don't know yet. He hasn't told them about me. He says they know about Pandion Capital and won't want him marrying into a scandal, and to an American to boot, so he's waiting for the news to die down."

"Hey, I'm all for waiting, but it sucks you have to keep hidden from the king and queen because you're American."

"They're *not* royalty."

"I meant the castle owners whose son won't stand up for the woman he wants to marry. Damn it, Elle, how can you take that?"

"It's not like that! You're not being fair!"

"Elle, I don't want to fight. I want to see you happy more than anything. I just can't stand anyone apologizing for you."

"He's willing to overlook our family, and I think that's very generous right now."

"Well, as one of the few remaining family members, I guess I have to thank him."

"Atti, you make me so angry sometimes!"

"You *should* be angry, but not at me."

"Elle!" Oliver called from in front of the gatehouse.

"Oliver's ready to leave," she said, "and, frankly, so am I."

Elle and Oliver said their goodbyes. Atti waved, feeling hollow and exhausted. Elle's news and her abrupt departure were two more ways the day had whipped him.

As evening came on, Father Giacomo went back to St. Bernard's with some neighbors. Q said he and Rooney would also go as they wanted to leave early to drive back to New York.

"I've got to stick around," Atti said. "The police want to meet with us tomorrow. Anyway, I could do with a few more days here. Lloyd gave me time off, and the gatehouse is comfortable. It'll give me a chance to spend time on the grounds."

"Sorry I can't stay with you. This place brings back great memories. But I suppose Ghost should drive back with us?"

Atti thought for a moment. "No, leave him here. It might be a hassle getting him on a plane but I need him with me right now."

Q looked at the dog, lying on the porch with one eye on them. "I think he feels the same," he smiled.

"So, I noticed Oliver bending Rooney's ear. What did she think of him?"

"Well, she suspects I once had a whopping crush on Elle…."

"Had?"

"Yeah, well, you know how *that* is. And I think she was curious what kind of guy Elle ended up with."

"And?"

"She says he's pretty smooth, with the accent and all, but she felt like he was putting the moves on her."

"That's *all* I need to hear."

"Concerned about our girl?"

Atti sighed. "Seems to be my lot in life."

When the guests had all gone and Martin wandered off, Atti helped Gabriel straighten up the house.

"What should we do with these flowers, do you think?" Gabriel said, holding a vase of lilies in his big hands.

"I don't know. Send them back to the church?"

"Aye, that's a generous thought. We'll collect them and bring them to Giacomo in the morning. Here, hand me those yellow ones there."

Atti reached for the vase by the fireplace but froze. Those flowers! They looked like… He put the vase on the table and pulled out his phone to call up an image of birdsfoot trefoil.

"Oh, God!" he exclaimed.

Gabriel turned to him. "What is it?"

"These flowers: they're from Crane!"

They hadn't noticed before, but there was a note attached to the vase. Atti read it out loud: "The Sins of the Father."

Atti felt his lungs constrict. That bastard wouldn't stop. He was out to kill them all!

He called the rectory. Father Giacomo said he brought over what had been left in the church and didn't know where the flowers came from. He asked his acolyte, who also hadn't seen them delivered.

Atti then called Detective Horace. "We got a note. It was on some flowers, the same kind as on the bag of maggots sent to my aunt."

"Flowers?" Horace paused. "Wait…yes. That's in the file, I think, but it's back in my office. But what about this note?"

Atti read the message.

"Listen," Horace said, "I'll get a squad car over to Pandion for tonight and will be out to meet with you first thing. But keep your eyes open and call me—at any hour."

In the morning Atti woke early. He went outside and found Ghost keeping Gabriel company while he repaired a fence. The world could come crumbling down but Gabriel would still meet it wearing his tool belt.

"Didn't expect to see you so early," Gabriel said with his kind smile. "The detective said he'd be here around nine?"

"Yeah, but I don't want to miss any of the time I have left at Pandion."

"Ah, you know, it'll possibly be some time before they sell the property. The trustee kept Enrique and me on for maintenance and security, so we'll know well before any new owners move in."

"Or bulldozers."

"Well, let's not be seeing the worst in things until we know. You and my favorite dog, in any event, are more than welcome to spend as much time as you like at the gatehouse, now and going forward. I love having you and really hope you'll treat this as your home."

"You've always been so good to me…to us."

"Ah, you know, Atti. Never having a family of my own, I always thought of you folks as mine. But come on now, and I'll cook you up a real Maine breakfast."

They sat over bacon and eggs while Martin slept in. When the detectives arrived, Atti roused him. Then they all sat together over coffee.

Detective Horace led the conversation. "To start let's address Harry Gooden. He claims he knew nothing about the Ponzi scheme but last spring started to suspect Hugo and his CFO were cooking the books. He approached your dad, who denied any fraud and played on Gooden's loyalty, but Harry didn't believe him and started liquidating assets and moving his money because he feared he'd be swallowed up in an investigation. Apparently, it all came to a head when Gooden and your dad met here in July and then Gooden was fired. He was broken up about that but had no intention of taking it any further; he planned even then to put distance between himself and the company to shield his money. He used a shell company to purchase a house and a car in a small town in Pennsylvania, all set up to live off the grid. Then, when your dad's plane went down, he panicked. He saw not only his wealth but his life in danger and he put his escape plan into effect."

"And lost the mustache," Atti said.

"Right. He was thorough, coloring his hair, shaving his face and dressing the part of the gentleman farmer. He flew out of the country and after several stops drove back in through Canada and started his new life. But when he heard the news about Ted, he felt he had to come to the funeral. He says he always thought of Ted as a close friend and another victim of Hugo's greed."

"So you don't think he was involved in the attacks?" Gabriel said.

"I just don't see it. The man has taken everything hard and seems too feeble. But we'll be sending him back to New York, where both the feds and NYPD have questions for him, and will do a thorough search of his new identity. After the criminal charges and the civil suits likely to follow, I doubt he'll have much left."

"But now…?" Atti said.

"Right," Horace continued. "The delivery of those flowers and the note tell us Lazlo Crane was in the village yesterday, or at least arranged to send along his threat. Even if he was here, he may have left the area, but we can't be sure so we've upped our patrols in and around the village and circulated an alert across southern Maine. We'll also keep a cruiser outside the gate here until we locate him."

"You can be sure we'll also keep a sharp eye out," said Gabriel.

"We know you will. And now, what else can you two tell us that might give us a lead to this man's whereabouts?"

Atti had given up trying to hide anything. He guessed Detective Lawrence had already passed on the main points, anyway. So he repeated what Ted told him about the man on the beach and the jewels and how they connected with the robbery at Pandion.

"I knew it!" Horace said. "That crazy ring! I was sure it meant something. We didn't dig deep enough." He frowned and said in an aside, "Blame it on poor record-keeping forty years ago."

Atti recounted delivery of the painting of Back Bay and the handbag full of maggots and the dogs being poisoned, but he left out his arrest, hoping Gabriel hadn't heard *that* story.

"Right, and we have copies of the case files on the two attacks. One thing they tell us is this perpetrator has resources and seemed to be on a mission to destroy Hugo and Ted. Now, however, it appears his rage extends to their children. Clearly, he has watched you two and Ms. Forester."

Atti began to think it was a mistake not telling them about his arrest, but revealing it now would just make him look foolish and wouldn't really add anything. He looked at Martin, who seemed more focused on his coffee than the conversation.

"Well, we appreciate the sit-down," Horace said. "We'll be checking in. I urge you stick to the compound or else let us know when you head out—so we can be ready for anything."

Chapter Nineteen

A storm picked up late in the afternoon and cut power to the gate-house. Atti sat on the window seat watching trees bend to the cold wind from the sea. Behind him Gabriel spread parts and tools over the table illuminated by an oil lamp. Martin stood in a heavy sweater close to the fireplace, as if he couldn't get warm. Ghost lay against the hearth, plenty warm enough.

"Why did you lose power?" Martin whined. "That never happened at the Barn."

"Well, lad," Gabriel responded, "we have issues with the weather, particularly this time of year, and the gatehouse hasn't the generator of the big house."

"You remember," Atti added, "how we used to light candles and oil lamps before they installed the backup?"

"Yeah…I guess," Martin said, beginning to pace the room.

Martin was a mess. He'd never been steady or strong, and as a teenager had a drug problem. He started at one college and then tried another and then came home and didn't do much of anything. But at least he was rich. Then the scandal and losing his father sent him reeling. And whatever he was using to self-medicate was not doing the job. He stepped toward Gabriel and watched him work, but his right arm twitched so badly he steadied it with his left. Two days of living together told Atti what that meant: he'd soon "go out for a walk." It couldn't happen soon enough for Atti. He didn't care what drugs his cousin used as long he did it somewhere else.

"I'm going to throw together a meal," Atti said. "What do you guys say to pasta?"

"That'll be lovely," Gabriel said. "While you prepare dinner, I'll run up to the Barn and install this fixture."

"Martin?" Atti said.

Martin looked up, startled, almost as if he didn't recognize his cousin. Then he took a deep breath and his face relaxed. "Not me," he said. "Not hungry."

"Man, you've got to snap out of it. You can't live on just coffee."

Gabriel clearly wanted no part of this conversation. He gathered his tools, threw a slicker over his jacket. Wind and rain swept in when he opened the door. This seemed to remind Martin of something. He grabbed his lighter from an end table and patted his breast pocket. Then he went up to the room he shared with Atti, came back down and followed Gabriel out the side door.

Before long Gabriel returned, and he and Atti ate a simple dinner. Martin wandered back some time later. He scoffed at the plate Atti had saved for him but poured a glass of water and sat until he finished it. Then he retired upstairs. Gabriel brought tea to the fireplace, where Atti had settled in with Ghost at his feet.

"So," said Gabriel, after a long silence, "have you got a court date yet?"

"Actually, the detective in New York got the charge dropped…Hey wait, how do you know about that?"

"Ah, you mentioned it to Detective Horace, didn't you?"

"Gabriel, tell me the truth."

Gabriel let out a deep sigh. "Yes, Atti, I heard about your run-in when your roommate called for bail money."

"It was you!"

"Aye, but it was no trouble." He smiled. "I knew you were good for it."

"But why didn't you say anything?"

"I guess I…How can I put this? I'm accustomed to helping from the shadows."

"What does that even mean?"

"Ah, well, you see…," he said and halted.

"What is it?"

"Well, what's important is about this thing with Crane, that you know you won't deal with this alone."

"What do you mean, alone? I have you—you've always taken care of me—and Q and Elle and Father Jake."

"That's not precisely it. I mean, well, you should know…."

"Is there more?" Atti said plaintively.

"There is just one more thing but this one's a corker."

Atti wondered what else could really matter with one cousin gone to Europe, the other shooting up in the woods and a madman tracking them all down. He wished he still had a sailboat and could shove off from the cove and not look back.

Gabriel looked down at his hands, working them together nervously.

"Tell me," Atti said. "I'm beyond being shocked by anything and would really like to get it all out at once."

"Okay then, you're right." Gabriel grimaced and rubbed his fist along his chin. "As you know, I've been at Pandion my whole life. I saw your dad grow from a headstrong boy into a wealthy and powerful man. From the time I met his young fiancée, I thought this man had everything: a fabulous home, a wonderful and adoring woman and a thriving business." He paused, as if to collect his thoughts. Atti was scared to speak, afraid of where this was heading.

"Well, years passed and your mother began to lose her way. Over the summers at Pandion, Hugo was gone for long stretches. She looked for consolation in her religion and her gardening, but it was clear she was lonely deep inside. I did what I could to amuse her and encouraged her to socialize with the neighbors, but she was listless and kept too much to herself. When she became pregnant with your brother, I thought Hugo would see he was needed at home, but this drove him farther away. He hired a young assistant around then and rumor was he turned his attentions to her. I only suspected until…well, there was one day when Marie had gone to Portland, and Hugo told me to make sure the gardeners stayed away from The Old Buck's Eyebrow."

He paused and rubbed his forehead, looking suddenly older. "Still, I only cared because of your mother. She was so trusting and loyal, and Hugo deserved none of it. He spent very little time here that summer, and no time with Marie when he *was* here. Then Bode was born and Marie threw herself into her new role, loving her newborn son to fill the void left by her husband.

"Well, Atti, I'm not proud to say this—but it felt right at the time, and I never for one moment regretted anything while Marie was alive…."

Atti became alarmed. "What are you saying?"

"Your mother was heartbroken when she learned Hugo was unfaithful. He was hardly ever at Pandion that next year, and she was so forlorn and so lovely. I just couldn't stand by and watch her sink."

"So, you and my mom…?"

"Yes, Atti. I was her crutch, and she became the love of my life, and you…"

"Oh, God!"

Gabriel shook his head and wrung his hands, tears in his eyes.

"Tell me!" Atti pleaded.

"You are my blood, lad. You're my son."

Chapter Twenty

Atti's head spun. He stepped back from the table and braced himself against the wall. Eyes closed tight he saw a swirl of images of Hugo sailing Calypso, at birthday dinners, playing croquet at the Picnic. This colored it all. The collapse of the fund and Hugo's disgrace were devastating but Atti still knew who he was. Now he didn't even know that.

He opened the side door. Gabriel draped a coat over his shoulders but said nothing. He held the coat closed and walked. He wandered toward the Barn in a fine drizzle and stepped up into the gazebo.

Gabriel was a good man; Atti knew that. He had been there throughout Atti's life, and now that he thought of it, in many ways had filled the father role better than ever Hugo did. But to carry on an affair with his mother! How could that ever be right? Could Gabriel be true and honest and yet do that? And what about his mom? If there was one center of faith in Atti's life, it was her. She was such a kind soul, taking on burdens, spreading patience, helping Atti negotiate Hugo's rigidity and Bode's malice. How could that goodness reconcile with having an affair while she was married to his father? All Gabriel had said about her loneliness and Hugo's neglect rang true—there was no denying it—but they were still married! And what did being fathered by someone other than his mother's husband make him? First he was an orphan, and now he was a bastard? There was so much he had to talk over with Gabriel, but first he needed to calm down.

When he returned to the gatehouse, Gabriel still sat by the fire, as if he hadn't moved. Atti didn't want to talk until he could make sense of things, but he didn't want to be rude and so he sat in one of the stuffed chairs.

Gabriel hesitated, but finally said, "You know, I've been proud of you your whole life but especially over the last few days."

"You mean because I brought Ted home?"

"That…and other things; how you've stood on your own; how you've cared for Elle and Martin."

Atti sighed and gazed into the fire.

"The tragedies of the last year have made you grow," Gabriel went on, "made you strong. You've taken control of your life. You've found you can live without all the trappings."

You call this living, Atti thought, getting kicked in the teeth over and over?

"I wish I could have told you long ago," Gabriel went on. "But it's the danger all around now, and how you've faced it that convinced me I had to tell you, that you deserved to know."

Atti had no response. His emotions were a muddle.

"And while we all have feelings for Elle," Gabriel went on, "I'm impressed with the responsibility you've taken for your other supposed cousin."

"Well, I *thought* he was my cousin."

"Aye, and it's clear he has no grip on what lies ahead. I've never been close to Martin myself, but I feel some responsibility for him. Like I said, I've always thought of you folks as family."

"I guess I still feel the same."

"This is what I mean. It took no Forester money for you to become a man, and I mean by caring as much as by strength. Here you've got this 'cousin,' who in his whole life hardly gave you the time of day and *you* try to pull him out of his squalid pit."

Atti had no reply. He had to get used to being Gabriel's son. The lessons and morals Gabriel had imparted all through Atti's life now seemed more important. And as to Martin…he might not be related to Atti but he still felt like a rotten appendage that needed attention. Elle, on the other hand….

"I attribute that to your mother," Gabriel said. "She never had the strength to stand up to Hugo, but she had a heart that took in all around her, and that was her gift to you."

"But I'm troubled she…"

"Yes, my boy, and isn't that natural? You should know it ate at her as well, being Catholic and all. For myself, well, I also had misgivings but no one to confide in all those years. I believe your mother confessed to Giacomo, and that was why—by silent accord—he and I kept an eye on you in shifts."

"And all the time Bode was bullying me…."

"You can imagine how it made me boil seeing another man's child oppress my own, but I had to respect Marie's commitment to keep her family intact and could only try to help you learn to fend for yourself."

Over the next two days Atti helped out around the property, trying to get past his feeling of betrayal. Gabriel and his mother had lied to him his whole life, but without that lie the family would have been torn apart. And who was really betrayed? Hugo? What consideration did *he* deserve? He was the villain in this story.

Atti missed his easy familiarity with Gabriel. He observed his father's kindness to Enrique or his quiet wit and asked himself if he shared those qualities. He had always believed he inherited ambition and dogged determination from Hugo; maybe he just learned that over twenty years. But could nurture black out what was inside, what had been passed down? What did he inherit from the union of the righteous Gabriel Oak with the kind and loving Marie? Atti had never been a "Forester man." Maybe he was something better.

And he'd have to tell Elle. Would this matter to her? Well, of course it would matter—they weren't related, although they always believed they were. He hated to think what his life would have been like without her. She was his accomplice in childhood schemes, his playmate over endless summers, his partner in finding a way to bring humanity and humor to being Foresters. But without the bond of family, how would their relationship survive the thousands of miles separating them now and the life she was building in Scotland?

Early the next week Gabriel arranged a ride to the city for Atti and Ghost with a local carpenter delivering furniture. Martin would stay on with Gabriel with the promise of getting clean, participating in Father Giacomo's support group and working with Enrique at Pandion.

Atti felt uneasy leaving Gabriel without resolving his feelings. But Lloyd had been incredibly patient about his absences and absolutely clear he must show up for work on Monday. Cell Block was gearing up.

And what would he say to Elle? That would just have to wait.

Chapter
Twenty-one

Atti was thankful Q was at the apartment when he got home. He was still reeling from his father's news and needed to unload to someone he trusted, someone apart from the Foresters and Pandion.

Q was shocked but quickly Atti could see his mind begin to process. "So you were only Hugo's stepson," Q said, "or not even that, really. Did you have *any* legal relationship? This has to help relieve your guilt about the fund."

"Oh, the guilt is real. I lived my whole life as Hugo's son, just as entitled as Bode. I think I'll always be trying to make up for that one way or another."

"But that wasn't you. You had no choice. And…and what about Elle? Holy crap! You've always said she was just your cousin, but now…?"

"Now that she's engaged?"

"Wait. You said he proposed, not that she accepted."

"Well, practically engaged." Atti fell silent, thinking of Elle and Oliver.

In the swirl of thoughts and emotions, Atti realized he had heard nothing more about Crane, which was good news but left him uneasy. It wasn't safe to let his attention wander. The attacks had been so varied and spaced out over time there was no way to prepare for them, but he couldn't let his guard down.

Wrapping up work one day, Lloyd reminded Atti he'd be receiving payment for his "inventor's share" in Cell Block and would be named as the inventor in the patent applications. On the train home he thought about his "inventorship." No matter how he tried to rationalize it, Cell Block was *not* his idea.

By the time he reached The Hall next day he had made up his mind. The world had gone to hell. The only thing he had to hold onto was this job and his integrity. There had to be more to success than money. Hugo and Ted only gave lip service to their 'noble cause,' but this was where he proved he was different, that he most emphatically was *not* a "Forester man."

"Morning, boss," he said, entering Lloyd's office with two cups of coffee.

"Thank you, Atti. How's the research going?"

"We're moving fast, but I need to tell you something."

Lloyd put down his paper and looked him in the eye. "This sounds serious."

"It's about the project." He paused, searching one last time for a way to avoid this, but then he blurted out, "When I told you about my idea…well…it was my idea to market a blocker but the idea for the device was not mine."

"You mean you developed it from the research?"

"Worse than that. The idea was Q's. He was sick of people in the audience being distracted. He may have even tried to build something."

Lloyd was silent for a moment. "I'm glad you told me this, Atti. We need to be open to ideas from wherever they come, but we won't steal, particularly from a friend. And especially not with Q as part of the team. I'm rather disappointed in you. Why hasn't *he* brought this up?"

"That's just Q. And I've come to see he's the best friend I ever had."

Lloyd sighed and looked at Atti sternly. "Well, so what do you propose we do with this?"

"I don't know. What if I sign over my profit share?"

"That would be noble, certainly, though you'd still be entitled to a finder's fee…and your regular salary, of course."

"I think that's fair, if you still want me to stay."

Next day Lloyd asked Q to join him and Atti in his office. "Atti has brought up a matter we need to discuss," he said to Q. "It seems the idea for Cell Block was actually yours—something to do with a vexatious audience—and Atti has asked me to transfer his share in the profits to you."

"No way!" Q said. "I bitched about noisy people but this is all Atti. I never would have made a blocker or tried to sell it."

"Still," Lloyd said, "if it was your idea, you merit the profit share, and the lawyers have to name you as an inventor for the patent to be valid. And if my intuition is correct, this will earn you a tidy sum."

"No," Q said. "That wouldn't be fair."

"How about if we split it?" Atti blurted out, seeing a way to be fair and still get a payoff. He could really use the money.

Lloyd looked at Q. "Well?"

"I can live with that," Q said.

"Deal," Atti said and reached out his hand.

"So let's get back to work," Lloyd concluded, "or there won't be any profits to share."

The space in Atti's mind freed up from guilt immediately filled with thoughts of Elle. The news from his father had turned everything on its head with the one person who knew him better than he knew himself. There was no time in his life she hadn't been there, encouraging him, helping him carry on. He had always loved her; that was now so clear. But it was too late. She had a life in Scotland and a fiancé. He saw her walking down the aisle in some castle with Oliver in his kilt. His anger at how Oliver treated her boiled to the surface.

Right on cue Elle called. She was happy Martin was staying with

Gabriel and helping Father Giacomo. "With the Father and Gabriel there, and the familiar surroundings," she said, "he *seems* good…but I'm still concerned."

"Gabriel tells me he's trying hard. I don't know if he told you he's thinking about renting an apartment in the village. I guess the trustee pays him for gardening; Father Jake sure has no money for salaries."

"I'd say he needs a *real* job, so he can start supporting himself. But maybe the physical activity is good for him now, and working with addicts might help him see what happens if he slips again."

"Well, in the end he'll have to find his own way. There's only so much Gabriel and Father Jake can do, and *you're* not coming back."

"What does *that* mean?"

"Just that you've got your own life, and it's not in Maine."

"So, you think I'll forget about my brother?"

"No, of course not, but Oliver doesn't want anything to do with him."

"Atti, this is getting old. We can't talk at all without you criticizing my boyfriend! For your information, Oliver *is* concerned about Martin. He asks about him all the time."

"But I'm guessing he hasn't mentioned your brother to his parents."

"I can't keep having this conversation. I need to hang up. You just have to accept my choices."

Atti put the phone down and smacked his forehead. It was bad enough fighting with Elle when she was supposedly his cousin; now it felt like masochism. And he still hadn't told her! He couldn't stop thinking how badly he was handling everything.

One surprising result of his focus on Elle and work was Jordan began warming to him. Her teasing eased up, and she started finding excuses to share a room or a table with him. One afternoon he looked up to see her across the veranda staring at him.

"I was thinking," she said, lowering her glasses seductively, "maybe we should cut out early. MOMA has an exhibit on new directors and new films, and a friend gave me two passes."

A month earlier Atti would done somersaults for a chance to spend time with Jordan away from work—and he still found her attractive—but somehow he was no longer interested. She wasn't landing any more Hitchcock roles.

But then he wished he knew his own mind. This made no sense. Elle was far away and probably engaged by now while Jordan was right there and hotter than ever, and she finally seemed interested. He concluded he must have the capacity—or the weakness—for only one crush at a time, and fight it as he might, when he closed his eyes he only saw Elle.

"I really need to keep at the research," he said. "But thanks for asking; it sounds like a great exhibit."

On the roof the next night, Q was philosophical. "It's human nature. Jordan senses you're no longer interested and so now she wants you."

"That's sick, especially since Elle's going to get married."

Still, Atti wondered if Jordan's new attitude might help him stop thinking about Elle.

While Atti had agreed to split his share of profits with Q, the import of this didn't come clear until Lloyd called him into his office one day. "I have your paycheck," Lloyd said. "But wouldn't you like to set up direct deposit? It would save you the trouble of going into the bank and avoid misplacing checks."

"But I enjoy going to the bank. This is only my second real job, so it's all new."

"Well, if that gives you a thrill, I wonder how you'll react to this." He handed Atti a second envelope. Inside was a check attached to a financial statement.

"What's this?"

"It's your first distribution: your inventor's share from Cell Block."

Atti looked at the amount of the check and his eyes went wide. "But how? We haven't sold even one."

"Well, when we brought in Arcade Technology as a partner to handle manufacturing and distribution, there was a buy-in that went partly to shore up the business but was mostly a windfall."

"But what about Q…and Jordan…?"

"Q will receive a similar check next time he comes in. Jordan is not credited as an inventor, but trust me, she'll be thrilled with her bonus. It looks like fair sailing ahead for all of us *if* we can bring discipline to our efforts to see the project through on schedule."

Going home Atti held on to his wallet in his pocket; after Lloyd's comment about misplacing checks, he was afraid he might lose it. But Lloyd's metaphor about fair sailing brought him back to the Maine coast and taking the Guppy out with Elle on days when the sea was calm. She was always so full of life. He had never enjoyed sailing with anyone as much as with her.

This vision expanded to take in Pandion and the village, and he thought about Father Jake. He couldn't imagine how the priest had been able to make up what he lost with the fund. How was he keeping St. Bernard's afloat, and wasn't he in trouble with his superiors for losing that money? Atti was sure the priest had cut back on living expenses and maintenance to keep providing his outreach. And unlike Atti's supposed "friends" from the soccer team and school, Father Jake never blamed *him* for anything. He just offered support and understanding. Atti felt the wallet in his pocket. This profit money could be a real start to gaining a foothold, but was this really the way to a fresh start?

But morning brought a reminder Atti had more serious things to think about than his love life or how to spend his windfall. Detective Lawrence called. "We traced Crane to Long Island City," he said. "He took a lease under a false name and presumably organized the attacks from there."

"So you got him?"

"He was one step ahead of us. But we found bomb-making materials and arsenic along with clothes he left behind. So, we flushed him out but we don't know where he landed. I suspect this guy will simply revise his plans."

Over the next week Atti had trouble concentrating on work. All he could think of was the threat from Crane and the prospect of losing Elle. One afternoon Lloyd pulled him aside. "You're distracted, Atti. I'd have thought you'd be energized by our progress and seeing some of the rewards."

"It's not that. I'm just…I don't know…."

Lloyd looked at him kindly. "I've heard you had some startling news about your lineage."

"Yeah," Atti sighed. "When was anything ever ordinary about *my* family?"

"Well, Jordan had it from Rooney that this has particular bearing on the pulchritudinous young lady who visited in December. If you'll forgive an old man intruding, I believe you've learned your 'cousin' is *not* actually related to you?"

"That's right."

"And while you've known her for some time, you now find you have feelings for her?"

Atti was surprised by Lloyd's perception but only for a moment. "My whole life; I've always known."

"Ah. So what are you doing about it?"

"What *can* I do? She's got a boyfriend…who's probably a fiancé by now."

"The young man with the ascot and the attitude?"

"Oliver MacNash," he spat out. "And anyway, she's in Scotland."

"So, if she's in Scotland, why are *you* in New York?"

Atti looked up. Lloyd's eyes twinkled and his mouth curled into a roguish smile.

Chapter
Twenty-two

Twelve hours later Atti was on a flight to Glasgow Airport, via Heathrow. After a long day of travel, he dragged himself off a plane and onto a bus headed northeast. The highway wound through rural villages and farmland where fields were mostly green with spring crops starting to sprout.

Outside the bus station in St. Andrews, he found a coffee shop with free Wi-Fi, sat down with a café Americano and a scone, and pulled up a map on his phone. It was a ten-minute walk to University Hall, the address he had for Elle. Seeing how close he was made him suddenly apprehensive. He had remained resolved all the way across the ocean, but now that he was near, this felt desperate, like something that could only work in the movies. Wouldn't she resent him for showing up unannounced? Would she be off somewhere in the countryside with Oliver?

"Too late to turn around," he said out loud.

"What's that, laddie?" the middle-aged waitress said. She wore a checkered apron around her broad hips and was collecting cups off the next table.

"Oh, sorry. I've just, well, come a long way, and I seem to have lost my nerve."

"American, is it?"

"Yes, ma'am."

"Well, is it the university you're after or, no…I see from that sad puss it's something more important." A sly smile spread across her jowly face.

"It's a girl."

"Ah, isn't love braw?" She circled behind him to clear another table. "So what's holding you up, laddie?"

"I'm afraid I'll look like a fool."

"But then," she laughed, "there's no shame in being a fool for love, now is there?"

Atti looked back at the address on his phone. He had to see her, now that he'd traveled all this way. But should he call first or just show up? And should he see her like this? He must look like hell. This was nuts. He didn't even know when she went to classes or where.

His pulse was racing, whether from coffee or nerves or lack of sleep he didn't know, but he had to move this along. If Elle was going to send him away, he might as well get started back to the airport. And what else *could* she do? Who was he to descend on her out of nowhere?

He looked around to make sure no one could hear him and dialed.

"Atti! Hi!" she said. "What a surprise hearing from my favorite cousin!"

"Yeah, Elle, about that…."

"About what?"

"Actually, there are a couple of things. Have you got a minute?"

"Sure. No more classes today so I'm all yours. Everything okay? Is it about Martin?"

"Everything's fine, or the same, anyway. They're still after Crane, and I'm sure they'll catch him soon. And Martin: well, he seems better, living in his own place and working with Father Jake."

"That's good to hear. So, what else?"

"Look, Elle, it would be best to do this in person."

"You're *not* going to tell me you have a big announcement and then make me wait until I come home! Can't you tell me over the phone?"

"Well, there are a few surprises, and the first one—and I'm sorry to spring this on you—is I'm *in* St. Andrews right now. I'm a few blocks from your dorm."

"What? What are you talking about?"

"I'm here. I came to see you."

"See me! But why didn't you tell me? Atti, you're scaring me."

"It's nothing bad, just…kind of a shock. We just need to talk."

He followed her directions to a gray stone building with gables and what looked like a guard tower. It seemed appropriate he should have to storm a castle to complete his quest.

Elle met him at the door. Atti dropped his backpack. She hugged him and backed off to look him up and down. "You look like you've been on the road for days. Can I get you something? Where are you staying?"

"I'm not staying."

"*Not staying*? Atti, what is it?" She looked confused as she led him by the hand to a bench in a quiet courtyard.

"So," he began, but faltered, suddenly lost in the crystal depths of her eyes and the strand of dark blonde hair blowing across her face.

"So…?"

"Right. So, like forty years ago, there was a jewel robbery in Portland…."

"You're going to tell me a story from forty years ago?"

"Just listen. This is a bit involved. So the thieves shot their way out of a store and killed a guard and then escaped. They made it down to Christmas Cove, stole a boat and headed out to sea, but it sank and one of the thieves washed up at Back Bay with the loot. And, well, when he was arrested, the guy was pretty beat up but he told the police two boys took the jewels."

"Two boys?"

"Hugo and Ted."

"And the thief?"

"Lazlo Crane."

"Wait, how do you know this is true?"

"Your dad told me the same story at the hospital. With Hugo gone, he wanted someone to know."

She took a moment to digest this. "So they took…?"

"They left Crane for dead and took the jewels, and kept them hidden, and that's why they got into the diamond business, to unload them. And that's also where they got the money to start Pandion Capital."

"So…that's why Crane came after them?"

"That's right." He took a breath and watched a bird pecking the ground by an ivy-covered wall. They were just getting started but he felt spent.

"Anyway, Crane went to prison, and I guess he had nothing but time on his hands to look at who lived near the beach. He pieced it together when Hugo and Ted emerged as diamond dealers, and then he started plotting his revenge."

"So, he placed a bomb on the plane?"

"Or had someone do it—the cops are still sorting that out. But then, yeah, with Hugo gone, he turned to Ted. He stalked him—remember the bag of maggots? Of course, you do. Then he poisoned that case of wine, which I guess was a sure way to get to your dad."

"So," she said and paused, "is that it? I mean, now that he's got his revenge, it's just a matter of catching him?"

He shook his head. "Well, then there were flowers at St. Bernard's for your dad's funeral. We saw them after you left. It was the same kind of flower as in the photograph glued to the handbag that came for Jillian."

"Oh my God!"

"And there was a note saying kids pay for the sins of their fathers. And, oh yeah, then there was the poisoned meat left for Ghost behind my building."

"Atti! This is awful! What can we do?"

"I honestly don't know. Gabriel and I gave the note to the police."

"Gabriel! That's right; you were at Pandion. What will *he* do now?"

"Well, let's take this one step at a time."

She cocked her head curiously.

"Yeah," Atti said, hesitating. "So this all led Gabriel to share a story—and *this* was the shocker."

She watched him, hardly breathing.

"Elle," he said, looking into her eyes. "Elle…Gabriel is my real father. He and my mother…."

She gasped out loud. Her eyes went wide, hand over her mouth. "Aunt Marie…and Gabriel Oak?"

He let this sink in, then reached gently to move her hand from her face. It fell limp into his grip. Her expression raced through a range of emotions.

Suddenly, she pulled back and peered at him. "So, you and I…"

"We're *not* related, not even really by marriage."

Elle stared blankly. Atti waited.

Her phone buzzed. She unconsciously raised it to her ear. "Oliver, yes," she said without changing her expression. "I had to meet my…cousin. Atti! Yes, he's here." She listened. "No, I didn't know. Right, yes, at seven."

She looked up at him. "Atti, I feel terrible about this, but Oliver planned a dinner for tonight. He made it a really big deal, got a reservation weeks ago at this posh restaurant."

"I understand, Elle. I gave you no warning."

"Look, I'll call him back, see if we can change the night."

"Don't do that. He already hates me."

"That's rubbish!"

"Sorry. I didn't mean that. No, you go to dinner. I'm tired. I'll find a room and get something to eat. I've got a flight back tomorrow night, but can you meet me in the morning? I'll be awake then and hopefully will make more sense."

"We can meet, sure, but…"

"Is that a problem?"

"No, it's just the timing. You see tomorrow is May first."

"And…?"

"Well, everyone will be at the May Dip." She sighed, seeing he didn't understand. "At dawn on the first day of May," she said, "the students swim in the North Sea, over at East Sands."

"Isn't it freezing?"

"Nothing new for us, right?" she said with a hint of a smile.

"So you—and I presume Oliver—will go swimming at dawn?"

"With thousands of others. It's meant to be good luck for exams… and cleanse your academic sins—of which I have none, of course."

"Of course. But…can I meet you at this East Sands?"

"Sure. Oliver and I will be there early for the bonfires—a lot of kids stay up all night. You're welcome to join in. It's incredible, the sun rising and the students running wild."

He wondered how he'd sleep and be able to get up so early after all the travel and changing time zones. But dawn here should feel like midday to him. In any event, he wouldn't let an early start and a little cold water stop him after coming all this way.

"Okay then," he said, "I'll see you in the morning?"

"I hope so, Atti, and I'm sorry about everything going on. It's just, with the year winding down and exams about to start, and Oliver, well, he has a particular way of doing things. Anyway, we'll find someplace warm for a quiet breakfast after."

Atti rented a bedroom in a modest house near Hallow Hill, left his backpack and wandered out looking for dinner. In a pub he ate a savory Scotch pie and drank a pint of lager. He felt desperately alone to be this close to Elle and yet so far away. When he ordered a second beer, the bartender struck up a conversation. Atti asked about the May Dip and found it was common knowledge. "The students have been at that for who knows how long," the bartender said. "Before my time anyway. They're all daft, of course, but it's harmless, and they love it."

Back at the house he set his phone alarm for four-thirty. He normally would have a terrible time getting to sleep with his emotions swirling, but that night he didn't even remember his head hitting the pillow.

It was pitch dark when he rose. This was unhelpful to setting his internal clock, but he dressed, left his backpack and made his way to the beach. There was no trouble finding the way; he simply fell in with people emerging from buildings, all walking the same direction. He felt caught up in the energy as groups of people, some dressed for the morning chill and others in crazy hats and shorts and wrapped in blankets, chattered and laughed. He joined a pack of nine or ten who came from a side street singing a drinking song. He envied Elle for being able to attend a college like this.

East Sands was a wide, flat beach of fine sand overlooked by castle and church towers. The beach was teeming with people, clustered around bonfires or wrapped together in blankets. Atti was wearing all the clothes he brought to Scotland but was still chilled by the predawn air.

He walked from group to group but couldn't find Elle. Then the sun poked above the sea, and the crowd began to undulate like a great flag rippling over the beach. People shed clothes and moved toward the water. Some wore bathing suits and others stripped completely, a few wearing odd hats and one a formal cape. A man in the crowd broke into a run, shouting and whooping, and others followed. The beach dropped off so slowly that people kept running in the water without it getting much deeper.

Atti stood by the water line, hoping to catch sight of Elle, and finally she came down the beach with two other girls, all in one-piece bathing suits, holding hands and laughing.

"Elle!" he shouted.

She looked up. "You made it!" she said, a little breathlessly. "Atti, this is Carol and Mary from my hall. Ladies, meet Atticus from America!"

"You'll be wanting to strip down," Carol laughed.

"Oh, I'm not…"

"Of course, you are," said Elle.

He couldn't resist Elle, especially seeing her in a bathing suit for the first time when she was *not* his cousin. He wondered if her figure had always been this stunning or if she had somehow blossomed over her years in Scotland.

He removed his jacket and began unbuttoning his shirt. Elle pulled at a sleeve to help, while the other two girls clapped and chanted, "Take it off!"

"But where's…?"

"Oliver? He said it was too cold, but I think he's sleeping off dinner last night."

This was all the motivation Atti needed. He upped the pace of undressing and soon stood in only his boxer shorts. "Surf's up!" he shouted, adding to the general din.

This brought smiles to them all, and together they turned toward the water. Elle's friends were effervescent, but she seemed almost to be putting on a brave face to mask her feelings. Atti wondered whether she was thinking about no longer being related to him or about Oliver's absence.

All around young people of all shapes and sizes were laughing and squealing, running and splashing. Many stood waist-deep in the water, dipping down and then bouncing up with shouts. Couples hugged. Women crossed their arms across bare breasts, apparently more from the cold than embarrassment.

In five minutes Carol and Mary went back to the beach, but Elle turned toward the open sea and dove. Atti took a deep breath and followed, swimming hard to try to warm up and keep up.

Elle stopped at the far edge of the crowd, where she could barely touch bottom. Atti reached her and stretched down to feel the sand. She looked at him with wide eyes and her face alight, once again the mischievous playmate of his childhood.

"Incredible?" she said.

"Brilliant!"

She looked to both sides. He knew she was confirming they had gone in deeper than anyone else, the competitive swimmer showing through. Apparently satisfied, she shouted, "Race you in?"

"I think…," he said, but she took off and left him to chase. He never could beat Elle at swimming but he pumped hard. When he reached the depth where he could walk faster than swim, he saw her emerge from the water, again marveling at her figure. He kept her in sight and followed her into the crowd.

He found her wrapped in a towel, standing with her two friends. He stepped up, shivering. Elle handed him a blanket, which he wrapped around himself.

"I should have known you'd take to the cold water," he said to Elle.

She turned to her friends. "Atti and I grew up swimming off the coast of Maine. He was always a little timid in the ocean."

"And she was the best swimmer in the village," Atti added, thinking how images of Elle now filled every one of his happy memories of Christmas Cove.

They dressed and stood by a bonfire until the sun was fully up and circulation had returned to Atti's limbs. Elle's friends were full of questions about Maine and what Elle was like as a young girl and he asked about the university. He felt awake for the first time in days and, after a sip of whiskey from someone's flask, he was ready to take on the world.

And the scene was breathtaking. The sea, the sunshine and these women of all types, in bathing suits or without. He wasn't sure if it was the brisk day or the water or the fever of the crowd, but they were all gorgeous. Still, the dazzling woman across from him, with the sky-blue eyes and Olympian build, filled his head, and he didn't care about anyone else. He longed to hold her, keep her from the cold and never let go.

The four of them walked toward the dorm, friends greeting them and strangers wishing them well along the way. Then Carol took Elle's wet blanket and towel, and she and Mary returned to the dorm, while Elle showed Atti to a café where they found seats by a fireplace. Atti ordered the biggest breakfast on the menu, suddenly starved by the cold and the sea and being with Elle.

"So," she said with a playful smile, "you've made a conquest."

He lost himself in this smile, in her full lips. Every time he looked at her now he found himself enchanted by another feature of her face or figure. "What?" he said, recovering himself. "What do you mean?"

"Carol thinks you're hot. She wants me to convince you to stick around."

He laughed. Then he sipped his coffee and said, "So, what's up with Oliver? That was incredible; where was he?"

"Oh, he meant to come. He's big on Scottish tradition, with his family and all. But he's done it before and we had a late night. When I called this morning, he said we could always do it next year."

"He heard what a good swimmer you are and didn't want to be shown up."

Elle pursed her lips. "Now, we're not going to start on poor Oliver again, are we?"

"No. I surrender."

"And…I'm happy you're here."

"Because," Atti said and paused, warily, "you've accepted Oliver's proposal?"

"I have, last night, and I'm deliriously happy! But we have to wait to announce until he tells his parents."

"He still hasn't…?"

"Atti, let's not start that again."

"But Elle, how can you marry a guy who's afraid of his parents?"

"You just don't understand."

"You're right, I don't understand. Oliver and his family are lucky to have you."

"Listen, I've got to go."

"Me too," he said with a deep sigh. "I'm heading to the airport."

"That's probably just as well, I'm sorry to say. But Oliver—who only *ever* thinks of himself—was thoughtful enough to offer you a ride to Glasgow. I have a seminar meeting or I'd take you myself. Of course, you don't have to sit in a car with him if he offends you."

"No, Elle. That's nice of him, and it will really help. I only need to pick up my pack and I'm ready."

"I'm sorry it has to be this way, that you came all the way here and have to leave before you even see the campus. But at least the drive will give you a chance to see what kind of person Oliver really is."

They parted with a hug that felt strained. He wished her luck with exams, maintaining his composure until she was out of sight. Then he went to pick up his backpack and stood on the sidewalk, thinking what a waste of effort this trip was.

He waited for almost an hour before Elle's fiancé showed up in a sleek black Audi. "Morning," Oliver said brightly from the driver's seat. "Hop in."

"Thanks. Good to see you again. I really appreciate the ride. This traveling has worn me down."

"It's no bother. Elle and I wanted to make sure you got off."

Atti didn't respond. It was clear Elle thought he should go, and Oliver would certainly want to make sure he was gone. As they started to roll, he asked, "How long will it take to the airport?"

"Ah, chum, here's the thing. I actually need to meet with an instructor in half an hour, so the best I can do for you is the bus station here in St. Andrews."

"But…," Atti said and stopped himself.

In the time he had waited, he could have walked back and forth to the bus station three times, and in that hour he probably had missed a connection to the airport. But this guy owed him nothing and there was no point complaining.

"Is there a problem?" Oliver said.

"No. Everything's fine."

"Glad to hear it. And next time you visit, old man, maybe you won't mind calling ahead so Elle and I can set aside some time for you."

"Sure, but I don't think I'll be visiting again."

Oliver looked over with great interest. "A shame," he said, sounding surprised and pleased.

Atti *did* miss a bus to the airport and had to wait three hours for another. The delay meant he would miss his flight home, so he called the airline to rebook. The next flight to New York was in the morning. He paid to switch the reservation and settled in for the night on an airport bench.

Chapter
Twenty-three

Atti traded a hard bench at Glasgow airport for a center seat between a sleeping woman and a man so fat his short-sleeved arms overflowed the armrest. The physical discomfort compounded the ache in his heart. Elle was lost. He had tried his best and was shot down. Elle would marry that—what did Jordan called him, a "wanker"? He'd just have to make peace with that and try to preserve his relationship with Elle.

He eventually arrived at Ludlow Street feeling like he was back from the wars, exhausted and knowing no one would understand what he'd been through. On the way upstairs he knocked at Rooney's door. Q was there with Ghost, who raised a commotion when he walked in.

"Well, you look like shit that something fell on," Q said.

"I can't even tell what time it is or what day it is."

"How did Elle react about your father?"

"Like the rest of us: shocked."

"But, about you and her?"

"So she realized we're not blood relations, but it didn't change anything."

"Still with Braveheart?"

"Worse than that; she accepted his proposal, although the laird and lady will object to their son marrying a commoner so he hasn't introduced her yet."

"That's screwed up. But at least they won't get married *now*. She'll have time to come to her senses."

Atti had no response so Q asked, "Should I make you a sandwich or something? I think there's cold chicken."

"I'd love anything but peanuts."

While Q set about preparing food, he said, "And hey, I'm sure Ghost will insist on coming upstairs with you. He's been out already this afternoon, but Roo or I will come by to walk him later so you can get some sleep."

"I don't know what I'd do without you, bro."

Atti felt as if his batteries were running out. Walking up the last flight of stairs took an effort.

He woke after noon the next day. Ghost wasn't there, so he figured Q must have him. He peeled an orange out of the refrigerator and pondered his situation. The one bright spot was his job. Considering how generous Lloyd had been about time off, he really had to buckle down at work and hopefully this would keep his mind occupied. He called and spoke with Jordan.

"Just wanted to say I'm back and will be in tomorrow morning."

"Okay, good. I'll tell Lloyd. And how was the trip?"

"Rather not talk about it."

Later he called Gabriel to tell him he went down in flames over Scotland. His father tactfully turned the conversation to the weather and spring plantings, which made the call a little less painful than Atti had expected.

The consideration everyone showed in avoiding mention of his debacle didn't remove the sting. After all the ups and downs—mostly downs—of the past year, it felt like Elle was now all that mattered. If he could just have gotten through to her, he could live with everything else.

But she had a new life, that fabulous school and a fiancé. She had no reason to look back.

At The Hall next day Atti forced himself to dig into work. Q and the product designers at Arcade had nearly finished the Cell Block prototype, and Lloyd was working his contacts to find a factory. Jordan was following the legal work, which suggested they should be able to market Cell Block for very localized uses, at least domestically. Lloyd assigned his Cool Tester to survey venues and develop a list of potential customers. This kept Atti busy contacting theater operators, concert halls and museums.

He got bored spending his evenings with Q and Rooney. While he was relieved Rooney had gotten over Chauncey's death, it was a little depressing to see how loving they were together. So one night he called Henry and they took a six-pack to Tompkins Square, but they ended up sharing most of the beer with the posse around the Krishna tree. The down-and-out park people and their bumbling guitar playing did nothing to lift his mood.

The next evening he took Ghost uptown to Washington Square. Atti hoped a park in the middle of the NYU campus would recreate the feel of St. Andrews. But this greenspace was urban and diverse, a boggling array of characters each doing their own bizarre thing. He also thought how Nick Emerson was at school here and must live nearby but would not want to see him. That evening didn't improve his mood either, although Ghost enjoyed a romp in the dog park.

Wherever he spent his evenings, he couldn't get his mind off Elle and how stupid he had been to go to Scotland and fight with her. He desperately needed a distraction and wondered about online dating. He had a good job now and an apartment; that had to be worth something. If he could find someone to maybe go to the movies, take a walk with Ghost or attend one of Q's shows, he could try to move on with his life.

But any hope for normalcy vanished when his phone rang while he was walking Ghost. It was from the 212-area code, so he guessed it was legitimate and answered.

"Rhamnousia," a raspy male voice said.

"I'm sorry," Atti responded. "Do I know you, Ram…?"

"Rhamnousia, you clodpoll. And you *do* know me…or soon will, along with the rest of the heinous Foresters."

"Crane!"

"So, you *do* know me. All the better."

"What do you want from us?"

"Retribution, young Forester. Cold and sweet, like steel. I just thought you should know, so you can enjoy that tingly feeling of anticipation."

"You're sick. Whatever happened between you and my father: you've already killed him. All the money's gone and everyone who's left wasn't even born…."

"We'll leave no demon progeny. It's time for a *complete* reckoning."

"It doesn't make sense! How can you…?"

The call clicked off. Atti stared at his phone. He could hear his heartbeat racing.

When he got home, he paced the room, trying to calm down, and then called Detective Lawrence. "I got a threat on the phone," he said. "He admitted he was Crane, though he called himself Rhamnousia, which must be more Greek drivel."

"See if your phone recorded the incoming number and tell me everything you can about the call," the detective said, "what he said and any sounds in the background. Now that he has your phone number, we should try to record his calls."

"I was out walking the dog and couldn't hear very well."

"Just tell me what you remember, and I'll see if we can hook you up with a portable recording device."

Atti looked up "Rhamnousia" and was not surprised to learn she was the Greek goddess of retribution. But that didn't help find Crane or predict what he might do next. This guy had his phone number and knew where he lived. Atti only hoped he hadn't followed him to The Hall.

He redoubled his vigilance on the street and on the train. There was no sense disguising himself since it would be simple to spot the guy with a big dog, but he watched carefully who got off in North White Plains and whether any car followed him from the station. It gnawed at him that he hadn't told Lloyd about the threat. But he still tried to forget about this while he was at The Hall and bury himself in work.

They had good results from the prototype, and a factory in Taiwan agreed to produce a first run of devices. Everything was set for token sales to begin in two months. This prompted Lloyd to announce a launch party at The Hall. He dubbed it the "Cell Block Breakout" and invited the Arcade team and the lawyers and asked Q to bring Rooney. He instructed the cook to go lavish and assigned Q to program the music. Jordan and Atti had to reign in his idea they should all wear orange prisoner jumpsuits, convincing him this would *not* be the best image for a new company.

Setting up for the party, Atti still had a nagging feeling he wasn't contributing enough. That, and his constant fear of Crane, dampened his enthusiasm but he tried to keep smiling. When the Arcade guests arrived, Q introduced the engineers to Atti and Jordan. Atti suppressed a laugh at seeing these two young men and a woman, who looked like the rest of Lloyd and Q's high school robotics club. Something in their awkwardness gave him confidence and he stepped in to make them feel welcome. This helped him relax and start enjoying the day.

He took a few photos on the veranda but his phone ran out of juice so he went inside. He plugged into his charger in the library as Jordan entered the room.

"Did you see the skinny guy with the thick glasses talking with Lloyd?" she said. "I thought maybe he was a clone."

Atti laughed. "He's actually pretty nice, but when they started taking about batteries and capacitors, I couldn't make any sense of it."

The doorbell rang. "That must be the accountant, Waverly," she said. "Have you ever noticed how much he sounds like a duck?" She looked at him seriously and quacked.

He laughed out loud, and she pushed him into the corner and shushed him with her hand against his mouth. "Listen. He's a duck."

"You're always getting me into trouble," he complained, struggling half-heartedly and laughing.

"Oh, you love it. And someone has to take our *Mr. Cool Tester* in hand."

"Yeah, well, you just watch those hands, missy."

She tickled his ribs, and he pushed her away, laughing, just as Jenkins appeared at the library door. He seemed distinctly unamused by their behavior and said in his usual officious tone: "Mr. Forester, a young lady to see you."

"A what?" Atti said.

Jordan looked at him with raised eyebrows. He shrugged. Jenkins gestured toward the rotunda.

Still laughing, Atti opened the door to find Elle! Her sky-blue eyes were vivid against a pale blue dress. Her expression layered affection and joy and secret knowledge. It was the most beautiful sight he'd ever seen.

"My semester finished and here I am!" she said brightly.

"I thought you were due tomorrow."

"I got an earlier flight when a mutual friend of ours invited me to your party."

Atti was speechless. Once again, he owed Q big time.

She shrugged and went on, "I'm going to close up Dad's apartment and then go see Martin."

"He's doing well?"

"Hard to tell from a distance but I'm hopeful."

"I could try…"

"No, this is on me, Atti."

"It is *impolite*, young man," Lloyd's voice boomed as he entered the rotunda, "to keep the loveliest woman at the party all to yourself." He offered his arm to Elle, who took it with an overflowing smile.

Atti followed them onto the veranda and watched as Lloyd introduced her around. Q gave her a huge hug, looking over her shoulder at Atti with eyes wide and mouth open. Ghost charged in for a greeting. Jordan shook her hand, casting a sly look at Atti.

The rest of the day passed like a dream. Lloyd was gracious, everyone was excited about Cell Block and Atti couldn't keep his eyes off Elle. After lunch Q proposed a croquet match. There were six mallets, so he suggested three teams of two. "But we have to split up the ringers," he said, gesturing at the two veterans of Forester croquet combat.

Watching Elle command the course, Atti was torn. She seemed so happy he felt he had to share her joy. He would have to get along with Oliver or risk losing her. Yet, he found the best friend of his childhood filling his thoughts with an intimacy he had never imagined. He felt a driving need to spend as much time as he could with her and wondered if he had any hope of subverting her engagement. He decided the best he could do was be her friend and let matters fall as they may.

After a buffet dinner on the deck, Atti pulled Lloyd aside. "Elle will be packing up her family's apartment for a couple of days, then driving to Maine to see her brother, and I was wondering…."

"You want to help her pack."

"And drive north too, if possible."

Lloyd's expression turned serious. "Look, Atti, I understand you have feelings for this woman, but unless I'm mistaken your forlorn hope in Scotland went for naught. And we'll be all hands on deck here for the next two months. If we don't nail the launch on schedule, we risk losing all our momentum."

"I know, I know, but she still feels like family, and there's no one else to help."

Lloyd looked intently into Atti's eyes. "You know I like you, Atti, and I told you I owe a debt to your father—or to your family at any rate—but I am foremost a businessman. So, here's the deal: you take the week—but remain available by phone—and you report back *first thing* a week from Monday ready to work around the clock."

"You got it, boss, and thanks! You won't be sorry."

Chapter
Twenty-four

Lloyd hired cars to take them home. Elle went to stay with neighbors in her father's apartment building while Atti rode to Ludlow Street with Q and Rooney and Ghost.

Next morning Atti subwayed up to Elle's apartment. He stopped in her neighborhood to pick up bagels and coffee, knowing she probably got right to work without thinking about breakfast.

"Bright and early!" she said, answering the door.

"And bearing sustenance," he said, holding up the bag.

They ate as they worked. Elle had made substantial progress already. Still, it was a long day of packing and throwing things out. They kept the service elevator busy carting donations to a very grateful thrift shop. Atti set aside two folding tables and a lamp for Ludlow Street, and Q and Rooney showed up to look over the remains and cart a big stuffed chair home on the subway. After they finished the next day, an auction house would take the rest.

On one trip to the thrift shop, Elle found Atti peering down the street. "You look like you're ready to pounce," she said.

"Oh," he said, jolted out of his watchfulness and trying not to look paranoid. "I'm just keeping a lookout. I didn't tell you I got a call from Crane."

"You're kidding! He called you?"

"Yeah. It was just for a minute. More Greek nonsense. I told the police but it doesn't add much, except we know he has my phone number. I don't think he'll confront us directly; we've seen how devious he is."

He rubbed his sore neck, shook his head and smiled, trying to lighten the mood. It was so good spending this time with her, almost like they were kids again; he wanted to cherish every minute. But she would go back to Scotland, that was unavoidable and for the best, at least for her. She'd be safe there and happy.

Through the day they talked about the Yankees and old friends, music and climate change, but neither of them mentioned Oliver or St. Andrews. They were like close friends who had been together just a moment ago, so there was also much they didn't need to say.

He reached for a heavy box of books she was moving, and she passed it to him with a grunt and an appreciative smile. She was so fit and strong, always had been, but she had nothing to prove and accepted his help graciously. When she turned away, he struggled not to stare. When had she become a grown woman?

In the early afternoon of the second day, they finished with the apartment. Elle looked satisfied. "Next stop, Christmas Cove," she said. "And I will see you soon, right?"

"Oh, I'm coming with," he said with a wily smile.

"Don't you have work?"

"I cleared it with Lloyd. He claims to be a staunch capitalist but he's really a pushover. I just have to chain myself to my desk next week."

"I see," she said with a look hard to decipher. "I welcome the offer, but I guess I didn't tell you I'll be driving up with Peter. You remember Peter Becker? He saw on Instagram I was in town and called. Turns out he's also headed north—to his family's house in New Hampshire—so we split the cost of a car to drive up together. I'll drop him off and return the rental in Maine."

Atti certainly remembered Peter, another of Elle's boyfriends who never treated her right. He wondered what Oliver would think about this plan. "But…why would you want to see him again?" he whined.

"It was cheaper for his father to rent the car and then for us to split the cost. I'm not made of money, you know."

Atti shook his head and frowned.

"He's all right, Atti. Look, I need all the friends I can get right now. He's nice enough…and he's still cute."

Atti steadied himself. It felt like he was taking punches to both sides of his head and he couldn't focus. How could this be? What about Oliver? What was going on here? "I know what you mean about holding onto friends," he said, "but why Peter Becker?" He wanted to add, "You've got me!"

"Atti, it's not your job to take care of me. I've got to find my way. And, well, there have been some changes, about me and school and especially about Oliver."

"What?" He wanted to close his eyes tight and wait for this. Another punch and he'd be reeling.

"You know what?" she said. "We're about done here. Let's take off. We can walk over to the park, go up to the obelisk. Remember when we used to call that spot 'Heliopolis?'"

He forced a laugh. "Just you, me and Thutmose the Great."

Elle led Atti into the park just south of the Met, and they walked up the mostly hidden knoll to Cleopatra's Needle. They had the small plaza around the obelisk to themselves and settled on a bench. A cool breeze stirred the trees. In the top branches a squirrel did a highwire act.

"You don't have to tell me if you don't want," Atti said when they were seated, "but…."

"You want to know about Oliver."

He tilted his head with a closed-lip smile.

"I guess you're entitled. But I don't want this getting around."

"Understood."

"But first my other news. I transferred to Bowdoin College for my last year. It's in Brunswick, just up the coast from Christmas Cove. They've got a great sustainable development program. That's what I want, not the hard science but the public policy side. And it'll save the cost of travel and help me keep an eye on my brother."

"So that means…?"

"I'm done with Oliver."

"Are you transferring because you broke up?"

"Not really. I mean, he was one reason to stay that doesn't count anymore, but I really feel like it's time to come home, such as it is."

"Look, *I'm* happy about it. I missed you." His emotions were racing. It could only be a good thing she'd be in Maine rather than Scotland, but he was still confused. "But tell me about Braveheart."

She smirked, and then took a deep breath, as if about to settle in for a long story. "Okay. So, you know there were tensions with his family."

He kept his mouth shut.

"To back up, as the days went by your visit really messed with his head. He thought you showed up just to upset the evening. It didn't matter I had no idea you were coming and that I accepted his proposal."

She looked at him as if expecting a comment, but he said nothing.

"Then later I found out he made you take a bus to the airport! And after he had offered to drive you! And he *lied to me* about it! We were on our way into a restaurant a week later when I found out and I just about slugged him right there in the street. I couldn't believe it, after you came all that way to talk to me and we treated you so shabbily. Why didn't you tell me?"

"What was there to say?"

"Anyway, that was only part of it. Ever since seeing you I'd been thinking about our shrinking family and how Martin was teetering. I mentioned something about how I should spend more time with my brother, and that blew his mind. He thought I was talking about transferring schools and couldn't believe I'd even *consider* giving up St. Andrews for some 'provincial' college. Of course, he mostly thought I'd be insane to babysit my derelict brother when I had a chance to join *his* family."

"The one you weren't allowed to meet."

"Exactly." She shot him a look saying to keep quiet and listen.

"I hadn't thought seriously about transferring until that moment—although I had been disappointed with the course selection at St. Andrews—but I resented how he denigrated *all* American schools; he was such a snob. But I wanted to make peace so we wouldn't sit across the dinner table steaming and so I said hopefully Martin would pull himself together on his own. Oliver was still angry, but he wouldn't show it in a restaurant where his family was so *very* well known.

"So we called a truce. He ordered wine—in his worldly way that was starting to feel pretentious. By the time the waiter brought it, we had both just about thawed out but then a woman's voice barked out his name. He sprung to his feet and gave the woman a kiss. It was his mother! She was big and well dressed, and stood in front of a kind-of stooped man in a three-piece suit.

"'This must be Vanessa Thorne,' his mother said. "We know your parents, dear, of course, and are so happy to meet you."

"'Ah, no Mother, Father,' Oliver said, 'this is Elena. She also attends St. Andrews.'

"She eyed me up and down like a side of beef and said, 'And I assume your friend has a last name?'

"I couldn't believe she was talking about me as if I weren't there. 'Elle Forester,' I said, putting out my hand, 'It's so nice to finally meet you, Mrs. MacNash. I've heard so much about you.'

"She ignored my hand. 'Forester,' she said, 'and you are American.' She said this as if it were both a brilliant deduction and an accusation.

"Oliver tried to divert the conversation, but his mother kept her eyes locked on mine. So I said I *was* American—from New York—and in my third year at the university.

"'Perhaps the young people will join us at our table?' Oliver's father put in cautiously.

"'Oh, no…,' Oliver spit out, but his mother interrupted. 'No, Edwin, our table won't seat four, and besides,' she again tried to peer inside me, 'we don't want to disturb this little *tête-à-tête.*'

"Her husband shrugged like he was used to taking orders. Oliver was relieved. The old lady started to turn, and then something snapped inside me. I thought of how the world used to bow down to our family for no reason other than our dads were rich. How many pompous, overdressed women had I seen kowtow to my father? Then I pictured Pandion with the flowers and birds and the sea and thought no drafty castle could hold a candle to where I grew up. And I saw you in our Secret Garden in the cellar when you were so funny showing Q and me how to taste my dad's wine, and then saw you sleeping in the airport while my fiancé laughed about it in a pub.

"'Oh, you aren't interrupting at all,' I said, probably sounding sarcastic. 'We'd love to join you. I'm sure we can find a table for four.'

"That was the moment. She exhaled hard. Oliver tried to hide. I thought I caught veiled amusement in his father's eye, but his mother said, 'No, my dear. Perhaps we will have an opportunity to see you some *other more convenient* time.' She spun on her heel—nimbly for such a formidable lady—and led her husband away."

Atti was trying hard not to laugh…or sing out. He could see the old battle axe meeting her match. "So, what happened?"

"Well, I never got to sample the 'finest *foie gras* in Scotland.' Then on the sidewalk Oliver yelled, 'Why did you push her? She's my *mother!*'"

"'That was clear,' I said, feeling my blood about to boil. 'And who's Vanessa?' I had heard that name before and suspected she was some girl from his own world who still visited the world where he wanted to marry me.

"'She's just someone I dated,' he said.

"'Dated, as in the past?' I asked.

"He shouted, 'That's not the point!'

"'You're so right,' I said, suddenly calm because I realized I didn't care anymore. 'The point is family will never mean the same for you and me. So let's quit pretending. I'm sure Vanessa will get on swimmingly with Mommy.' I wanted to tell him he was not only a liar and a momma's boy but also a coward. But instead I just walked away."

Atti felt a rush of blood to his head. The clouds had parted and sunshine streamed in. There was a fanfare from the horn section. Fireworks burst in the sky. But he tried to stay calm. "How did he react?"

"He shouted that no one walked out on *him*, and no girl could talk to him that way, and I was becoming 'hysterical.' He was the one shouting but he called *me* hysterical. Hysterical! It was more than I could take. I hit him with a few unladylike Americanisms that left him speechless. It was the last time I saw him."

Atti wanted to hug her off her feet, but instead he said, "I'm sorry it didn't work out. I know you hoped for much more."

She smirked. "You know I always pick the worst of the bunch."

Atti tried to suppress a smile and look sympathetic. It was true she had latched on to some deadbeats through the years. He wondered if that had to do with losing her mother so young or possibly her miserable male role models. He wished she'd let him show her another kind of man, someone who could be responsible and care for her. But now that she was free she was back to Peter Becker? That made him feel ill.

"So what about it?" he said, unable to keep the frustration out of his voice. This was starting to feel masochistic, but he couldn't help himself. Letting her drive off with Becker would be surrendering the field without a fight. "I've got the time off. I want to see Gabriel anyway. I wouldn't interfere with you and Peter."

"Atti," she said, losing patience. "Peter and I are *not* together. He's just an old friend and it happened to work out we could share a car. I don't know why you're acting all hurt."

Atti reminded himself he had to support Elle, be there for her and not pressure her. She was probably still processing that they weren't cousins. And maybe she'd never get past thinking of him that way. But there was hope, wasn't there? If so, his presence might keep anything from happening between Elle and Peter...and he'd still have time with her after they dropped him off. "No, it's fine," he said finally, "*if* you have room for me and Ghost. I don't want to leave him here."

"You're sweet, Atti," she said and hugged his arm. "We can certainly fit you and your old dog." She paused. "So, hey, why don't we go out to dinner tonight? Peter said something about a new place in Chelsea. You could ask Jordan."

"Jordan?" he said, confused. "Why do you think…?"

Elle's phone buzzed. She shrugged in apology and picked it up. She got up and talked as she walked down a path back toward the apartment house.

Chapter Twenty-five

Atti passed on joining Elle and Peter for dinner and spent the evening wondering what she had meant about inviting Jordan. She never used to be enigmatic. Now she seemed like her old self one minute and a complete stranger the next, speaking in riddles.

In the morning Elle and Peter took a bus to LaGuardia Airport to pick up the rental car. Atti met them at her apartment.

"Good to see you again, Forester," Peter said, stepping out of the passenger seat and extending his hand. Atti had forgotten how big he was. Peter grinned when he turned to Ghost. "And this is the famous dog," he said, reaching down to pet him. Ghost didn't seem to mind, but he wasn't always so discerning with people willing to scratch his head.

"Right," Atti said, feeling Peter squeeze harder than was appropriate. It seemed Elle's old boyfriend was staking a renewed claim, or else he was just still an ass. Atti smiled derisively.

"Something funny?" Peter said.

"Not at all." Atti realized how much the last six months had forced him to grow up, while Peter hadn't changed at all. He was still the pompous center midfielder from high school who never deserved Elle.

"You want to drive?" Peter asked Elle.

"Yeah, I'll start out. Someone can take over in a couple of hours."

"So Forester," he said, "the back seat's a little cozy so I'm going to call shotgun. Hope you don't mind; it'll be much easier on the legs." He actually gestured at his two long legs with a pompous grin. This was going to be a fun trip.

By the time they left Manhattan, Ghost had settled in for a nap, and Atti had tired of straining to hear the conversation from the front seat. He plugged in ear buds, cranked up his music and stared out the window. In time the cityscape turned to dense woods lining the thruway. He thought of how his apprehension grew as he had watched the Scottish countryside from the bus to St. Andrews. A lot had happened since then, a lot of good things, but the knot in his stomach now was just as tangled. Elle was back—on this side of the ocean, at least—and Oliver was out of the picture, but it took her no more than the blink of an eye to attract a loser from her past.

As they headed north past Hartford, Elle directed a comment to Atti. He took out his earbuds and asked her to repeat herself.

"It's nothing, I just thought it strange…that blue car behind us…I think it's the same one I saw near Bridgeport."

"Everyone's headed up to God's country," Peter said with a smile.

Elle didn't smile and neither did Atti. He looked furtively through the back window. A blue sedan was two cars back but he couldn't make out the driver. He cursed his lack of attention to whether they might be followed.

"You know, we should probably take a break for Ghost," Atti said, thinking a stop would make clear if the blue car was trailing them without making a fuss or letting Peter know what he and Elle feared.

Elle pulled into the next rest stop. Peter hurried inside while Elle and Atti lingered at the car watching the off ramp. After a minute, they hadn't seen the blue car, and they both relaxed.

"Just a coincidence," Atti said. "Maybe Peter was right: everyone is headed north today."

Elle sighed. "It's terrible we have to be on our guard like this. I'd hate to think we might lead Crane up to Christmas Cove."

Atti was pensive. He didn't point out Crane had no need to follow them to suspect they were headed to Maine. There was no use upsetting Elle further, though he was reassured she was keeping her eyes open.

"So you caught up on your sleep?" she said brightly.

"I didn't sleep. I plugged in to avoid hearing Peter's stories about Peter."

"You really don't like him, do you?"

Atti didn't care about Peter but he loved Elle. Why couldn't she see that? Why were they wasting what could have been a magical trip together by bringing along that toad?

She kept looking at him, obviously expecting an answer. He had no grounds to object. At least he got a ride and they'd both be in Christmas Cove. Maybe after they dropped Peter they could start over. Pouting would only put her off. "It's all good," he said. "I guess I kind of looked forward to driving with just the two of us."

Her smile started curious and turned affectionate. But then she turned on her heel to go find the ladies' room. Atti walked Ghost and then also used the restroom. He soon found himself back at the car, where Peter announced he would take over driving.

"Why don't you two men take the front," Elle said. "I'm ready to join Ghost for a nap."

Atti reluctantly took his place beside Peter. The seat was more comfortable than the back but left him where he couldn't avoid hearing about Peter's college, his fraternity and his summer internship. Atti wished they had stocked the glove compartment with carsick bags.

New Hampshire's Atlantic coast is barely thirteen miles long, but this was enough space for the Becker family to build a beach house. The detour off Route 95 was brief in terms of actual minutes, but to Atti it passed like hours.

Fortunately, Elle declined the invitation to stop for lunch and the only lasting pain from the drop-off was seeing Peter kiss Elle goodbye, winking at Atti over her shoulder.

Atti then took the wheel. He focused on the road and erasing Peter from his mind while Elle navigated, played music from her phone and reached back to pet Ghost, who had perked up for the last stretch.

As the miles passed, they shared memories of Pandion and she talked about her plans to study responsible development. Then she brought up her concern about Martin.

"You know," he said, "he must have the same kind of 529 plan as you, which means he could have his room and board paid for another couple of years, assuming he can manage to stay enrolled somewhere."

She cocked her head. "Hey, you really *are* an idea man."

"You're lucky your mom set up those accounts."

"I'm so grateful. She appreciated the money from the company—like the rest of us—but she never quite trusted it. I think her Midwest upbringing taught her to enjoy the harvest but prepare for times of drought."

There was much of her real mother in Elle, a pragmatism she never lost in the best of times and sustained her now in the worst. Atti looked over. Her smile filled the car. He was so totally in love.

"And so, what about you and school?" she said cautiously.

"Well, yeah," he said, recovering. "When things ever settle down, I'll get back to college. First, I have to earn a living and find a way to pay for it. And this whole mess: we need to put a stop to it. I don't think I could focus on school until Crane is locked up. Then maybe I could look at schools up here…like the University of Maine?"

She turned to him. Her eyes reflected the blue sky. "You know," he burst out, "I've got to say something."

She raised her eyebrows.

"Why did you bring Peter? I'm really kind of upset you didn't want to spend the time with me."

"With you? Atti, that's not fair. I came home to find you involved with a woman. I'm happy for you. Really, I am. But I need to keep an even keel here and not lose the few friends I have."

"*What* other woman?"

"You and Jordan. I heard you."

Atti unconsciously braked, making them both lurch against their seatbelts. He recovered and tried to understand.

"She's nice," Elle said, "smart and very attractive."

"I'm confused. What do you mean you *know* about us? What makes you think there's something between me and Jordan?"

"Look, I don't know how it happened. I never meant to eavesdrop. But I heard you two. I don't know how but I heard you."

"Heard me? Wait, where were you?"

"In that entry room, at your launch party."

"You were in the rotunda and heard us in the library! Damn. But no, Elle, Jordan and I: we were only messing around. I like her fine. And you're right, she's attractive and smart, but we're not together, never have been. I couldn't…not after I f–f–found out…." He was embarrassed at stuttering for the first time in months. He clenched his teeth and gripped the steering wheel hard.

"I see," she said, her smile turning thoughtful.

They reached South Bristol in the early afternoon. Atti dropped Elle and the boxes they were moving at Martin's apartment in the village and took the car to Pandion. Gabriel was gone, along with his Jeep, so Atti let himself in.

An hour later Elle called. "Believe it or not," she said, "Martin gave up his bed for me and is sleeping on the couch."

"This is *Martin Forester* we're talking about?"

"I know. Incredible, right?"

"This might be the first time he and I have ever been able to talk," she said, sounding hopeful. "I mean really talk. I told him I'd stay a few days and help fix up the place."

"That's great, Elle. I'll be at the gatehouse until Monday and am ready to help any way I can.

"Right, back to the grindstone, young man. And, of course, you will have to give me my car back so I can drive you to the airport; just tell me the time."

"Thanks," he said and added seriously. "And Elle, please keep your eyes open and remember Crane could be in the village."

When the afternoon wore on and Gabriel still hadn't returned, Atti drove into the village to see Father Giacomo. He was about finished with a mass, and Atti slid into the back pew. He contemplated praying a prayer, but that would be insincere. He was there for counsel—and a friend—not prayer to an impervious God.

When mass was done, the priest smiled and walked up the aisle. "We haven't seen you in church for some time, Atti, but you know I've been praying for you."

"I know, Father, and I need it."

The priest looked at him with the unsettling perception Atti had so often seen in the past. "I think," Father Giacomo said, "we should have a cup of coffee. Come over to the rectory."

Ghost had waited outside the church. When Atti stepped out, he whistled and the dog trotted around the corner. They all walked next door to a two-story house where the priest and his acolyte lived and kept a simple office. Father Giacomo set out a bowl of water for the dog and then made coffee while he passed village gossip through the doorway.

Atti laughed at the stories from a shaky chair in the dining room. He looked around at the tired furniture and thought how the priest denied himself so much.

"How are things at the church?" Atti called out.

"With the Lord's help, we get by. In a rainstorm last Sunday, we sprung a new leak in the middle of my sermon. We had to pause the service to move the lectern three feet to the left." He laughed "We had drip-in-the-pail percussion accompaniment to the word of God."

Atti thought about the endless repairs to the roof, the plumbing and *Organo*, and how his father's fraud had made things worse. Could he help? He still had the Cell Block check, but that was his start to getting back on his feet.

Finally seated at the wooden dining table, the priest said, "So, Atti, the reason for this visit?"

"What do you mean?"

"You did not come by for just a quick hello."

Atti wondered how Father Giacomo could always see through him. "Well, since you mentioned it," he said, "I had a conversation with Gabriel." He paused to gauge the priest's reaction but saw nothing. This man's a pro, he thought, and plunged on. "He told me he's my father."

Father Giacomo nodded. "I had hoped you two would have this talk."

"Gabriel said he thought you knew all along."

"Let's just say I heard your mother's confession for many years and also tried to help her through the dark times."

"Did she confess to an affair?"

"That I cannot say."

"Well, obviously she did, but what did *you* say about it?"

"As a minister of the Church, I counsel respect for the sacrament of marriage...."

"But...?"

"But as a bridge-builder between God and humanity, my love and respect for your mother left me deeply concerned. I couldn't help but see how Gabriel brought life into her tired eyes, along with hope and that joy in her that bedazzled us all. And when *you* were born, I had no doubt. Really, anyone paying attention would have seen. Marie loved you like a gift from God, something pure, beyond Hugo's money and, as it turned out, his greed. I counseled your mother to try to make the marriage work but also to take great care in whatever she did. Perhaps I was complicit, and this was my failure as a priest."

"You know, Father, you and Gabriel were two constants in my life, two bulkheads I could always tie on to. I hate the thought of my mother cheating on my dad, but maybe I just don't understand it, maybe she did what she had to do. And what does it matter now anyway?"

"Well, it matters a great deal to you and your father."

Atti took this in but had nothing to say.

He drove the short way to Pandion still not sure he could forgive his father or whether he even had a right to judge. Gabriel was in the yard when he and Ghost pulled up at the gatehouse. Let out of the backseat, Ghost ran for him, barking out his joy.

Atti followed the dog and without a word grabbed hold of his father and hugged, in more of a boxer's clinch than a friendly greeting.

He hadn't planned this. Gabriel and he had always been close, but they kept a physical distance, maybe because Gabriel was a retainer or just because that was the northern way. And then the revelation about the affair overturned Atti's lifelong admiration for him. But holding this big man against him felt right to Atti, and Gabriel gave in to it as well. After a moment they both looked at the dog, who watched curiously.

"He thinks he's the only one to get hugs around here," Gabriel laughed.

Atti smiled. "Not anymore."

Gabriel grilled salmon while Atti made a salad, and they enjoyed a quiet dinner. They talked about the village and Atti's work. "I hate leaving tomorrow," he said, "but I've got to get back."

"The job is busy?"

"Yeah, we're in a crunch, about to launch this product. Lloyd has been really tolerant in giving me time, for Ted's funeral and to fly off to Scotland, and then this week to help Elle pack and drive up here, but his patience has run out. Are you sure it's not a problem to leave Ghost with you?"

"Less than not a problem, it's a gift. That critter and I have an understanding. And he'll keep me company on the drive down to see you in New York."

"I've warned you: you won't be impressed with the accommodations."

"Atticus, I know what you've been through and yet you're so young still. I'm proud of how you've made your way. The police will catch this criminal. And for the rest, I'm going to help every way I can. And don't you worry about Elle, either. Now that the truth is out, things will fall into place; I'm sure of it."

"I wish I had your confidence, but I can't offer her anything unless I at least keep my job, so I guess that's it. I fly out of Portland at eight. Elle will drive me to the airport, so we'll have time to talk. It's funny. Our whole lives, when she was just my cousin, I could read her like a book, no secrets, no ambiguity. But now I have no idea what she's thinking or what she'll do next."

"Sounds like things are progressing," Gabriel said with a grin.

Atti smiled, a little embarrassed, but then became serious. "But she's also headstrong and I worry she won't be careful enough."

"Crane?" Gabriel said, frowning.

Atti nodded. "In New York I had a call from him. None of us will be safe until he's back in prison."

In the darkest part of the night, the telephone rang. Atti reached for his phone but saw his battery was dead. Ghost was pawing at the bedroom door. Gabriel's muffled voice came through the wall. Then Gabriel burst through the door. "It's Martin!" he said. "Get dressed. I'll meet you downstairs."

Atti stumbled out of bed, pulled on his pants, grabbed his shoes and hurried down the stairs. He heard the Jeep start up in the garage. He closed the dog in the house and hurried out to the driveway, one shoe still in his hand. The Jeep stopped and he jumped in. Gabriel threw up gravel accelerating through the gate.

"Who called?" Atti said. "Was it Elle?"

"No, it was nurse at Miles Memorial. She said he was taken in by ambulance."

Atti was out of the Jeep the moment it stopped at the hospital. The two of them jogged into the emergency room. They didn't see Elle so Atti assumed she was with Martin.

A doctor stepped into the waiting room. "Gabriel," he said, extending his hand. "I assume you're here for Martin Forester?"

"That's right, Joe," Gabriel said. "Atticus, this is Doctor Humbold. Joe, this is Atticus Forester."

"How is he, doctor?" Atti said. "Do you know what happened?"

"We're not permitted to give out medical information without express approval of the patient," the doctor said, "but I can tell you he is stable for the moment."

Atti was frustrated. "Can we at least talk with his sister?"

"She's not here as far as I know. The only one who's been in is a detective. I believe he's still in the building."

Detective Horace then came down the hallway. He joined them as the doctor excused himself.

"Do you know what happened?" Atti asked Horace.

"Let's step aside here for a minute," Horace said. He led them to an empty room and spoke confidentially. "First, we know Martin has been struggling with addiction…and I understand he had been making progress. But someone approached him last night with a deal. He said he fought the urge but gave in, thinking he could keep the drug for 'special occasions.'" He paused. "Well, he decided to sample his purchase in the sacristy at St. Bernard's—apparently Father Giacomo had given him a key."

"Were the drugs bad?" Atti asked.

"Bad," Horace said, "or too good. Martin knew base cocaine, but this lot was laced with fentanyl. Smoking laced crack cocaine—particularly after staying clean for several months—almost made Martin's heart stop. Luckily, the acolyte heard noise in the church around one this morning and found him unconscious."

"Who'd sell that kind of poison?"

"Someone who didn't care what damage it caused, or *intended* to kill."

Atti went pale. Gabriel said, "Did the doctors say anything about Martin's condition? All they'd tell us was he's stable."

"He arrived unconscious but they think they gave him naloxone in time. They expect him to recover in a few days. The long-range prognosis, I would say, depends on his own choices."

Atti was incensed. "That devil!" he growled.

"Aye," Gabriel said, "it could be Crane but…"

"But it could be a dealer," Horace said. "We've had plenty of trouble with that sort around here."

Atti wasn't buying this could be a coincidence, that Martin was poisoned by the local cocaine dealer. No, this was Crane; he was sure of it. It was clear he was after the whole family and…" He stopped and suddenly panicked. Elle! Where was she?

"Have you seen my cousin?" he asked urgently. "We were sure she'd be here. She was staying with Martin."

"I haven't seen her."

"Oh, my God," Atti said, mostly to himself. He called Elle but her phone went to voicemail. He looked at Horace and Gabriel and shook his head.

Horace immediately sent a patrol car to Martin's house, and Gabriel sped off to follow. Atti said he'd stay at the hospital in case she showed up.

An hour later, Martin had stabilized and was sleeping, but Elle was missing. The patrol car and Gabriel had returned with no news. The taxi company reported Elle had called for a car at two in the morning but wasn't there when it arrived.

Chapter
Twenty-six

Detective Horace put out a bulletin that Elle was missing and presumed kidnapped by Lazlo Crane. Gabriel and Atti spent the night driving in and around the village, hoping against the odds to see some sign of them.

By morning they were exhausted and frustrated. Gabriel convinced Atti they needed to regroup, so they returned to the gatehouse, where Gabriel cooked breakfast and Atti checked his phone. Atti had texted Q about Martin when they first got to the hospital. Q responded, asking for news, but Atti couldn't bring himself to reply, not until they had a plan.

There was also an email from an unknown sender titled "Sins of the Father." Atti walked up to the guest room and sat on the bed to read:

Plutus-became-Icarus too close to the sun
And Dionysus drowned in wine
But the sins of the fathers leave redress undone
And the debt to their breed intertwines

Narcissus inconsequent
To her image succumbs
The lotus-eater imbibes,
His verity benumbed

Now Eros-become-Hermes
Guides the hunt, but she'll
Only draw savior Zelos
To doom all with his zeal

Mind, last of the line,
Don't share, Come alone!
Bring on Astynomia
And lose sweet Eros to the loam

The email had to have come from Crane, given the Greek gibberish, and it must hold a key to what happened to Elle. The end sounded like a threat. And if Atti was "the last of the line," the last of the Foresters, did that mean Elle was Eros and was she dead? Why then the message? And what about "Come alone"? Come where? Where would he even start? The one word he looked up on his phone was "Astynomia," which was the Greek police, so it was clear the message said Atti shouldn't share this with Detective Horace.

"Breakfast is on!" Gabriel called from downstairs. Atti pocketed the phone and tensed. Could he do what the email said and not share the message, even with Gabriel, and go after Elle on his own?

He went downstairs. They ate silently until Gabriel said, "Chin up, Atticus. We have to believe she's alive and well, that Crane intends something other than to hurt her. And how far can he have gone with the police everywhere?"

Atti looked down at his plate. The warning said to act alone, not to share, but that was hopeless. Gabriel had friends—he knew everyone—and maybe someone could help. Atti *needed* help.

"I got a message," he blurted out.

"What do you mean, a 'message'?"

"An email on my phone a few minutes ago. It says I have to act on my own if I want to save Elle, but I can't even understand it."

"Can I see it?"

Atti handed over his phone. Gabriel read with growing bewilderment and anger. "That blackguard is deranged. But this gives us hope. He's playing with us, which says he's still holding Elle. You've got to share this with the police."

"No!" Atti almost shouted. "He's watching. He's been watching all along. He'll know if we tell Horace; I'm sure of it."

"What else can we do?"

"You must know people, friends we can trust?"

"But if a lot of people start poking around, won't Crane know that too?"

"Damn, you're right." He paused. "But I know someone who can help."

By not showing up for work that day, Atti had effectively left Lloyd's employment. But he had such a good excuse he was sure his boss would understand and cut him some slack. Even if he didn't, he might be the *only* one who could make sense of Crane's message. The police would be no good and telling them was exactly what Crane warned him *not* to do.

"Lloyd, it's Atti," he said when he got through on the phone.

"Telling me you're on your way in?"

"No. Something terrible happened. Elle was taken!" Atti filled Lloyd in about Martin's overdose and Elle's disappearance, and then described Crane's email.

"You got a message from the kidnapper," Lloyd said, "and haven't told the police?"

"It says I have to act alone. He says specifically I should *not* tell the cops."

"But you can't handle this yourself!"

"Lloyd, I can. I just…look, will you help me or not?"

"Atti, I know you're frantic about Elle but you need law enforcement to apprehend this man. I won't encourage you to act irresponsibly and get yourself hurt."

"Thanks, Lloyd. Thanks for nothing," Atti spit out and hung up.

Gabriel looked over, concerned.

"I was sure my boss would help," Atti said, "since he's the one person I know who would understand the message. But he refused."

"So what now? We call Detective Horace?"

Atti buried his face in his hands and then looked up. "No, wait. There's one other person."

Q answered the phone. "S'up, dude?"

"Trouble," Atti said. "Crane took Elle...."

"Damn! I'm on my way!"

"No, no, listen. He sent a riddle. It says I shouldn't tell anyone, but I need help with it."

"Anything, dude."

"I'll forward it. It's all Greek god stuff, so you...."

"Take it to Lloyd."

"I tried. I got fired for not coming in today and Lloyd says I have to go to the cops, but I just can't. The message says. You'll understand when you see it.

"Okay, send it on. I'll get right back."

Atti hung up and forwarded the email. Gabriel rose, cleared the dishes from the table and unlocked the gun case mounted on the wall. He removed a shotgun, loaded it and pocketed several shells.

"Have you got a gun for me?" Atti said.

Gabriel turned, biting his lip. "I'm not giving you a gun, Atticus," he said. "I saw you at the traps and skeet and, frankly, you'd as likely shoot yourself as anything else."

"What the hell?" Atti erupted. "What if I find him?"

"If *we* find him, you'll leave the guns to me. Let's hope we can keep everyone safe without any shooting."

Atti stewed over Gabriel's lack of trust; he had thought his true father would have faith in him. But he forced himself to put that aside and focus on the message. He was still fidgeting and feeling helpless when Q called back. Atti put the call on speaker.

"Here's what I've got," Q said. "There's a lot; you might want to write it down." He paused. "To start, think about what we already knew. "'Ithaca' on the painting frame. I don't know how we missed this, but Ithaca is where Odysseus was left on the beach after twenty years at the Trojan wars. Crane thinks he's Odysseus, washed up on the beach and fighting gods and enemies all around!"

"And he taught Greek literature."

"Right, and needs to show us he's smarter than we are. The ring he left as a warning was in the design of a 'Greek eye.' The customer who set you up was "Act-less," which sounds like 'Achlys,' the goddess of poison and death. The Dionysus bag? Dionysus was the Greek version of Bacchus, god of a good time, which was perfect for sending a bat to Ted's trophy wife."

Atti pondered this. "And there was the postcard with the constellations."

"Right, which Lloyd already explained was a threat against you and Ghost."

"But what about the email?"

"Okay, so Plutus was the Greek god of wealth, which fits with Hugo, and then "becomes Icarus and flies too close to the sun" could be him piloting his own plane, where the bomb got him. Next line is about Dionysus again, the god of wine or your uncle. And the third line says Crane is not satisfied killing your father and your uncle but is out for the whole family. Next, Jillian was booby-trapped by a luxury handbag because she's Narcissus—lost in her own reflection. And then the lotus eaters; they were people addicted to a narcotic that lulled them to live their lives in a daze. I don't know how that makes sense, although 'verity' means truth or, I guess in this case, reality."

"It's Martin! He overdosed last night on coke laced with fentanyl. The cops think it was Crane."

"Holy crap, dude. It's a war zone up there."

"What about Eros-become-Hermes, and Zelos? Is that Elle and me?"

"Anybody who's seen her," Q said, "knows Elle is Eros, the goddess of attraction. But she transforms into Hermes, who is—let me get this straight—the god of trade, thieves, travelers, athletes and border crossings, and also a guide to the Underworld. This gets me nowhere. Hopefully, it doesn't mean Crane smuggled Elle into Canada."

"How could he do that?" Atti said.

"How has he done any of this? Anyway, next is Zelos, the god of jealousy and zeal. You must realize we *all* know how you feel about Elle."

"I have no secrets anymore," Atti said resignedly.

"So you're Zelos, and with Elle engaged to someone else…"

"Yeah," Atti interrupted, "there have been some changes there."

"What? What changes?"

"Later. I'll explain it all later, but assume Crane doesn't know about it either. So if I'm Zelos…."

"Crane is warning that you trying to rescue Elle will bring disaster, which is I guess what he means by losing her to the "loam," which is clay or the soil. And the warning at the end, like you said, is not to tell anyone else, particularly the police."

"Right…'Astynomia'; I looked that up. But other than telling Gabriel and asking you about the note, I have no idea where to go or what to do."

"We have to think. The key is in the line about Hermes guides the hunt. Something must point the way."

Atti said, "Thanks for all this. It's amazing how fast you were. We'll check whether the cops have anything new. Then I'll call back."

Atti didn't need to call the police because as he hung up Detective Horace arrived at the gatehouse with a Detective Orlansky.

Horace introduced his colleague, and said, "We wanted to fill you in. We've put out a notice throughout Maine and New Hampshire and at all the airports and train stations. I spoke with Detective Lawrence in New York, who's spreading the word there. We believe Crane rented a car in Portland on at least two occasions in the last year, but paid cash and returned the cars on time. What we don't know is how he's getting around now. Assuming he's got the funds, he may simply have bought a vehicle. In any case, given the incident with the cameras three years back, we're guessing his surveillance of the property has been extensive and long-term. There was no useful information from the local hotels or inns, but he's got to be holding Elle somewhere. I trust you haven't heard anything more from him?"

Atti looked at Gabriel, whose expression gave nothing away. When it mattered more to Atti than anything in life, his father was leaving it to him to decide whether to divulge the email.

He would just have to chance that Crane was bluffing and couldn't know if Atti shared the message. "We've got something to show you," he said, pulling out his phone.

Atti forwarded the email to Horace and then passed along Q's analysis. The detectives assured him they'd keep the message to them-selves but would give its meaning their full attention. As they drove off, Atti still worried Crane might have bugged his phone, but he had already forwarded the message to Q and needed to do something. He couldn't live with himself if Elle was hurt while he sat on his hands.

The afternoon wore into evening. Gabriel made calls to friends along the coast, but there was so little to go on. On top of that, a nor'easter was bearing down and everyone was preparing for the storm.

Gabriel and Atti sat before a dinner they hardly touched, reading the email out loud to each other, racking their brains. Ghost suddenly sprang to his feet and barked, and then they heard a car pull up. They opened the door to find Q, wet hair hanging down his face and a knapsack over his shoulder. He started to speak but Atti pulled him inside and hugged him, almost in tears. It took the worst of times to recognize a true friend.

Ghost forced them apart and jumped up on their visitor. Q's som-ber expression broke into a smile as he tussled with the dog.

Gabriel warmed some food for Q, and they talked late into the night trying to make sense of the message, especially the line about Elle. Atti went over again all he could remember of his uncle's story about Back Bay and the recounted each time Crane had disrupted their lives. The email still didn't give them any clue to where Crane was holding Elle.

In the morning the wind and rain picked up. Gabriel nonetheless drove down the coast to ask friends to put out the word.

Q sat with a cup of coffee, diagraming the email. "If Eros means Elle," he said haltingly, "then why does she become Hermes?"

"And how does she 'guide the hunt'?" Atti rejoined.

"But wait!" Q said. "Hermes was a guide to the Underworld. So what's the 'Underworld'?"

"Hell, of course, where that psycho wants to see us all."

"But no, not the Greek Hades; what could you call an 'Underworld' here?"

"Why here?"

"We have to start somewhere. Anyway, it sounds like he wants to meet you face-to-face, so he must be near."

"Good point." Atti pondered this. "So what about the cave?"

"The cave?"

"Yeah, where Hugo and Ted had their clubhouse, where they buried the loot. And that's right by Back Bay!"

"Would Crane know about that?"

"He seems to know more than he should. But yeah, that's got to be it. He could hold her there and no one would know!"

"We've got to go!" Q barked.

"Right. Damn it, I wish Gabriel were here."

Q was pulling on his boots. "Should we call the cops?"

"Yeah, we'll call on the way."

Atti had watched Gabriel hide the key to the gun locker and quickly retrieved it. He pulled out a double barrel shotgun and a handful of shells. Q grabbed a flashlight, and they each put on a slicker. They shut Ghost in the house and ran out into the sheets of rain sweeping in from the sea.

"You drive," Atti said. "I'll call."

They sped in Q's car through the gates and hurried along the road to the village, their windshield-wipers straining to keep up with the deluge. Atti reached Detective Horace. "We think the 'Underworld' in the message is a cave out past Back Bay. We're headed there now."

"Atti, hold up. You shouldn't be out in this storm, especially on the coast road."

"We can't wait! We'll see you there!" He hung up and held tight as Q sped through the village, dodged a fallen tree and careened onto the coast road. The torrent coated the windows, obscuring any view of the ocean.

After a few frightening curves in the road, Q started to pull over above the cliff at Back Bay. But Atti shouted, "Not here! Drive to the end!"

Q spun the wheel back onto the road but ran through a large puddle. Water splashed over the windshield and blinded them. Q missed the turn onto the road and drove onto a dune. He put the car in reverse and hit the gas, but the wheels spun.

"Damn it!" Atti yelled. "Come on!" He jumped out of the car. Q flipped on his warning lights and followed.

Rain whipped their faces as they jogged up the road. Atti led the way down a path into the scrub, which turned toward the sea. Around a large boulder, Atti turned and sidled along the cliff face to where they could climb up to the cave. Holding the gun in one hand, he climbed with the other and soon reached the outcropping hiding the cave entrance. He stopped with his back against the cliff and the wind in his face to load the gun, hoping it would still work even though it was soaked. Q caught up. He had armed himself with a branch and looked ready for a fight.

Atti called into the wind, "Watch your step but don't turn on the light until we get to the opening. He won't hear us coming. Flip it on inside, and I'll have the gun on him."

"Don't shoot Elle!"

Atti scoffed at this but girded himself to take extra care.

They got up the last few steps and burst into the cave. Q flipped on his flashlight, and Atti held the gun to his shoulder.

But there was no one there.

Atti lowered the gun and grabbed the flashlight. He stepped farther into the cave, shining the light into all the corners.

"Damn it!" Atti growled, handing the light back to Q.

"It was worth a try," Q said in both sympathy and growing frustration.

Back at the road they saw the flashing lights of Detective Horace's Jeep.

"No one there," Atti shouted.

"But I see you buried your car," Horace replied. "I told you not to go out in this storm."

"We had to try," Atti said.

Horace called for a tow truck as he drove Atti and Q to the gate-house. He dropped them at the door and returned to the village. Inside, Ghost jumped up on Atti, almost frantic at being locked up with so much going on outside. Q collapsed on a chair. Atti was exhausted but couldn't sit. His heart was still racing.

Gabriel returned shortly. He was angry when he saw the shotgun on the table. "I told you to leave that to me," he said firmly.

"I know, Gabriel. I'm sorry." Atti was almost in tears, not so much from disappointing his father as from feeling helpless about Elle. Atti pulled the shells from his pocket and laid them on the table.

Gabriel still stood, dripping on the floor. "Where did you two go?" he demanded.

"Out to the cave. We thought *that* was the 'Underworld.'"

"You drove the coast road in this storm? Are you crazy?"

"We had to do something!" Atti paused. "I'm really sorry about taking the gun."

"No matter," Gabriel said, back to his controlled, determined tone as he removed his hat and shook off the water. "We've only one task now. Nothing else matters."

"Wait…," Q said, his eyes suddenly wide.

They both turned to him.

"The Underworld!" he said. "We thought Crane would take his revenge at Back Bay because it was close to the Forester property, but what "underworld" is even closer, right here at Pandion?"

They looked at him urgently. "Just say it!" Atti pleaded.

"The Secret Garden," Q said.

"Holy shit," Atti shouted, "the wine cellar!"

Gabriel's face flashed recognition and then resolve. "Atti, grab a flashlight and bring Ghost; we may need help tracking. Q, you call Horace and get him back here. I'll handle the gun."

Gabriel and Atti jogged up the driveway, Ghost darting silently ahead. Gabriel unlocked the kitchen door and led the way into the Barn. They tried to cross the floor quietly but Ghost sounded like a tap dancer on the wooden floorboards.

Gabriel gestured to keep the dog still. Atti held Ghost's collar. He wondered where the key to the cellar would be since the old clock had probably been sold, but then he remembered Gabriel always had the keys.

It didn't matter because they found the door to the cellar unlocked, and this led Gabriel to hold up. The door creaked on old hinges when he slowly pulled it open. He descended the stone staircase, gun pointed down. Atti waited, holding Ghost.

The light in the cellar went on. "Come down," Gabriel called up, his voice dripping with disappointment.

Atti let go of the dog, who scuttered down the stairs, and then he followed. What he saw was a large doll with blonde hair, stupid blue eyes and unnaturally rosy cheeks. It was propped up on a barrel, and pinned to its gingham dress was a note:

Zelos-become-Sisyphus.
Naught left but to call on Baucis and Philemon.

"Damn him!" Atti shouted. "More fucking riddles?"

Atti almost broke down when he saw around the doll's neck a gold necklace Elle got from her mom and always wore. What if Crane hurt her? He had to find them!

There were confused footprints in the dust. "There are smaller prints here," Gabriel said, "which must be Elle's, and it looks like there was a scuffle, like she was resisting."

That was reassuring. Elle was tough, but the thought of her struggling against that man enraged Atti. When they got back upstairs where his phone worked, he called Q with the newest puzzle. Q said he'd talk to them back at the gatehouse. He added that Horace had called to say the road from the village was blocked by the storm but they were working to clear it.

Atti and Gabriel pushed their way through the storm back to the gatehouse, almost propelled by the wind. In the house they didn't bother removing their slickers. They sat heavily on chairs in the kitchen, dripping on the floor. Atti had tucked the doll under his coat. He took it out and stared at the note, trying to calm his heartbeat.

"Okay, I have to say this," Q said, "everything I told you before came from Lloyd. I guess he mentioned your call to Jordan and she wouldn't leave off until he helped us. But he was pissed off and didn't want me to tell you. I called him again about that last note. He said Zeus punished Sisyphus for cheating death by making him roll a boulder up a hill from Hades forever. And Baucis and Philemon lived somewhere remote where they were the only ones to recognize Zeus and Hermes as travelers."

Q looked up to see if this made sense to them. They stared back.

"The Sisyphus part is easy," Q said. "You cheated Crane when you escaped the drug charge but then went down to the Underworld to find Elle, and now you're doomed to remain there, at least figuratively. But the other part…?"

"I don't know," Gabriel said, "but if Crane was in the cellar just hours ago, he can't have gotten far, not in this weather."

"He's staging the final act at Pandion," Atti said gravely.

"How do you know that?" Gabriel asked.

"It's all about his delusion, his retribution. Pandion belonged to Hugo and Ted, and it's where the family has always been. He wants it to end here."

But how could he be on the compound and still in a remote place?" Gabriel said.

"The property is pretty big," Q said.

"And drenched by a storm," said Gabriel.

"I won't wait," Atti said decisively. He rose and picked up a flashlight.

Gabriel and Q looked at each other and Q nodded.

"Okay," Gabriel declared. "We'll check the grounds. In this blow he'd have to hold Elle in a structure, so we're looking at the cottages and the boathouse, or he could be holed up somewhere in the big house. We'll split up. Atti, you start at The Lookout and work your way up the trail behind Cliff Dweller. Q, you look through the main garage and the shed buildings. I'll check the boathouse and the cove side cottages. Then we'll meet on the porch of the Barn and search the house together."

Atti and Q nodded.

"But if you find Crane," Gabriel said gravely, "do *not* approach him. We have to be smart here. Just head straight for the Barn, and we'll come up with a plan and wait for Horace. Hopefully he'll have cleared the road by then. Understood?" He stared Atti down until he agreed.

Chapter
Twenty-seven

Atti took the beach trail. After two steps he fell down painfully on his side and came up wet to the waist. His hands dripped mud.

Continuing on, he found The Lookout locked. The sea had covered the beach and raged against the rocks on the shoreline. Saltwater sprayed into the wind and mixed with driving rain. He picked up a walking staff lying by the steps in hopes it would keep him upright.

With the wind lashing the shore, he could barely make out the cliff trail. Wet branches slapped his arms and legs. Water dripped down his face and into his slicker. His boots were sodden. As the trail rose along the cliff face, Ghost ran out of sight ahead. Atti leaned hard on the staff, trying not to slip again. It would be a hard wet fall to the shoreline.

The storm echoed Atti's panic. Where was she? Had he sealed her fate by telling the cops? Was he dooming everyone by rushing to find her? He began to doubt the wisdom of walking the cliff trail. He could barely keep his footing, and there was no way Crane could have hauled Elle down here. But he was half-way along so there was no sense turning back. He would come up behind Cliff Dweller and then move to the open lawn and the Barn. It felt like a nightmare.

Ghost came running back to walk the trail ahead of Atti. As glimpses of the cottage came into sight through the trees, he thought he saw a flickering light through a window. Was someone there? His heart leaped. Had he found her? He gripped his staff and pushed on with a tight-lipped smile.

If she was there, then so was Crane, and Gabriel said not to approach him. But he still had to get close enough to see.

Lightning cast the trees and cottage into stark relief. It came at the same instant as thunder, which made him freeze and look around for a tree on fire or falling. Seeing nothing, he pushed on. When the trail turned inland, the wind shoved him from behind. He wished he could call Gabriel to tell him he saw a light, but his father didn't carry a phone.

Reaching the side of the cottage, he peered in a window. The curtains and the rain dripping down his face obscured his view. Still, he could make out a figure that could be Elle seated by an oil lamp. He rubbed water from his eyes and made out a second figure standing.

Could it be his father? Could Gabriel have doubled back and reached the cottage? But then why was Elle sitting? Was she hurt?

Gabriel had said to go to the Barn and get the others, but Atti thought he heard a muffled groan. With a surge of adrenaline he rushed to the front of the cottage, cast aside his staff and threw open the door. Ghost dashed in ahead of him.

The dark shape turned, startled. Atti saw a mangled ear! The deranged fire in Crane's eyes froze him for an instant.

Ghost barked and ran to Elle, struggling against ropes that tied her to a chair! She was trying to yell but something was stuffed in her mouth. Crane kicked the dog. Ghost yelped and fell against the wall in a heap.

Atti stepped forward, yelling, "What the…?"

Crane wheeled on him with a knife. Atti jumped back, pulling a hat rack over between them. Crane lunged. Atti batted at the knife with the flashlight, but a searing pain went up his arm.

Ghost sprang up again, barking and snapping at Crane, who pulled a pistol from his belt. Ghost jumped at him, knocking the gun from his hand. Crane had the knife in his other hand and swung it wildly, at the same time kicking at the dog but missing. He turned and ran out the door.

Atti rushed after him but Crane moved too quickly. Atti stumbled to the clearing. Lightning lit up another dark figure in the distance.

"Gabriel!" he shouted. "Help!"

Thunder shook the ground, drowning out any reply, but Gabriel approached at a run. In another lightning flash, Atti saw Crane disappear down the beach trail.

"Get him!" Atti shouted, shining the flashlight on Crane as he ran into the trees.

Ghost took off as if shot from a bow.

"Where?" Gabriel yelled as he came clearly into view.

Atti pointed the light at the trail. "Ghost is on him!"

Gabriel gave chase. Atti tried to follow but slipped on the mud and fell. The pain in his arm was almost blinding. When he reached to grasp his arm with his other hand, he saw the cottage door bang open and closed. When it opened again, there were flames!

He staggered back to the cottage and through the door. Elle had knocked over her chair and the oil lamp. Curtains were on fire. He pulled open a drawer by the sink but there was no knife!

Elle gagged as if she couldn't breathe. Atti fell to his knees, yanked the rag from her mouth and pulled at the ropes, but they wouldn't budge. He struggled back to his feet, tilted the chair back and dragged it toward the door.

"Hold on!" he tried to shout but smoke choked out his breath.

The flames spread quickly to a bookshelf and pillows on the window seat. Smoke was filling the room. With all his remaining strength, he yanked the chair over the saddle of the doorway and away from the cottage. In a few more steps, he fell backward on the grass, the chair and Elle on top of him.

As carefully as he could, he rolled the chair to the side. Coughing, he labored to his knees. To get at his phone he tore off his slicker and leaned over Elle, shielding them both from the rain as he dialed for help.

"A man with a knife!" he shouted. "He's on the trail!"

"Please slow down, sir. What's your name? Where are you?"

"Atti Forester! South Bristol! Pandion! Tell the cop at the gate! There's a fire! Send an ambulance!"

He dropped the phone and tried again to untie Elle's ropes. She coughed violently. Q came running, fell to his knees and cut the ropes. Q then lowered Elle to the grass and covered her with his coat. Atti crawled to her and lifted her head to rest in his lap, his tears flowing into the rain and salt spray. She looked up with cloudy eyes, losing consciousness.

In another minute flashing lights of the police cruiser came down the driveway, followed by Horace's Jeep. They both stopped on the lawn. Two cops and Horace jumped out of the cars.

"Where is he?" Horace shouted into the wind.

"Gabriel chased him toward the beach," Atti said and pointed before coughing made him double over.

One cop turned the cruiser's floodlight on the trees and Horace ran down a trail. The other cop raced to Elle, strapped an oxygen mask over her face and knelt to check her pulse.

A siren approached from far off. Then a shotgun blast came from the direction of the beach. Soon an ambulance pulled up and two men jumped out.

They lifted Elle onto a stretcher. Atti and Q stood beside it, each holding one of her hands. The driver motioned for them to step aside, and as they lifted her into the ambulance, she opened her eyes and looked at Atti, a universe of longing and thanks blanking out the pain and the storm and the evil.

One of the EMTs paused to put an oxygen mask on Atti and place a large bandage against his arm. "Hold this tight," he said.

"I can do that," Q said, taking hold of the bandage. "Get going. We'll be right behind you."

The ambulance left with its lights flashing. Atti felt dizzy and sat heavily on the ground.

Gabriel came out of the woods into the floodlight, pushing a man before him with his gun. Crane's long hair streamed across his face. He recoiled from the dog, who prowled at his side, growling and snapping.

Horace emerged from another path and hurried to take hold of Crane and handcuff him. One of the cops placed him in the cruiser.

Atti still sat on the lawn, and Ghost ran to him and licked his face.

"Your arm," Gabriel said when he reached them, gesturing with his head. "Come on. We'll get you inside."

Blood trickled from beneath the bandage Atti held against his arm. Relief spread across his face. "You got him," he said to Gabriel.

"*We* got him, Atticus. I only shot over his head after our defender ran him to ground and sunk in his teeth."

Chapter
Twenty-eight

Gabriel and Q helped Atti to the gatehouse. In the light of an oil lamp, they removed the slashed raincoat and Atti's shirt. Gabriel put on a dry bandage and wrapped the arm in gauze. Then he helped Atti into dry clothes.

"Do you think she'll be okay?" Atti said as they drove to the hospital.

"I'm sure of it, Son," said Gabriel, "thanks to you."

Gabriel navigated fallen trees and downed power lines. The hospital staff were waiting when they arrived. Thankfully, they had backup generators. A nurse treated Atti right away, telling him Elle had arrived and was stable. She cleaned and disinfected the wound and gave him a tetanus shot, and then a doctor sutured the arm. After he was bandaged, the nurse placed a sling around his shoulder.

"That's just to keep your arm in place for a few days and let the healing begin," the doctor said, "mostly to remind you you've been injured and should take it easy."

When Atti came out to the waiting room, Gabriel and Q were speaking with another doctor. "Ah," Gabriel said. "Doctor Hazelback, this is Atticus Forester, your patient's cousin."

Atti looked at Gabriel curiously but sensed he shouldn't correct him.

"Good to meet you, Atticus," the doctor said. "I was sorry to hear about your uncle, well, and all your family troubles. Actually, we've met before. I've made a few visits to Pandion in my time."

Atti didn't recognize the doctor but held out his left hand to shake.

"Seems every year there are new rules about patient privacy," the doctor said. "But Gabriel tells me you're the only living relative of Ms. Forester and her brother, who's also in our care, so I'm making an exception."

"Thank you, Doctor," Atti said, now understanding the continued ruse. "So, is she okay? Can I see her?"

"Ms. Forester has been sedated and should sleep through the night. She suffered bruises and minor burns along with smoke inhalation, but the worst of this should pass with a little rest."

Gabriel and Atti looked at each other, relieved.

"Your other cousin, by the way, is resting comfortably but will remain with us a few more days for observation. As to Ms. Forester, Gabriel tells me she'll be staying with you two at Pandion until she's feeling better, and I think that's the best medicine she could have. You can plan to pick her up tomorrow—assuming this storm passes and all her vitals are back to normal—say about eleven?"

Gabriel drove Atti and Q back toward the gatehouse. The wind was letting up. The radio reported over three inches of rain and even some snow at higher elevations. The Saco and Presumpscot Rivers had both approached action stage but didn't flood. The storm surge had inundated low-lying areas near Portland and damaged sea walls, boardwalks and bulkheads. Low clouds and fog still made driving hazardous and had grounded flights as far south as Baltimore.

Gabriel drove carefully, and they arrived home to the great joy of the hero of the night. Ghost seemed ready to race back outside and chase more villains, but his attention was easily turned to the large soup bone Gabriel happened to have in the refrigerator. The power was back on, and Gabriel cooked up grilled cheese sandwiches, which they devoured with mostly silent smiles. Then Q and Atti went up to the guestroom.

Atti lay in bed with Ghost on the floor beside him. It felt like the universe was finally coming back into alignment. The last year had been so filled with horror it had been hard to see a way out. His mother was gone, and he'd never stop missing her. But now, with Crane in custody and Elle back home and free from Oliver, maybe there was promise ahead. He thought about Gabriel and how different life seemed with his father as a foundation and a refuge.

By morning the rain had passed, and Atti felt better, but the arm hurt and he moved gingerly. The sun came out on what promised to be a beautiful day. Out the window he saw Ghost and Q helping Gabriel cut up a tree that had fallen on the driveway. None of the recent drama altered the dog's energy or Gabriel's incessant industry.

Q came into the kitchen while Atti sat with a cup of coffee. "You got him," he said in a voice filled with relief and congratulations.

"It was Gabriel and Ghost who got him. He was a tough old bird but apparently not up to fighting off a shotgun and a mad Australian shepherd."

"I'd love to have seen the teeth marks on his ass."

Elle would not be released until eleven o'clock, and Gabriel insisted he and Q needed no help in the yard, so Atti turned to two chores.

First, he picked up his phone.

"I've been waiting for your call," Lloyd said. "Fill me in."

"First, Q told me it was you who deciphered the messages."

"You must have known I couldn't pass up a puzzle built on Greek mythology…and for such a cause."

"I guess I knew before he told me. He's smart but he's *not* the smartest person I know."

"I can do without the encomium. Just give me a summary."

Atti faltered for a second. Where did Lloyd get those words? Then with a smile he recounted everything from the poisoning to the arrest.

"Ah, Lloyd said, "I applaud your quick reasoning…and action."

"We couldn't have made sense of his twisted mind without your help. And look, as to my job, I know I'm unemployed. I promised I'd be back.…"

"And instead you lured my technical advisor away with you."

"Well, there's that, too."

"And the two of you ignored your responsibilities and solemn promises…all to save the girl you love."

"That's pretty much it."

"So, when you come back to The Hall—by *mid-week*—I will require full attention from both of you until Cell Block goes to market. After that, we'll see how it goes."

Atti almost laughed out loud hearing Frank Bruno's line again. "Lloyd, you're a life-saver."

"Sounds like that term better fits you, young man. I am proud to know you. You give my best to the young lady, and pass along my edict to my other truant employee. We'll see you both this week."

Atti was beside himself with gratitude. Things really had turned his way. There was only one more thing he needed to do. He told Gabriel he had to run a quick errand in the village.

"The roads should be cleared," Gabriel said, "but take the Jeep, just in case, and stay clear of power lines!"

"Understood, Dad." It felt great saying that.

Gabriel grinned but turned away as if he were embarrassed.

Atti found only one tree blocking the road and was able to use the Jeep's four-wheel drive to go around it. When he parked in front of St. Bernard's, Father Giacomo and his acolyte were collecting roof tiles in a pile on the lawn. There was a long ladder leaning against the church and puddles in the graveyard.

"It hit you hard," Atti said with concern.

Father Giacomo looked up, surprised. "Atti!" he said, rising to his feet to hug his young friend but then backing off to arm's distance, gesturing with concern at the sling.

"It's nothing. Just a cut. You heard about Elle and Crane?"

"I did, and I'm so relieved it turned out. How is our Elle?"

"She'll be fine, Father. We'll pick her up from the hospital this morning. She's got burns and bruises but that's most of it, physically at least."

"And she's strong."

"You got that right. She may be the strongest person I know. But what about your roof?"

"Ah, the bane of our existence. It needs a complete renovation, but we'll paste it together again, and I'll keep giving sermons under an umbrella."

The latest damage to the church removed any doubt about what Atti had to do. "Father," he said, "there's something else."

The priest straightened and looked at him apprehensively. "Not more troubles?"

"No. In fact, this should bring some relief."

Father Giacomo cocked his head.

Atti handed him the Cell Block check, endorsed over to him. "This is to make up some of what you lost in the fund…and is so much less than we owe you."

"Now hold on. The trustee told me I can expect to recover a good portion of the initial investment. The church will be fine."

"Fine, as in duct-taping the roof to keep the congregation dry?"

"Our business is protection from the devil, not the rain."

"That may be but you'll put up a better fight if you're dry."

The priest looked down at the check and his eyes went wide. "But we don't need all this," he said. "You'll be wanting to pay for college."

"That will happen sometime; I'll work it out. I've still got my watch from my parents, and my boss says there'll be more payouts if our product takes off. I couldn't spend this money without thinking about you, St. Bernard's and *Organo*, besides what Hugo did."

"You are truly your mother's son," the priest said, with a look of pride.

"And my father's?"

"*And* your father's."

Driving slowly back to Pandion Atti thought about his family. The Foresters had been on this land for three generations, flying so high and crashing notoriously low. Then he wondered who got the three sailboats in the end, and whether the new owners had kept them safe from the storm. But that made him realize one thing the auditors would never find: the ammo box buried on Peregrine Isle. There had to be a few hundred dollars' worth of whiskey in that box—along with enough equipment to camp in peace, out of sight of the world. The last of the Forester fortune, he laughed. But since it turned out old Preston Forester was *not* his grandfather, maybe he had no right to it. Then again, he also had no hereditary duty to sail around the world and fight off hurricanes. But he was the only one alive besides Martin who knew about the buried treasure, so maybe he'd hire a boat someday and go dig it up.

Atti showered before they went to the hospital. His arm looked like hell and felt like it too, so he took some painkillers. Gabriel helped him re-bandage his wound.

When they arrived to pick up Elle, she was dressed and ready to go, looking fragile but with resplendent eyes. She recoiled at Atti's sling. "Did *he* do that?" she asked, gently touching the arm.

"Nah," Atti shrugged. "Twisted my elbow lifting tree trunks this morning."

She frowned and hugged him gently on his left side. Then she turned to Gabriel and hugged him full on. Atti laughed quietly at his expression, showing joy this time instead of surprise. His father was getting used to conspicuous affection.

"So, where are my other guardian angels?" she said.

"Ghost was a little too excited to wait in the car," Atti responded, "so he stayed home with Q, but they're planning a welcome for you."

She laughed, which started her coughing. Atti and Gabriel exchanged secretive concerned looks but both smiled when she looked up at them.

At the gatehouse Atti held Elle out of the way when Gabriel opened the door so Ghost wouldn't bowl her over bursting from the house. The dog rushed out as soon as he was freed but turned back to jump up on Elle like he hadn't seen her in ages. Gabriel grabbed his collar to hold him down on all fours, where all he could do was lick and whine.

After lunch, Atti and Elle sauntered around the grounds, while Ghost chased squirrels but kept his people in sight. The gazebo and the big lawn looked empty, except for scattered broken branches. They stopped where water had pooled in a large puddle in front of the Barn. Elle gazed up at the windows, much as Atti had done days before. It gave him a warm feeling to know someone shared his memories of Pandion at the Apex, when the Foresters ruled the world.

"What are you thinking?" he asked.

"About our Secret Garden. You know that's where he held me?"

"We figured that out, finally, but by then he had moved you to the cottage."

"I wish we could have preserved the cellar somehow and been able to still use it as our refuge from the world." She paused. "Then again, after being tied up down there, I don't think I could go back."

"We can never go back to what Pandion was," he said sadly. "And I'm so sorry you had to go through all that. How did Crane find you?"

"I don't know. I called for a car and he showed up. I should have recognized him, but I was only thinking of Martin, and we both had our hoods up against the rain. Once he got me in the car, he pulled a knife, tied my hands and put a bag over my head. Next thing I knew it was dark and cold, and at first I didn't recognize where I was." She seemed to concentrate hard to remember. "All I cared about was getting my hands free. But Crane kept muttering it was all perfect, and I realized he was waiting for *you* to show up. I wanted to warn you, but I could barely move, and my gag made it hard to breathe. Still, why did he hold me at Pandion, where you were most likely to find me?"

"Well, we only figured that out after Lloyd deciphered his note.

And anyway, Crane's mind was so twisted he forgot you and I weren't alone here. His fatal error was not accounting for my father."

"And your dog."

"*And* my dog."

"And then there was also Q."

Atti laughed. "Yeah, I just can't seem to lose that guy."

"Lucky for us all."

"That's so right. And by the way, he made clear he's counting on *me* to watch out for you from now on."

"You two are so funny, appointing yourselves my guardians. But I guess I needed it in the end. I'm really glad he's found someone. Rooney seems good for him."

Elle took his left arm, and they headed down to the ocean beach, trading reminiscences. The sun had dried the ground so it wasn't so slippery. They stepped around broken branches partly blocking the trail. In the cove a rowboat was smashed against the rocks, but The Lookout had weathered the storm. The ocean was strangely calm, and the familiar call of seagulls filled the air.

"Remember when Bode tried to show off by standing on a kayak?" she said.

"That may have been the finest cold dunk in the history of Pandion." They both laughed.

After a time, they ambled up the cliff trail. Atti relished the view of the ocean that seemed priceless now that it was no longer theirs. When they reached the pile of stones and charred embers that once was Cliff Dweller, they both stared, lost in thought.

Finally, she looked at him tenderly. "You saved me, you big lug."

"Oh, I don't know. It feels like you've been saving me ever since it all went to hell."

"The last best hope for the Foresters," she said with a tight-lipped smile. Then she looked at the dog. "So, is it for Ghost to show us where he caught Crane?"

Atti nodded and pointed toward the beach. Ghost scampered off, happy to lead the way. This trail was fairly clear of fallen branches, but Atti wasn't sure exactly where the dog took Crane down and Ghost didn't understand he was supposed to explain his part of the story.

"He tends to live in the moment," Atti apologized, turning with her to return to the big lawn.

"Well, what moment could be better than this?"

He stopped. The look in her eyes, a look only for him, made his knees go weak. She kissed him once on the cheek and then full on the lips. With his left arm he held her close, finally after a lifetime feeling her body against his.

When she looked up, he said, "Elle, I have to say…."

"Say what, sailor?"

"It's just…when Gabriel told me we weren't related, it all came rushing in. I've loved you as long as I can remember."

"That's nice," she said with a sweet smile.

"Nice?" he said, almost in desperation.

"Yeah. I'm thinking this time around I might have picked the *best* of the bunch."

They held each other for what seemed like all the hours and days and years of their lives. When they finally stepped back, joined by their hands, Elle gestured at Ghost, watching them and tilting his head with one of his inscrutable looks.

"You think he's okay with this?" she said.

"Just try and get away. He'll run you down."

THE END

Acknowledgments

For this, my third novel, I have to thank some old friends and also some new contributors with specific expertise. Robbin Collens Howard shared her childhood memories in helping me create the Pandion property in its setting on the coast of Maine. To make certain I didn't confuse port with starboard, I thank Tommy Goldstein for introducing me to Nicole Breault, who certainly knows her way around a boom vang. Brian Driscoll took time away from teaching gemology to help me pull a jewel heist and launder the loot. Peter Gordon lent a hand to my lovelorn protagonist wandering around the University of St. Andrews in Scotland. And Martin Whitley, of Dartmoor Hawking, taught me everything I know about flying raptors while delivering one-liners. Others helped with one-off questions: Doug Lyons on guitar electronics, Dave McCabe on the law of trusts and estates, Chelsea Taylor on the terminology of financial services. But special thanks go to Drew Dawson, Mary Behan, Richard Maki and my brother, Greg Ried, for their long support of my writing efforts and in particular for kicking the tires on early drafts to help mold *Pandion* into a workable story. Lorenzo Contessa inexplicably again agreed to put up with my inchoate notions of how to create the book's central image of the *pandion haliaetus*; it means a lot to have you contribute to the effort. César Pardo deserves all my thanks as well, for designing the cover through my hundred revisions. Alyce Townsend Kay did the detailed work of proofreading the manuscript. And once again my editor, Christine Keleny at CKBooks Publishing, saw me through the birth pangs of writing, formatting and publishing a novel. I am indebted as always for your help. Finally, my wife Megan helped enormously, from imagining the story while we hiked in Maine to proofing the galleys back home in Murray Hill. Nothing works without Megan.

About the Author

William Michael Ried was born on Long Island, graduated from the University of Michigan and Georgetown University Law Center and practices law in New York City. His first novel, *Five Ferries*, was a finalist in the 2019 American Fiction Awards for Best New Fiction. In 2021 his second novel, *Backstory*, won the New York City Big Book Award for mystery, a Silver Medal from the Wishing Shelf Book Awards for adult fiction, was a semi-finalist for the Kindle Book Award for literary fiction, and was named a 2022 Eric Hoffer Award category finalist. Bill lives with his wife in Manhattan.

For book club suggestions, cover stories, and more information see wmrauthor.com.

www.ingramcontent.com/pod-product-compliance
Lightning Source LLC
Chambersburg PA
CBHW050820190726
48286CB00007B/1939